Who's Kitten Who?

*A **Reigning Cats & Dogs** Mystery*

Cynthia Baxter

BANTAM BOOKS

WHO'S KITTEN WHO?
A Bantam Book / October 2007

Published by
Bantam Dell
A Division of Random House, Inc.
New York, New York

This is a work of fiction. Names, characters, places, and
incidents either are the product of the author's imagination or
are used fictitiously. Any resemblance to actual persons, living
or dead, events, or locales is entirely coincidental.

Bantam Books and the rooster colophon are registered
trademarks of Random House, Inc.

ISBN: 978-0-553-59034-0

Printed in the United States of America
Published simultaneously in Canada

www.bantamdell.com

OPM 10 9 8 7 6 5 4 3 2

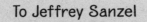

To Jeffrey Sanzel

Acknowledgments

Whenever Jessie Popper gets involved in something new, I get to jump right in alongside her and learn everything she learns. Researching this book required becoming a fly on the wall to observe firsthand how a musical comes together. I would like to thank Jeffrey Sanzel, Executive Director of Theatre Three in Port Jefferson, for welcoming me into his theater and patiently answering all my questions as he expertly created his fine production of *Annie Get Your Gun*.

I would also like to thank the members of Theatre Three Productions, who are all as warm as they are talented: Jean P. Sorbera, Choreographer; Ellen Michelmore, Music Director; Maureen Spanos, Production Stage Manager; Robert W. Henderson, Jr., Lighting Designer; and the entire cast and crew, especially Douglas J. Quattrock and Brent Erlanson.

Jessie Popper's medical expertise is the result of being allowed to be a fly on the wall at the Woodbury Animal Hospital in Woodbury, Long Island. Thank you, Dr. Marc A. Franz, Wendy M. Niceberg, Denise

Doughten, Dorene Evans, Anne McLoughlin, and Kim Marino, as well as your clients, for letting me see how real-life professionals care for their patients.

And, as always, thanks to my partners in crime, Caitlin and Faith.

Who's Kitten Who?

Chapter 1

"Man is the most intelligent of the animals—and the most silly."

—Diogenes

"O uch!" I cried. "Stop, I'm begging you! You're torturing me!"

"Hold still!" my attacker insisted.

I glanced around desperately, wondering if there was any way out. But I was afraid that continuing to resist would only anger my assailant—who was armed, dangerous, and clearly determined to make me her next victim.

"You are moving too much, *signorina*!" she exclaimed. "I can not make the neckline straight if you will not stop—what is the word?—fidgeting!"

I have every right to fidget, I thought crossly. First I get roped into spending my Saturday morning standing on a ridiculous pedestal in the middle of a bridal shop, surrounded by enough ruffles and veils to make me break out in a rash. Then I get turned into a giant pincushion. As if that's not bad enough, I'm periodically forced to twirl around like an Olympic ice skater to make sure the skirt of this preposterous dress swirls in just the right way.

But I knew I'd get no sympathy here. In fact, from the relentless way Gabriella Bertucci kept sticking me, you would have thought she was a voodoo priestess instead of a fashion designer whose wedding dresses were well known all over Long Island.

"Take a look in the mirror, *signorina*," Gabriella said with a sigh. "You look so beautiful, no?"

I screwed up my face before forcing myself to peer into the three-sided full-length mirror. When your idea of sprucing up is putting on a freshly washed Polarfleece jacket and a sparklin' new pair of chukka boots, being encased in a Barbie doll frock that reaches down to the floor and is cut nearly as low is about as much fun as changing a tire on a twenty-six-foot veterinary clinic-on-wheels. In the dark. In the rain. And sleet.

But after all the time, energy, and emotion I'd invested in having this dress made, I figured it was time to check out the results. Maybe, I hoped, I would even look something close to *nice* . . .

"E-e-ek!" I cried.

"*Signorina!*" Gabriella sounded as if she was about to burst into tears. "You don't like?"

I stood a little straighter and forced myself to take another look. An objective look. Even though my dark-blond hair hung limply, and even though as usual I wasn't wearing any makeup, I was startled by what I saw. The dress Gabriella Bertucci had custom-made for me fit beautifully, making me look more like Cinderella than I ever would have thought possible.

Her creation was made from a silky fabric that draped around my various body parts in a surprisingly flattering way. It skimmed over my torso and waist and hips, giving me a womanly shape that a comfortable pair of jeans just didn't capture. Even the low-cut neckline looked good on me. At least, once I finally stopped tugging at it after remembering that the petite *fashionista* had a sharp pair of scissors in her possession and that even she had a breaking point.

The only problem was the dress's color.

Mint green.

When it came to planning her wedding, my dear friend Betty Vandervoort was turning out to be a real traditionalist. Instead of an edgy event with, say, a justice of the peace who did a rap version of the ceremony or a hippie minister who recited the poems of Charles Bukowski, she surprised me by insisting on something out of a fairy tale. And it included a bride in a long white gown accompanied by bridesmaids in pastel shades like baby pink and pale yellow and my own mint green, colors that made us look more like dishes of candy than grown women.

I'd pleaded with Betty to let her bridesmaids wear a more dignified color.

"How about black?" I suggested hopefully. "These days, bridesmaids dressed in black are considered the height of sophistication."

"Black is for funerals," she returned with a frown. "When I married Charles, longer ago than I care to admit, we eloped. This time around, I want the kind of wedding I've dreamed about since I was a little girl. And that means a maid of honor who looks like an angel, not the Grim Reaper!"

The other details of Betty's spring wedding, now just three weeks away, were equally traditional. The ceremony in which she was marrying Winston Farnsworth, a charming British gentleman I completely approved of, would take place in the garden of the estate on which we both lived. The area was going to be festooned with garlands of gauzy white tulle and hundreds of flowers. The music would be performed by a string quartet dressed in tuxedos or black gowns.

She was even demanding that the canine guests come formally attired.

In fact, it seemed as if Betty had put more thought into deciding exactly what my snow-white Westie, Max, and my black-and-white Dalmatian, Lou, would wear on the big day than she put into choosing her own dress. She'd finally decided on red bow ties for both of them, and for her fiancé Winston's dog, a wire-haired dachshund named Frederick, she'd selected a bright yellow bow tie that would complement his soft fawn-and-tan fur.

Personally, I thought all three dogs looked just fine naked.

But it wasn't my wedding. Betty had already pointed that out several times. And a few of those times, she'd suggested that I'd have much more leverage if I'd consider making it a double wedding. That certainly put an end to my complaining.

Now that I was officially engaged to Nick, ideas like that probably shouldn't have surprised me. Yet becoming engaged had been a big enough step, one I was still trying to adjust to. I hadn't gotten used to wearing the small but tasteful antique diamond ring that had belonged to Nick's grandmother, so the idea of shopping for caterers, squealing excitedly over bridal shower gifts, and enduring fittings for my own white dress— not to mention contemplating actually *being* married— was way beyond me.

For the moment, the role of maid of honor was about all I could cope with.

"What you don't like?" Gabriella asked hopefully, studying my reflection with the same intensity as I was. "Maybe I can fix."

"The dress is beautiful," I assured her. "It's just that it's so...so *green*."

The tiny native of Milan, Italy, with the build of Pinocchio and the determination of Julius Caesar, folded her arms against her chest. "*Signorina,*" she replied crisply, "is not me who choose the color. If you no like, you talk with *Signóra* Vandervoort and see if she change."

Fat chance, I thought. There was no reasoning with a woman who, in her eighth decade of life, was suddenly subscribing to magazines like *Over-the-Top Bride*.

Still, Betty had promised to meet me at Gabriella's shop this morning so she could see the dress. I supposed this was my big chance to make whatever constructive criticisms I could come up with, but I was torn. Up until a few minutes ago, I'd believed I was willing to do anything in the world for her.

I was pondering the possibility that the one thing I *wasn't* willing to do was risk being arrested for impersonating Scarlett O'Hara when I heard a car door slam outside the shop. Seconds later, the bride-to-be—and the person responsible for my transformation into a life-size after-dinner mint—came dashing through the door.

From Betty's fringed lime-green capri pants, lemon-yellow linen blouse, and orange espadrilles, no one would ever have guessed that at that moment Gabriella was busily stitching up a wedding dress for her that had enough satin, Belgian lace, and tiny beads to make my dress look like a military uniform by comparison. Just looking at her was enough to provide me with the day's minimum requirement of vitamin C.

I was mustering up the courage to register my concerns over the dress when I noticed the expression on her face.

"Betty, what's the matter?" I demanded. "You look like you've just lost your best friend!"

"Simon Wainwright may not have been my best friend," Betty replied seriously, "but that doesn't make the fact that he's been murdered any easier to take."

It took a few seconds for the meaning of her words to sink in.

"Someone you know was *murdered*?" I cried. I lifted my skirt and started to step off the pedestal.

"*Scusa, signorina,*" Gabriella burst out, sounding completely exasperated. "We will never finish the dress if you do not stop moving around like a . . . a puppy!"

"Let's take a break," I suggested, more calmly than I felt. Apparently, the dress designer's English vocabulary didn't include the word *murder*.

But mine did.

"Sit down," I instructed Betty. "Take a few deep breaths and tell me exactly what happened."

"*Signorina!* The pins—"

"I'll be careful," I assured Gabriella. Suddenly, getting poked with a few straight pins didn't seem to matter at all.

As soon as Betty and I perched on the brocade-covered couch that graced one corner of the shop, I turned to face her.

"First of all, who is Simon Wainwright?" I asked.

"A member of the amateur theater group I belong to," she replied, wiping away a tear. "Someone who was so charismatic he would light up a room the moment he walked into it. Yet he never let any of it go to his head. Everyone loved him. He was one of the kindest, most charming, most down-to-earth people I've ever met.

"He joined the Port Players about a year ago, five or six months before I first got involved with them. From what I hear, it didn't take long for everyone to see what a talented actor he was. And then, a few months ago, he mentioned to Derek Albright, the executive director, that he'd written a play. Derek was completely blown away by it, and he begged Simon to let the Port Players put it on."

"Is that the play you've been rehearsing?" I asked gently.

"That's right. The play I've been living and breathing for the past six weeks. It's called *She's Flying High*, and it's based on the life of the famous aviator Amelia Earhart. It was scheduled to open in two weeks, and it was going to be the world premiere. Simon was playing the male lead, Amelia's husband, George Putnam."

Betty sighed. "Simon Wainwright was a 'triple threat,' one of those rare individuals who's a gifted actor, singer, and dancer. The fact that he was also such a talented writer only made him that much more amazing. There was even talk of *She's Flying High* being produced on Broadway!"

"And now he's dead," I said softly, still trying to take it all in.

Betty nodded. "His body was found at Theater One early this morning. The police won't know the actual cause of death until an autopsy has been performed, and they're refusing to release any details at the moment, even to those of us in the cast."

"Who discovered his body?" I asked.

"The costume designer, a young woman named Lacey Croft. She opened a trunk that was stashed in one of the dressing rooms and..." Betty swallowed hard. "Simon's body was stuffed inside."

"That's awful!" I exclaimed. "You must be so upset, Betty. What a horrible thing!"

She covered her face with her hands. "Simon was such a dear friend!" she cried in a choked voice. "I thought the world of that young man. I'd known him for only a few months, but I was already starting to think of him as a son, much the way I think of you as a daughter, Jessica. And if it isn't hard enough trying to cope with his death, all of us in the company also have to face the possibility that someone in the Port Players killed him!"

I gasped. "Do you really think so?"

"The theater was his life," Betty said sadly, lowering her hands, "so it seems likely that someone who was part of that world was responsible for his death. Simon spent every moment he could at Theater One. To support himself, he took whatever part-time jobs he could find: working as a waiter, a barista at Starbucks, an office temp...He had no real investment in any of it. It was just a way to pay the bills."

Shaking her head, she added, "All his friends were involved in theater. His enemies too. Not that I would have expected that he had any, but there was apparently at least one."

"Betty, I'm so sorry," I said. "If there's anything I can do—"

She took a deep breath and looked at me intently. "As a matter of fact, Jessica, there is."

• • •

Theater One in Port Townsend had begun life as a button factory a hundred years earlier. Since then, the freestanding red brick building had also been a warehouse, a vaudeville house, and a movie theater. Its last incarnation was still in evidence, thanks to the big marquee jutting out over the glass and wooden front doors, the large glass-covered displays with posters publicizing the next production, and the old-fashioned box office in the middle of the tiled entryway.

Betty and I walked through the side entrance marked STAGE DOOR. I knew it was business as usual for her, since decades earlier she'd been a Broadway dancer in shows like *South Pacific* and *Oklahoma!* But I felt a little flutter in the pit of my stomach. Even though the circumstances that were responsible for me being here in the first place were tragic, I couldn't help feeling a twinge of excitement over getting a behind-the-scenes look at a theater company.

True, the Port Players was only a local group, run by amateurs. But theater had always held a certain mystique for me, mainly because I couldn't fathom anyone actually having the guts to go onstage in front of an audience and perform. Personally, I was one of those behind-the-scenes people. Of course, the only real theatrical experience I'd had was in college, when I'd worked backstage at the Bryn Mawr College Junior Show.

Betty and I made our way past a few dressing rooms, stepping carefully over the ropes and cables that littered the wings and, finally, traipsing along the side of the stage. As we walked down the short set of stairs off to one side, I glanced out at the audience. At least twenty-five people were scattered throughout the first four or five rows, some sitting alone and others clustered in small groups.

The lights were low and the air was somber. It seemed fitting that the entire stage was black—not only the floor but also the tremendous backdrops hanging behind the stage.

As Betty and I sat down in red velvet seats, a tall, gangly man rose from the first row and turned to face the audience. He had gaunt features, piercing dark eyes, and curly dark brown hair that was so thick I wondered how he managed to get a comb through it. It kept falling into his eyes and he resolutely kept pushing it back.

He was wearing beige pants and a white turtleneck,

an outfit that screamed *Director*. At least to me, who'd learned most of what I knew about the theater from movies.

As if she'd read my thoughts, Betty leaned over and whispered, "That's Derek Albright. The Port Players' executive director."

"This is truly a sad day," Derek began somberly. "We have lost a man who was more than a member of our troupe. Simon Wainwright was our spiritual leader. Yet even in this time of deep despair, it's imperative that we continue. The expression *the show must go on* has never been more true. I don't think any of us doubt that's exactly what Simon would have wanted. Jonathan, who's been playing Charles Lindbergh, has agreed to step into the role of Amelia Earhart's husband, George Putnam. I'm hoping you'll all agree that the best way we can remember Simon is to bring his work off the page and into this theater. Let's work together to honor the man who was our friend and mentor by finishing what we started—"

"How *can* you?"

The high-pitched female voice that rose up from the back of the theater startled everyone, cutting through the somber mood. As I craned my neck to see who had spoken, I noticed that everyone else in the audience was doing the exact same thing.

Halfway back, a young woman had stood up. She was dressed entirely in black, wearing a long dress that looked as if it was from another era. Either that or it was one of those bridesmaid's gowns I'd been wishing Betty would opt for.

Still, there was no way I would have traded my mint-green frock for her getup. Not when the dress was accessorized with a dramatic black velvet cape edged with silver sequins and a black felt hat that swooped down over one eye and was decorated with a huge feather that some poor ostrich was undoubtedly still looking for.

Once I managed to get past her startling outfit, I saw that a cloud of wild and wavy jet-black hair hung halfway down her back. Her features were pretty enough, if not particularly outstanding. That is, except for her green eyes, their striking emerald color no doubt the result of tinted contact lenses. Even though her eyes were ringed in thick black eyeliner, I could see that they burned with fury.

"How *can* you?" she repeated, gliding down the aisle. "How can you possibly go on as if nothing has happened?"

"That's Aziza Zorn," Betty whispered. "Simon's girlfriend. They were very close. At least if the fact that Aziza was always hanging all over him is any indication."

"Does she always dress like that?" I asked.

"I understand her day job is working at the Port Townsend branch of the Bank of Long Island," she replied. "I have a feeling their dress code isn't quite that liberal."

Aziza had reached the front of the theater. She planted herself firmly next to Derek, and, throwing her arms out dramatically, she cried, "Simon is dead! He's gone! Some vile person has taken his life. And with that cruel act, he's taken a part of our lives too! So how can we be expected to proceed as if . . . as if life could possibly go on in exactly the same way?"

"I agree with Aziza," a male voice added. I turned in time to see a tall, lean man with sandy-colored hair and blue eyes rise from his seat. "If you ask me, the best way to honor Simon would be to admit that we can't possibly continue without him."

Instantly, the entire theater erupted into chaos. People rose to their feet, shouting about what Simon would have wanted and what Simon wouldn't have wanted. I had to admit, this was turning out to be much more interesting than I'd expected.

"People, please!" Derek finally yelled, his voice loud enough to rise above the racket. "Take your seats. Please, we must discuss this reasonably!"

Once everyone had quieted down, he held up both hands. "I hear what you're saying, Aziza. Kyle too. When you come right down to it, I think we all have to mourn our loss in our own private way. But for me, that means continuing the work Simon started. He was so excited by this production, and I think it's vital that we keep it going. Those of you who agree with me, I invite you—no, I *beg* you—to stay. Those of you who don't, you're welcome to leave, with no hard feelings."

Aziza bobbed up from where she'd perched in the front row. "You all know what I think," she said, turning to address the audience. "I'm just too sickened by what happened to go on. But if you truly believe this is what you have to do, I wish you the best."

With that, she squared her shoulders and stalked out of the theater, heading up the aisle and disappearing behind the double doors that I surmised led to the lobby.

"Anyone else?" Derek asked.

The room was so still you could have heard one of Gabriella Bertucci's pins drop.

"Good. Then I suggest that we all go home and try to get over the shock of the terrible news we received this morning," Derek said firmly. "A wake is being held tomorrow from one to four at Bingham Brothers' Funeral Parlor in Sandy Point. I urge everyone to stop by, not only to pay their respects but also to try to get some closure. As for our production, we'll stick to our schedule and meet for our next rehearsal Monday at seven."

As the cast and production crew stood up and the room buzzed with their conversations, Betty turned to me. "Well?" she asked anxiously. "What did you think?"

I just shook my head. "I'm sorry, Betty. I didn't get much of a sense of who any of the other members of the company are or what their relationship with Simon was, not enough to even begin to guess who might have wanted him dead."

"Of course not. How could you?" Betty frowned. "I knew this wouldn't be an actual rehearsal, but I didn't think Derek would end it so quickly. Maybe he wouldn't mind if you came back another time, perhaps even to our next rehearsal on Monday evening. Would you be willing to come?"

"Certainly," I assured her. I pretended I was simply being polite. Somehow, admitting that I'd found the drama that had just unfolded before me surprisingly entertaining didn't seem appropriate, given the circumstances. Not to mention that, though I didn't want to worry Betty, the possibility that one of my dear friend's castmates was a killer made me more than a little concerned for her safety.

"Oh, thank you, Jessica! Let's check with Derek to make sure he's comfortable with having you there."

We walked over and waited while Derek continued the conversation he'd been having with a slim, forty-something woman.

"We've lost our Amelia!" he wailed. "I can't believe Aziza is doing this to us!"

"We'll figure something out," the woman assured him. "Elena Brock is the obvious person to take over the lead. I'll start working with her right away."

"Then who'll take Elena's role?" he asked, sounding just as woeful. "Who'll play Anita?"

The question remained unanswered as he let out a loud sigh, then turned and noticed Betty and me.

"Derek," Betty began, "if you have a moment, I'd like to introduce a friend of mine, Jessica Popper. Jessie is interested in coming to Monday night's rehearsal—"

I stuck out my hand to shake, expecting him to do the same. Instead, he just stared at me, his face lighting up as if Greta Garbo herself had just walked in.

"Perfect!" he cried.

Something about his sudden burst of enthusiasm made me nervous. "Uh, what's perfect?"

"You are! You're perfect for the role of Anita Snook, the aviation pioneer who gave Amelia Earhart her first flying lesson."

"But I never—"

"I won't take no for an answer," Derek insisted. "Whoever you are, *please* say you'll join the cast!"

Chapter 2

"I love cats because I love my home and after a while they become its visible soul."

—Jean Cocteau

I was still trying to reconstruct exactly what had gone on in that theater as I steered my little red Volkswagen off Minnesauke Lane and bumped along the quarter-mile driveway leading to my stone cottage. My tiny hideaway was nestled among the trees that still covered much of the historic Tallmadge estate, a sprawling property that dated back to the early 1800s. The mansion and all the outbuildings had been built by the grandson of Major Benjamin Tallmadge, the head of the Culper Spy Ring, which, during the Revolutionary War, sent George Washington vital information about the British soldiers' whereabouts. Tallmadge's grandson had clearly taken to the capitalist system, and his success as a businessman had earned him an estate that was pretty impressive even by today's standards.

These days, four of us lived on the property. Betty and her fiancé, Winston Farnsworth, lived in the Big House, as I couldn't resist calling the dignified mansion, with Winston's dachshund, Frederick. And Nick and my animals and I holed up in the caretaker's cottage, which made up for its lack of space with enough charm to rate its own show on the Home & Garden Channel.

But coming home to such a cozy little cabin was only partly responsible for the feeling of relief that swept over me as I neared the end of the driveway. I've always been a strong believer in that old saying, *Home is where the heart is.* And even more than the softest pillows, the comfiest bed, and a freezer stocked with Ben & Jerry's, that means my loved ones, both human and animal.

After an afternoon that still had me in a fog, I was even more anxious than usual to surround myself with all the elements in my life that really mattered. I was glad to see that Nick's car was in the driveway, a sign that he was home from another long Saturday at the library reading up on torts and contracts and whatever other obscure topics law schools drum into the ambitious heads of their first-year students. His black Maxima was parked next to my clinic-on-wheels, the twenty-six-foot white van that served as my office. Blue letters were stenciled on the door, spelling out the words:

REIGNING CATS & DOGS

Mobile Veterinary Services
Large and Small Animals
631–555-PETS

As I let myself into the cottage, I was serenaded by Eric Clapton, thanks to the CD player Nick had no doubt switched on the moment he'd gotten home. That man is positively addicted to classic rock, I thought. I was also instantly smothered in kisses as my two dogs rushed to greet me, both so happy I was home that their claws skittered across the hardwood floor as if they were the Keystone Kops.

"Hey, Louie-Lou!" I cooed, throwing an arm around my one-eyed Dalmatian. Max, my tailless Westie who, like Lou, was a victim of his previous sub-human owner, jumped up and down as if he were a marionette rather than a crazed terrier. "Hello, Maxie-Max. Were you afraid I'd forget to say hello to you?"

As soon as he realized his favorite playmate was now available for fun and games, Max sprang across the living room to retrieve his most treasured toy, a pink rubber poodle that was eternally covered in saliva. He never got tired of chasing after it. I dutifully wrested it from his jaws, then tossed it back to the other end of the room. Both he and Lou scampered after it, their body language communicating, *Don't you just love playing Slimytoy?* The fact was, I loved it as much as they did.

All this commotion prompted my blue-and-gold macaw, Prometheus, to start squawking his own greeting. "*Awk!* Who's the pretty birdy?"

I went over to his cage and stuck my hand in so he could climb on.

"Welcome home, Jessie," he greeted me, mimicking my voice perfectly. "*Awk!*"

"I've got a special treat for you," I told him, running my hand along the bright, silky-smooth feathers covering his back. "I'll get you a piece of apple as soon as I get my bearings."

"*Awk!* Prometheus loves apple!"

As I put him back in his cage, Catherine the Great, better known as Cat, crept over. My lovely gray kitty was clearly feeling her arthritis. Even so, as she made her way toward me, she carried herself like a *grand dame,* someone along the lines of Queen Elizabeth—or perhaps her namesake, the enlightened empress of Russia during the 1700s.

Cat's quiet dignity was emphasized by the sudden appearance of the latest addition to my household, Tinkerbell. The spunky orange tiger kitten had joined our family a few months earlier, after Nick found her abandoned in a cardboard box in a field on his university's campus.

At the time, she'd been so tiny she fit into the palm of my hand. But that hadn't stopped her from taking over the entire household. And now that she was nearly grown, she had size on her side as well as attitude. I wouldn't have thought it was possible, but she'd found a way to wield even more power over the other members of my menagerie. The one exception was Cat, whom she seemed to recognize had earned herself a place at the top. The way the two felines managed to cohabitate was by giving each other a wide berth.

"Hey, Cat!" I crooned. "Hi, Tink!" As I stroked them both, I cast a fond glance at the most retiring member of my menagerie, Leilani. Of course, her failure to extend a personal greeting was largely based on the fact that she lived in a glass tank. But I was pretty sure the Jackson's chameleon Nick and I had smuggled home from Hawaii in a sock gave me a little wink. Not that it was easy to tell, given the fact that her eyes were on opposite sides of her head.

I flopped on the couch with Cat in my lap, basking in the feeling of being home. While most people would have taken this action as a sign of complete exhaustion, Max, being a terrier, decided it meant I was looking to play a few more rounds of Slimytoy. Given his obsession with his pink poodle, it was no surprise I'd had to replace it several times. Fortunately, Max never questioned how its head had been reattached or its squeak had mysteriously returned.

I'd given the poor slimy poodle a few more tosses by the time Nick emerged from the bathroom, drying his dark hair with a white towel. A second towel was wrapped around his waist, giving him a sexy beach-boy look I kind of liked.

"Hey," he greeted me, turning the volume on the CD player way down. "I didn't hear you come in." Tinkerbell meowed loudly, then wound herself through his legs.

"You're never going to believe what I did today," I returned, stroking Cat's fur distractedly.

But from the stricken look on his face, I got the feeling he hadn't heard me. Not when he clearly had something much more pressing on his mind.

"What's the matter?" I asked, sitting up straighter. A hundred different possibilities flashed through my head. He'd failed an exam at law school, something terrible had happened to one of his friends...

"It's my parents," he announced, picking up Tinkerbell and plopping down on the couch beside me.

"What about them?" I asked cautiously.

He cleared his throat. "You know they've been anxious to meet you for a really long time," he said. "And now that we're engaged, they can't wait."

"I can't wait to meet them either," I said sincerely. My own parents had been killed in an automobile accident years earlier. All the more reason I was looking forward to getting to know Nick's, even though he'd been warning me for years that his mother was—what was the word he always used? Oh, yes—difficult.

"No, they *really* can't wait," he continued. "They're coming here to meet you. All the way from Florida. Soon."

Something about the way he said the word *soon* made my stomach tighten. "How soon?"

"Monday. The day after tomorrow."

"The day after tomorrow?" I squawked, sounding an awful lot like Prometheus.

Nick winced. "I'm afraid so. My parents figure they've been waiting so long to meet you that there's no reason to postpone it any longer. Now that my dad's retired, he and my mother are constantly looking for ways to fill their time. Apparently they'd been talking about taking a trip to Long Island. Ever since they moved down to that condo in Fort Lauderdale, they've been on the go so much they haven't even had a chance to check out the swimming pool. My dad told me they're even considering buying an RV so they can travel around the country."

I was having trouble listening to all these details, since I was still stuck on the day-after-tomorrow part.

"But, Nick, they can't come that soon!" I protested. "I've got a full schedule of appointments this week and...and a *Pet People* segment that's airing on Friday...and Betty's wedding is exactly three weeks from today! And you're in the middle of the spring semester, with classes every day. How on earth are we going to find time to see them?"

"Funny you should bring that up," Nick replied nervously. "There's, uh, something else."

"Which is...?" I prompted.

"They're planning on staying with us."

"What?" Now I really sounded like Prometheus. Especially when he's got a seed caught in his throat.

"They feel it's the best way to really get to know you," Nick explained. "And since they're coming all that way..."

"Nick, the cottage is barely big enough for you and me, much less Max and Lou and Catherine the Great and...and..." I was so flustered I couldn't even remember the names of all my pets. "We have exactly one small living room, one tiny bedroom, and a kitchen the size of a linen closet. The bathroom is microscopic, so it doesn't even count. Where are we supposed to put them?"

He shrugged. "I figured we could give them our room."

"And where will you and I sleep?" I demanded. "In Lou's water bowl?"

"The couch folds out," he said, in that annoyingly cheerful *let's make the best of this* way of his.

"Now, there's a good option." I didn't even try to keep the sarcasm out of my voice. "Especially if you enjoy sleeping with a metal pole in your back that makes you feel like you're being tortured by the Spanish Inquisition."

"It's only for a few days," Nick insisted. "We'll manage." He cleared his throat before adding, "Even with Mitzi."

Mitzi? I thought. I couldn't remember Nick ever mentioning anyone in his family named Mitzi.

"And Mitzi would be...?"

"Mitzi is my mother's dog," Nick explained. "A Maltese."

"Is *that* all?" I was so relieved I actually laughed. "You may have noticed, Nick, that I feel pretty comfortable around dogs. In fact, some of my best friends are dogs."

He wasn't laughing. "I know that. But I'm not sure you're going to take to Mitzi."

"Relax. I've met very few dogs I haven't liked," I assured him.

"It's not actually Mitzi that's the problem," Nick went on, frowning. "It's more...well, you'll see." He was clearly anxious to change the subject, because he suddenly asked, "So what was your news, Jess?"

"My news?" I repeated distractedly. At the moment I was too busy trying to digest the fact that my beloved home was about to be invaded by a tribe of barbarians known as the Burbys. I glanced around, trying to picture four adults and six—no, *seven*—animals stuffed into a cottage that would have been too small for the Three Bears.

"When you came in just now," Nick explained, "you said something like, 'You won't believe what happened to me today.'"

"Oh. Right." I gently placed Cat on the cushion beside me to free up my hands, which I've been known to use to emphasize what I'm saying. In fact, I was beginning to realize I possessed somewhat of a theatrical streak myself. "This morning I got some terrible news: A member of Betty's theater group was murdered. They found his body at Theater One early this morning. His name was Simon Wainwright, and he wrote the show the Port Players have been rehearsing for the last few weeks, *She's Flying High*. It's about Amelia Earhart, and it opens in two weeks.

"But the most disturbing part is that Betty is pretty sure that someone in the theater company is the culprit," I went on breathlessly. "Apparently just about everybody Simon knew was part of that world. Anyway, I agreed to go to this afternoon's rehearsal with her, and the next thing I knew, I got railroaded into joining the cast so I can help investigate the murder.

"But there's more. It turns out that Simon wasn't only the playwright; he was also the lyricist. Because, believe it or not, *She's Flying High* is a musical. A musical! Do you know what that means, Nick? It means that before I had any idea what I was getting into, I agreed to go onstage and sing and dance in front of a real live audience!"

I was so focused on the horror of what I'd gotten myself into that it took me a few seconds to notice the expression on Nick's face, which had morphed into a look of utter fury.

"You're investigating another murder?" he asked in a strained voice.

"That's right," I replied, nodding. "I'm doing it for Betty. She's totally distraught over Simon's death, and she begged me to look into it, since I have some experience in that area and the police apparently aren't giving out much information. It's so important to her that she even asked me to make it my wedding present to her. Of course, I had to say yes."

"But what about my parents?"

I looked at him and blinked. "Do you think they'd like to help?"

"No, I don't think they'd like to help! What I meant is that you're spreading yourself a little thin, aren't you? Here's your big chance to spend some quality time with my mother and father, and . . . and instead of looking forward to getting to know your future in-laws, you're making plans to traipse around Long Island, trying to solve the murder of someone you don't even know!"

I had to admit, I hadn't seen this one coming.

"Nick," I said, making a point of keeping my voice as calm as if I was talking to a frantic pet owner, "don't you remember how supportive you were in Hawaii? And how rewarding we both found it solving a murder case together?"

"Yes, but that was different," he insisted. "We were on vacation—and you were in danger. Now we're back to real life."

"What difference does that make?" I demanded.

"Jessie, what are my parents going to think if it turns out you're too busy to, I don't know, have dinner with them because you have to go talk to some murder suspect? You're a veterinarian, not a homicide detective!"

By this point, the concept of controlling my voice in the name of maintaining harmony had completely flown out the window. Nick's parents hadn't even arrived yet, and they were already causing problems. "If you mean I'm going to be too busy to spend every moment of your parents' unplanned visit playing dutiful daughter-in-law to be, you're absolutely right. I *am* a veterinarian, and I have a veterinary practice to run; I have a TV show on Friday that I have to prepare for; I have a life!"

"Exactly. So why clutter it up even further by taking on one more thing to do?"

"I'm sorry, but I don't see helping out a dear friend who's grieving over the death of someone she really cared about as 'one more thing to do.' Especially since Simon's killer could turn out to be the person who's been standing onstage right next to Betty during all these weeks of rehearsal!"

"Yes, but..."

I could see we weren't going to get anywhere with this. And I wasn't in the mood to argue. I much preferred to take advantage of a Saturday night when, miraculously, neither of us was swamped with work or a zillion other responsibilities. Renting a DVD, ordering in some Chinese food, and opening a nice merlot sounded like a lot more fun than spending the evening trying to convince Nick that what I was doing made perfect sense.

"Trust me," I said, leaning over and nuzzling against his chest. "I won't let doing a favor for Betty get in my way. I'll find a way to make it work. In the meantime, what do you say we order up some garlic triple crown and a couple of spring rolls?"

"Okay," he agreed, only a little bit begrudgingly.

There, I thought with satisfaction. Mission accomplished, at least for now.

I only hoped I could manage to live up to the promise I'd just made.

Chapter 3

"To his dog, every man is Napoleon; hence the constant popularity of dogs."

—Aldous Huxley

That night I kept having the same nightmare over and over again. It was one I'd had before, but this time it took on new meaning.

In my dream, I was standing in the wings of a theater only minutes before I was supposed to go onstage. But I was perfectly aware that I hadn't learned my lines or gone to a single rehearsal or bothered to get a costume....

I was relieved when I woke up, although I was bathed in sweat. It didn't even matter that the cottage was so cold it felt like December, not April. The alarm clock told me it was nearly nine. Beside me, Nick was sleeping peacefully with Tinkerbell curled up on his chest and Cat stretched out next to his leg, resting her chin on his ankle.

Since Sunday morning was the only day of the week he allowed himself to sleep late, I climbed out of bed as gently as I could. Fortunately, my dogs limited their early-morning activity to staring at me expectantly, as if worried I might forget that letting them out was always the first order of the day. They both wagged their tails furiously, although Max, having only a stub left, actually wagged his whole butt. How the two of them managed to do that with full bladders, I couldn't imagine. It was some canine secret that hadn't been revealed to us in vet school.

As quietly as possible, I let them out the back door, checked the water bowls for all my winged and four-legged loved ones as I gave each of the others a pat and a cheerful "good morning," and headed straight for the coffeepot. While my good pal Mr. Coffee gurgled away, working his usual magic, I stuck an English muffin into the toaster oven and hunched over the tiny kitchen counter, watching the peaks and valleys on the surface darken.

You have a friend in need and a murder to solve, I reminded myself firmly. No matter what Nick thinks, no matter how busy you are this week being welcomed into the Burby clan, no matter how many clients you have to see, and no matter how far behind you are in coming up with a topic for Friday's *Pet People* spot on Channel 14, you made a promise to Betty.

I tried not to dwell on the fact that the first step I was going to have to take was contacting one of my least favorite people—a vain, self-centered man with a Napoleon complex. After all, Lieutenant Anthony Falcone, Chief of Norfolk County Homicide, was most likely the best source of information about what the police were doing to solve Simon Wainwright's murder. Even if I was sure he wouldn't be inclined to share very much of it with me.

I hoped Falcone would be working despite the fact that it was Sunday. I was pretty sure that the Norfolk County Homicide Department, like the Big Apple, never sleeps.

I waited until after nine, which seemed like an

appropriate time to begin conducting business on a weekend morning. By that point, my two cups of coffee and my two halves of an English muffin had brought me fully into consciousness.

But even a healthy dose of caffeine can only do so much. I was still filled with dread as I punched in the familiar number.

"Homicide. Officer Delaney speaking." Not surprisingly, the officer who answered the phone sounded less than cordial. I figured he probably wasn't very happy about having to work on a Sunday morning.

"I'd like to speak to Lieutenant Falcone," I announced confidently.

"He's not here," the crusty officer at the other end of the line informed me. With a great deal of satisfaction, it seemed to me. "Want his voice mail?"

"Where is he, if you don't mind me asking?"

"Actually, I do mind. But since he just left for a ten o'clock press conference, that's not exactly top secret information. Anybody with a TV or a radio will be able to figure out where he is."

"May I ask where it's taking place?"

"You'll probably see it in the background when you turn on your TV."

"Thanks for all your help," I replied dryly before hanging up.

I coudln't be positive, but I had a feeling that if Lieutenant Anthony Falcone was holding a press conference, it was almost certainly related to Simon Wainwright's murder—and that he'd be sure to stage it at a place that would provide him with the greatest possible sense of drama. I was beginning to suspect there were a lot of actors out there who had never set foot in a theater.

* * * *

Adrenaline surged through my veins as I wriggled into an outfit that was more or less respectable, depending on how high your standards were, and jumped into my red VW Bug. Sure enough, as I pulled into the parking lot of the Norfolk County Courthouse less than half an hour later, I saw two Channel 14 vans, along with vehicles from three Long Island radio stations. I wasn't surprised that the murder of an up-and-coming actor–playwright who was headed for Broadway was big news in Norfolk County. I also wasn't surprised that I'd been right about Falcone intending to squeeze every possible ounce of publicity he could get out of it.

I parked and ran up the steps of the large, imposing building, whose facade boasted more columns than the Parthenon. Inside was a cavernous lobby, complete with a shiny marble floor, more columns, and a large statue of Lady Justice. Way in back, I saw a camera crew setting up. Lieutenant Falcone was nowhere to be seen. But my eagle eyes zeroed in on a pair of shiny shoes poking out from behind one of the columns at the lobby's edge. I was pretty sure I'd seen them before.

However, the two feet that wore them were separated from me by a large police officer who looked as if he was no stranger to the weight room.

Nevertheless, I strode confidently toward what I surmised was a makeshift dressing room. I did my best to appear much too busy and much too important to engage in any chitchat, even with a cop who, at the moment, was playing the role of guard dog.

"I need to speak to Lieutenant Falcone," I said breathlessly, as if the mere act of bothering to explain was a waste of my time.

"He's kinda busy right now," the burly brute announced, folding his arms across his chest in a manner that most people, including me, would interpret as menacing.

"That's okay," I assured him. "The lieutenant and I are friends."

"*Friends?*" I heard a familiar voice repeat from the other side of the column.

I cringed over the way that voice pronounced the word, stretching it out to at least three syllables and using a tone that was so dry we could have used a humidifier in there. But at least I'd gotten his attention.

Lieutenant Falcone popped his head out from behind the tall marble structure, which suddenly seemed embarassingly phallic, and scrutinized me with the dark piercing eyes of a bird of prey. Even though he had a jockey's build, the man carried himself like a four-star general. In honor of this morning's press conference, he was decked out in a gray suit that had the distinctive sheen of polyester. His blue-black hair was just as shiny. In fact, it looked as if it had been spiffed up for the occasion with a thick coat of shoe polish. Today there was one unusual addition to his outfit: a small white towel draped around his neck.

"Well, well, well. If it isn't the famous—or should I say *infamous*—Dr. Popper." As usual, Lieutenant Falcone pronounced my name without the Rs, so it came out sounding like "Docta Poppa." I wondered if somewhere out there, there was also a "Docta Mama."

"See?" I told the guard, forcing myself to smile. "We really are friends."

He just grunted. Falcone didn't help much by growling, "Whaddya want, Dr. Popper?"

I blinked in surprise as I suddenly noticed something else about Falcone.

Makeup. He was wearing makeup.

Not the Alice Cooper variety. This was more subtle. A thick layer of foundation that was a tad too orange for his natural olive skin tones had been smeared all over his face. And, I couldn't help noticing, not exactly blended along his jawline.

If I wasn't mistaken, he also had a faint dusting of pink on each cheek, just enough color to give his cheekbones definition—and to make him resemble a Swiss milkmaid posing for a hot chocolate ad. It was even possible that the reason the lashes framing his piercing eyes looked especially dark today was that they, too, had been chemically enhanced.

In a way, the attempts at subtle improvement were even more shocking than if he really had ringed his eyes with thick black circles à la Alice Cooper.

"You look...different," I couldn't help blurting out.

"Hey, welcome to the media age," he replied defensively. He stood up straighter, puffing out his chest like a rooster intent on proving who was king of the barnyard.

"That's something I happen to be familiar with," I replied cheerfully, recognizing the need to stay on his good side. "A few months ago I started doing a weekly spot on Channel Fourteen TV—"

"Yeah, yeah, I know all about that." Eyeing me warily, he added, "I'm kinda busy here, Dr. Popper. I'm goin' on camera in about five minutes. What can I do for you?"

"You want her outta here?" his beefy bodyguard offered gruffly.

"No, we're okay." He hesitated before adding, "So far."

I decided to jump in before I was muscled out. "Lieutenant Falcone, I'm trying to find out whatever I can about Simon Wainwright's murder. You see, I'm—"

"Then you're in the right place at the right time," he returned with a smug smile. "I'm about to go on TV to tell the people of Norfolk County that we've got this investigation under control."

"So you know who the killer is?" I asked hopefully.

His smile vanished. "I didn't say that, did I?"

"Well, no, but you implied that you—"

"I can assure you, the same way I intend to assure all the county's residents, that Norfolk County Homicide is doing everything in its power to find out who was responsible for the death of Simon Wainwright."

In other words, I thought, reading between the lines, he didn't have a clue.

"How was Simon killed? Who are you questioning?" I asked. "Do you have any suspects?"

"You got a TV?" he shot back. "Go home and turn it on."

I decoded his response to mean that the answer was no.

In other words, at this point Falcone and his posse of homicide detectives didn't know any more about Simon Wainwright's murder than I did.

"Thanks for your time," I said, recognizing a dead end. "If you don't mind, I'll call you in a few days to see how the investigation's going."

"Whoa, whoa, whoa," Falcone protested. "Whaddya talkin' about? The investigation of Simon Wainwright's murder's got nothin' to do with you."

"I'm just a concerned citizen," I assured him. "And I happen to be particularly interested in this because Simon was a friend of one of my dearest—"

"*Madonn'*," Lieutenant Falcone muttered. "Here we go again. Dr. Popper, don't tell me I'm gonna be running into you at every turn. I hope this isn't gonna be another one of those murder investigations where you're gettin' in my way every time I try to do my job."

My eyebrows shot up so high they nearly collided with the dome-shaped ceiling. Rather than "getting in his way," as Lieutenant Falcone characterized our past interactions, I had actually *solved* several of the crimes that were part of that job he alluded to so proudly. But instead of getting any appreciation, aside from the occasional begrudging acknowledgment, all I got was attitude.

Fortunately, I had other options. In fact, I was contemplating the best way of taking advantage of them when I noticed the most obvious one entering the lobby of the courthouse, looking as if he'd received a personal invitation to be there.

• • •

"If it isn't the very person I was hoping to see!" I called out to Forrester Sloan.

Turning my back on Lieutenant Falcone, both literally and figuratively, I strode across the tremendous lobby. As I did, I wished I were wearing shoes with heels that clicked loudly. Somehow, trying to make a statement with rubber soles just didn't cut it.

As soon as Forrester glanced in my direction, his face lit up. "He-e-ey!" he greeted me. "If it isn't my favorite vet and amateur sleuth. How's it goin', Popper?"

He did indeed look glad to see me. Too glad. While I'd always done my level best to keep our relationship professional, the *Newsday* reporter didn't exactly see things the same way I did.

Still, that didn't keep me from picking his brain every time he happened to be covering a homicide investigation I was interested in.

"What brings you here?" he asked jovially. "You're not on trial, are you?"

As usual, Forrester looked remarkably cool, calm, and collected. It wasn't just his natural good looks, his gray-blue eyes, and his thick blond hair that softened into a mass of curls at the back of his neck. It wasn't his preppy style of dress either—the khaki slacks, white button-down shirt, and loose-fitting tweedy jacket that hung from his broad shoulders as if he'd thrown it on as an afterthought. Even more than his appearance, it was the easy self-confidence he naturally exuded. He always looked as if he'd just sailed in from his summerhouse on Nantucket and, underneath his leather Top-Siders, still had sand between his toes.

"Actually," I replied, "I'm trying to find out whatever I can about Simon Wainwright's murder. Which I understand is the topic of Falcone's press conference today—and which I assume is a story you're covering for *Newsday*."

"Right on both counts. I guess you didn't see my article in this morning's paper."

"Sorry. I didn't have time to pick it up."

"No problem. We don't know much yet, aside from the fact that the poor guy turned up Saturday morning stuffed into a trunk full of costumes as if he were a toga left over from *Antony and Cleopatra*."

I cringed at the image. Forrester didn't seem to notice.

"The results of the autopsy aren't in yet," he continued, "but the police think the murder occurred sometime Friday night. There was no rehearsal that evening, so the theater would have been empty."

"Makes sense." My mind was already clicking away, picturing a dark, lonely theater late at night, with only two people there: Simon and some nameless, faceless figure with evil intentions. "How did he die? What about the murder weapon?"

"It hasn't been found yet. Apparently the poor guy was bashed in the back of his head with something heavy. But the cops have yet to locate it or even to determine what it was.

"Y'know, Popper," Forrester went on breezily, "I thought our paths might cross again. I had a feeling this case would turn out to be your cup of tea." He was wearing a grin so wide it made the Cheshire Cat look like the Mona Lisa.

"And why is that?" I asked coolly.

"Three reasons, actually. One, because the murder occurred within spitting distance of where you live. Two, because your pal Betty Vandervoort is involved in the same theater group as the victim. And three," he added, leaning closer, "because you haven't had a chance to poke around a murder for, what is it, three or four months now? That must be driving you nuts."

For some reason I had yet to uncover, Forrester Sloan had an uncanny ability to irritate me. Yet it seemed critical to act as if nothing he said fazed me. Especially when I wanted something from him—which was pretty much all the time.

So I laughed. "Cut it out, Forrester. You make it sound as if I'm obsessed with solving murders."

"Not obsessed, exactly," he returned. "More like... eternally intrigued."

"It just so happens I have other things to think about these days," I shot back. "Important things."

"Like what?" he asked. "I'm all ears."

"Like being engaged."

A look of total shock crossed his face. But his expression quickly melted into one of skepticism. "Uh-huh."

"You sound as if you don't believe me."

"Maybe that's because I don't."

I raised my chin a little higher in the air. "Don't you think I'm the marrying kind?"

"As a matter of fact, I don't."

"Maybe this will help convince you." I stuck my left hand in his face, figuring the ring I was wearing was bound to make an impression.

He took my hand in his, squinting as he examined it. "Not exactly the Hope diamond, is it?"

"I'm not big on flashy jewelry." I yanked my hand away. "The point is, I love Nick and he asked me to marry him."

"On bended knee?"

Even though Forrester's wheedling tone made me want to smack his nose with my cell phone, I tossed my head haughtily and replied, "Yes, as a matter of fact. His marriage proposal was extremely romantic."

"Don't tell me. A quiet, candlelit restaurant, with violins playing the background?"

"A canyon, actually. And it was certainly quiet. In fact, the only sound in the background was the skittering of geckos."

"Now that's definitely what I call romantic." That same annoying grin was back on his face. "Nothing says undying passion like lizards."

"You don't seem to be taking any of this very seriously," I said petulantly. I hated the fact that Forrester always seemed to make me react this way. Almost as much as the fact that I didn't seem capable of doing anything about it.

"I'm not," he replied, chuckling. "I know you better than you think I do, Popper. And frankly, I won't believe this business about you getting married until I see you strolling down the aisle in a long, white dress."

By this point, I figured, there was probably steam coming out of my nose, just like in the Saturday morning cartoons. "Well, that's not going to happen, mainly because I don't expect you to make the guest list."

"In that case, maybe I'll use my press pass to sneak in." He tapped the laminated picture ID hanging from his neck. "It's amazing the places this thing gets you into. But don't worry. If I do crash your wedding, I promise I'll bring you and your lucky fiancé a nice wedding gift. A blender, maybe, or even an ice cream maker."

"Very thoughtful. But I already have a blender."

"Then maybe I'll bring you something else. Like information about the murder investigation."

His words grabbed my attention. "What do you know, Forrester?" I demanded.

"Like I said, not much. At least, not yet. But whatever I do find out, I promise I'll have it engraved and wrapped in silver paper with a big white bow."

"No, seriously. The reason I'm here is that I promised Betty I'd find out whatever I could about Simon Wainwright's murder. She's really broken up about it. Would you help me?"

"I've already said I would." Looking at me with what I was certain was great amusement, he added, "On one condition."

"What's the condition?"

"That if and when your engagement gets called off, you'll let me take you out on a real date."

My eyebrows shot up to my hairline. "What makes you think my engagement will get called off?" I asked as indignantly as I possibly could.

He laughed again. Actually, it was more like a smirk accompanied by a few throaty sounds. Whatever it was, it was certainly a lot more irritating than a normal laugh. "Like I said, I know you," he replied simply.

I folded my arms across my chest. "Okay, Forrester. I agree that if—*if*—I ever call off my engagement to Nick, I'll go out on a real date with you."

"Or if he calls it off," he interjected. "Let's be clear about that."

As if *that* would ever happen, I thought.

"Either one of us, then. But you'd better buy yourself some warm socks, because that'll be the same day hell freezes over. In return for agreeing to this ridiculous occurrence that will absolutely, positively never happen, you'll tell me everything you learn about Simon Wainwright's murder. Deal?"

"Deal," he agreed. "Whenever I find out something about the case, you'll be the first to know. But at the moment, I have a few other important things to figure out."

"Like what?" I asked, even though I knew that was exactly how he wanted me to respond.

"Like which restaurant I'll take you to on our first date."

With that, I really did hit him with my cell phone, jabbing him in the ribs harder than I'd intended. I suppose it was childish. But somehow I just couldn't help myself.

Given the fact that it only made him laugh, I wished I hadn't bothered.

Chapter 4

"Animals are such agreeable friends—they ask no questions, they pass no criticisms."

—George Eliot

I hung around the courthouse just long enough to catch the first few minutes of Lieutenant Falcone's press conference. That was all it took to confirm my hunch that the police didn't have a clue about who had killed Simon Wainwright. At least, not yet.

Then I hurried home to change my clothes and pick up Betty and Winston for Simon's wake. As Derek had claimed, the sad gathering would give everyone a chance to pay their respects and, hopefully, get some closure. But I also saw it as an opportunity to find out more about Simon's friends, his enemies, and perhaps even some of his enemies who had disguised themselves as friends.

I pulled up in front of Betty's house, expecting to park my VW and dash inside to retrieve her and Winston. But I'd barely stopped the car before she came running out.

"Let's go," she said, yanking her seat belt over her black blazer.

"Isn't Winston coming?" I asked, surprised.

She just shook her head. It was only then that I noticed the pink patches on her cheeks.

I didn't say anything. She didn't either. We drove the entire length of the driveway and turned onto Minnesauke Lane without speaking.

In fact, I was debating whether to switch on the radio or make a comment about the lovely spring weather when she volunteered, "Winston and I just had an argument." After a moment's hesitation, she added, "He thinks I should drop out of the Port Players."

"No way!" I cried. "Why?"

"Because he feels it's not safe," Betty replied. "This morning I mentioned that given the circumstances of Simon's death, as well as his life, it seems likely that he was murdered by someone who's involved with the theater company. Winston was beside himself when he learned there could be a killer in the cast. He said he's worried sick that something will happen to me, but..."

Her voice trailed off. Then she turned to me and said, "Jessica, you have to do everything you can to solve Simon's murder—the sooner, the better. I can't drop out of the Port Players! Winston is right, of course. It's terrifying to think that Simon's murderer could be someone I know, even someone standing on-stage right next to me! But being in the theater again after all these years is simply too important to me."

She sighed. "Then again, Winston is important to me too. We're getting married in less than three weeks. I don't want to spend every minute between now and the wedding being angry at each other."

I nodded. After all, I was no stranger to the tension that seemed to seep into even the best of relationships in the weeks before a marriage ceremony. In fact, I was beginning to think we needed a medical term for it: Pre-Wedding Syndrome, or PWS.

The difficulties Betty and Winston were having only made it clearer than ever that that I had serious work to do. Opening night was a mere two weeks away. If Betty's theory was correct, if Simon's murderer really was someone who was involved with this production, it would be that much harder to determine his or her identity once rehearsals were over and the run of *She's Flying High* ended. Not only for me, but also for the police.

And solving this crime was crucial if I was going to keep things rosy between Betty and Winston—not to mention protecting my dear friend from an unknown killer. Which meant I needed to put everything I had into finding out who had murdered Simon.

With or without Nick's support.

• • •

The Bingham Brothers' Funeral Parlor occupied a rambling hundred-year-old building that had originally been a charming Victorian home. The three-story building had a big, friendly porch, a frosted oval-shaped window set into the front door, and stained-glass panels framing the windows. I liked the fact that the people who had known Simon Wainwright would be able to say good-bye to him in such a warm, homey place.

The scene outside, however, was anything but warm and homey. So many people had turned out for the wake that the parking lot was full. Drivers were fighting for spaces, with some abandoning their cars in nonexistent spots and even on the lawn. As for the cars, they were an interesting mix of Mercedeses, BMWs, flashy sports cars, and broken-down jalopies that looked as if they might need to be towed away. I figured the diversity reflected those who'd made it in show biz versus those who had yet to get their big break. I also spotted a few limousines, their drivers congregating near a fence where they smoked and chatted as they idly watched the crowd.

As Betty and I walked arm in arm toward the front door, I realized that it wasn't only the parking lot that was filled to capacity. The sprawling Victorian building was so packed that people actually spilled out onto the lawn. It was a warm spring day, with the oppressive humidity that was guaranteed to characterize the next several months already in evidence. But the sun was nowhere to be seen, hiding somewhere in a sky filled with gloomy gray clouds.

We wove through the crowd, murmuring "Excuse me" over and over again as we tried to get inside. Something struck me as out of the ordinary: Many of the mourners were wearing outfits better suited to a stage than a wake. A man with bright orange-red hair sported an outrageous kelly green plaid suit. If it hadn't been for his black velvet armband, I would have thought he was here to audition his vaudeville act. Several of the women wore long black gowns, some with trains and others decorated with sequins or feathers or fringe that made Aziza Zorn's outfit from the day before look positively drab. I wondered if they'd bought them in a department store or rented them from a costume shop.

"I guess a lot of the people who came here today are in the theater," I commented to Betty as soon as we squeezed through the doorway. So many people were crammed inside, standing around and chatting animatedly, that I felt as if I were crashing a cocktail party.

"Simon had developed quite a name for himself," she replied. "His career was about to take off. Which makes this whole thing even harder to..." Her voice trailed off, ending with a choking sound.

"Are you all right?" I asked anxiously, putting my arm around her shoulders.

"I'm so sorry." Sniffling, Betty scrounged around inside her purse for a tissue. "I thought I'd be able to handle this better."

"You have no reason to apologize!" I assured her. "I know how fond of Simon you were." Glancing around, I added, "So were a lot of people."

She wiped her eyes. "Maybe I should take a minute to pull myself together. If you don't mind, I'm going to pop into the ladies' room."

"Take your time, Betty."

After she disappeared into the throng, I glanced around the front room of the funeral parlor, wondering how to occupy myself while I was on my own. I'm not generally that good at large gatherings, and the fact that this one was a wake made it even more difficult than usual.

But I was curious about whether I'd see anyone I recognized. I immediately spotted Aziza Zorn, who was draped in black and standing alone in a corner, looking mournful. Derek Albright, the director, stood with a group that included some familiar-looking faces I was certain belonged to cast and crew members I'd seen at the theater the day before.

I also noticed a man in an ill-fitting sports coat hovering in the corner, scanning the crowd. One of Falcone's men, I figured. No doubt he was just as anxious as I was to see if anyone interesting had turned up to say good-bye to Simon Wainwright.

I decided to head in a different direction. Beyond the front room was the main room, which was separated from the entryway by large double doors that were wide open. People were milling around in there as well. I wandered inside and, as I'd suspected, discovered that Simon Wainwright's body was lying in an open casket. The room was covered with flowers, bouquets and wreaths and elaborate sprays that filled the air with a sickly-sweet smell.

I edged over to take a look at the man I'd already become so focused on yet had never actually met. In fact, I'd never even seen his picture. Peering into his casket, I saw that he was extremely good-looking, with light-brown hair and attractive features. Still, it was hard to imagine him as full of life as I knew he had been.

My eyes filled with tears, and I was about to move away when a man standing nearby commented, "He looks very peaceful, doesn't he?"

I thought he was talking to me. But before I had a chance to respond, I heard a woman respond, "Very peaceful." She snorted, then added, "To look at him, you'd never guess what was really going on."

"Gloria, this isn't exactly the time and place," the man said crossly.

I took a step sideways, as if I were trying to make room for them. In reality, I wanted to see who they were, this duo who not only lacked diplomacy but also seemed to know something about the details of Simon's life.

The man and the woman were both in their late forties or early fifties, I estimated. Even though they were holding hands, the strain between them was obvious. The man was dressed in an expensive-looking suit that fit him so well I wondered if it had been custom-made. The woman was also well-heeled, but in a much more obvious way. She, too, wore a suit, but hers looked as if it had been created by some high-priced designer. Chanel, maybe, although I was hardly an expert in garments that cost more than three months' take-home pay. Her dark, meticulously coiffed hair, worn in a short pageboy, was tastefully streaked with silvery highlights.

But it was her jewelry that made me wonder if she and her escort were among the visitors who had arrived in one of the limousines parked outside. On her left hand, she wore a diamond that looked like a boulder compared to the pebble I had on mine. On the same finger, she also wore a wide gold wedding band that was studded with more impressively large diamonds. Around her neck was a string of large black beads I recognized as Tahitian black pearls. As for the gold bracelet dangling from her wrist, the diamonds were so voluminous I was surprised she could lift her arm.

"He does look peaceful," I commented, determined to hone in on their conversation. "Goodness, what a tragedy!"

The woman looked at me curiously and frowned. "I don't think I know you. Were you one of Simon's *suburban* acquaintances?"

"He and I were in the same theater company," I replied, ignoring her condescending tone.

"Ah." She sniffed. "An aspiring actress."

"You're with the Port Players?" Her husband sounded genuinely interested.

"That's right," I replied. "At least, for this production. What I mean is, it's my first time onstage."

"Really? And what prompted this sudden interest in the theater?" he asked.

"Actually, the reason I got involved is that a friend of mine who's in the company asked me," I explained. "Otherwise, I never would have attempted acting, much less singing and dancing. I don't really think I've got what you'd call star quality."

"I'm curious," the man continued. "Which cast member convinced you to join?"

"Betty Vandervoort," I replied. "She and I live on the same property in Joshua's Hollow. She's in the main house and I'm in the cottage. Which means she's my landlady as well as my friend."

"No wonder you couldn't say no," he said, smiling. "What role are you playing?"

"Anita Snook, Amelia Earhart's first flying teacher."

"That's a good role. Not a major one, but at least you have a few lines. It sounds like a great way to get started."

Just then, a cell phone burst into song. As I was wondering who was insensitive enough to keep a cell phone turned on in a funeral home, the shiny woman snapped open her beige purse. It was emblazoned with the name *Prada* in large enough letters that just about anyone would be able to read it, even without glasses.

"Damn," she muttered, pulling out her phone and checking the caller-ID screen. "I thought everyone knew I was coming to a wake today."

"Apparently not," her escort muttered, looking embarrassed.

"Yes, Harvey, what is it?" she snapped into the phone, stomping toward the other end of the coffin and stopping when she reached Simon's feet.

"You'll have to excuse my wife," the man apologized, stepping away from the coffin to allow other people to drift over to pay their respects. "She's been under a lot of stress lately."

I moved away, following him. "People express their grief in different ways."

He laughed. "You're much too kind."

"It sounds as if you and your wife were close to Simon."

"We were business associates," he said. "Not that

we weren't fond of him. We both were. But we were planning to produce *She's Flying High* on Broadway." He extended his hand. "I'm Sheldon Stone. And that's my wife, Gloria."

My eyebrows shot up involuntarily. Even I recognized those names. Sheldon and Gloria Stone weren't just Broadway producers. They were *the* Broadway producers. Long before I'd joined the theater world, Betty had talked my ear off about how influential the couple was. At the moment, they had no fewer than four phenomenal hits on and off Broadway.

"It's an honor to meet you, Mr. Stone," I said sincerely, wanting him to know I knew who he was. "I'm Jessica Popper."

"I'm pleased to meet you too. And call me Sheldon. Or Shel. Tell me, what do you do when you're not onstage?" he asked with a kind smile.

"I'm a veterinarian. I have a clinic-on-wheels, and I travel all over Long Island, treating animals."

"How fascinating!" he exclaimed. "You must find that rewarding. I admit, I'm an animal lover myself. In fact, my wife and I happen to be owned by an extremely engaging bull terrier."

Just then, Gloria came bustling over. "Shel, you're not going to believe the games Harvey's lawyers are playing. He just told me—"

"Gloria," Sheldon Stone said calmly, "we're at a wake. I suggest we behave in a manner that's appropriate for this sad occasion. You can conduct all the business you want once we're on our way back to the city."

She cast him a scathing look but refrained from finishing her sentence. Instead, she set her mouth into a thin straight line that convinced me that later on she'd have more to say about being chastised in front of someone else—even a *suburban* someone else.

"I just noticed Sutton and Nathan over by the front

door," Gloria said abruptly. "No doubt they're here because they're still hoping *She's Flying High* will go to Broadway. Not that either one of them is even remotely right for the show. But I should go over and say hello anyway. I mean, they did come all the way out to the sticks just to impress me."

"Be my guest," her husband replied. "I'll join you in a minute."

As she stalked off, he smiled at me woefully. "I should be off as well. Good luck, Jessica. I'm sure you'll be terrific as Anita Snook."

"Nice meeting you," I called after him.

He'd barely disappeared into the crowd when Betty joined me, her eyes clear and her face dry. "I see you were talking to Sheldon Stone," she commented. "Is he as nice as people say he is?"

"He seems to be," I replied. "Too bad I can't say the same for his wife."

"Yes, I've heard that Gloria Stone is as nasty as her husband is charming. But apparently she's an amazing woman. Rumor has it she can tell whether a show is going to be a hit within the first five minutes." Ruefully, she added, "Or a flop."

The viewing room was filling up, so after Betty took a few moments to say good-bye to Simon, we nudged our way toward the front room once again.

"I'm sorry, Jessica," Betty suddenly said. "I know we just got here, but I think I've already had enough. Would you mind if we didn't stay?"

"That's fine, Betty," I assured her. "We can go right now if you're ready."

I had to admit, I'd pretty much had all I could stand of this mob scene myself. Still, I was glad I'd come. What I'd seen had reinforced that what I'd heard about Simon Wainwright being on the verge of great success hadn't been an exaggeration.

How sad that he didn't live to see his dreams realized, I thought. To see his musical staged on Broadway, to listen to the wild applause as he sparkled onstage in a starring role, to hear theatergoers stream down the aisle humming the tunes that had been written to go with his lyrics—what a tragedy.

But at that same time, another thought nagged at me: that maybe the timing of Simon's demise wasn't simply a coincidence.

Chapter 5

"Cats regard people as warm-blooded furniture."
—Jacquelyn Mitchard

The bleating of my alarm clock early on Monday morning was a harsh reminder that there was more to my life than joining a theater company to investigate a murder. True, the day's to-do list was filled with bizarre tasks like *Memorize your lines so you don't make a complete fool of yourself at your first rehearsal tonight* and *Find some footwear other than chukka boots for mastering dance steps.* But I also had a career.

After sending Nick off to law school, I climbed into my van. My veterinary practice consists of driving all over Long Island, treating animals at their owners' homes or, occasionally, at their workplace. Usually, I love every minute, with only a few minor exceptions like cranky clients or patients that are seriously ill. Yet something hung over me all day like a little black cloud. It was the same feeling I got when I had a dentist appointment coming up, that low-level sense of dread that just wouldn't go away.

This time, the cause was the imminent arrival of Nick's parents later in the day.

According to his phone call with them Sunday evening, they expected to arrive around dinnertime. I was determined that every aspect of the Invasion of the Burbarians would go perfectly. My strategy was to wow them with my hospitality, welcoming them into such a warm environment that they'd immediately accept me as their daughter, rather than just their daughter-in-law.

All day, my head was swimming with plans. By the time I let myself into the cottage late Monday afternoon, I actually felt I had the situation under control.

Then I stepped inside and saw what was waiting for me.

"A-a-r-g-gh!" I shrieked.

• • •

As I took in the chaotic mess in my living room, my first panicked thought was that DEA agents had mistakenly believed this was the home of a heroin dealer or a crystal-meth factory. A throw pillow had been ripped to shreds and its feathers strewn all over the living room, making it look as if it had snowed while I was traipsing around Long Island, plying my trade. Toilet paper streamers were draped across the floor and furniture like snowdrifts. And bird seed was scattered all over the floor in Prometheus's corner of the room.

It took me only a second or two to realize it wasn't federal agents who were responsible for the horrific state of my house. It was my pets.

As Max came rushing over to greet me, I could see a few telltale feathers stuck in his beard—hard evidence that he was the perpetrator who'd pulverized that poor pillow. Tinkerbell had clearly played the role of sidekick, since she was wearing a few feathers of her own. The seeds were the result of Prometheus overturning his seed dish, one of the ways he liked to amuse himself when he got bored. And Lou had obviously gotten into the toilet paper again, something he hadn't done since the first week or two he'd moved in. Why he had to revert to such negative behavior today of all days, I couldn't begin to imagine—unless he was picking up on my high level of stress over the impending in-law invasion.

"Guys," I moaned, "how could you? Why did it have to be today? It's going to take me forever to clean up this mess!"

Lou just wagged his tail, while Max picked up his pink rubber poodle hopefully, as if he sincerely believed that a few rounds of Slimytoy could smooth anything over. Cat, regally draped across the middle cushion of the couch—her favorite spot as of late—looked on from afar. Her disdainful expression said she wanted no part of such shenanigans.

Meanwhile, Prometheus squawked, "I'm gonna give you my love!" While I recognized how impressive it was that he was one of the few birds on the entire planet who knew all the lyrics to every Led Zeppelin song ever recorded, I wasn't exactly in the mood for a concert. Especially an X-rated one.

As for undoing the havoc my fun-loving animals had wreaked, I didn't have time. At least not now. At the moment, I had more important things to do to make this place scream "Welcome" from the moment my future in-laws walked through the door. I also had to shower and change in order to make myself look like a solid, upstanding candidate for the job of Nick's wife, instead of a hired hand who'd just come in from plowing the lower forty.

I headed straight for the kitchen, where I began by taking the assortment of expensive cheeses I'd bought out of the refrigerator so they could get warmer and putting a bottle of red wine into the spot that had just been vacated so it could get cooler. I'd splurged on that too, buying the best wine I could find from Thorndike Vineyards, one of Long Island's most acclaimed wineries.

Part of me was disdainful of the way I was trying so hard to convince Nick's parents that he was marrying someone who deserved him. Someone who knew her way around a cheese shop, someone whose pets were as well-behaved as our children, if we ever had any, would be—in short, someone who was capable of creating a good home.

But part of me knew that our first meeting could well define the relationship I had with Nick's parents forever. In their eyes, the fact that I'd spent my life pursuing a meaningful career that made me feel both fulfilled and proud mattered a whole lot less than what kind of wife I'd be for their son. And that part of me was willing, even eager, to pull out all the stops.

With such thoughts in mind, I'd decided on the way home that I'd use the time I had before Dorothy and Henry Burby arrived to make brownies. True, it's generally something I'm foolhardy enough to attempt only once or twice a year, usually when there's a holiday lurking in the not-too-distant future. But I figured that if anything spelled homeyness, it was the smell of chocolate wafting through the air.

Which meant the first order of the day was locating my eight-inch-by-eight-inch square brownie pan, which was so rarely used that I tended to stick it in the most out-of-the-way place I could think of.

If I remembered correctly, that happened to be under the sink. I crouched down, opened the cabinet door, and peered inside. Sure enough, there it was, tucked away with a pie tin that had never seen the inside of an oven and a Bundt pan I'd gotten free with the purchase of some cake mix.

Before I could reach it, however, I had to pull out a gallon of paint Nick and I had bought a few weeks earlier after deciding that a fresh coat in a cheerful color was exactly what the kitchen needed. But as soon as we opened the can, we saw that that particular shade of orange, one that had looked so warm and inviting in the store, was much too bright. Instead of livening up the room, it would have made us feel as if we'd just walked inside a huge cantaloupe.

I put it on the counter, out of the way. But Nick and I must not have closed the lid tightly enough when we'd stuck it under the sink, because when I bumped it with my arm and it fell onto the linoleum floor with a loud bang, the cover flew off and bounced across the room. I watched with horror as thick orange liquid sloshed across the floor, splattering into long, menacing fingers that reached into every corner.

"*No!*" I wailed.

My two dogs, who had pretty much been minding their own business up until that point, interpreted my outburst as a cry for help. Either that or they thought something involving food was going on.

At any rate, they both came loping in. Even though I instantly knew what was about to happen, there was no way to stop it, since there was no actual door in the doorway. Within seconds, my kitchen floor was covered with orange paw prints, both Westie-size and Dalmatian-size.

"Max, get out of there!" I shrieked. "Lou, stop!"

Max froze, looking up at me guiltily. As for Lou, the sharpness of my tone sent him skittering across the wet floor. Before either of us knew what was happening, he slipped and ended up lying on his side.

In addition to large orange smears all over the floor

in front of the refrigerator, I now had a large, gangly dog who was orange along the left side of his body.

What's black and white and orange all over, I thought morosely.

I scooped up Max, figuring I'd minimize the damage by getting my dogs out of there as fast as I could. It would have been a good plan, except for the fact that his fluffy white paws had become fluffy paintbrushes, turning my shirt, pants, and most of the skin on my arms the same bright color that everything else was quickly turning.

Lou began barking furiously, no doubt sensing how upset I was and not having a clue that his canine enthusiasm was part of the reason.

"Quiet!" I barked back.

His sweet face tightened into an expression of remorse. I could have handled hurting his feelings, just a little bit. What I couldn't handle was the fact that he decided to try getting back in my good graces by sitting down in the middle of the paint-covered floor and holding up one orange paw as if responding to the command "Shake."

Somewhere in the back of my mind, I realized that at any other time I might have considered this whole scene hilarious. And I might even have found comfort in the fact that this was water-based paint, which wouldn't be all that hard to clean up as long as it didn't dry.

But this wasn't any other time. This was now, when Nick's parents were due in only a couple of hours.

"Stay!" I commanded Lou. He gave a hopeful little wag of his tail, as if the fact that I was paying attention to him meant he was back on my A-list. Determined to give it his best shot, he remained sitting, his orange butt glued to the orange floor.

I took a few steps toward the kitchen doorway and

kicked off my shoes, which now had squishy orange soles. Then I carried Max across the living room, opened the front door, and deposited him outside. Cat and Tink watched in silence, as if wondering what poor Max had done to deserve banishment.

Next I dashed into the bathroom and grabbed the biggest towel I could find, cajoled Lou into lying down on it, and dragged him across the living-room floor so he could join Max in the great outdoors.

Thanks to two and a half rolls of paper towels, a lot of water, and a bottle of some magical cleaning fluid that smelled like something an undertaker would use, I managed to turn the linoleum floor back to its original shade of grayish-white. Of course, the dangerous chemical smell from the cleaning fluid lingered in the air. I could practically feel the brain cells dying off.

But at least my kitchen looked as if normal people lived in it instead of Smurfs.

I'd just gotten the floor back to its normal color—but hadn't had a chance to even start on my pants and shirt—when I heard a car door slam right outside the living-room window.

Nick! I thought, overcome with relief. He's home early. He's going to help me clean up the feathers and the toilet paper before his parents get here, and then I'll have time to get those brownies in the oven and rinse out these clothes and scrub my skin back to its normal color in the shower....

I froze at the sound of a second car door slamming.

I raced through the living room. But even before I reached the window, I saw a white car I didn't recognize. Two people had just gotten out: a towering, broad-shouldered woman with short dark hair that looked as if it had been sculpted out of plaster of Paris and a lean, white-haired man who was as gangly as Lou.

At least seventeen suitcases were piled on the lawn next to their car.

"Oh, my God!" I cried aloud. "It's the invasion!"

The first thing I noticed was that Nick's mother was dressed entirely in white. A white skirt, a white blouse, white shoes, and even a white hat. She looked as if she was on her way to Ascot, not enduring a fifteen-hundred-mile road trip.

It was at that moment that I noticed she also carried something white in her arms. White—and fluffy. While it could have been a trendy pocketbook, my bet was that it was Mitzi, the Maltese Nick was so sure would be one of the few dogs I couldn't find a way to bond with.

I glanced down self-consciously, fully aware that I, on the other hand, had chosen the color of prison garb for my fashion statement.

A wave of excruciatingly horrible heat rushed over me as I suddenly remembered the whereabouts of my dogs.

The fear had barely formed in my mind when the nightmare became a reality, right before my eyes. Max, as usual, had run up to greet our visitors. But my friendly little terrier was so excited over having company that he broke the number one rule that I'd tried desperately to impress upon him since the day I'd adopted him.

He jumped up on Nick's mother, painting her blindingly white skirt with orange paw prints.

"Agh-h-h!" she yelled.

"Max!" I cried, bursting through the front door. I ran over and scooped him up, hardly caring at all that the sharp edges of the gravel in the driveway were cutting into my shoeless feet as if I was undergoing some test of faith.

When Lou came loping over, I grabbed his collar,

trying to exercise at least a little damage control. Then, not quite knowing what to do next, I just stood there clutching my two canines, wondering what the odds were that the ground would open and swallow me up at what would have been a really good time.

"My skirt!" Dorothy Burby exclaimed, peering downward over Mitzi's fur. "This...this *glop* will never come out!"

She looked at me expectantly. And, I might add, accusingly.

"You're early," I greeted them in a soft, defeated voice.

"We got lucky," Nick's father, Henry, said heartily. "Hardly hit any traffic." He stiffened, as if he'd just realized that maybe they hadn't been lucky at all. That maybe if they'd delayed their arrival by even a few minutes, things would have turned out differently.

I turned to say something to Nick's mother, hopefully something that would sound much more welcoming. As if on cue, Mitzi began barking her head off.

"Poor Mitzi!" she cooed. "I know, Mitzi-Bitzi, it's so upsetting, isn't it? To come all this way just to have our favorite skirt *ruined.*"

She paused to take a deep breath, as if she'd suddenly remembered who she was. She stood up straighter, extended her hand, and said, "You must be Jessica."

I just nodded.

She looked me up and down. "You're certainly not what I expected."

"I don't usually wear this much orange," I returned, smiling. And hoping my future mother-in-law would do the same.

No such luck.

"Is Nicky here?" she asked, her voice strangely high-pitched and tinged with desperation.

I knew I was about to let her down even further by announcing that for the moment she was stuck with me.

"He should be home any minute," I replied, hoping that just saying the words would make them come true. "Why don't you come inside and get settled?"

It was only then that I remembered what "inside" looked like. But I couldn't very well leave my future in-laws standing in the driveway, no matter how tempting that proposition might be.

"I loved this skirt," Dorothy moaned as she and Mitzi-Bitzi followed me inside.

Henry, who'd been left behind to deal with every single piece of luggage, said, "But, Dottie! You were just saying in the car that you thought it made you look ten pounds heavier!"

"I said no such thing," she snapped. "I would never own a garment that didn't show off my figure to its best advantage!"

As soon as she strutted inside with her little white dog still in her arms, she froze, causing me to bump into her and transfer orange paint from my clothes onto hers. She didn't seem to notice.

"Heavens!" she cried. "Your house has been vandalized!"

"I'm afraid not," I said. "The dogs got a little rambunctious today, that's all."

She turned around and studied me for what seemed like a very long time. "I thought dogs were your business."

"Yes, but..." I didn't see any point in trying to explain. Instead, I swept as many of the feathers and toilet paper garlands off the couch as I could and said, "Why don't you sit down? What can I get you? Coffee? A cold drink? Wine?"

I must admit, I was kind of hoping for the wine option.

"Coffee would be fabulous," Dorothy replied, settling into one corner of the couch with Mitzi in her lap. "In fact, I need some liquid refreshment before I can muster up the energy required to unpack and put on some *clean* clothes. I take my coffee light but not too light, about two-thirds half-and-half and the rest one percent milk. One and a half packets of Equal. And stir it really well."

She thinks she's in Starbucks, I thought scornfully, translating her order as coffee with milk and sugar. I glanced over at Henry, who had collapsed in the toilet paper—strewn upholstered chair, no doubt exhausted from hauling in a good portion of the suitcases. I wondered if it was simply coincidence that he'd sat as far away as a person could get from Dorothy without leaving the room. "What about you, Henry? Milk? Sugar?"

"Black."

I was starting to like this man.

"Dottie," I heard him say as I retreated to the kitchen, "I don't suppose you brought any antihistamines. If I didn't know better, I'd think there were cats in this house. . . . Ah-ah-ah-*choo*!"

I froze in the doorway. "Don't tell me you're allergic to cats," I said weakly.

"Deathly allergic," Dorothy snapped. "He can't tolerate being around them. Most people think it's the fur that's the problem, but it's actually the dander. Those are teensy-weensy flakes of dried saliva on their skin—"

"I know what cat dander is," I muttered.

"But you don't have any, do you?" she asked anxiously. "Cats, I mean?"

"I have two," I admitted.

"Don't worry, Jessica," Henry said. "If I can just take something for my allergies, I'll be—ah-choo! Ah-choo! Ah-*cho-o-o-o*!"

"I think I have some Benadryl," I said. "Will that help?"

"Definitely," Dorothy replied.

"It does tend to make me a little tired," Henry added.

"Take it," his wife ordered. "I can't stand to listen to all that annoying sneezing."

First I went to the bathroom and got the Benadryl, along with a glass of water. Then I grabbed poor Cat and Tinkerbell and jailed them in the bedroom. I knew it wouldn't make much of a difference, since the cottage was covered with cat hairs, but at least it would look like I was trying to do something constructive. Next I went into the kitchen to get Mr. Coffee going. Once that was done, I got serious about cleaning as much orange paint off my dogs as I could without putting them through the gentle cycle of a washing machine.

I also scrounged around in the freezer and found some chocolate chip cookies the size of saucers. I couldn't remember how they'd gotten there, but they were going to have to fill in for the freshly baked brownies. I considered microwaving them but decided that Dorothy wasn't likely to eat them anyway since she was so concerned with keeping her girlish figure. As for Henry, before long he'd be too drugged to notice.

"Here you are, Henry," I said as I came out of the kitchen a few minutes later, bearing a tray. "And, Dottie, this mug is yours—"

She stiffened. "Only my husband calls me Dottie," she said crisply. "Everyone else calls me Dorothy."

"Sorry," I said. Nick, where *are* you? I thought mournfully.

Just then Max picked up his beloved pink poodle in his jaws and tottered over to Mitzi, who was still curled up in her owner's lap. He glanced up at her hopefully, as if he was asking, *Wanna play?*

I heard a low growl, which quickly escalated into a sharp, high-pitched bark.

"Aarf!" Mitzi complained. "Aarf! Aarf!"

"Get that horrid animal out of here!" Dorothy shrieked. "It's clearly upsetting poor Mitzi!"

"I can see that," I returned, nearly tripping over poor confused Lou as I leaped across the room to retrieve Max.

But my feisty little terrier had ideas of his own. He wasn't about to let some interloper call the shots, something that clearly violated terrier code. Instead, he started barking too, making it clear he was ready to go *mano a mano*—or paw to paw—with the cranky white lapdog.

His challenge only escalated Mitzi's fury. "Aarf! Aarf, aarf!" her deafening bark continued.

The more she barked, the tighter Dorothy held on to her. "Go away!" she cried, waving her hand at my sweet little doggy as if he were a cockroach. "Get away from here, you vile beast!"

Nick! a voice inside my head shrieked, sounding as desperate as Stanley Kowalski wailing for his wife, Stella, in *A Streetcar Named Desire*.

I tried to soothe Max, meanwhile carrying him to the bedroom—which at this point was starting to get crowded. "You're better off in here, hiding under the bed," I muttered. "In fact, save a place for me."

As I shut the door firmly, I tried to compose a calm, logical way of explaining to Nick that this arrangement simply was not going to work. Maybe I was so miserable that he actually heard my thoughts, because just then I heard a car door slam right outside.

"It's Nick!" I cried breathlessly, charging toward the front door. Never in my entire life had I been so happy to see him.

"Mom? Dad?" he cried as he stepped inside.

"Here's our boy!" Dorothy announced gleefully. She seemed to be having a religious experience. Her face lit up with joy and she ran toward him with open arms. "Oh, Nicky, it's so wonderful to see you!" She was so glad, in fact, that she actually released Mitzi, dumping her unceremoniously in poor Henry's lap.

"It's great to see you too, Mom." He gave her a big hug, then went over to his father, who was looking very relaxed and was in fact listing to one side, Mitzi and all. The Benadryl was clearly starting to kick in. "Dad, good to see you too." Nick leaned over and gave him a hug. Henry just looked at him with glazed eyes and blinked.

"Well," Nick said, glancing at what looked to the unenlightened eye like a pleasant afternoon tea party, "I see you've had a chance to make yourselves at home." Glancing at me and frowning, he said, "Don't you think you should shower and change? And what's with the feathers? And the toilet paper?"

"The dogs," I replied.

"Speaking of the dogs, why is Lou so...so *orange*?"

"I was just as surprised as you are to find that Jessica has so little control over her own pets," Dorothy observed, grabbing Mitzi out of her husband's arms and regally lowering herself back onto the couch. "Especially since she's in the dog grooming business."

"That's not what I do," I said in a strangely high-pitched voice.

"Don't you? I thought your job was cutting poo-dles' fur into those horrid little poofs."

I bit my lip. "I'm not a dog groomer," I replied, sounding so polite even I was impressed. "I'm an animal doctor. I'm sure Mitzi has a veterinarian you bring her to regularly."

Dorothy sighed tiredly, as if this topic of conversation was so boring it was exhausting her. "I've never been a pet person. Aside from Mitzi, of course. But she's not a dog, is she? You're my little girl, aren't you, Mitzi-Bitzi? *Aren't* you?"

I opened my mouth to speak. But before I had a chance to give my future mother-in-law a piece of my mind, Nick reached over and squeezed my hand.

"Getting into vet school is even more competitive than getting into medical school," he said calmly.

"Animals always seem so *dirty* to me." Dorothy cast poor Lou such a scathing look that he dropped his head and slunk away. "Not my Mitzi, of course," she continued. "But she thinks she's a person, don't you, Mitzi-Bitzi? And that's because we've always treated you like a member of our family. You're the sister Nick never had, aren't you?" Pointedly she added, "And she's as clean as any other little girl."

Perhaps the cleanliness standards at the local Holiday Inn would be more to your liking, I thought, feeling my blood heat up from simmer to boil. Or we could always set up a tent outside.

In fact, I was just about to suggest that alternative housing might be a good idea when the room suddenly exploded with a deafening "*AH-CHOO!*"

We all looked over at Henry, who had rallied from his stupor just in time to grab a dish towel–size hand-kerchief out of his pocket and thrust it against his face with alarming ferocity.

"Ahchoo! Ahchoo! Ah-ah-ah-*choo*!"

"Are you okay, Dad?" Nick asked anxiously.

"It's my allergies," Henry replied. "I'm sure the antihistamine effects of the Benadryl will kick in soon, but sometimes it takes a while—*ah-choo*!"

"What are you allergic to?" Nick asked. He glanced at me accusingly, as if I'd gone out of my way to spray pollen throughout the house or something.

"Cats," Henry and I said in unison. He'd barely gotten the word out before he broke out into another string of sneezes.

I cast Nick a look of total desperation. One that was designed to communicate, *Plan A is not working. It's time to come up with a Plan B.*

But he didn't seem to be able to read my expression. Either that or he chose not to.

You can still back out of this, I told myself. Getting engaged is not like getting a tattoo. It can easily be undone.

A more mature voice reminded me that it wasn't Nick's parents I was planning to marry; it was Nick. And I liked Nick. I loved Nick.

Still, I thought grimly, in-laws, like diamonds, are forever.

• • •

"Nicky," Dorothy cooed, after she'd drunk two cups of coffee that she begrudgingly admitted tasted just fine and downed no fewer than four oversize chocolate chip cookies, "would you bring in the rest of my luggage? Henry and I might as well start making ourselves at home—as much as that's possible, of course."

"I'll help," I volunteered, jumping out of my seat. Anything to avoid being left alone with Dorothy and Henry.

"Nick," I said breathlessly as soon as we were

outside and out of earshot, "I don't think this is going to work. It's just too crowded."

My attempt at diplomacy didn't work. "She's not as bad as she seems," Nick said with a pleading look in his eyes.

No, I thought grimly. She's actually a heck of a lot worse. If this is Dorothy Burby on day one, while she's still on her best behavior, I don't dare imagine day three.

"Just wait until she gets to know you better," he added. "I'm sure that the two of you will become the best of friends."

"It's probably just as well that I'll be out this evening," I said, resigned. I hauled a duffel bag out of the trunk. It was so heavy I decided the Burbys must have brought along their favorite bowling balls. "That'll give your parents some time to get used to our place without me getting in their way."

" 'Out'?" Nick repeated, blinking. "Where are you going?"

"I have a rehearsal. For the musical Betty roped me into, remember?"

"But what about my parents?"

"The three of you can spend the evening catching up," I said cheerfully. "It's obvious that you're the light of your mother's life, and I'm sure she'd like nothing better than having you all to yourself. You can tell her all about law school and . . . and you can show her the photos from our trip to Hawaii!"

Nick grumbled something I didn't actually hear, since he'd stuck his head into the backseat to retrieve one more suitcase. I figured it was probably just as well.

Having a rehearsal to go to practically every night of the week was starting to seem like a real stroke of luck. Compared to feeling like one of the characters in *No Exit*, the Sartre play in which three people who hate one another are trapped together in a room for eternity, an evening of acting and singing and, yes, even dancing, suddenly didn't sound half bad. Even if it *was* likely I'd end up making a complete fool of myself.

Chapter 6

"A dog is the only thing on this earth that loves you more than he loves himself."

—Josh Billings

I hope you're not nervous, Jessica," Betty said later that evening as I drove the two of us to Port Townsend for my first rehearsal with the Port Players.

Actually, I'd been on the verge of saying something along those exact same lines. Ever since she'd gotten into my VW, I could sense her anxiety. But I suspected it had nothing to do with whether she'd mastered all her dance moves. Instead, what was undoubtedly responsible was the fact that she was still upset about the tension in her household, as well as the possibility that someone in her theater group was a cold-blooded killer.

I decided to do my best to distract her.

"I'm a little nervous," I told her. "But maybe you can take my mind off the butterflies in my stomach by telling me about Amelia Earhart. I don't really know that much about her, aside from the fact that she's one of the world's most famous aviators—and probably the best-known female aviator of all time."

"You're right on both counts," Betty said. "She racked up quite a long list of achievements. In 1932, she became the first woman to make a solo transatlantic flight. She was also the first person to fly solo from Hawaii to the American mainland, which made her the first person to fly solo anywhere in the Pacific and the first person to solo both the Atlantic and the Pacific Oceans." Her voice was becoming more animated, a sign that my ploy was working. "On top of all that, she held several transcontinental speed records and a women's altitude world record.

"To me," Betty continued, "she's a symbol of adventure, a spirited role model who proved that women can do anything men can do."

"Then I guess Simon Wainwright had a real brainstorm when he came up with the idea of writing a musical about her," I observed.

"Definitely. Have you read through his fabulous script yet?"

"So far, all I've had a chance to look at is the scene with my speaking part." I cleared my throat and, in my strongest, most self-assured voice, boomed, "Come on, Amelia. Let's show these men the stuff we're made of!"

"That's very good, Jessica!" Betty exclaimed.

"Thanks. I've only said it about eight thousand times in the last twelve hours," I admitted. "All day I kept muttering it under my breath as I drove from one house call to another."

"At least you'll get your scene out of the way early on," Betty said. "Anita Snook gives Amelia her first flying lesson in scene four, I believe. You see, the play starts with George Putnam—he's Amelia's husband—narrating. He announces that Amelia Earhart is about to embark on a historic flight that will make her the first woman to fly around the world. Onstage behind him, the ensemble is bustling around, reading newspapers and talking about her groundbreaking flight. You and I are both in that scene.

"But then the play goes back in time, to Amelia's childhood. She was only ten when she saw her first plane at the Iowa State Fair. A darling little girl named Wendy plays Amelia as a child. Then we see Amelia at twenty—that's Elena's first scene. She's at a stunt-flying exhibition, and the pilot of a small plane deliberately heads toward her to give her a scare. But she stands her ground, not even flinching. There's a famous quote about the experience, something like, 'I didn't understand at the time, but I believe that little red airplane said something to me as it swished by.' "

"So that's where her passion for flying began," I commented.

"Exactly. Then the play follows her through all the events in her early adult life: becoming a nurse's aide in Toronto during World War Two, going up in a plane for the first time in Long Beach, California, with a pilot named Frank Hawks, and then her first flying lesson with Anita Snook—that's you.

"The rest of the play takes the audience through her achievements, as well as her relationship with George Putnam. He was a publisher who started out doing public-relations work for her. But before long, they fell in love and married."

"She died on that flight around the world, didn't she? The one the play begins with?"

"That's right. It was in 1937. She'd gone more than twenty-two thousand miles with her navigator, Fred Noonan, and she only had about seven thousand miles to go. But something went wrong and she never made it. She was never found either, which resulted in all kinds of speculation. One theory is that she and Noonan were captured by the Japanese and killed. Another is that they both came back to the United States but used assumed names."

Betty shrugged. "As tragic as her untimely disappearance was, it adds to her mystery. She was truly larger than life."

At least I didn't get roped into playing Amelia Earhart, I thought as I pulled into a parking space in front of Theater One. Compared to playing Amelia, spitting out a few lines as Anita Snook should be a snap.

As soon as I walked inside, I sensed that the atmosphere was markedly different from the first time I'd been there, right after everyone got the tragic news about Simon Wainwright. That time I'd felt like I was attending a memorial service. Today there was a buzz in the air that practically screamed, *It's showtime!*

As I trailed down the aisle after Betty, swerving out of the way of the sewing machine someone had set up near the stage, I realized that the butterflies in my stomach weren't the only ones doing warm-ups. The other members of the company were scattered around the first ten or fifteen rows stretching, doing breathing exercises, or earnestly studying their scripts.

"How come everyone's sitting out front, instead of backstage?" I asked.

"Derek likes the cast members to sit in the audience as much as possible during rehearsals," Betty replied. "Watching the rest of the cast rehearse helps familiarize everyone with the entire production. This way, everyone can also hear all his comments, so he doesn't end up saying the same things over and over."

Nearly all the cast members were dressed casually in T-shirts and jeans or sweatpants. In fact, Betty was one of the few who looked the way I'd expect performers to look during a rehearsal. She wore a black leotard and a pink chiffon skirt specially made for dancers, along with beige high-heeled dancing shoes with a strap across the foot.

"I'll just tell Derek we're here," she said, dropping her bag onto one of the red velvet seats. "I'm sure he'll be grateful that you showed up. Maybe even a little surprised."

No more surprised than I am, I thought, once again wondering how on earth I'd gotten myself into this.

I was doing my best to reason with those annoying butterflies when I heard the woman sitting a few seats away from me say something. It sounded an awful lot like, "Ah, aw, oh, oo." I wondered if she was in pain.

"Excuse me?" I said politely.

"Ah, aw, oh, oo," she repeated. Apparently I'd heard her correctly the first time. "Ah, aw, oh, oo. Mah, maw, moh, moo. Mah, maw, moh, moo."

"Sorry," I said, trying not to let my embarrassment show. "I'll just leave you to your..." I let my voice trail off, not certain how to refer to the voice exercises I'd finally figured out she was doing.

"Pah, paw, poh, poo," she continued, glaring at me as I moved away as quickly and as quietly as I could.

I was actually relieved when Derek stood up in front of the stage and clapped his hands. "Okay, people. Everybody onstage. Jill is doing the choreography for 'Wild Blue Yonder.'"

"Let me give you a quick overview," Betty whispered after she and I shuffled up the aisle and onto the stage with all the other actors. "That platform up above is called a catwalk. It's mainly used for lighting and sound equipment. Those balconies on either side of the stage are called juliets—as in *Romeo and Juliet*. And those three trapdoors on the floor open into the basement. By the way, *upstage* refers to the back of the stage. *Downstage* is closer to the audience."

I simply nodded.

"Jill D'Angelo, the choreographer, changed some of the steps in the 'Wild Blue Yonder' number," Betty continued in the same low voice. "She's going to teach them to us right now. That's Jill over there."

She pointed to a slender, dark-haired woman standing on the stage. Like Betty, Jill was dressed like a pro, although her leotard, sheer skirt, and high-heeled dancing shoes were all black. I remembered that the director had been talking to her on Saturday, right before he'd decided to make me a star—or at least a member of the cast.

"This is what's called a choreography rehearsal," Betty added.

I blinked. "You mean there's more than one kind of rehearsal?"

"That's right. First comes the read-through, where the actors sit around a table, reading through the script. Next there's a blocking rehearsal. The director blocks out the entire production, positioning everyone onstage for each scene. Of course, it's all subject to change as rehearsals continue and it becomes obvious that some blocking works while other blocking doesn't.

"After that," she continued, "there are music rehearsals, choreography rehearsals, and integration rehearsals. When opening night gets close, we'll start doing actual runs, which means going through the whole show. And the final week—tech week—is when the lighting people and the sound people come in to do their thing. That week, the members of the orchestra also come in."

My head was reeling with all these new terms, not to mention the pressure of catching up. I was going to have to learn what everyone else had already been doing for three weeks, and fast.

I was still trying comprehend the challenge I'd taken on when Jill clapped her hands.

"Okay, my darlings, give me your beginning positions for scene four, please," she said. "Jessie, you'll be standing over here, next to Elena."

I took my place, then proceeded to copy Jill's movements as she began teaching all of us the dance number. I couldn't help looking around at the other people onstage, wondering if any of them was harboring a horrifying secret. Was Simon Wainwright's murderer the lanky, red-haired young man who played one of the two pilots who accompanied Amelia Earhart on her famous transatlantic flight? Was it the intense middle-aged man who played Will Rogers, the comedian and folk philosopher who was one of her contemporaries? Or was it possible that Elena, who'd been moved out of the role of Anita Snook and into the role of Amelia Earhart, was ambitious enough to have killed Simon, knowing that Aziza would drop out and she'd be the most likely replacement?

I had to remind myself that even though my main reason for being here was to answer all those questions, at the moment I had something much more pressing to attend to.

You'd better focus on dancing, I scolded myself, or you're going to look ridiculous.

"Listen to me, my darlings," the choreographer said, demonstrating the opening steps that accompanied the song "Wild Blue Yonder." "It's step, pivot, step, uh-*huh*. Got it? Let me just count it out, sweethearts, to the count of eight. If you start on the right, go left, and if you start on the left, go right. So cross over...that's five, six, seven, eight...and one, two, three, four. I know I'm throwing a lot at you, and I know it's busy, but you'll catch on. And it will help if you start coming to rehearsals in clothes you can move in. Let's take it from where Amelia sings the words *learn to fly*. And one, two, three, four . . ."

My head was swimming. This way, that way, step, pivot—I'd always thought that when it came to coordination, I was at least average, if not slightly above. Why, then, did I find myself going left when all the other members of the ensemble were going right?

"Umph!" one of the other dancers cried as I smashed into her, surprising myself as much as I surprised her.

"Jessie, that's stage left," Jill called with just a hint of impatience. "Stage left means left while you're standing on the stage, facing the audience."

I knew that, I thought, embarrassed. At least, I used to know that.

"Let's do it again."

This time, I managed to cross the stage without causing anyone bodily injury. Maybe I wasn't exactly graceful, but at least I wasn't dangerous.

"You'll get it," whispered one of the other members of the ensemble, a lithe blond woman named Courtney who looked as if she was still a college student. "Sometimes it takes a while."

"Thanks," I whispered back, genuinely appreciative of any encouragement I could get.

All of us in the ensemble continued to copy Jill's moves, at the same time memorizing where our hands were supposed to be, which way we should be facing, and what our facial expressions should be. Never before had it occurred to me that every moment of a stage production—every word, every hand gesture, every smile, every step—was planned out in advance.

"Okay, my darlings, that's good." Jill extended her right hand with her fingers spread, as if she were imitating a gecko. "Then we go into a Fosse," she continued, bending from the waist and freezing. "*Pose*. Then, for a completely different feeling, extend your arm—we'll call it a Freddie."

"What's a Fosse?" I asked Betty, who happened to be standing right behind me.

"She's referring to the kind of move the Broadway choreographer Bob Fosse would have used," she returned in a low voice. "And a Freddie—"

"Don't tell me. Fred Astaire?"

Betty beamed. "Now you're getting it."

"It's kick and cross, pivot and pose," Jill called. "Got it? We'll end with a button."

"Translate, please," I whispered to Betty, growing increasingly frustrated over my inability to understand this foreign language.

"It means you wait until the very end of the song to strike your pose. You snap into it at the last second."

"Got it," I returned, wishing I felt as certain as I sounded.

"Okay, my darlings," Jill exclaimed, clapping her hands, "let's take it from the tippy top. Jessie, we'll start with your line."

The tiny amount of satisfaction I'd gotten from learning a five-minute dance routine vanished as I stepped forward as stiffly as a robot. As I gazed out at the endless rows of seats, I was suddenly gripped with fear.

It wasn't because I hadn't learned the few lines my character had. Unlike in my nightmare of a couple of nights before, I'd memorized not only my opening line but my entire part. But saying those words to an audience—*acting*—was something else entirely.

My weekly live television spot felt like a piece of cake by comparison. At the Channel 14 TV studio, there were generally only a couple of people in the room, so it was easy to ignore the fact that out there in TV land, thousands were watching me. Here in the theater, I could actually see the faces of the people in the audience. True, there were no more than six at the moment, since most of the cast was onstage. But from this vantage point, I could judge their reactions by their expressions, their posture, even how much they were fidgeting.

"It begins, 'Come on, Amelia,'" Derek prompted from the front row, where he was sitting with a script in his lap.

I swallowed hard. "Come on, Amelia," I said aloud, aware that my mouth had become as dry as desert sand. "Let's show these men the stuff we're made of." I tried to make the words sing out loud and clear. I really did. Instead, they came out a near-whisper.

"Good, but not quite loud enough," Derek said patiently. "Let's try that again."

"Come on, Amelia. Let's show these men the stuff we're made of!" This time my words came out like a squawk. An audible squawk, but a squawk nonetheless.

"You wouldn't get me in a plane with an instructor who had so little confidence," some unknown person behind me commented.

"Come on, Amelia!" I cried in a powerful voice that surprised even me. "Let's *show* these men the stuff we're made of!"

"Excellent!" Derek exclaimed. "Let's continue! Amelia—Elena—this is where you start singing. Can we get a music cue?"

I did it! I thought, experiencing such a rush that I was tempted to try a couple of handsprings right then and there. I actually did a good job of delivering my line!

I glanced over at Betty, who gave me an approving nod. I just grinned, glad that I hadn't let her down.

We did a run-through of the entire number. Even I could see that it was still ragged. But I could also imagine what it was going to turn into once we'd all perfected our dance steps and added costumes, makeup, lighting, props, and hopefully a humongous surge of opening night adrenaline.

"Okay, my sweeties," Jill finally said. "Let's take a ten-minute break."

"Wait!" A short, plump young woman bobbed up from the front row. "Before anyone leaves, I'd like President Coolidge and President Hoover to come backstage for their final costume fittings."

Lacey Croft, I surmised. The costume designer who had found Simon's body.

I studied her with interest. For someone who was so involved with clothes, she certainly didn't appear to have put a lot of thought into her own outfit. She was dressed in a dark pleated skirt that did little to downplay her ample girth. Her white blouse was rumpled, and the burgundy cardigan sweater she wore over it looked a couple of sizes too big. Her dark-brown hair was twisted into a haphazard bun and loosely held in place with a plastic clip, allowing wisps of hair to frame her round, almost childlike face.

She was definitely on my list of people to talk to, and I made a mental note to do so the very first chance I got. But now was not the time, mainly because I wasn't playing one of the two presidents who had honored Amelia Earhart for her splendid achievements. It was just as well, since I was suddenly aware of how much energy the thirty-minute ordeal I'd just undergone had taken out of me.

Still, I was itching to get a look at the crime scene. But Derek's policy about cast members watching all the rehearsals made it difficult to slip backstage. Besides, finding an excuse to go into the men's dressing room would be kind of a challenge. But checking it out was a high priority, and I intended to see it for myself the very first chance I got.

As I dropped into one of the red velvet seats, one of the actors I remembered from Saturday afternoon's rehearsal strolled up the aisle. He was lean and on the tall side, probably in his mid-thirties but clearly striving for a slightly younger look by wearing his sand-colored hair on the shaggy side. Like most of the other actors, he wore jeans and a T-shirt. He was the man who'd agreed with Aziza Zorn that the production should be shut down. Yet here he was, enduring the grueling rehearsal, just as I was.

He stopped and offered me an encouraging smile, his blue eyes shining. "That wasn't bad, especially since you're new to the company," he commented. "I take it you've got some serious acting experience."

"You're too kind," I assured him. "I believe the last time I appeared onstage was in my first grade class's production of 'The Food Pyramid.' I played a carrot."

He laughed. "Then I guess you're simply a natural." He held out his hand. "I'm Kyle Carlson. Also known as Fred Noonan, the navigator who accompanied Amelia Earhart on her final flight."

As we shook hands, I commented, "I guess this rehearsal is difficult for everyone, the first one since Simon..."

Kyle's cheerful expression faded. "Yes. He and I were really close friends."

"Then you must be devastated."

"Frankly, I'm still in shock."

"So is Betty Vandervoort," I said. "She's a good friend of mine. In fact, she's the person who got me involved in the Port Players. She was really fond of Simon."

"I know Betty. She's a really nice person."

Trying to sound casual, I said, "Betty thinks somebody who's involved with the Port Players must have murdered Simon."

"Duh!"

The vehemence of his response stunned me. "You mean you agree?"

"Of course! It's obvious. In fact, I'm furious that the police haven't gone ahead and arrested her. I can't imagine what they're waiting for."

"You know who did it?" I asked, sounding as surprised as I felt.

"It doesn't take a rocket scientist—or Sherlock Holmes—to know that Lacey killed him."

"Lacey Croft?"

"Of course!" he exclaimed angrily. "She was standing over his body when the police came in Saturday morning. If that's not holding a smoking gun, I don't know what is!"

"I thought she was simply the person who had the bad luck to find him," I said, carefully measuring my words.

"Ha!" he cried. "There was a lot going on between those two. Believe me, I know. Simon gave me an earful, especially over the last couple of weeks. That woman is not stable.

"In fact, looking back, I'm not surprised." He clenched his fists tightly. "I should have seen it coming. Simon should have seen it coming."

I blinked. "Why? What was—"

"I can't believe how incompetent the police are!" Kyle was apparently too wrapped up in his tirade to notice that I'd asked a question. Or at least tried to.

"All they have to do is ask anyone who knew him! There's no mystery here.

"The way this whole thing is being handled is an abomination," he continued bitterly. "In fact, I was even furious with Derek at first. I couldn't believe he wanted to continue with the production. I thought it was really bad taste. I was seething when I walked out of here on Saturday."

"Yet you decided not to quit, the way Aziza did," I said gently.

"That's right." He sounded a tad defensive. But at least he'd calmed down. "After I got home and had a chance to think about it, I realized that Derek was right, that going ahead with the production really is the best way of honoring Simon's memory."

"I suppose it is," I agreed. "And it's a great show. I didn't know Simon, but I think he would have been pleased that this production of *She's Flying High* is going to live on."

"I suppose," he agreed gruffly. "But I still think it's a travesty that they've allowed Lacey to remain part of this production." And then, after an awkward silence, he asked, "So what do you do when you're not thrilling audiences with your innate acting talent?"

"I'm a veterinarian."

"No kidding! How cool is that?" Kyle seemed to have completely recovered from his tirade over Simon's death. He hesitated for a few seconds, then asked, "Be honest: Would I be overstepping the bounds of polite conversation if I asked you for some free advice?"

"Not at all," I replied. "I give out advice all the time—even some that's completely unsolicited. What's the problem?"

"A couple of days ago, Monty, my Weimaraner, was chasing a squirrel and he squirmed through a hole in the metal fence around my property. I guess it had some sharp edges, because he got a couple of pretty bad cuts. I've been trying to clean them with bacitracin and hydrogen peroxide, but they don't seem to be getting any better. What do you think I should do?"

"I hate to make recommendations without actually examining the animal," I told him. "Monty might need stitches, but I can't tell without seeing how bad his cuts are. If you'd like, I could check him out."

"Where's your office?"

"All over Long Island. What I mean is, I operate a mobile services unit. A clinic-on-wheels. I travel to my clients' homes to treat their animals."

"Wow. I've never heard of that. But it sounds great, not only for your patients and their owners but for you too."

"I enjoy it," I agreed. "It's certainly better than being holed up in an office all day. If you'd like, I'd be happy to stop by your house to take a look at Monty. How about tomorrow? It's a fairly light day, so I'm sure I could fit you in."

The vehemence with which Kyle Carlson had insisted that Lacey killed Simon had piqued my interest. I sensed that making a house call to treat his dog would be an excellent way to begin my investigation.

"Tomorrow would be great," Kyle said. "I often go home for lunch, since the place where I work is so close to my house in Melton. Would twelve-thirty work for you? I'll give you my address and phone number...."

I'd barely had a chance to copy the information down when Derek clapped his hands.

"Okay, everyone, let's run through the opening scene," he boomed.

This time, going up onstage didn't seem nearly as frightening. I wasn't sure why. Maybe it was because

I'd already broken the ice by delivering my first line. Or maybe it was because my little chat with Simon's pal Kyle had helped me put things in perspective, reminding me of the real reason I was here.

I hoped going to his house to check out his dog the following day would give me a chance to find out more about Simon and the rest of the cast. At the moment, however, my focus was Lacey Croft. The fact that she'd reported Simon's murder to the police and been found standing next to the body, combined with Kyle's contention that she was the culprit, had earned her the honor of becoming the very first person on my list of suspects.

• • •

While Theater One was the obvious place to corner Lacey, I didn't think it was the best place. For one thing, she was almost always surrounded by other cast members, and most of the time they were either stripped down to their underwear or up to their necks in straight pins. But I also wanted to catch her with her guard down by talking to her in a completely different environment than the one she'd shared with Simon Wainwright.

That meant calling in the big guns.

"Forrester?" I said as sweetly as I could after dialing the *Newsday* reporter's cell phone number on Tuesday morning. "It's Jessie."

"Hey, Popper!" he returned with his usual enthusiasm. "Always a treat to hear from you. What's up?"

"I was wondering if you could tell me where I can find Lacey Croft during the day. She's the costume designer at Theater One."

"I know who she is, since she also happens to be the person who discovered Simon Wainwright's body."

"Good memory," I commented.

"That's why they pay me the big bucks," he returned. "And it just so happens I have that piece of information."

"I thought you might," I said, gritting my teeth and wishing he would just tell me.

Instead, he said, "If I tell you, it's part of our deal, right?"

"What deal—oh, that." I realized he was referring to the ridiculous terms he'd laid out when I first asked for his help: that in exchange for his assistance, I'd agree to go out with him if Nick or I ever broke off our engagement. "Sure, Forrester," I said impatiently. "Whatever you say."

"Just checking. Lacey Croft runs workshops at the Yellow Brick Road. It's a school for kids who are interested in the theater arts."

"That's a relief," I returned. "For a minute there, I thought you were telling me Lacey's day job was being a Munchkin."

"Good one, Popper. See, that's just one of the things I like about you. You're as sharp as a tack."

"I try." Jotting down the name of Lacey's workplace, I added, "I don't suppose you have an address or phone number?"

"I've got both." Once he'd delivered that information, Forrester said, "So tell me, Popper. How are things going with you and that fiancé of yours?"

"Just fine," I shot back.

He chuckled. "Am I imagining things, or do I detect a little defensiveness in your tone?"

"Things between Nick and me have never been better," I insisted.

"Goodness gracious, I do believe I'm sensing trouble in paradise. Be still my heart."

"Oh, why don't you go…interview someone." I knew I sounded childish. But it was better than telling him to go jump in a lake, which was the first thought that had popped into my head.

He laughed. "As a matter of fact, I was about to do just that. Your pal Anthony Falcone, in fact. At the moment, I'm parked right in front of police headquarters."

"Do they have the results of the autopsy yet? Are there any leads in the murder investigation?" I asked anxiously.

"If there's anything new, I promise you'll be the first to know. Later, Popper!"

As usual, my conversation with Forrester left me feeling both angry and flustered. On top of that, my body was reacting as if I'd just chugged five cappuccinos. My heart was pounding, my head was spinning.... Frankly, I found my reaction to him totally confusing.

What is it about that man? I wondered, staring at the phone as if it had the ability to answer my question.

At least there was one thing I wasn't confused about, and that was what my next step would be. It was simple: just follow the Yellow Brick Road.

• • •

Not surprisingly, the Yellow Brick Road was made out of bricks and painted bright yellow. The children's acting academy was located in a maze of industrial buildings in Barnwood, a spot of sunshine amid one-story warehouses and forklifts and huge trucks that made annoying beeping sounds as they backed into loading docks.

As soon as I walked through the front door later that morning, however, I forgot all about the forklifts and trucks. The interior walls of the anteroom were painted turquoise and lime green, the hallway just beyond was hot pink, and the rooms that jutted off it were painted similarly bright colors that made me wish I'd brought along the leftover orange paint to donate.

The uplifting sound of a tinkling piano wafted into the front hallway. On the walls hung eight-by-ten glossies of exceptionally well-groomed children, little girls with perky bows in their hair and little boys wearing T-shirts that looked as if they'd been ironed. The academy's success stories, I surmised.

Off to one side, through a closed door with a window, I could see the business side of the operation. Two women sat at desks, their eyes glued to their computer screens as if they'd been hypnotized.

I stepped away before they noticed me, figuring I'd get much further without their assistance. I slunk along the hallway, following the sound of dreamy music, then peered through the glass in the door of the large, sunny room at the end of the corridor. It had an expansive wooden floor and not a stick of furniture. One wall was completely covered with mirrors, making it look like every dance studio I'd ever seen in the movies.

The twelve or fifteen little girls whirling around in circles weren't exactly dancing. But they were definitely in motion, some twirling gracefully and others milling around with the randomness of puppies. They all had their arms spread out, and the colorful silk scarves attached to their sleeves with safety pins fluttered around them.

"Okay, butterflies!" cried the only grown-up in the room. She, too, had flowing squares of fabric wafting from her arms. As she whirled and twirled among the little girls, the undulating chiffon looked surprisingly like the wings of a butterfly. In fact, even though the instructor didn't have the willowy build of most dancers, she almost floated across the room, her pink ballet shoes barely touching the ground. "We've just spotted a bunch of beautiful flowers over in that corner. Let's all fly over to them!"

I lingered in the doorway, fascinated by the energy in the room. The innocence too. I watched, mesmerized, as the sweet-faced little girls did their best to emulate the colorful butterflies they were no doubt picturing in their minds.

I was so busy enjoying the charming scene that I didn't notice that someone had snuck up behind me until I heard, "Can I help you?"

I whirled around, instantly feeling guilty. The person who'd spoken was a sour-faced woman who accessorized her beige sweater set with a pair of glasses hanging on a clunky gold chain. I recognized her as one of the two office workers I'd spotted on my way in.

"I'm looking for Lacey Croft."

The woman frowned. "As you can see, she's tied up at the moment. But if you can wait, her class ends in a few minutes."

Confused, I peered into the studio again. Was it possible that the head butterfly, the woman who practically floated through the air, was the mousy wardrobe mistress I'd seen at the theater?

Sure enough, as she fluttered in my direction, followed by a flock of younger, smaller butterflies, I saw that the woman with the look of pure joy on her face was, indeed, Lacey Croft. A completely different version of her, perhaps, but the same person nonetheless.

"Perhaps you'd be more comfortable in the waiting area," the woman from the office suggested coolly.

It was only then that I remembered that I didn't exactly belong there. In fact, I suddenly felt as if I was intruding on a special moment that belonged only to Lacey and her young charges.

"Of course."

After a few minutes of sitting dutifully beneath a photo of a freckle-faced boy I was sure I recognized from a Cheerios commercial, the door to the dance studio opened. The little girls scrambled out of the room and into the arms of the mothers who had been gathering all around me. I took that as my cue to seek out their instructor. Weaving through the chattering crowd, I made my way back to the end of the hall.

I found Lacey in the big, mirrored room, keeping a watchful eye on her reflection as she practiced a few dance steps.

"Lacey?" I said gently.

She glanced over, startled at the interruption. But as she dropped her arms to her sides, her moon-shaped face lit up with a smile, causing two huge, distinctive dimples to appear in her cheeks.

"Sorry to disturb you," I began.

"Not at all. What can I do for you?"

Lacey's words were colored with a hint of an accent, one I couldn't place. "I'm Jessie Popper," I began. "I'm—"

"I know who you are," she replied. "You just joined the cast of *She's Flying High*, right?"

"That's right. I'm a friend of Betty Vandervoort's. She's the one who got me involved."

Lacey nodded. "Betty's great. A really terrific dancer too. What about you? Have you done much theater?"

"Practically none," I admitted. "But when Aziza dropped out and Elena became Amelia Earhart, Derek and Betty railroaded me into making my stage debut."

"Gee, that was awfully nice of you. To help Derek out like that, I mean." The muscles in her forehead tensed as she added, "That horrid Aziza. It's so typical of her to do something like that."

I recognized an opportunity when it fell into my lap.

"Really? I don't know Aziza very well. What's she like?"

Lacey snorted. "Self-centered. Dramatic. Inconsiderate. I mean, look at the way she left Derek in the lurch. After weeks of rehearsal, she walks out two weeks before opening night! Not only do a whole bunch of cast members have to switch roles to accommodate the prima donna; now I have to do major alterations on all their costumes, including yours. You'll need to try on the Anita Snook outfit tonight so I can see if I have to make any adjustments."

Shaking her head disapprovingly, she added, "*Aziza* isn't even her real name. She made it up. Her real name is Ann or Anna, but that's too ordinary for her. It just goes to show what a phony she is."

"In that case," I commented casually, "it's hard to understand what Simon ever saw in her."

"You're telling me," she said, sounding surprisingly bitter. "Their relationship was practically a play in itself. The drama queen was always picking fights with him over the stupidest little things—like if he was five minutes late or . . . or if he didn't look happy enough to see her. She was incredibly possessive too. She was always going ballistic, accusing him of flirting with this woman or that woman. And she sure wasn't shy about embarrassing him in front of other people. Everybody in the theater company got used to their shouting matches. She was always making a scene over some imagined transgression of Simon's."

I blinked. "So why *do* you think Simon put up with behavior like that?"

Lacey's eyes were blazing as she replied, "According to Aziza, it was because he was madly in love with her. When he wasn't around, she'd go on and on about how she was his muse and how he couldn't live without her. But I think it was just because Simon was such a nice guy. He had more tolerance for that kind of thing than most people. But none of *us* could understand it."

"How long were they together?"

"About a year, off and on," she said. "Aziza was constantly breaking up with him, although I'm sure she just did it so he'd beg her to come back to him. Which he did, over and over again. Once, when we were rehearsing another production a few months ago, he even showed up at the theater with an armful of roses. He got up onstage and on bended knee recited Romeo's famous lines: 'But soft! What light through yonder window breaks? It is the east, and Juliet is the sun!'" She twisted her mouth into a sneer. "Only he substituted *her* name, saying, 'It is the east, and Aziza is the sun!'"

It sounds as if Simon had a flair for melodrama himself, I thought.

"But every once in a while, he would be the one to break it off," Lacey went on. "Simon was capable of putting up with a lot, but sometimes even he'd had enough. Of course, that would make Aziza furious. She'd cry, she'd threaten to kill herself, she'd do anything she could think of to convince him to take her back."

I'd clearly touched a raw nerve. Yet I was still taken aback when she added, "I wouldn't be surprised if it turned out Aziza killed Simon."

"Why would she have done that?" I asked, surprised.

She shrugged. "Maybe he finally dumped her for real. Maybe he realized once and for all that there was no room in his life for such a high-maintenance relationship now that he was finally about to achieve the success he longed for. I always believed that sooner or later, Simon would come to that conclusion. If he told her that on Friday night, and if she understood that this time he really meant it, I could easily imagine her going nuts and attacking him. In fact, she was the first person I thought of when I found him Saturday morning."

"Lacey," I asked gently, "can you tell me about that? What it was like finding him in the dressing room?"

Instantly her shoulders slumped and all the muscles in her face sagged. The anger was gone. In its place was sadness.

"It was horrible," she said, lowering her voice to a near-whisper. "I went into the men's dressing room to check if this old trunk that had been stashed in the corner for as long as I could remember had any costumes or props inside that might be useful in *She's Flying High*."

A faraway look came into her eyes. "As soon as I walked in, I knew something was wrong. There was this horrible smell..." She made a choking sound, as if she was reliving the entire scene. "But I went over to the trunk anyway. I noticed immediately that it wasn't in the spot where it had always been. Someone had obviously moved it.

"It seems funny now, but my first thought was that I was glad it was in a more convenient place. It hadn't been moved very far, just a few inches away from the wall. But that meant I didn't have to drag it out of the corner myself. Anyway, I went ahead and opened it."

And in the process covered it with your fingerprints, I thought cynically. Just in case you needed to explain how they got there.

But I kept my theories to myself. "Was the trunk difficult to open?" I asked.

"Not at all. I mean, it wasn't locked or anything. As I was lifting the lid, I noticed that the smell got much worse. And then I saw what was inside. Simon, all crumpled up in this really unnatural position. That was what struck me most. That and the horrible expression on his face. He looked . . . surprised."

As any of us would be, I thought, if someone bashed us in the head from behind.

"I only looked at him for a second," Lacey went on. "My main thought was that I had to get away. From the horrible sight, I mean. And that I had to call 911."

"Which is what you did," I noted.

"That's right. From my cell phone. In the hall, right outside the dressing room."

"Lacey," I asked, "did you happen to see anything odd?"

She looked startled. "Finding a dead body in a trunk isn't odd enough?"

"I mean anything that might have indicated who the killer was. A scarf, a button, a hair—anything at all?"

Lacey shook her head. "I didn't have enough time to see anything like that. Like I said, I just wanted to get away. It was such a horrible sight."

"I understand completely," I assured her. "It must have been awful for you."

"I'll never forget it," she agreed solemnly. "Look, I'm finding this really painful. Maybe we'd better stick to talking about whatever it is that brought you here today."

I froze. I'd been so busy trying to locate Lacey that I'd forgotten to come up with a good reason for showing up at her workplace like this.

I glanced around frantically until my eyes lit on one of the photographs of the school's alumni hanging right outside. It featured a cute little girl in a black-and-white polka-dot dress and fluffy blond hair with a big white bow.

"Uh, I have two nieces, named Maxine and Lou—

Louella," I stuttered, glad that I was fairly fast on my feet, if not always exactly inspired. "I'm, uh, thinking of enrolling them in an acting class to help them build up their confidence. They're pretty shy."

It was true that Lou could be described that way. However, the idea of my pushy little terrier Max being anything close to shy was laughable. Unless there was a thunderstorm, of course. Then all his feistiness vanished, sending him under the bed, quaking.

"Anyway," I continued, "somebody mentioned at rehearsal the other night that you conduct acting workshops for kids here at the Yellow Brick Road, and I thought I'd come check it out."

Lacey beamed. "The Yellow Brick Road is the top acting school on the island, as far as I'm concerned." She pointed to the row of photos right outside the door. "We've had kids go on to do commercials, soap operas, movies, Broadway shows . . . Of course, a lot of them just take a class or two for the same reason as your nieces. It's a great way to build confidence. It also helps them improve their social skills and their communication skills. Acting is a great way for children to increase their self-esteem."

"You're so good with them," I observed. "They really seem to respond to you."

"The kids are great," she said, her face lighting up again. "Working with them, helping them explore their creativity—it's almost as rewarding as being onstage myself."

Surprised, I said, "But I thought you just did costumes."

"For this production. But I've been in a lot of the Theater One productions. In fact, when I was in college in Alabama—that's where I'm from—I majored in theater arts. At least, until my junior year."

That explained the lingering accent. "What happened during your junior year?"

Her expression twisted into one of disdain. "My father announced that if I didn't find a more practical major, he wasn't going to pay for the rest of my college education." She sighed. "I suppose I could have become one of those students who carry a full course load plus work thirty or forty hours a week. But I guess when it came right down to it, I had serious doubts about whether I'd ever be able to make it in the theater. So I just switched majors to education."

"I take it your father was happy with that?"

"Oh, yeah. He thought becoming an elementary school teacher was the ideal career path for his drab little daughter." The bitterness that had crept into her voice made me cringe. "Working here, at least, is a version of that I can live with."

"Besides, you're still involved in theater," I pointed out. "You have the Yellow Brick Road during the day and the Port Players at night."

"And *She's Flying High* is such a fabulous show." Her expression darkened. "Simon was a real genius."

"Yes, it sounds as if he really was," I agreed.

She was silent for a few seconds. "Jessie," she said hesitantly, "since you're part of the show and all, someone's bound to tell you sooner or later that Simon and I had a—we dated for a while. Theater people do so love to gossip." Hastily, she added, "But we remained on good terms after we broke up. We turned out to be one of those unusual couples that manages to stay friends."

"I see." Simon and Lacey? They struck me as an unlikely duo. Still, her revelation explained her anger over his relationship with Aziza.

It also made the fact that she had been the one to

call in his murder after reportedly stumbling upon his body much more interesting.

As if she'd been reading my mind, she added, "Which made finding him like that all the more horrifying. I always felt that Simon and I were destined to get back together." Her big brown eyes filled with tears. "Once he got away from that witch Aziza, that is."

Aha, I thought. The intrigues of the cast and crew of *She's Flying High* were getting more and more complex every minute—especially with respect to the two women who had competed for Simon's affections. Who was the wise writer who said, *Hell hath no fury like a woman scorned*?

I remained silent, hoping for more detail. Instead, Lacey blinked hard a few times, then said, "Anyway, I'm glad you're part of the show. And Maureen up front will give you a copy of the Yellow Brick Road's schedule. Classes are broken down by age group. I'm sure you'll find something that's right for your nieces. We have classes in comedy, magic, voice, movement, acting for television...If you have any questions, we can talk more at rehearsal tonight."

Definitely comedy for Max, I thought, getting caught up in the charade. He's a natural clown. As for Lou, he's so gawky he could probably benefit from a movement workshop.

I had to remind myself that as much as I loved them, they were dogs, not children. And that I hadn't really come to the Yellow Brick Road to enroll my Westie and my Dalmatian in theater classes.

I'd come because Lacey Croft had seemed like such an obvious suspect. Not only was one of Simon's closest friends convinced she was guilty; she'd found the body and called the police.

Now I'd learned there was a third reason she

deserved a prominent place on my list of possible killers. Simon, Aziza, and Lacey had been caught up in a love triangle, and neither woman had been ready to let go. And as even amateur sleuths know, since the beginning of time that's been a very strong motive for murder.

Chapter 7

"A kitten is chiefly remarkable for rushing about
like mad at nothing whatever, and generally
stopping before it gets there."

—Agnes Repplier

I spent the rest of the morning zigzagging around
Long Island, making house calls. I often brought
Max and Lou with me, but the last thing I wanted
was to get railroaded into taking Mitzi-Bitzi along too.
I was afraid Dorothy would decide that her beastly
Maltese felt left out, especially since she couldn't very
well bring Mitzi while she and Henry went sightseeing.
Even she realized that her surrogate daughter wasn't
likely to be allowed in museums, restaurants, or other
establishments that had health codes to adhere to.
Since Mitzi and my menagerie would be spending the
day together, just to be safe I'd arranged for Betty to
stop in at the cottage from time to time to make sure
that no fur was flying—literally.

I was particularly anxious about my eleven-fifteen
appointment in Metchogue. Grace Washington, a dignified octogenarian with the demeanor of a queen, was
a favorite client of mine. She had been understandably

traumatized when her sweet eight-year-old Lhasa Apso's back legs became paralyzed a few weeks earlier.

I'd discovered that poor Sugar had intervertebral disk disease, which had resulted in a ruptured disk. The ailment is common with the breed, as well as with French bulldogs, basset hounds, Welsh corgis, and several others. The first step, a course of corticosteroids, hadn't been successful in reducing the inflammation. So two weeks earlier I'd surgically removed what was left of the disk from Sugar's spinal cord. It was time to see if his body had taken over, filling in the area with scar tissue and enabling him to walk again.

Mrs. Washington was peering out her living room window when I drove up to her house. Even before I'd parked, she rushed out the front door with Sugar in her arms.

"Dr. Popper, you're right on time." She greeted me with a nervous smile as I climbed out of the van. "I've been waiting for you all morning. I'm so anxious to hear how you think Sugar is doing."

"Bring him inside and we'll find out."

As I expected, she insisted on carrying Sugar up the steps herself. Even though my van is only twenty-six feet long, it houses an entire clinic: examining table, cabinets stocked with medications and supplies, and, thanks to a generator, running water, heat, and air-conditioning. I sometimes arrange to borrow another veterinarian's surgery room, and I often use an outside lab for testing. Other than that, I have everything I need to treat animals right here.

"When is Sugar going to walk?" she asked apprehensively as I gently lifted her dog onto the examining table. As usual, she was wearing a dress, stockings, and a pair of pumps with a low heel, and a long string of pearls hung around her neck. Her salt-and-pepper hair was neatly sculpted into a short pageboy.

"I know you're worried, Mrs. Washington," I replied. "But as I've said, his recovery will probably take six to eight weeks. Let me take a look and see how's he doing."

I stroked my patient's soft gray and white ears, noticing how closely his coloring matched his owner's. He wagged his tail, meanwhile gazing up at me uncertainly with his big brown eyes. "Hey, Sugar, how's my boy? Have you been trying to walk?"

"He certainly has," Grace answered, sounding like a proud mom. "Stand up, sweetie. Show Dr. Popper how well you're doing."

"Has he recovered his ability to urinate?" I asked.

"Yes, he has. I don't have to massage his bladder anymore, the way you showed me."

"That's good news." I put my hand under Sugar's paw and was encouraged when I felt him push against me.

Grace toyed with her reading glasses. "What should I be doing to help him?"

"Put him on the floor, pull him to his feet, and help him stand there. That will help Sugar start walking again by strengthening the muscles in his legs and back. Can you sit on the floor with him? Or kneel?"

"Not with my back." Grace thought for a few seconds. "But I have a low bench. I can use that to sit with him."

"That's perfect. Put your hand on the side of his groin and let him move his legs. The more he moves them, the faster he'll recover. And until he's able to walk, he shouldn't be allowed to pull himself down the stairs or climb on the couch, since his legs are still weak and we don't want him to fall.

"Mrs. Washington, Sugar will walk again," I assured her. "He's making excellent progress. Just give him some time."

I didn't know which I found more rewarding: the

fact that the gentle, even-tempered dog was on his way to recovery or the look of gratitude in his owner's eyes.

As I was about to head to my next appointment, I suddenly remembered that I had to call Patti Ardsley, the producer of the fifteen-minute television show I host every Friday morning. I always check in with her early in the week to tell her what topic I plan to talk about on the next show.

"How are you going to wow our viewers this week, Dr. Popper?" she asked after the show's production assistant, Marlene Fitzgerald, put me through. As usual, Patti exhibited all the energy and enthusiasm of a terrier who'd OD'd on caffeine.

"I thought I'd do a segment on CPR for animals," I replied, relieved that I'd finally come up with a topic. I got the idea from a television show I'd seen recently, a police drama in which a paramedic saved someone's life. "It's a skill that's really helpful for pet owners to learn, but most people don't even know it can be applied to animals."

"I like it," Patti said. I could picture her nodding. "It's unusual, but not too unusual. And we can do a great teaser. Something like, 'CPR—for cats and dogs? Tune in to *Pet People* for breaking news in the medical field.'"

"It's not exactly breaking news," I corrected her. Still, I'd learned enough about the world of television in the six or seven months I'd been doing this to know my pleas about sticking to reality were likely to fall on deaf ears.

"Our audience is always interested in something new," Patti noted.

No use arguing, I thought. At least it'd be new to most of the viewers.

"One more thing," I added. "I'll need a mannequin to demonstrate on."

"A mannequin?" Patti repeated.

"A fake dog or cat," I explained. "You know how life-size dummies are used for practice in regular CPR classes? I'll need one to show how the technique is done. I can't use a real dog or cat, since it would be next to impossible to demonstrate on a conscious animal."

"Got it," Patti said crisply. "Fake dog or cat. That shouldn't be too difficult. I'll put Marlene on it right away."

As I hung up the phone, I wondered if I'd been explicit enough in defining exactly what I needed. But at the moment I had too many other things on my mind to worry about it—like my next house call, during which I'd have to share some very discouraging test results with a cat owner. Even after all my years as a vet, that still took an emotional toll.

I finally took a break around noon, when I stopped off at one of my favorite delis to grab a sandwich. I devoured it in the driver's seat of my van, washing it down with a bottle of iced tea. Then I headed for my twelve-thirty appointment with another cohort of Simon Wainwright's. I didn't know whether to consider Kyle Carlson a suspect or merely a potential source of information. But I hoped that by the time I treated his dog, Monty, I'd have a better idea.

Kyle lived in a ranch house with a fair-size yard in Melton, an undistinguished community known for its abundance of big box stores. From a distance, Kyle's home looked like every other house on the block—which wasn't surprising, since they had obviously all been built at the same time with the same blueprints.

Still, most of the homeowners had found ways to distinguish their cookie-cutter houses. One had hung a wreath made of dried flowers on the front door, while his next-door neighbor had recently painted the shutters bright blue. Another had added a porch with hanging plants and an old-fashioned swing. The houses looked lived-in, with a tricycle on the lawn or gardening tools left on the front steps that gave clues about their residents.

Kyle's house showed no such signs of homeyness. With its brown shingles, white shutters, and nondescript shrubs, I got the feeling it looked pretty much the way it had the day it was built. I suspected that Kyle lived here alone, without any females to add cozy touches or children to scatter their colorful toys around.

I spotted a hole in the cyclone fence that surrounded the property, no doubt the one that was responsible for Monty's gashes. Fortunately, it had been patched up with chicken wire.

When I opened the car door, I heard loud barking, the kind that can only come from a large, chesty dog. Sure enough, a sleek silver-gray Weimaraner that easily weighed eighty pounds waited for me at the front door, watching me intently through the screen.

"Quiet, Monty!" Kyle scolded as I got closer. Grabbing the dog's collar, he added, "He won't hurt you. As the old saying goes, his bark is worse than his bite."

"I'm usually pretty good with dogs," I assured him, adding, "In this line of work, I'd better be."

The moment Kyle opened the door to let me in, Monty stopped barking. Instead, he wagged his tail furiously, skittering on the wooden floor and tripping over his own paws as he pranced around and jumped up on me. From the way he acted, you would have thought we were long-lost friends reunited.

"You were right," I said, laughing as I leaned

over to scratch Monty's ears. "He's nothing but a big pussycat."

"Yeah, he is," Kyle agreed.

He pushed back his shaggy sand-colored hair and crouched down in front of Monty. He placed his hands on either side of the dog's long, graceful neck, then pressed his human proboscis against Monty's gray, wet, throbbing one so they were nose to nose and forehead to forehead.

"Get over here, y'big goofus," Kyle said, using a deep, throaty voice to address his beloved canine. And then he proceeded to emit a string of sounds that were somewhere between baby talk and the utterings of some otherwordly being. I did manage to make out several syllables that sounded like, "Goofus, moofus, woofus." I wondered if these particular terms of endearment had been inspired by the elocution lessons from acting classes he'd taken.

Still, I couldn't help smiling. I'd noticed that most of my clients had a special voice they used only to communicate with their pets. In fact, a lot of them had developed their own vocabulary as well, using terms of endearment for their cat or dog or rabbit or gerbil that wouldn't be found in any dictionary. Words like *moofus* and *woofus*, for example. It was possible that no other human being on earth had ever spoken them, yet Monty seemed to know exactly what they meant.

Instead of being embarrassed that he'd been caught speaking a language that was comprehensible only to him and his dog, Kyle looked up at me and grinned. "He's a great dog, isn't he?" he asked.

"He certainly is," I agreed. Glancing around, I added, "And this is a terrific place you've got here."

Actually, the interior of Kyle's house was similar to the exterior in that it had few homey touches aside from a bedraggled fern on the windowsill and a fairly worn recliner chair that looked as if someone loved it too much to part with it. Then again, the living room was so cluttered that it was difficult to focus on the actual decor. Papers and books were scattered everywhere, even in piles on the floor. A stack of DVDs as high as a floor lamp towered in one corner of the room.

"It suits our purposes," he replied with a little shrug. "There are three bedrooms in back, so my roommate and I each have our own space."

"I assumed you lived here alone," I remarked.

"Nope. Got a roommate—Ian Norman. He and I rented this place together about a year and a half ago."

"Is Ian interested in acting too?" I asked, trying to steer the conversation toward Simon's world.

"Not these days. He used to be, back when we were in college. In fact, the three of us—Simon, Ian, and I— were inseparable. We took acting classes together. We went to plays together. We pretty much ate, drank, and breathed the theater.

"But Ian took a more practical route and became a computer geek. He runs his own business. He started out working for a few Long Island companies, but now he also has clients all over the country. He's one of those lucky people who's able to work from home, so the third bedroom serves as his office."

"I didn't realize you and Simon had gone to school together." Automatically, I glanced toward the back of the house, expecting to see Ian clicking away at his keyboard. "Maybe we should talk more softly," I said, "so we don't bother Ian."

"He's running some errands," Kyle explained. "Actually, we do a pretty good job of keeping out of each other's hair. I'm pretty much out all day at the printing firm where I work. That allows Ian to have the place to himself. So when I'm chilling here at home, like in the evening, he often goes out to give me some space."

"I didn't know you worked at a printing firm," I said.

"It's not the most exciting job in the world, but it supports my acting habit." In the resonant voice he used onstage to portray Amelia Earhart's copilot Fred Noonan, he added, "Advertising flyers by day, Macbeth by night!"

I smiled. "You're lucky, Kyle. It's nice that you have something you're so passionate about. I guess I feel that way about animals."

"Then you're the lucky one." Kyle had grown serious. "Your job and your passion are one and the same. Very few of us aspiring actors get to live out that dream.

"But you're not here to listen to a grown man whine, are you? You're here to look at those cuts Monty got while he was chasing squirrels."

"Right. Let's get him into the van so I can check him out."

Once inside, Kyle lifted Monty onto the examining table. "Whoa. Take it easy, boy," he murmured, holding the animal in place as his paws skittered across the stainless steel surface.

"Any change in appetite or water consumption?" I asked as I examined Monty's eyes and ears, checked his teeth, and ran my hand along his vertebrae. "Any vomiting or diarrhea? Coughing or sneezing?"

Kyle's response to all my questions was no.

I weighed Monty—82.5 pounds—and took his temperature, which was normal at 101 degrees Fahrenheit. Then I studied the two wounds on his right thigh. Both were filled with pus, a sign that they were infected. But there was good news too. The cuts were only about an inch long. And they weren't very deep, just penetrating the skin but not the muscle beneath it. I cleaned them both with an astringent called ChlorhexiDerm, applying compresses saturated with the warm blue solution.

"How bad are they?" Kyle asked anxiously. "Does Monty need stitches?" He hesitated before adding, "I feel awful that I didn't have these looked at sooner."

"They're not that bad," I assured him. "I don't think we'll need to suture him up. But I am going to put Monty on oral antibiotics. He's eighty-two pounds—let's try five hundred milligrams of cephalexin every eight hours for ten days. In addition, apply warm compresses twice a day. And you'll need to restrict his activity while those wounds are healing. Can you keep him inside the house?"

"Monty won't like it, but we'll manage. You're going to bandage those up, right?"

"Actually, I'd like to leave them open so we can see how they're coming along. If he keeps licking them, we can get him a collar or put him in a T-shirt. But you should see them start healing in three or four days."

"What about a tetanus shot?" Kyle asked. "Does he need one? I mean, it was a metal fence."

"Tetanus is really uncommon in dogs," I told him. "They naturally have a high resistance to the tetanus toxin, so it's not something we normally worry about." Holding Monty's head in my hands, I looked into his amber eyes and cooed, "Okay, Monty, my boy. You're all done. You were such a good boy!"

"Thanks, Dr. Popper." Kyle lifted him off the table. "I promise I'll keep a close eye on him. I wouldn't want anything bad to happen to my best pal."

"You can take him inside," I said. "I'll join you after I jot down some notes in Monty's file."

When I went back into the house, I found Kyle rummaging around the living room. "Believe it or not, my checkbook is somewhere in this mess," he said apologetically. "Why don't you have a seat while I look for it? If you can find a place to sit, that is."

"I'll just move this . . ." I reached down to remove a stack of white paper from a big upholstered chair, the type that makes you feel as if it's embracing you with its soft, padded arms. As I picked up the stack of paper, I noticed that typed on the front page were the words *Two Boys and a Girl. A One-Act Play by Kyle Carlson.*

"I see you're a writer too," I observed, placing it on a stack of books as I sank into the chair. It was just as comfortable as I expected, aside from the spring sticking into my butt. "Like Simon."

"Yes, like Simon," he repeated sadly, pausing in his frantic search through a desk drawer. "In fact, Simon's the one who got me interested in writing in the first place. But that was what he was like. He could get anybody fired up about anything. His enthusiasm—his *passion,* to use your word—was contagious. I wouldn't be exaggerating if I told you Simon did more to shape me, to turn me into who I am today, than anyone else in my entire life. He was really a special person." With a sigh, he added, "It's hard believe almost twenty years have passed since we were both theater majors at Brookside University."

"My boyfriend goes to law school there," I interjected.

"Great school," Kyle said, nodding. "Anyway, we hit it off right away. Simon and I had so much in common. We both loved theater and we were both determined to have successful careers. After we finished school, we got an apartment in Manhattan together—although calling it an apartment is stretching the truth. It was actually more like a room. A very small room.

"But I think of that period as one of the best times

of my life," Kyle went on wistfully. "During those years we lived in the city, Simon and I both continued taking acting classes. We also went to auditions together, rehearsed together, spent hours discussing different theories of acting and planning what our lives would be like when we were both rich and famous. We were inseparable. Which is one of the reasons it's so hard to believe—" He stopped when his voice deteriorated into a choking sound.

From the emotional way in which Kyle spoke about his long-term friend and one-time roommate, I couldn't help wondering if there had been more than friendship between them. At least from Kyle's perspective. He seemed so filled with admiration and awe that he almost sounded as if he'd had a crush on Simon.

Which led me to wonder if Kyle and Ian were more than just roommates. True, they could have simply been two single men in their thirties who found it more convenient to share a place than to live alone, longtime friends who still enjoyed each other's company.

But the intensity of Kyle's feelings for Simon made me suspect he was gay. I also sensed that it was something he didn't want widely known.

The fact that he'd let his guard down prompted me to probe a little further. "Kyle, did you happen to see Simon last Friday, the night he was killed?"

What I meant was, *Okay, dude, what's your alibi?*

If he saw through me, he didn't let on.

"No," he replied, shaking his head. "There was no rehearsal that night. I came back to the house straight from work, around five-thirty. I didn't budge until the next day." Sounding a bit defensive, he added, "Ian was here with me the whole time. In fact, when the police asked me that question, I gave them the exact same answer."

So Kyle had an alibi, one that sounded fairly solid.

Although the idea that Ian could simply be protecting Kyle did pop into my suspicious mind.

Along with the idea that Kyle could be protecting Ian. Especially if my suspicion about them being more than just roommates was correct.

Another possibility occurred to me: that Simon, Kyle, and Ian had been involved in a love triangle, just like the one the Simon, Aziza, and Lacey were apparently part of.

"What about Ian?" I asked, trying not to sound too eager. "Did he and Simon remain friends after college?"

Kyle cast me an odd look. "Yes," he replied uncertainly. "Of course, Ian wasn't as close to Simon as I was. He never had been. But the three of us stayed friends. And we began spending more time together once Ian and I began rooming together."

Before I had a chance to think up another question, he commented, "You seem quite interested in Simon."

I tried to maintain a neutral expression. "Simon and Betty were friends, and she and I are close. She's extremely upset about what happened. I just wish I could help her cope better by getting some closure. And I don't think that will happen until the police identify his killer."

"None of us will get any closure until then," Kyle said bitterly. "And I firmly believe the answer is staring the cops in the face. For some reason, they're just not getting it."

From our conversation at rehearsal the night before, I knew he was referring to Lacey. But I didn't want to pursue the topic of Simon's murder any further, since I didn't want word to get around that I was showing an unusual interest. Blowing my cover would make it impossible to get the other Port Players to open up to me.

The fact that Kyle had already made that observation made me uncomfortable enough.

Fortunately, he resumed his search for his checkbook, which he found hiding underneath a throw pillow.

As he wrote me a check, I studied him closely. He apparently had an alibi that, as far as I knew, the police had accepted. Still, there was something about Kyle Carlson that didn't sit right with me. Something about his relationships with both Simon and Ian too. And it went far beyond the possibility that the three men were gay—or in Simon's case, perhaps bisexual—and that Kyle seemed determined to hide it. Even more, it was the intensity with which he spoke about Simon. I couldn't help feeling he was an unusually emotional person. Maybe even emotional enough to be considered disturbed.

I didn't know if the police had kept Kyle's name on their list of suspects despite his alibi, but he definitely had a place on mine. And I was inclined to add Ian Norman's name as well. At least in pencil. Even though I hadn't met the man, his past was apparently closely intertwined with Simon and Kyle's. Which meant his present might have been too.

• • •

Instead of looking forward to going home, as I usually did, I felt nothing but dread as I turned into the driveway of the Tallmadge estate. Even the idea of seeing my animals after a long day away didn't make up for the fact that there were currently other forms of life at the cottage that made the idea of going home a pretty unsavory prospect.

My stomach tightened at the sight of the Burbys' white car in the driveway, next to my red VW. Meanwhile, Nick's black Maxima was nowhere to be seen. So instead of pulling into my own driveway, I trundled a little farther along the road and pulled up in front of the Big House.

I shut the van door silently, not wanting to alert anyone on the premises to my arrival. Then I sneaked around to the side of the house, hoping I'd find Betty in her kitchen.

Sure enough, through the back door I saw her sitting at the kitchen table, nursing a cup of tea. As soon as she noticed me through the window, she jumped up.

"Jessica! What a lovely surprise!" she exclaimed as she opened the door.

Betty wasn't the only one who gave me a warm greeting. Frederick, Winston's spirited wirehaired dachshund, came scurrying across the kitchen floor on his short legs. He jumped up to say hello, wagging his tail wildly.

"Hello, Frederick," I cooed, stroking him. "How's my favorite four-legged next-door neighbor?" He was such an engaging and affectionate animal that it was difficult to believe dachshunds had originally been bred to hunt badgers—*dachs* in German—slipping into their narrow burrows and dragging them out.

As soon as I'd dropped into the chair opposite Betty's, she said, "I'm glad you stopped by, Jessica. I'm anxious to hear how the investigation is going. Have you developed any theories about who might be responsible for what happened to Simon?"

"I'm afraid I haven't gotten very far," I told her apologetically. "In fact, the only people I've had a chance to talk to so far are Lacey Croft and Simon's friend Kyle Carlson. Maybe after I've gone to more rehearsals."

"I'm sure you're doing a fine job," she insisted. "I certainly don't mean to pressure you. It's just that it's so unnerving, not knowing who I can trust and who might have..."

Her voice trailed off, as if she couldn't bring herself

to say the words. "So many of those people are my friends, Jessica. Yet throughout the rehearsals, I can't stop thinking about poor Simon and the fact that someone in the Port Players could be a murderer. Sometimes I wonder if Winston's right that I should just drop out of the production."

"You can't be serious!" I cried. "Betty, you can't drop out! Not only would you leave Derek in the lurch, you'd also feel terrible knowing that a wonderful play you've been rehearsing for weeks was going on without you." I sat up straighter and squared my shoulders. "I'll just have to try harder."

"I really appreciate it," Betty said. "Especially since I know how busy you must be entertaining your future in-laws. Are you having fun getting to know them?"

She'd barely asked the question before my hands flew to my cheeks and I wailed, "Betty, they're driving me absolutely insane!"

"Oh, dear. You sound like you need a cup of my special tea."

What made it special, I knew, was the shot of whiskey she always added, one of the critical ingredients in her tried-and-true recipe. Given the way I was feeling, I wasn't about to protest.

She filled the kettle with water, put it on the stove to boil, and joined me at the table. Frederick, who'd been watching her every move, curled up under the table between us and sighed contentedly.

"Tell me," Betty ordered. "What have they been doing to you?"

"It's—it's everything about them!" I exploded. "I can't do anything right. And of course Nick, their beloved son, can't do anything wrong. Every word Dorothy says to me, or even about me, is a put-down. She hates my animals, and she acts like my cottage is a—a cardboard box on a street corner. She complains about everything and somehow finds a way to blame it all on me!"

"I know how you feel," Betty commented. "I've gotten the exact same reaction from Winston's children."

I blinked. "You have?"

She shrugged. "It's not that surprising. After all, I'm an interloper, just like you."

"I didn't know you'd met Winston's children. In fact, I didn't even realize he had any."

"Two. A son and a daughter, both of whom live in England. James is a barrister—a lawyer—in Bristol. Chloe runs a bookshop in London. She's married to a very wealthy man she apparently treats like a servant. He's an investment banker who, for reasons that are entirely incomprehensible to me, dotes on her. Chloe came to New York a few weeks ago for a trade show, and James came with her expressly to meet the woman they're certain is marrying their beloved father for his money."

My mouth dropped open. "But, Betty, you hardly seem like someone who needs to marry for money!"

She shrugged. "I must admit, Winston did his best to convince them that we're very much in love. But the minute his daughter got me alone, she looked me right in the eye and said, 'Have you and my father discussed how your marriage is going to affect our inheritance when he dies?'"

"Oh, my! What an awful thing to say!"

"Especially since Winston has always been so generous with both of them," Betty agreed. "They have tremendous trust funds that have made it possible for them to pursue whatever interests them. Chloe's shop is apparently more of a hobby than anything else. And James has a good job, but he's quite adept at spending money on expensive toys like Ferraris and yachts and fashion models."

"They both sound like people who can't imagine anyone not being attracted by someone else's money," I mused.

"That was certainly my impression." The teakettle had started to whistle, and Betty hurried over to the cabinet and took down two delicate Limoges cups decorated with pink roses.

"You'll feel better after a cup of my tea," she reassured me as she made her signature drink, Earl Grey meets Jack Daniel's. "And please let me know if there's anything I can do to make this 'invasion,' as you call it, easier for you. Maybe I could stomp over and pretend to evict you."

"If that happened, Dorothy would probably insist that we get a single room at a hotel so we could continue with all this togetherness," I muttered. "It's bad enough tripping over them in that tiny cottage. But now Nick is insisting that we all go out for dinner at the Bayside Bistro tomorrow night. Since only the principals are rehearsing, I can't even use the play as an excuse. I happen to love that restaurant, but I can already imagine Dorothy complaining about the menu, the decor, the waiters..."

"At least you'll eat well," Betty commented. "I've heard wonderful things about that place."

"I'd better not eat too well," I replied, "or I might not fit into my costume."

"Speaking of the show," Betty said, "I have a couple of things I'd like to give you. Follow me—and bring your tea."

Frederick padded after us as Betty led me into the front parlor, a large, sunny room decorated with gilt-framed mirrors, a dramatic marble fireplace, and ornate Victorian couches upholstered in silk brocade and strewn with beaded silk pillows. But today it also contained an old-fashioned wooden trunk she must have dragged out of some closet.

"I think this might help," Betty said, reaching into the trunk and pulling out a piece of flowing pink chiffon.

"What's that?" I asked nervously.

"A skirt," she replied. "One that's especially made for dancing. You can wear it at tonight's rehearsal."

I cast Frederick a look of desperation. But he seemed enthralled by the fluttering fabric. In fact, his soft dark-brown eyes remained fixed on it and he began wagging his tail, as if he hoped that it might be earmarked for him.

I sighed. The pink skirt was a far cry from the jeans I was so much more comfortable wearing, but I could see where this was going. If Betty had the power to dress me up in a mint green frock, there was nothing to stop her from decking me out in pink chiffon.

"Here, Jessica. Wrap it around your waist, like this—there! Doesn't that make you feel like doing a few *jetés*?"

"I can hardly stop myself."

"And now for the *pièce de résistance* . . ." She pulled out a pair of beige shoes with a strap across the top. They also had heels that were ridiculously high, as far as I was concerned. I'd seen some of the other women in the show wearing them, and I'd been dreading the moment I'd have to affix a pair to my feet.

"We're suppose to dance in these?" I asked, sounding as woeful as I felt.

Betty laughed. "You'll get the hang of it. I promise. In fact, why don't we run through some of the dance numbers right now? Let's start with 'Wild Blue Yonder.' "

I had to admit, all the pressures of the day vanished as I worked with Betty, sliding and turning and pivoting across her living room floor. I even got a kick out of the way the skirt flared out when I twirled. As for the shoes, I reminded myself that I'd overcome more difficult challenges in my life than aching feet. Surely I could conquer this one!

By the time I said good-bye to Betty and Frederick and climbed back into my van to drive the few hundred yards to my own driveway, I felt a thousand times better. I experienced a real sense of triumph over having mastered the dance steps that up until that point had seemed impossible. Even the prospect of an evening with the Barbaric Burbys didn't dampen my mood.

I'd just turned the key in the ignition when my cell phone trilled. Glancing at the caller ID, I saw it was Forrester.

My euphoric mood faded as I remembered that the reason I was swishing around in a pink chiffon skirt in the first place was that I was investigating a murder. And that Forrester was one of my main sources of information.

"What's up, Forrester?" I answered eagerly.

"Whatever happened to, 'Hello! How are you? It's so nice to hear from you!' " he replied.

"Hello! How are you? It's so nice to hear from you. What's up, Forrester?"

"What a shame the social graces have fallen to such a low level." He sighed. "What's up, Popper, is that I've got something I think you might be interested in."

"What is it?" I demanded, not even trying to disguise my eagerness.

"Our deal is still in place, right?"

"Forrester, if you don't tell me what's going on in the next two seconds, I'm going to—"

"I'll take that as a yes," he replied. "So here it is: There's been a break in the case."

Chapter 8

"If you think dogs can't count, try putting three dog biscuits in your pocket and giving Fido only two of them."

—Phil Pastoret

My heart pounded furiously as I waited for Forrester to go on. Listening to the seemingly endless silence that followed was pure agony.

"So are you going to tell me or do I have to beg?" I finally asked.

He laughed. "You know I love it when you beg, Popper."

"Hey, we made a deal," I reminded him sharply. "One I expect you to live up to, if you have any sense of honor whatsoever—"

"Okay, okay! It seems a witness has come forth."

The news stunned me. This *was* a break. A major break.

"A witness to the murder?" I asked anxiously.

"Not exactly. More like a witness to what happened right *before* the murder. Apparently there's a cleaning woman who comes into the theater a few times a week. She told the police that on Friday evening, she was cleaning backstage. When she went into the women's dressing room, she overheard Simon arguing with a woman."

My head was spinning with all the questions I was dying to ask. "What did the woman Simon was arguing with look like?"

"The cleaning woman didn't see her. She couldn't identify her by her voice, either. She said she recognized Simon's voice but not the woman's."

"What were they arguing about?"

"She didn't hear enough to know. She said she figured that what was going on in the next room wasn't any of her business, so she put on her earphones and turned up the volume on her iPod."

"What time was this?"

"Around nine. The police think Simon was killed shortly afterward. She wasn't wearing a watch, so she couldn't be exact."

"Did she hear what they were arguing about?"

"Apparently not."

"Was there any particular phrase she heard? Or maybe a name? Anything at all?"

"Hey, I'm beginning to feel like I'm getting the third degree here. I can picture a single lightbulb hanging over my head—"

"Two more questions," I interrupted. "What's her name and where can I find her?"

"Her name is Sunflower McGee—"

"Did you say Sunflower?" I asked, not sure I'd heard him correctly.

"That's what they tell me. As for finding her, that might be a little tricky. She works for a cleaning company called Home Maid, so the folks at the theater aren't in direct contact with her. She has a key to the building and she comes and goes as she pleases. She works around the acting company's schedule, so she won't be in the way.

"Actually, I wouldn't mind talking to her myself," he continued. "But she's ignored the messages I've left on her cell phone. And I don't have time to keep going to the theater, hoping I'll run into her."

"The fact that she doesn't have a regular work routine does complicate things," I agreed.

It certainly complicated them for Forrester. But as a member of the Port Players, I was in possession of the company's rehearsal schedule. And I planned to study it the first chance I got to see if I could figure out a likely time a cleaning woman would be taking advantage of an empty theater to mop and dust without getting in anyone's way.

"So did I earn some brownie points with that piece of information?" Forrester teased.

"Definitely," I assured him. "And if I find out anything interesting, you'll be the first to know. Thanks a million. Later."

I hung up before he had a chance to make some unseemly comment about cashing in those brownie points of his.

I knew that Sunflower McGee could turn out to be an important witness. The fact that Simon had had an argument with a woman right before he was killed obviously pointed to a female murderer. Two names immediately popped into my head: Aziza Zorn and Lacey Croft, two sides of the love triangle that Simon had been embroiled in.

There was another name that came to mind: Gloria Stone. I still had a lot to learn about her, as well as her relationship with Simon. But there were two things I did know. One was that Gloria and her husband were largely responsible for the success he was about to realize at the time he was murdered. The other was that when I met her at the wake, she had definitely impressed me as someone who was unusually coldhearted—perhaps even coldhearted enough to commit murder.

As far as I was concerned, the combination of those two things made her someone worth looking at very closely.

Of course, the woman arguing with Simon could also have been one of the other twelve or fifteen females in the cast or crew. Or even someone who wasn't in the Port Players but had followed him to the theater or even accompanied him there.

But I was determined to narrow down the possibilities. And while Theater One's cleaning woman couldn't identify whose voice she'd heard that night, it was possible that by asking the right questions, I could.

I certainly intended to try.

● ● ●

"How was your day?" I asked my future in-laws Tuesday evening, trying to sound genuinely interested in how Dorothy and Henry had occupied themselves.

Even though it was almost six, Nick wasn't home yet. So the three of us sat in the living room, me with Cat in my lap, Tinkerbell on one side, and Max on the other, gnawing on the squeaky pink poodle. Henry was settled in the big, comfy upholstered chair he'd monopolized since he'd arrived. His allergies hadn't kicked in yet. Neither had the Benadryl he'd popped as soon as he walked in the door. In fact, he was energetic enough that he'd taken on the never-ending task of scratching Lou's ears, making a friend for life in the process.

Dorothy, who'd staked out her usual spot in the corner of the couch, was cradling Mitzi in her arms lovingly, no doubt recovering from having spent an entire day without her alter ego. And Mitzi was equally enraptured over her reunion with Dorothy. Yet I noticed Mitzi kept eyeing Max's favorite toy in a way I didn't like. Poodle envy, I figured.

"Did you enjoy the Cradle of Aviation Museum?" I added, trying to encourage pleasant conversation. That morning I'd suggested they check it out, gushing about Long Island's historic role in aviation history. I'd told them all about how its flat terrain and windy conditions had made it the home of numerous aviation milestones, including distance records, speed records, and the first U.S. airmail flight. And Charles Lindbergh had taken off on the first nonstop transatlantic flight ever from Roosevelt Field—a plot of land that these days was occupied by a sprawling shopping mall.

I'd developed an interest in aviation since accepting the role of Anita Snook. But when it came to the Burbys, I had an ulterior motive. Suggesting an airplane theme for their day of sightseeing was my subtle way of encouraging them to travel—as far away from here as possible.

"I don't know why you sent us to that horrid place, Jessie," Dorothy complained. "It was filled with airplanes. *Old* airplanes."

"I thought it was interesting," Henry piped up. Five points for Henry, at least in my book. "And I'm not usually much for museums."

"You're just saying that to be contrary, Henry," Dorothy retorted. Turning back to me, she said, "Do you have any ideas about what Henry and I should do tomorrow? Perhaps something *fun*?"

I had several ideas, but I didn't dare say any of them out loud. "You could drive out to the North Fork and visit some wineries," I suggested. "A lot of them have tours and tastings. And there are some wonderful farm stands out there—"

"Jessie, I'm exhausted," Dorothy interrupted. "Why

don't you make me a cup of coffee? You actually manage to make it the way I like it."

Was that a compliment? I thought, amazed. But I simply said, "Of course, Dorothy. I'd be happy to."

"Some of those chocolate chip cookies from yesterday would be nice too," she added. "Just something to nibble on before dinner. That is, if you haven't finished them all off yourself."

"No problem." Nothing like carbohydrate loading, I thought as I headed into the kitchen. Especially if it improves someone's mood.

I was actually pretty exhausted myself, having put in a long day of calls all over Long Island in addition to all the detours I'd made to further my investigation of Simon's murder. But I was the hostess, I reminded myself. Besides, waiting on Dorothy hand and foot would give me an excuse to escape into the kitchen for a while.

In addition to making Dorothy a cup of coffee using the same recipe I'd already dazzled her with, I made a cup for myself and some black coffee for Henry. Then I brought our snack into the living room, setting up the cups and cookies on the coffee table as if I were serving tea.

"These cookies are quite good," Dorothy remarked, pouncing on them the moment the saucer hit the table's surface. "I usually eat only homemade sweets. I don't suppose these are homemade...?"

I was so tempted to lie. Instead, I said, "They're from a really terrific bakery that's not far from here."

"I must give Mitzi a taste," she said, breaking off a piece the size of a hockey puck.

Not surprisingly, Max and Lou were watching with great interest. My brave little Westie went so far as to approach Dorothy and park himself at her feet, in case she decided to share with everybody.

"But, Dorothy," I protested, "it's not a good idea to feed dogs people food. Especially chocolate. Did you know that chocolate—"

"Nonsense," she interrupted dismissively. "I've been feeding Mitzi people food for years, and she's the picture of health. Besides, she loves her chocolate, just like I do. Don't you, Mitzi-Bitzi? *Don't* you? *Don't* you?"

"But chocolate can cause serious problems," I insisted. "Chocolate contains theobromine, which is poisonous to dogs. It affects the animal's central nervous system and the heart, it can cause epileptic seizures—"

"For heaven's sake, a little bit won't hurt. Some people just worry too much." Dorothy smiled triumphantly as the little white Maltese eagerly gobbled up the huge chunk of cookie.

I was about to rip Mitzi from Dorothy's arms when the sound of the front door opening distracted us all.

"Nick!" I cried, rushing over to him. Dropping my voice to a whisper, I pleaded, "Would you please make your mother stop feeding chocolate to Mitzi? I was just about to tear that poor dog away from her myself."

"Calm down, Jess," Nick returned, patting my shoulder. "I'm sure Mitzi is fine."

"Come sit with us, Nicky," Dorothy called from the couch. "We're having such a lovely time."

"Taking care of animals' health is my job, Nick," I reminded him through clenched teeth. "Actually, it's more than my job. It's my life. It's probably the thing I care about most. So how can you expect me to sit by and watch—"

"Okay, okay! You've made your point. My mother is a terrible person."

"What are you two being so secretive about?" Henry asked.

Nick and I both ignored him. "I didn't say that," I

hissed. "The fact is, chocolate is seriously dangerous for dogs."

Nick cast me an odd look, then strode over to the coffee table and scooped up the plate of cookies.

"Where are you taking those, Nicky?" Dorothy asked petulantly.

"Back into the kitchen," he replied. "I don't want you to spoil your dinner, Mom, since I'm about to order in the best Chinese food you've ever tasted. Sound good, Jess?"

I forced myself to smile. "It sounds great. Unfortunately, I, uh, have to get to the theater."

"So soon?" Nick cried. "But it's not even six o'clock!"

I did some quick thinking. Rehearsal didn't start until seven, but I was sure Betty wouldn't mind me killing the extra time at her house. She'd probably even feed me dinner. "I know, but, uh, since I joined the cast so late, the director asked me to come in early this evening. He wants me to work on a few things."

"But I just got home!"

My fake smile got even wider. "Which means you have the whole evening ahead of you to enjoy your parents' company."

"What about dinner?"

"I'll pick up something in Port Townsend." Grabbing my jacket off the back of Henry's chair, I added, "You know what they say. The show must go on!"

I never thought I'd live to see the day, I thought as the front door closed behind me, but I can't *wait* to put on my dancing shoes.

• • •

My second rehearsal with the Port Players went considerably better than the first one. It was actually fun, now that I was starting to get the hang of it. Surprisingly, I managed to wear the beige dancing shoes all evening without developing a single blister. However, prancing around in public in a pink chiffon skirt was definitely going to take some getting used to.

The following morning, I made my first stop of the day the Port Townsend branch of the Bank of Long Island, hoping for a chance to talk to Lacey Croft's romantic rival. And since Aziza was no longer involved with *She's Flying High* and wasn't coming to rehearsals, I had to seek her out on her own turf.

Lacey had used some pretty strong words to describe Aziza Zorn, saying she was a "drama queen" who was "always going ballistic." Her characterization, along with Sunflower McGee's claim that she'd overheard Simon arguing with a woman shortly before he was murdered, made me anxious to find out whether Lacey's claims were valid or merely the result of jealousy. Besides, the police always took a close look at the wife or girlfriend of a man who'd been murdered, so I figured it made sense for me to do the same.

The bank was quiet, with only three other customers. Eight tellers sat behind bars, rows of deposit slips were neatly lined up on counters equipped with pens on curly cords, and, along the back wall, a big banner read, *The Bank of Long Island: Make Your Money Work for You!*

I cased the joint, feeling kind of like a bank robber. But I finally spotted my target sitting at one of the half-dozen desks in back, the area in which customers sat down with bank employees to talk one on one about new accounts and loans and other topics of interest to people who were trying to make their money work for them.

Aziza was tucked away in the corner. I was glad her desk had a plaque with her name on it, since it was hard to believe this ordinary-looking woman was the same individual I'd seen dressed like Morticia Addams at the theater and again at Simon's wake. While that Aziza Zorn had filled the room with her presence, adorning herself with feathers and capes with the same ease most of us wear Nikes and jeans, this Aziza Zorn blended into her surroundings with the finesse of a chameleon.

She was wearing a nondescript dark blue suit and an off-white blouse, and her wild black hair was pulled back into a severe bun. As I got closer, I saw that her eyes were a pale gray-green this morning, rather than the brilliant green I'd noticed the first time I'd seen her. And the only makeup she wore was a slash of dark red lipstick that made her look like a little girl playing dress-up.

Her desk was as neat and as serious-looking as she was. There were two silver picture frames on it, placed at different angles. I could see that one contained a photograph of Simon Wainwright, smiling warmly at whomever was taking the picture.

"Aziza?" I asked hesitantly as I walked toward her desk, exercising the same caution I'd use in approaching a Rottweiler.

"Yes, I'm Aziza Zorn," she replied, looking puzzled. "Do we know each other?"

"I know you, but there's no reason for you to know me."

She blinked. At that point, she was probably trying to decide whether to call security.

"My name is Jessie Popper, and I recently joined the Port Players," I explained. "It's kind of a long story, but basically I went to one of the rehearsals with my friend Betty Vandervoort. Even though I've never been in a play before, much less a musical, the next thing I knew I was part of the cast."

"I know Betty," Aziza replied guardedly. "She's very nice."

"Betty's the best."

Aziza studied me, frowning. "So you're in the play? I don't remember you."

"I've taken over the role of Anita Snook," I replied. "Elena Brock took over the role of Amelia, so Derek needed someone to play Anita." I hesitated, then added, "I hope you won't hold it against me that I'm in the play. Since you didn't think the production should continue, I mean."

"Not at all," she replied stiffly. "I understand that Derek felt the need to go on." She hesitated before adding, "I don't happen to agree with him, but he's entitled to do what he thinks is right."

She glanced around nervously, as if she'd suddenly remembered she was at work. "Maybe you'd better sit down. I don't want to get in trouble."

I lowered myself into one of the two chairs opposite her desk. My new location afforded me a good look at the second silver picture frame on her desk. When I saw the photograph in it, my heart skipped a beat.

"I don't blame you for not having the heart to continue with the play," I said. I took a deep breath, wondering how far I dared push this. "But I guess I don't really understand why you're so against the production continuing."

"Simon was killed just days ago!" she exclaimed, her voice tinged with bitterness. "It seems so . . . so callous to go on as if nothing happened. If Derek and everybody else have any feelings at all, I don't see how they can continue."

"I didn't actually know Simon," I said. I was trying to keep her from lumping me in with the other Port Players who'd stuck with the production, since she clearly saw them as disloyal. "But it sounds as if a lot of people really cared about him. Admired him too."

"That's certainly true. But I'm sure you didn't come here to talk about Simon or his play," she said impatiently. She sat up straighter and folded her hands on her desk. "Are you here to open a new account?"

"I'm thinking about it," I replied, hoping I sounded convincing. "I wanted to get some information about fees and interest rates, things like that. I'm shopping around for a new bank, and I want to visit a few and compare their services."

"Very wise," she said, nodding. She opened the top left drawer of her desk and pulled out several glossy booklets. Each one featured pictures of people who were smiling, presumably because they were so delighted to be customers of the Bank of Long Island.

For the next five minutes, I pretended to listen with interest as Aziza explained all the different checking and savings account plans to me. I nodded and said "Uh-huh" a lot, but, frankly, the experience made me glad that I was satisfied with my present bank.

"Thanks for all the information," I told her when I was pretty sure we'd covered all the options, including the one that would afford me an attractive plastic travel mug with the bank's logo on it as soon as I signed on the dotted line. "Like I said, I'm going to be looking at a few banks, so I'm not ready to make a decision yet."

"Of course," Aziza replied woodenly. "But if I were you, I'd think carefully about the Savvy Savings Plan. It's perfect for you."

We'd exhausted the topic I'd been pretending had brought me here in the first place, which meant it was time for me to strike. So after stuffing the pamphlets into my purse, I gestured toward the second photograph on her desk.

"I see you have a cat," I said in what I hoped was a friendly manner. "Looks like a purebred Persian."

Aziza's eyes narrowed. "What about it?"

"I'm always interested in people's pets," I replied. "I'm a veterinarian."

"Really?" For the first time since I'd spotted her, I could see her letting her guard down. "Ophelia is an absolutely amazing cat. She's so smart. Her vocabulary is incredible. She knows the names of different kinds of food, the names of the different rooms in my apartment—I swear she even knows the days of the week. Monday through Friday, when I have to go to work, she comes into my room at seven to wake me up. But then, on Saturday and Sunday, she waits in the living room or the kitchen until I get up!"

She was smiling as she studied the photograph of her cat. But her expression suddenly tightened. "I should bring her in for a checkup. It's been almost a year since she's been to her vet. It's just so hard when you work a nine-to-five job. I've been busy with the Port Players, and of course Simon and I spent every spare minute we could find together."

"Has Ophelia experienced any health problems?" I asked.

"She's fine," Aziza insisted. Then her forehead tensed. "Except for this one thing. I've noticed a few white scabs on her skin lately. I suppose it's just dry skin."

A warning bell instantly sounded in my head. Ophelia's white scabs could indicate ringworm, since the condition was particularly common in Persians. Ringworm caused skin lesions, itching, and hair loss, and it was nothing to fool around with. Not only was it difficult to treat in long-haired cats; the fungal infection could easily be transmitted to both other animals and humans.

"Actually, it could be a sign of something more serious," I told her. "Maybe even ringworm, which is a common problem in Persians."

"Really?" She sounded alarmed.

Even though I'd reacted to her cat's skin problem the same way I would have with anyone else, I was secretly pleased that I'd gotten a rise out of her. I was hoping to be invited to Aziza's home, since it would undoubtedly help me get a better sense of her. I was still disturbed by Lacey's claim that Simon's announcement that he was breaking up with Aziza could have driven the woman to violence. Then again, something else might have pushed her over the edge—like learning that Simon was involved with Kyle or Ian or both.

"I'd be happy to take a look at Ophelia," I volunteered. "I have a mobile services unit—a clinic-on-wheels—instead of a regular office. I make house calls, which saves my clients time and travel. It also makes the treatment much less stressful for the animal. And I'm pretty flexible about hours."

"Could you really?" Aziza asked, her eyes widening. "I live pretty near here, in Pond Grove. My apartment is only about a half mile off the Expressway. When would you be able to come?"

We agreed on five-thirty that evening, right after she got home from work. I wrote down her address and phone number in my appointment book.

"Thank you so much, Doctor—Pepper, is it?" she said as I stood up to leave.

"It's Dr. Popper, but you can call me Jessie. And you're very welcome." I hesitated, then said, "You know, when I first came in here today, I didn't recognize you at first."

She offered me a weak smile. "This isn't really me. Whenever I'm here, I just pretend I'm in a movie, playing the role of someone who works in a bank. It helps me get through the day."

Glancing around with a forlorn look on her face, she added, "Sometimes I feel like it's the best acting I've ever done in my life."

• • •

Mission accomplished, I thought with satisfaction as I left the bank, loaded down with pamphlets but, alas, no plastic travel mug. I hoped I would do as well at what would be my second stop of the day related to my investigation of Simon Wainwright's murder.

I'd planned that one for much later, however. Close to noon, in fact. After studying the schedule Derek Albright had given me when I'd first signed on with the Port Players, I decided that late morning looked like a good time for a freelance cleaning person to descend on Theater One. It was right after a group of high school students would have gathered there to watch a play about drunk driving and a few hours before Jill had scheduled a special choreography rehearsal with the show's two principals, the actors playing Amelia Earhart and George Putnam. From what I knew about high school students, the gum wrappers alone undoubtedly warranted a thorough cleansing before grown-ups would be able to use the space.

When I stopped by, I found that, as usual, the front door of the theater was open. I walked right in and wasn't surprised to see someone standing on the stage, sweeping.

Bingo, I thought.

Then I did a double take. Sunflower McGee wasn't exactly what I'd imagined when I heard the term *cleaning woman*. She certainly wasn't the apron-wearing, Windex-wielding type. She was tiny, barely five feet tall, and looked as if she hadn't yet celebrated her twenty-first birthday. Her outfit consisted of a black T-shirt printed with the words *If You Can Read This, You're Too Damn Close,* baggy black jeans studded with way too much metal, and a pair of heavy black boots, footwear that, by comparison, made my chukka boots look like ballet slippers.

Not that she was completely without splashes of color. Her short black hair was highlighted with a single brilliant blue streak. She wore it in a deliberately disheveled bed-head style, with bangs that nearly obliterated her eyes. Gold stud earrings curved around her entire left ear like a constellation. They occasionally glinted in the light, as did the silver rings she wore on each finger, including both thumbs.

She didn't appear to notice that I'd come in. That was probably because a pair of earphones was clamped around her head, with the music turned up loud. So loud, in fact, that even before I reached the stage, I was able to identify the group as the Red Hot Chili Peppers.

I stepped onto the stage and waved until I caught her attention. She immediately pulled off her earphones.

"Sorry about that," she said with a grin. "Are you looking for somebody?"

"You, I think," I replied. "Are you Sunflower McGee?"

"Sunny," she said, grimacing. "Hardly anybody calls me Sunflower."

"It is kind of an unusual name," I commented.

"My parents were hippies," she explained matter-of-factly, leaning her broom against the wall and wiping her hands on the front of her T-shirt. "Sometimes it seems like they still are. They're always listening to these old guys like James Taylor and the Who and Crosby Stills and whoever else. And they listen to *records*! I mean, they're like the only people in the universe who still own a turntable! Can you imagine?"

I had to smile. Nick was such a fan of classic rock, including the performers whose names Sunny had just rattled off, that I'd grown to appreciate the oldies almost as much as he did. He also owned a few vinyl versions, although in most cases he had the CD as well.

"If you have a couple of minutes," I said, "I'd like to ask you a few things about the night Simon Wainwright was murdered."

Sunny's big brown eyes widened. "Are you a cop?"

"No."

"But you work with the cops."

"Not exactly. I'm just trying to help a close friend of Simon's figure out exactly what happened."

She nodded. "Yeah, I don't blame people for being upset. The whole thing is pretty creepy. Well, ask away. Anything to break up the monotony of chasing down dust bunnies!"

I sat down on one of the wooden chairs that edged the stage. "I understand you were here at the theater last Friday night, cleaning."

"Yup." She dropped into the chair closest to me. "That's one of the things I like about this job. The fact that I can work weird hours." Sounding a bit defensive, she added, "See, I'm not your normal cleaning lady. I'm just doing this until I find something more interesting to do with my life."

"Sounds like a good plan."

"What about you?" she asked, studying me. "What do you do when you're not trying to find murderers?"

"I'm a veterinarian."

"No way!" Sunny's face lit up like one of the spotlights up above. "That is, like, the coolest thing ever. How long did you have to go to school for that?"

"Four years. After four years of college, that is."

"Whoa, that's a long time. Where's your office?"

"I don't have an office. I have a mobile services unit, which is basically a clinic-on-wheels. I travel all over Long Island to treat my patients."

"Wow! That is beyond cool!" she exclaimed. "Taking care of animals must be so great. Do you absolutely love it?"

"I do. Sunny, what time did you hear Simon and the woman he was arguing with?"

"Do you use the van for regular driving too? I mean, like when you drive to the library or the supermarket or someplace like that?"

"I use the van only for business," I explained. "I have a little red Volkswagen I use for regular driving."

"Those are so cute," she commented. "Hey, what school did you go to? To learn how to be an animal doctor, I mean?"

"The College of Veterinary Medicine at Cornell University. It's upstate, in Ithaca."

"Do you need to take a ton of science courses to be a vet?"

"Yes," I replied as patiently as I could. "Sunny, would you mind telling me exactly where you were when you heard Simon quarreling?"

Instead, she said, "I was never that good at science. In school, I mean. But I love animals. It would be amazing to work with them. I can't think of a better career."

"I can't either." As frustrated as I was about her reluctance to focus on the important issue at hand, I couldn't hold it against her. Not when she was clearly interested in the vet biz—and as enthusiastic as I was about the notion of working with animals.

"Do you ever need help?" she asked suddenly. "When you treat animals, I mean."

Her question gave me pause. Sure, I needed help on

occasion. But that didn't mean I actually had any. Hiring a vet tech seemed far too expensive at this point in my career. So far, I'd managed on my own.

Still, sometimes I had to ask owners to help, usually by restraining their pets. And every once in a while, especially in an emergency, I really could have used a second pair of hands.

Before I had a chance to answer, she said, "Because I could help out. With your practice, I mean. I'm really good with animals. And I'm very reliable. You can even ask the people at Home Maid. They'll tell you. All my clients love me. I'm always on time, I always get the job done..."

"I'll keep that in mind," I told her sincerely. "But for now I'm curious about what you told the police. I believe you said you couldn't identify the woman you heard arguing but that you're sure the man was Simon. How can you be so certain?"

"Because I knew Simon's voice," she replied matter-of-factly. "I didn't overlap with the people in the theater company very often, but whenever I did, Simon was one of the few people who bothered to say hello to me. In fact, he'd take the time to chat with me every now and then."

"Did the two of you talk about anything in particular?"

Sunny shrugged. "Not really. Just the usual stuff about the weather and how bad traffic's gotten, that kind of thing. But he was always so *nice*, you know? When you're a cleaning lady, most people treat you like you're a bug on the wall. They just pretend they don't see you."

That, I knew, was probably true.

"Sunny, if you don't mind me asking, why were you here on a Friday evening? I know you like working at odd hours, but isn't that an unusual time to be cleaning? I mean, wouldn't you rather go out with your friends on the weekend?"

"Like I said, this job gives me a ton of flexibility," she explained. "That's the best thing about it. We can pretty much work on our own schedule, once we've been assigned certain clients. As long as the clients are okay with it, of course. This Theater One gig is really easy, since this place doesn't get very dirty.

"Not unless they're putting on special performances for high school kids, like this morning." Rolling her eyes, she commented, "If I were you, I'd stay out of the bathrooms until I get a chance to clean in there. But normally, when they're in rehearsal the way they are now, it only takes me a couple of hours to clean the entire place. So I can sleep late, do a couple of jobs in the afternoon, come here after dinner, and be done by nine. That gives me plenty of time to go out with my friends afterward."

I suddenly felt very old. For me, nine o'clock was time to think about climbing into bed with a good book—and Nick.

"What about the female members of the cast?" I asked. "How well do you know them?"

"Which ones?" she asked. "There're a lot of them, and they change all the time, depending on who's in which show."

"I was thinking of Aziza Zorn."

"Ugh."

That wasn't the reaction I'd expected. "So you do know Aziza," I said noncommittally.

"She makes sure *everybody* knows her. Aziza thinks she's the new Cate Blanchett or something," Sunny sniffed. "A real drama queen. Not to mention the fact that she always acts like she's better than everybody else."

"Would you have recognized her voice?" I asked.

"If she was the woman who was arguing with Simon that night?"

Sunny shook her head. "I'm really sorry, but it's like I told the police. I couldn't tell whose voice it was. I was in the dressing room next door, for one thing, so I heard them through the wall. There are two dressing rooms, one for men and one for women. I was in the women's, cleaning the big mirror. Somebody had gotten lipstick all over it. Can you imagine? It's such a pain to get that stuff off too. And to answer your other question, it was around nine. I wasn't wearing a watch that night, so I'm afraid I can't be any more precise than that. But I know I was running late, because my friends were teasing me about it when I finally caught up with them afterward."

"What about Lacey Croft?" I asked patiently. "How well do you know her?"

"Not much better than I know Aziza," she replied. "She sure seems a lot nicer, though. She does the costumes for a lot of the shows, so a lot of times she works here late. In fact, sometimes it's just me and her, both of us working away long after everybody else has gone home."

"I see," I said, thinking, So no one would find it unusual if Lacey was here after hours.

"Hey, have the police figured out what the murderer used to kill Simon yet?" Sunny asked eagerly.

"No, not yet."

"I have a theory of my own, you know," she announced with pride. "Not that the cops were interested in hearing it. Especially that obnoxious guy who's named after a bird and is only about as big as one."

Her characterization of Lieutenant Anthony Falcone made me smile. "I'm interested in your theory," I told her.

Lowering her voice to a conspiratorial near-whisper,

she said, "There's this really cool place backstage called the props closet. Have you ever been in there?"

I shook my head.

"Well, I have. I go in there to dust every once in a while. It's where all the props from the show are stored every night after rehearsal. But lots of old props from other shows are in there too. There's all kinds of great stuff! And my theory is that somebody took something out of that closet and bashed poor Simon in the head with it. Then they put it back, probably pushing it behind a bunch of other old props. For all I know, the killer's fingerprints are all over it and it's just sitting there, waiting to be discovered!"

It was an interesting theory—especially since it raised the question of whether or not Simon's murder had been premeditated. From the first, I'd assumed that Simon had been killed in the heat of the moment, mainly because of where he'd been struck down. An empty theater wasn't the best place to commit such a heinous crime, since it wasn't exactly private. People went in and out of Theater One all the time. Simon, for example, who had shown up there even though no rehearsal was scheduled for that night, as well as the mysterious woman who had gotten involved in a shouting match with him. The killer must have been aware that someone could walk in at any time.

Then there was the problem of hiding Simon's body. The killer had stashed it in a trunk. Once again, not a good choice, especially for someone who wanted to keep the crime a secret for at least a little while.

There was another possibility, of course. And that was that the murderer was making a statement by killing Simon inside Theater One. After all, this theater was undoubtedly the most important place in the victim's life. Within these walls, he was witnessing the musical he had created on paper come to life. It had to have been a thrilling time for him—and his killer had to have known it.

"What did the police say about your theory?" I asked.

"Actually, that bird guy hardly let me say anything," Sunny said, grimacing. "Aside from answering his stupid questions, that is. When I tried to tell him I had an idea about how the murder went down and where the weapon was, he gave me this little speech about how I should leave the investigation to the pros—like him."

Been there, done that, I thought. Aloud, I said, "That sounds like something Falcone would say."

Sunny's eyes suddenly grew big. "Wanna see it?"

"See what?"

"The props closet. I'm telling you, it's a really cool place. Maybe you'll even be able to pick out the murder weapon."

"Sure. Let's go."

My heart was pounding as I followed her into the left wing and through a doorway that led backstage. Not only would this impromptu tour give me a chance to see the props closet. It also afforded me the first opportunity I'd had to get a good look at the crime scene without arousing suspicion.

We walked along a hallway lined with doors, including one marked WOMEN'S DRESSING ROOM and one marked MEN'S DRESSING ROOM. As soon as we passed them, she made a sharp left onto a much shorter corridor. At the end was a closed door.

She flung it open, revealing a closet that measured about four feet by four feet. Three of its walls were lined with floor-to-ceiling shelves. A single bulb in the ceiling provided enough dim light to see the amazing assortment of items packed in there. There were trophies, a globe, a silver Viking helmet, and an elaborate crown that could have been worn by King Arthur. The rolled-up flags of several different nations stood in one corner. One shelf was crammed with fake food, including a big bowl of fruit and a rubber fish, as well as empty boxes of Cheerios and other familiar name-brand products. I saw wineglasses, umbrellas, eyeglasses, an old-fashioned radio, a teddy bear, paper fans, guns, busts, a guitar, plastic lizards, a rubber snake, and a stuffed bird that looked really fake up close but probably worked just fine onstage.

"What's that?" I asked. I pointed to a good-size metal box with a handle that was sitting on the floor, shoved beneath the shelves. It looked more like a piece of electrical equipment than a prop.

"That's a fog machine," Sunny explained. "See? It says *Pro Fogger* here on the side. I accidentally flipped the switch once when I was cleaning up in here. A couple of minutes later, all this fog started pouring out of it. Once I figured out what was happening, it was pretty cool." She laughed. "See, it's things like that that keep this job interesting."

The amount of stuff packed in the props closet was mind-boggling. And Sunny was right. Many of the items sitting on the shelves could have been used to commit murder.

"So what do you think?" Sunny asked, holding out both hands to indicate the incredible assortment of items. "Did Miss Scarlet use the lead pipe, the candlestick, or maybe that bust of Socrates over there? Of course, it's only papier-mâché, so you'd be lucky if you could kill a mosquito with it. But how about this clock? It's made of brass, I think. You could easily bash somebody's head in with that. And check out this metal sword. It's pretty heavy. That's what I'd use if I wanted to kill somebody."

I suddenly realized that our impromptu backstage tour presented me with a golden opportunity.

"Sunny," I said, "could you show me exactly where you were standing when you overheard Simon arguing with a woman?"

"Sure," she replied brightly. "Follow me."

We retraced our steps, this time stopping in front of the door marked WOMEN'S DRESSING ROOM. As I stepped inside, I saw that it looked just like the ones I'd seen in the movies. A counter lined one wall, and directly above were large mirrors framed with round white lightbulbs. The counter was littered with makeup, hairbrushes, bobby pins, cotton balls, and tissues. Plastic bins sat on a shelf high above, labeled *Beauty Products: Wipes, Etc; Hair Spray/Gels;* and *Wigs, Hats, Q-tips, Fabric Freshener.*

"Where were you standing when you heard the altercation?" I asked.

"Right here." Sunny took a step sideways, then stood up straight as a soldier once she got into position. "I remember exactly where I was, because I was struggling to get this stupid lipstick stain off." Frowning, she leaned forward and ran her finger over the mirror. "Look, you can still see a smudge."

"And you heard the argument through here?" I pointed at the wall behind the mirror she was still scrutinizing.

"Yup. I guess these walls aren't that thick. Besides, Simon and whoever else was in there were both pretty loud."

"But you didn't hear what they were saying."

"Nope. As soon as I realized a fight was going on, I drowned it out with my music." With a shrug, she added, "I come here to clean, not eavesdrop. I figured I'd give them some privacy, since they seemed to think they were the alone in the theater."

No doubt, I thought.

"Can you also show me the spot where the police found Simon's body?" I asked.

"Sure. It's right next door, in the men's dressing room."

The other dressing room was almost identical to the first. But they were mirror images of each other.

"This is it," Sunny said ruefully. "The room where the argument took place and the room where Simon was killed. From what I understand, the trunk his body was found in was right about here." With both hands, she indicated an area toward the back of the small room, near the counter. "Of course, the police took it with them as evidence. But it had been sitting in this corner for a long time. Certainly as long as I've been working here, which is, like, seven or eight months."

We were both silent for a few moments, as if each of us was contemplating the awful event that had transpired right in this spot just a few days earlier. I had hoped that finally visiting the scene of the crime would provide me with some insights I wouldn't have had otherwise. Instead, being here just made me feel sad.

"Simon was really a nice guy," Sunny finally said, speaking with a kind of reverence. "I know everybody's talking about how great he was, now that he's dead. But that always happens when someone dies. Simon *was* pretty great, though. He had a terrific smile, and he never walked by me without saying something friendly. He had a way of making me feel like I mattered—"

Suddenly she gasped. "Oh, my gosh. What time is it?"

I glanced at my watch. "A few minutes past noon."

"I gotta get busy. I just took on a new cleaning job

at a law office. I'm supposed to meet with them at three to find out exactly what they want me to do."

When we returned to the stage, where Sunny had left her broom, she turned to me and said, "Hey, have you got a business card?"

"Sure." When I handed her one, she studied it. "Wow. *Jessica Popper, DVM*. It must be so cool to see your name like that. With those letters after it, I mean. It makes you seem really important, y'know?"

"The main thing is that those letters mean I can do a job I really enjoy."

"You're so lucky," she said wistfully.

"I guess I am," I agreed. "Anyway, thanks for the tour. And thanks for sharing your theory about the murder weapon with me."

"No problem. Think about my offer, okay?" she called after me as I headed down the aisle. "If you ever need help, I'm your girl."

"I'll keep that thought in mind," I told her.

And I did file it away, just as I'd promised. Even if it was way in back.

Chapter 9

"No animal should ever jump up on the dining-room furniture unless absolutely certain that he can hold his own in the conversation."

—Fran Lebowitz

As I left the theater, I checked my schedule and saw I had some time before my next appointment. I decided to use it to pay Kyle another visit.

Making a second house call so soon after the first was only partly legitimate. True, it wasn't a bad idea to check up on Monty and see how the Weimaraner's wounds were healing. But my real purpose was trying to pump a little more information out of his owner. I'd been interested in his claim that Lacey was the guilty party ever since I'd first heard him voice his opinion. Now that I knew Sunny had overheard Simon arguing with a woman Friday night, I was anxious to find out more about the status of Lacey's relationship with Simon at the time he was killed.

I decided to call first to make sure he was home. After pulling into the first parking lot I spotted, outside a supermarket, I punched Kyle's number into my cell phone. I was greeted by the usual "Hello?" at the other end of the line.

"Hello, Kyle?" I said. "This is Jessie Popper. I'm close to your house, and I thought I'd stop by to see how Monty is doing, if this is a convenient time."

"Sorry, Kyle's not here right now." It was only then I realized the man I was speaking to had a British accent. After a pause, he added, "This is his roommate, Ian.

"But if you'd like to check on Monty," he continued, "you're welcome to come over. I'm sure Kyle wouldn't mind. In fact, he'd probably be grateful that you're taking such good care of that beloved beast of his."

"Great. I'll be there in ten minutes."

I was mildly disappointed that I wouldn't have a second chance to pump Kyle for information. But the opportunity to meet his roommate was at least as valuable. While Ian Norman wasn't part of the theater world in which Simon traveled these days, I was still curious about just how "friendly" this trio of college buddies was—and whether the intrigues within their little group could have driven either Kyle or Ian to murder.

I'd barely pulled up in front of the tiny brown house when the door opened. A man in his thirties stood in the doorway. He was dressed in very dark jeans that looked crisp and new. The same went for his navy blue sweatshirt with *Massachusetts Institute of Technology* emblazoned across the front in white letters. If that old saying about the clothes making the man was correct, then Kyle hadn't been exaggerating when he'd described his roommate as a computer geek.

Yet the rest of his look didn't quite fit the nerd template, as if he was trying not to succumb to it fully. Underneath his baseball cap, he had curly hair with a reddish tinge that made him look like a throwback to the 1960s. His scraggly beard, also reddish-brown, was sorely in need of a trim, which went even further in giving him the look of an aging Flower Child. Then there were his wire-rimmed glasses. They weren't at all the type of spectacles favored by the computer nerds I'd encountered.

"Dr. Popper, I presume," Ian said, his dark eyes peering at me through his thick lenses as I neared the door.

"That's me," I replied. Smiling, I added, "For some reason, that big old van parked outside always gives me away."

"It does, rather, doesn't it?" he replied, chuckling. "I'm Ian Norman. Ian Michael Norman, if you want the complete introduction."

"Nice to meet you, Ian," I said, shaking his hand. "Especially since I've already heard so much about you."

"Oh, dear," he said, sighing. "Now I have to worry about what Kyle's been saying about me."

"Nothing but good things, I assure you."

"That's a relief. But, goodness, I'm certainly not being much of a host, am I? Please, come inside." As he opened the door, he added, "And I should mention that Kyle has also told me wonderful things about you. Mainly that you've taken good care of Monty."

I had to smile at his proper way of speaking. He reminded me of Winston, who epitomized the proper English gentleman. You couldn't help expecting this man to suggest tea and crumpets—if not a tour of Buckingham Palace.

In fact, I found it absolutely charming. But my focus quickly shifted to Monty, who had raced over to greet me.

"Hey, Monty," I said, crouching down and fondling his soft silver ears. "How's my boy? How's my fella?"

Glancing up at Ian, I asked, "Has Monty been staying inside? I told Kyle that was important to help his wounds heal."

"Goodness, yes," Ian replied. "The little devil's been underfoot constantly." Rolling his eyes, he added, "It's been positively maddening."

"But the best way to help the poor guy get better," I commented. "I'm anxious to see how he's coming along."

"Maybe you'd like to take him into the kitchen to examine him," Ian suggested.

"Normally I'd bring him into the van," I said. "I've got an entire clinic in there. But for something like this, I can check him out right here."

Still crouching beside the dog, I examined the wounds on his thigh. There was almost no pus, a sign that the infection was clearing.

"Monty looks great," I told Ian. "But it might not be a bad idea for me to check on him again in a few days. In the meantime, please tell Kyle to continue giving him the antibiotic and to keep up with the warm compresses twice a day."

"Will do," Ian assured me. "Now, how about a cup of tea? Or do you have to run off?"

I generally don't avail myself of my clients' hospitality, largely because I simply don't have the time. But Ian wasn't just any client. He was the friend and roommate of one of the suspects in Simon Wainwright's murder. He was also the person who'd provided Kyle's alibi—and possibly a suspect himself.

"Tea would be great," I told him.

"Why don't you sit down?" he suggested. "I'll just toddle into the kitchen for a moment to get things started."

"Thanks."

As Monty settled happily into a corner, I took

advantage of being left alone to do a little snooping around the living room, something I hadn't had a chance to do during my first visit. I started with the wooden bookshelf tucked away in the corner, next to what appeared to be a nonworking fireplace. Not surprisingly, many of the tattered paperbacks were plays. I spotted the works of Samuel Beckett, Anton Chekhov, Sam Shepard, Eugene O'Neill, Tennessee Williams, Tom Stoppard, Neil Simon, and, of course, William Shakespeare. I didn't know much about acting, but I knew a comprehensive collection of the world's greatest plays when I saw one.

The collection also included books about acting theory by such masters as Sanford Meisner, Uta Hagen, Konstantin Stanislavsky, and Stella Adler. Interspersed were books on computer programming, biology, and chemistry, including some textbooks I recognized from my own days as an undergraduate.

I took one down from the shelf. The name *Ian Norman* was scrawled on the inside cover.

"Caught me red-handed," I quipped when Ian strode into the room, carrying a tray. "Sorry to be so nosy. I love books, and I can't resist looking through every bookshelf I come across."

"Be my guest," Ian replied, setting the tray down on the table. "As long as you don't mind all the dust. Neither Kyle nor I are particularly committed to housekeeping."

"I figured these books belonged to Kyle, since they mostly seem to be about acting," I observed. "But I noticed your signature inside this one."

"Somehow Kyle's books and my books have gotten all mixed up together," he explained. "I'm not even sure which ones are mine anymore, especially since books seem to find me, like stray cats and dogs. And some of these are quite old, going all the way back to my college days."

"Isn't that where you and Kyle met?" I asked, returning the book to the place I'd found it.

He looked surprised. "Yes. How did you know?"

"I think Kyle mentioned it," I said. "What about Simon Wainwright? Did you know him too?"

"Yes," he replied. "We'd drifted apart in recent years, but I knew him well back in college." His voice suddenly sounded strained. "I still saw him from time to time, once Kyle and I began sharing this house."

"Did you take acting classes at Brookside too?"

For some reason, Ian seemed to react strangely to this question as well. "Oh, yes," he answered. "That's how Kyle and Simon and I met: studying acting as undergraduate students at Brookside University. We were in so many productions together—*Glengarry Glen Ross, Our Town, The Iceman Cometh, The Skin of Our Teeth*...In fact, we used to joke about being a modern-day version of the Three Musketeers. We even got really drunk one night and dubbed ourselves the 'Three Musk-Actors.'" Smiling sheepishly, he added, "I guess that's only funny after you've been doing tequila shots."

Suddenly, the muscles in his face hardened. So did his voice as he concluded, "But all that was a long time ago. I eventually decided that the cutthroat world of theater wasn't for me. I'm involved in computers now. Not only is that a much more practical way of making a living; the nature of my job also enables me to work from home."

The topic of acting seems to be a bit of a sore point, I observed, filing that factoid away. Was it possible that Ian had been jealous of Kyle's continued interest in the theater—maybe even because of his roommate's strong attachment to Simon? I couldn't help feeling that I'd stepped into a plot as intriguing as a long-running soap opera.

And Ian struck me as one of the more mysterious

members of the soap opera's cast. I was frustrated by my inability to put my finger on exactly how he fit into Simon's world, and the rest of our conversation over tea yielded little more information. So I decided to check in with the one person who was mostly likely to know.

Even though it went against my better judgment.

• • •

"Falcone," the Chief of Homicide barked when he picked up the phone. Five seconds of interacting with me and he already sounded impatient.

Frankly, I was surprised he'd even taken my call. When I'd been put on hold while the officer who answered checked to see if he was "available," I expected to get the brush-off.

But now that I had his attention, I wasn't about to let go of the opportunity to find out whatever I could. No matter how minimal it might turn out to be.

"Thanks for taking my call," I began, figuring a little buttering up never hurt.

"You got five minutes, Dr. Popper," he replied, as usual not bothering to pronounce the *r* at the end of my name.

Somewhere out there, I mused, there's a tremendous warehouse filled with all the *R*s that people living in the New York area have discarded.

"That means *five*," he repeated, "not six or seven or ten. And the clock's already started ticking."

Great, I thought. I'm trying to solve a murder, and instead I'm suddenly a contestant on a game show.

I dove right in. "You know how upset my dear friend Betty Vandervoort is about Simon Wainwright's murder," I began. "And naturally she finds the possibility that one of the Port Players may have killed him terrifying. You also know that, as a result, I've taken a real interest in the investigation."

"You seem to do that quite often," he commented.

I let that one pass.

"I've taken the liberty of speaking with a few people in the theater company," I continued. "People who strike me as suspects. I'm sure most of them have also been a focus of your investigation."

"We're questioning a number of individuals who are of interest," he retorted, sounding as if he was reading the stock phrase off an index card.

"I wanted to know what you think about Kyle Carlson and his roommate, Ian Norman."

"Dr. Popper, surely you don't think I'm going to discuss this case with you."

Actually, I thought, I was hoping you'd do exactly that.

Aloud, I said, "What *about* Kyle? Do you consider him a suspect?"

"Kyle Carlson has an airtight alibi," he replied, sounding almost smug. "His roommate, Ian Norman, swears Kyle was at home with him from Friday after work until Saturday morning, when they both heard the news from somebody in the theater company."

"But how do you know Ian's not just covering for Kyle?" I persisted. "After all, the two of them are obviously close friends. Why wouldn't they lie for each other?"

"Look," Falcone huffed, "we had both of them come into the station. Separately, of course. And they managed to convince us they were both telling the truth. They were consistent on even the smallest details."

"You talked to Ian Norman yourself?"

"That's right."

"And you didn't sense anything...strange about him?"

"Aside from his accent?" From the way Falcone sounded, I could tell there was a big smirk on his face. As if *he* was one to talk. "He seemed perfectly believable. By the way, according to my watch, you got about forty-five seconds left."

"How about Lacey Croft?" I tried, talking faster than usual. "Did you know she was Simon's jilted girlfriend?"

"We're looking closely at the female suspects," Falcone admitted begrudgingly, "based on what the cleaning lady told us about the argument she overheard." Sourly, he added, "Speaking of Sunshine McGee, Forrester Sloan told me you may have had a conversation with her."

I ignored that too. Share and share alike, as far as I was concerned. And he wasn't exactly doing a great job of sharing.

"And Aziza Zorn? What about her?" Falcone knew at least as well as I did that the victim's love interest is almost always a suspect. Especially given Sunny's report about Simon's argument with a member of the female gender.

"We're looking at her as well. Sorry, Dr. Popper, but your time is up."

"Wait!" I cried. "What about Sheldon and Gloria Stone? What about other people in the theater company, like Derek Albright and Jill D'Angelo and—and—"

"Look," he interrupted petulantly. "When are you gonna learn to leave the police work to the police, Docta Poppa?"

Neva, I thought. But I kept my response to myself.

• • •

As I climbed back into my van after making my afternoon calls, I glanced at my watch and saw that I still had some time before I was scheduled to go to Aziza's house. It seemed like the perfect time to focus on two individuals whose relationship with Simon I hadn't yet had time to explore. While love was often a motive for murder, money was probably an even more likely factor. I'd been curious about Sheldon and Gloria Stone since I'd met them at Simon's wake. And it wasn't the extreme difference in their personalities that had intrigued me. It was the fact that they were about to become very important people in Simon's life.

And he, in turn, was about to become important to them—especially their pocketbooks. The two producers were on the verge of taking a huge risk by putting *She's Flying High* on Broadway. Of course, that would have been the case with any theatrical production. But I wondered if in this instance there was some backstory, some goings-on that weren't part of the obvious plot, that could possibly have erupted into murder.

My local public library seemed like a good place to start. Since I didn't know much about the theater world, I started by strolling through the periodicals section, perusing the slick, colorful magazines that lined the shelves to see if anything caught my eye.

I stopped when I spied a magazine called *Theater World*. I picked up the current issue, which was right on top, and saw that the previous five or six issues were stacked underneath. Whose faces did I find smiling out at me from the cover of the November issue but Sheldon and Gloria Stone's.

NEW YORK'S HOTTEST PRODUCERS BRING *THE HOTTEST SUMMER* TO BROADWAY, the cover copy read.

I leafed through the glossy magazine until I found the article. It was mostly about the play, which had been written fifty years ago but never produced. Gloria had reportedly discovered it at an antiques shop, retrieving the dust-covered manuscript from the bottom drawer of a rolltop desk where its author, Arthur

Nimsley, had apparently stashed it years and perhaps even decades earlier.

The second paragraph quoted her as saying, *"A chill ran through me as I stood in that dark, musty little store. I only had to read the first few pages to realize I'd stumbled upon a surefire hit. As I read the opening monologue, in my head I could hear Chucky Winthrop saying the words. I could see how the entire production should be staged. I knew then and there that we had to make it into a musical. Maybe Mr. Nimsley hadn't realized it, but that's what he'd written."*

I read on, soon finding a comment by some hotshot producer who was apparently a competitor but still had the greatest respect for her. *"Glo has a real instinct for what works and what doesn't,"* he was quoted as saying. *"And with the minimum cost of producing a Broadway musical somewhere around $10 million, being able to pick a hit has never been more important. Understandably, backers are only interested in investing in shows whose producers have a strong track record. That's something the Stones can offer."*

I continued looking through the rows of magazines until I spotted another likely candidate. Sure enough, *Behind the Footlights* had done a piece on the Stones in its January issue. When I flipped through the magazine, I found that facing the article was a full-page photograph of Sheldon and Gloria, standing back to back. *She has the nose, while he's the financial wizard,* the caption read.

I read through the first few paragraphs and learned that Sheldon and Gloria Stone did, indeed, play different roles, each complementing the other's talents. According to the article, Sheldon was a master at raising the tremendous pot of money required to stage a production on Broadway. But it was Gloria who was the real genius when it came to picking hits.

Gloria Stone has yet to make a mistake, the article claimed. *The consensus among her peers is that she was born with a natural instinct that very few people in the business are lucky enough to possess.*

Instinct. There was that word again. The people who knew about these things agreed that Gloria Stone practically had a sixth sense about the theater.

As I tucked the magazines under my arm so I could photocopy the relevant pages, I wondered if these two articles were simply a case of theater people being kind to other theater people. After all, both were clearly magazines read only by insiders who lived and breathed the industry. But when I expanded my search to the thick red volumes of the *New York Times* index, I found an article from the Sunday Arts & Leisure section that had run the year before. I tracked down the correct microfiche reel, threaded it into the machine, and began to read.

BROADWAY PRODUCERS ATTRIBUTE SUCCESS TO "INSTINCT"

While musical theater seems as much a part of the American landscape as rodeos and state fairs, the art form actually dates back less than 150 years. In 1866, William Wheatley, the manager of a 3,200-seat auditorium in downtown Manhattan called Niblo's Garden, was worried about filling his tremendous theater. Fearful that the play he was producing would never bring in the crowds, he came up with the idea of adding songs, dance numbers, and lavish sets to the mediocre dialogue. The result was the world's first musical, *The Black Crook*. The five-and-a-half-hour production instantly became a huge hit, running for over a year and bringing in over a million dollars.

Mr. Wheatley was probably not aware that he was setting a precedent. Yet over the past century and a half, the magic of the Great White Way has been kept alive by gifted individuals with his same sensibility, Broadway producers who possess the innate ability to recognize a potential hit and then pour their blood, sweat, and tears into bringing it to the stage. David Merrick, who produced such Broadway phenomena as *Gypsy, Oliver!, 42nd Street,* and *Hello, Dolly.* Joseph Papp, who produced *Hair, The Pirates of Penzance,* and *A Chorus Line,* in addition to creating the New York Shakespeare Festival. Hal Prince, the genius who gave us *West Side Story, Fiddler on the Roof, Cabaret,* and *A Funny Thing Happened on the Way to the Forum.*

The latest names on that impressive list are theatrical impresarios Sheldon and Gloria Stone. This duo of dynamos has been waving its magic wand over Broadway for nearly three decades, lighting up the Great White Way with one record-setting hit after another. From *Red Riding Hood* to *Sad-Faced Clowns* to *Elizabeth the Queen,* the Stones have set a new standard. The couple has also made stars like Chucky Winthrop and Della Dormand household names, at least in households whose members enjoy this all-American form of entertainment.

Given their history, it's hardly surprising that the Stones have done it again, this time with *Strange Bedfellows,* which opened at the Gower Champion Theater . . .

I skimmed the rest of the article, finding it packed with accolades. Then I checked more thick red volumes of the *Times* index. During their three decades in the Broadway biz, one article after another had appeared in the *Times*'s Arts & Leisure section, raving about the plays and attributing their success to the Stones' genius.

The last article I read on the microfiche screen caught my interest for an entirely different reason. It was entitled, WEEKENDS IN THE BROMPTONS RELIEVE THE STRESS OF SHOW BIZ. This article, which turned up in the *Times*'s Real Estate section, was about the Stones' second home, which was located in the chic and ridiculously expensive village of East Brompton on the east end of Long Island's South Shore.

But it wasn't the detailed description of the stainless steel Sub-Zero freezer in the four-hundred-square-foot kitchen or the three different living rooms overlooking the beach—or even the collection of Tony Awards crammed onto the mantel—that intrigued me. It was the simple fact that the famous impresarios spent significant amounts of time on my home turf of Long Island.

That meant the Stones and their bull terrier were neighbors. And as far as I was concerned, it was definitely time to act neighborly.

• • •

After I finished at the library, I saw there was still time before my appointment with Aziza to check on my animals. Betty had been too busy to stop in at the cottage during the day, since she'd had a long list of pre-wedding errands to run, so I was anxious to see how Max and Lou and Cat and the rest were coping with their uninvited guest.

I was relieved that Max and Lou met met at the front door, as usual. And Prometheus started squawking some incomprehensible greeting, a mishmash of his favorite expressions. Within seconds, Tinkerbell came running in from the bedroom, where she'd undoubtedly been lounging in her favorite location: my pillow. Leilani looked as contented as usual, draped across a large twig in her tank.

Only Cat wasn't in sight. As I glanced at her preferred spot—the middle cushion of the couch—I saw why.

It was occupied by Mitzi.

"Hi, guys," I said, but without my usual enthusiasm. I couldn't explain it, but I had a funny feeling something was wrong beyond Mitzi ousting the queen of the castle, no doubt exiling her to the rug in front of the refrigerator.

My feeling of doom was confirmed when Max failed to grab his pink plastic poodle in the hopes of engaging his favorite playmate in a rousing game of Slimytoy. After all, that's generally the first thing he does when I come home. Instead, he just looked at me expectantly, his sturdy little body jerking every few seconds as if he was more agitated than usual. For a terrier, that's saying a lot.

"What's the matter, Maxie-Max?" I cooed, crouching down and scratching him behind the ears. "Don't you want to play Slimytoy? Where's the poodle? Go get the poodle, Max!"

Instead of bounding off to find his beloved toy, he let out a sharp little bark.

"Max, where's the poodle?" I asked uneasily.

I was afraid I already knew the answer. A feeling in the pit of my stomach told me that some terrible fate had befallen his favorite toy. And I was pretty sure I knew who was behind it.

My eyes automatically drifted to the ball of white fluff nestled on the couch. Mitzi was watching us both with what I was certain was a look of defiance.

"Max, did Mitzi steal your poodle and hide it?" I demanded.

I knew my Westie couldn't understand me. At least not the words I was saying. But something about the way he barked halfheartedly told me he knew exactly what I was talking about.

I spent the next ten minutes searching everywhere for that poodle. Max padded after me hopefully, following me from room to room and sticking his nose under the bed and behind the couch right along with me as if he was trying to be helpful. Even Lou joined in the search. Of course, he was even less help than Max, since he had no idea what this new game was all about.

But I did. So I looked everywhere. Behind the cushions. In the bathtub. Even in the refrigerator, carefully stepping around my lounging feline.

Nada.

Meanwhile, Mitzi didn't budge. She just watched us from the couch, looking amused.

Okay, fuzzball, I thought, anger rising inside me. The jig is up.

I went over to the couch and got on my knees so we were eye to eye.

"Mitzi," I said, trying to remain calm, "be honest. Did *you* take Max's poodle?"

She growled.

Her reaction got my hackles up even further. And when it comes to dogs, I have a lot more patience than most people. Still, I found myself wondering if somewhere there was a reform school for dogs.

"Mitzi," I tried again, "I know what you did. Now, where is it? Just tell me—I mean show me—where you hid Max's poodle. I promise there'll be no hard feelings."

I was lying about that last part, of course. But it showed how desperate I'd become.

Mitzi, however, remained unmoved. She continued staring straight at me, then let out a single yap. I could only imagine what it meant in dog language.

And then, with a haughty toss of her head that sent her ears flapping, she stood up and turned her back on me. After leaping off the couch, she strolled into the kitchen nonchalantly, shaking her furry little butt.

By that point, I was fuming. I've had more than my share of negative interactions with animals. I've been bitten, drooled on, peed on, pooped on, vomited on, hissed at, snarled at, scratched, kicked, and pecked. But never in my life had I encountered such attitude.

"That's it, Cujo," I called after her. "If that poodle doesn't show up by tomorrow morning—unharmed—you just may be making an unscheduled stop at the pound."

Of course, my bark was much worse than my bite. But I didn't expect a Maltese to know that.

"Don't worry, I'm going to tell Nick about this," I promised Max, who continued to stare at me with woeful eyes.

But I knew it wouldn't do much good. And that for better or for worse, Mitzi the Malicious Marauder was about to become my dog-in-law.

Chapter 10

"A dog wags its tail with its heart."

—Martin Buxbaum

I made it over to Aziza's residence in Pond Grove just in time for our five-thirty appointment. Even though I wasn't familiar with that area, I tracked down her street easily with the help of my trusty Hagstrom map.

But it wasn't until I got there that I discovered she lived in a nondescript garden apartment complex called Norfolk Knolls. As I pulled my van into a curb-side parking space, I couldn't help wondering if the developer had thought of naming it *Knorfolk* Knolls. At least a catchy name would have added a little character. The half dozen two-story brick buildings packed onto the meager piece of land were as plain and angular as if they'd been built with Legos. They were grouped around large courtyards, but the grass was sparse and brown. The few trees that were planted on the property looked scraggly.

The buildings themselves weren't in much better shape. The dark green paint on the exterior doors was peeling in spots, and chunks of concrete had broken off the steps in front of them. The only splash of color was a pair of lime green paisley curtains someone had hung in one of the windows. I knew all about "curb appeal" from watching the Home & Garden Channel, and, frankly, this place had none. In fact, I got the impression this apartment complex had been built in the 1970s and hadn't had a face-lift since.

I was struck by the contrast between the flamboyant persona Aziza adopted at Theater One and the reality of her life as a disgruntled bank employee with a humdrum job and a shabby apartment. I wondered how she had really felt about Simon's imminent success. Had she expected to ride on his coattails, finally launching the acting career she clearly longed for?

Or had she feared she'd be left behind?

I was also curious about which of the two Aziza Zorns I'd find at home this evening. I got my answer as soon as she answered the door. In fact, I got the definite feeling I'd just done some serious time travel and ended up not in the 1970s but in 1920s Hollywood.

Aziza was wearing a cream-colored silk kimono, a garment I believe used to be referred to as a dressing gown. But it was the matching turban on her head that really made me wonder what decade I'd stumbled into. I half-expected her to croak, "I'm ready for my close-up, Mr. DeMille."

As for her eyes, once again they were the color of emeralds.

Her shiny, dark red lips stretched into a smile. "You're right on time, Jessie. Thanks for coming."

While her apartment complex didn't quite live up to her glamorous image, she had clearly done her best to create a living room that was the perfect backdrop for the role she was playing. In addition to the usual furnishings—a couch, a TV, a couple of nondescript end tables—tucked into one corner was a champagne-colored upholstered chaise longue. Thanks to my inex-

plicable fascination with watching other people deco-
rate, I knew it was called a fainting couch. Since fainting had gone out of style long ago, they no longer
enjoyed the popularity they had in, say, Victorian
times.

Both the fainting couch and the more traditional couch
were festooned with satin pillows in rich jewel tones like
purple, dark blue, and green. I would have bet my stetho-
scope that Aziza referred to them as "amethyst," "sap-
phire," and "emerald." Hanging on the off-white walls
were black-and-white photos of the greatest actresses of
the past century. Marilyn Monroe and Jean Harlow
peered down at me from the wall near the fainting couch.
Greta Garbo and Katharine Hepburn both had a place of
honor above the TV. I even recognized a few stars from
the silent-movie era, clustered near the entrance to the
kitchen: Lillian Gish, Clara Bow, Mary Pickford, and a
few whose names I didn't know, even though they looked
vaguely familiar.

But what really struck me about the place was the
number of mirrors the apartment contained. I wondered if Aziza constantly watched herself out of the
corner of her eye as she lived her life. It was possible
that in addition to enjoying being an actress, she also
got a kick out of being a director.

At the moment, however, it was the role of actress
she appeared to have stepped into. And apparently
part of playing the role of a star was being gracious.

"Can I get you something to drink?" she offered as I
settled into one of the more ordinary chairs. She gestured toward the kitchen with a dramatic sweep of her
hand. "I just got home a few minutes ago, so I'm dying
for something. Coffee? Tea? Or perhaps something
more interesting?"

Since I was working, I wasn't exactly ready to start
happy hour. "Tea sounds great," I said, glad that the

effects of my midday caffeine infusion with Ian Norman had worn off long before. Forcing myself to drink another cuppa would give me a chance to hang around for a while, trying to pump information out of the woman who had supposedly been the love of Simon Wainwright's life.

"Then tea it is," Aziza declared. "Do you take milk or—oh, here she is. Ophelia, I was wondering where you were hiding, you naughty girl!"

A fluffy white cat with the distinctive blue eyes, flat face, and tiny ears of a Persian had just wandered in from what I assumed was the bedroom. Despite her thick fur, I could see she was wearing a pale pink collar studded with huge rhinestones.

"What a gorgeous cat!" I remarked. And she was. Persians are generally a lot of work, since they require daily grooming. Yet Ophelia had a beautiful coat. Because keeping their fur snow white can also be a chore, special grooming powders are available to maintain the bright white color and prevent stains. Aziza had clearly availed herself of whatever was required to keep Ophelia looking like she was posing for a cat food ad.

"She can keep you company while I make the tea," my conscientious hostess offered. "And I'll see if I have a special treat for you, Ophelia."

As soon as Aziza disappeared into the kitchen, Ophelia sauntered over to check me out. I was relieved that she decided I wasn't worth her time, since I hadn't yet had a chance to determine whether or not she had ringworm. She leaped onto a cushion that was probably a favorite hangout, choosing to study me from afar. Meanwhile, I studied the room's intriguing decor, hoping I could use it to get Aziza talking about theater in general and the Port Players specifically.

Yet she was strangely quiet when she returned with

a tray. After giving her beloved kitty a treat, she gracefully draped herself across the couch so that she was half sitting, half lying down. We were separated by a coffee table laden with a teapot, two delicate china cups, and a plate of bland-looking cookies that had *afterthought* written all over them. Her sudden reticence told me I was going to have to do all the work.

It was a good thing I'd worked out a strategy for making conversation. "I love all the photographs of old movie stars," I commented, glancing around the room. "Which one is your favorite?"

"Theda Bara," she said without hesitation, pointing to the cluster of actresses I had recognized from the silent era. "She's the mysterious-looking one with the big eyes and the exotic makeup."

She rose from the couch and, daintily lifting the skirt of her satin dressing gown, floated across the room. I nearly fell off my chair when I noticed she was wearing cream-colored satin mules with huge feather pom-poms at the toe.

She stopped in front of the photograph, her eyes glazing over as she gazed at it in awed silence. "Theda Bara was the original vamp," she finally said in a reverent voice. "She created the role of the 'bad girl' in the movies at a time when ingenues reigned. You know, the sweet young airheads with pretty faces and great figures but not much else going for them. Yet she dared to play women of depth, like Salome and Cleopatra. She was even cast as a character named Madame Mystery."

Aziza turned to me and smiled. "Her studio, Fox, told everyone she was a member of Egypt's royal family, but she was actually born Theodosia Goodman in Cincinnati, Ohio. The deception was revealed early on in her career, yet she quickly became Fox's biggest star. She made as many as ten movies in a single year." Aziza looked back at the photograph and sighed.

"And she had the perfect life. Not only was she wealthy; she was happily married to a man she truly loved."

Her message was all too clear. A girl from Ohio named Theodosia Goodman had completely reinvented herself, becoming someone totally different—not unlike someone named Ann or Anna becoming Aziza. She then went on to have everything she wanted, including a successful acting career and a loving husband. Aziza obviously idolized Theda for having had two important things that appeared to have eluded her.

As she returned to the couch and poured me a cup of tea, she asked, "How are you finding your foray into Theater One?"

"I've been enjoying the play rehearsals much more than I ever expected," I told her. I was glad she'd mentioned Theater One, since it was the most direct way to bring the conversation around to Simon. "And everyone's been so nice to me."

"Really." She raised one eyebrow about a quarter of an inch, an ability I often wished I'd mastered somewhere along the way. "If I were you, I'd be careful."

"What do you mean?" I asked, surprised.

"Not everyone who's involved with the Port Players can be trusted." She shrugged, a movement that caused the creamy silk fabric of her dressing gown to shimmer. "I suggest that you watch your back."

I wondered if she was referring to the likelihood of someone in the troupe being Simon's murderer or something of a completely different nature.

"I'm sure there are all kinds of intrigues within the group," I remarked. "Friends, enemies, jealousies—even love affairs."

"Like Simon and me," she noted.

I decided to jump in, feetfirst. After all, a person

could nurse a cup of tea for only so long. "But that sounds like it was one of the smoother relationships within the group," I observed. I paused before adding, "I was surprised to learn from Betty that Simon and Lacey used to be an item."

The way Aziza bristled confirmed that I'd just brought up an extremely sensitive topic.

"That's right," she finally replied, frowning. She stirred her tea so frantically that some of it spilled into the saucer. "About three months ago, during rehearsals for *A Chorus Line,* Simon and I had a silly disagreement and we split up. But only for a very short time," she added hastily.

"That seems surprising," I commented, "given how close Betty told me you two seemed to be."

"Betty's right; we were extremely close. But Simon had, shall we say, a real sense of drama."

Talk about the pot calling the kettle black, I thought.

"Anyway," she went on, clearly still agitated, "it was just a silly lovers' quarrel, but Simon was known to overreact on occasion. He demonstrated just how angry he was with me by taking up with that fat, mealy-mouthed Lacey Croft.

"It was pathetic, really," she went on, her green eyes narrowing. "That woman isn't even *close* to being in Simon's league. Not only is she one of the most unattractive people I've ever seen in my life; she has absolutely no acting talent. I mean *none.* She can't even make a decent costume. I'm sure Derek only keeps her around because he can't find anybody else willing to work as hard as she does. And that's only because she has no life. When I think of her and Simon together, it's all I can do to keep myself from . . . I don't even know what."

I could practically see Aziza's face turning green,

like the Wicked Witch character in TV ads for the Broadway musical *Wicked*.

"Of course, she'd been throwing herself at him for months." The way Aziza spat out her words reminded me of my pussycat Catherine the Great, back in her feistier days. "And when Simon suddenly found himself alone, well, you know how men are. They're not very good at saying no. Especially when someone is obviously panting for them. Add in the fact that he was trying to find a way to hurt me, and you've got your motivation for their tawdry little affair."

"So Simon and Lacey started going out as a result of your breakup," I prompted, hoping for more detail.

Aziza smiled coldly. "From what I hear, they didn't go out much. They mostly stayed in. It seems their relationship was based primarily on, shall we say, carnal pleasures. Not surprising, considering the woman's complete lack of personality." She sighed. "Fortunately, it lasted only a few weeks. It didn't take Simon long to realize that he'd traded a silk purse for a sow's ear. Just as I expected, he came running back to me.

"You see, Simon and I were made for each other," she went on, throwing one arm into the air in an embarrassingly histrionic movement. "We both realized that the moment we met, on the same day he joined the Port Players. He used to call me his muse. He said he would never be able to create without me at his side to inspire him. We're a real life Romeo and Juliet." Her voice thickened as she corrected herself by saying, "I mean, we *were*."

The tears that suddenly filled her vibrant green eyes seemed genuine. Then again, I wasn't the most insightful person around when it came to evaluating someone's acting abilities.

"He never really cared about Lacey," Aziza continued. Her vehemence made me wonder if she was trying to convince me or herself. "He just used her to get back at me."

"And yet it seems like poor Lacey never got over him," I said softly, as if I was simply thinking out loud instead of trying to understand their love triangle as well as I could.

Aziza let out a raw, throaty noise that sounded so much like a bark that it took me a few seconds to realize it was a laugh. "Now, that's what I call an understatement."

My confusion must have been written all over my face, because she added, "You don't know, do you?"

"Know what?" I asked.

"That for the past few weeks Lacey had been stalking him."

I wasn't sure how to respond, since I didn't know if Aziza's version of "stalking" meant giving him a call every few weeks to see how he was doing or taping her underwear to his bedroom window. Frankly, Lacey struck me as someone who was much too levelheaded to do anything extreme, let alone stalk someone.

"What exactly do you mean by 'stalking'?" I asked cautiously.

Aziza's expression darkened. "As soon as Simon came back to me, the woman went absolutely berserk. She started calling him on his cell phone thirty or forty times a day. She constantly followed him in her car, so that wherever he went he'd find her waiting for him when he came out. She also sent him letters."

"What kind of letters?" I asked, puzzled.

"Threatening letters," she replied, her emerald-colored eyes growing round. "Letters that were filled with phrases like *I'd rather see you dead than with her* and *One day you're going to regret what you've done*." She paused, no doubt for dramatic effect. "Then there were the phone messages."

"What kind of phone messages?"

"The ramblings of a deranged mind," she replied bitterly. "Simon and I would come home from an evening out together and she would have filled up his answering machine. She'd say things like, 'I know you're out with her. I followed you, so I know you went to such-and-such restaurant.'" She shuddered. "It was terrifying."

"Where are the letters and tapes now?" I asked, my interest piqued.

"Oh, Simon got rid of them." Once again, she waved her hand in the air in a gesture that was considerably more dramatic than what was called for. "He acted like they were nothing. He never did see her for what she really was. He had such a kind heart that he probably couldn't even imagine anyone that malicious."

"So he never went to the police?"

"No." Shaking her head slowly, she added, "I tried to get him to file a report. Or even to get a restraining order. But he insisted that Lacey was harmless. I considered going to the police myself, but I knew that without his cooperation I wouldn't get very far."

"But you must have told the police about Lacey's harassment after he was...after last weekend."

"I tried," Aziza insisted. "But the officer I talked to—an absolutely unctuous man, by the way—didn't seem very interested. Not when he found out I couldn't actually produce the letters or the tapes as evidence." With an indignant toss of her head, she added, "He acted as if I was making the whole thing up."

As much as I hated to agree with Anthony Falcone on anything, this time around I was leaning toward his way of thinking. There was no proof that Lacey was stalking Simon aside from Aziza's version of what had gone on. And the fact that it happened to incriminate her rival for Simon's affections made it extremely questionable.

Then again, Kyle Carlson had also alluded to Lacey's extreme behavior. At Monday night's rehearsal, he'd mentioned that Simon had told him a lot about Lacey—"an earful," was the way I remembered him putting it—over the last few weeks before he was murdered. Enough that Kyle had also concluded that Lacey Croft wasn't a stable person.

Still, the bottom line was that Aziza was accusing Lacey of killing Simon, while Lacey thought Aziza was most likely the culprit. I supposed that was par for the course in a love triangle that ended in murder.

I would have liked to hear more about Aziza's take on Lacey's frightening behavior, but she suddenly put her teacup down on the table. "It's getting late. I suppose you should take a look at Ophelia. I haven't been able to stop thinking about what you said all day. Ringworm is pretty awful, isn't it?"

She was right. Once Aziza and I were in the van, I pulled on a pair of rubber gloves before touching Ophelia. She, meanwhile, stood on the examining table with her muscles tensed and her eyes darting around nervously.

As I palpated the cat's internal organs, I went through my usual list of questions. "Any change in appetite? Any vomiting or diarrhea? Any coughing or sneezing? Any changes in her water consumption?"

Aziza answered no to all of them. "What about itchy skin?" I tried. "Has Ophelia been scratching a lot?"

"No. The scabs don't seem to bother her."

I put Ophelia on the scale and recorded her weight of 8.2 pounds. Then I took her temperature, which was a healthy 101.8 degrees. Next I checked her eyes. After switching off the lights, I examined her skin with a bar of ultraviolet light called a Wood's lamp, which causes some skin lesions to glow.

But it was when I checked inside her tiny ears with an ear videoscope that things began to make sense.

There on the screen, dramatically magnified and in full color, was the interior of Ophelia's right ear—complete with the horde of tiny crablike parasites living there.

"She has ear mites," I informed Aziza. "They can cause bacterial and yeast infections, as well as lesions in the ear. But they can also cause skin lesions on the body. It's not common, but it's possible that that's what we're dealing with in this instance. I have to treat the ear mites anyway, so for now let's focus on getting rid of them and assume that they're responsible for the scabs. If she doesn't improve, then we'll start looking for other causes."

Ophelia patiently allowed me to wipe out her ears with a cleaning fluid called OtiCalm. Then I poured a second liquid into her ears called MilbeMite, a one-shot treatment consisting of a solution of milbemycin oxime that kills ear mites.

"Ophelia should be rechecked in three weeks," I told her. "She may need a second treatment of milbemycin oxime at that point. In the meantime, I'd like you to clean her ears twice a day with OtiCalm. I'll show you how. I'm also going to give you some ear drops to help get rid of the ear mites and yeast. It's an antifungal, an anti-inflammatory, and an antibacterial.

"And continue to keep an eye on her skin lesions. We still haven't completely ruled out ringworm, so if you see what you think may be a flare-up, either your regular vet or I should have it cultured. That will give you a definitive answer."

I glanced around my clinic-on-wheels. It suddenly seemed extremely large, mainly because I knew that my next step would be cleaning the entire interior with bleach—a necessary precaution whenever there's even a suspicion of ringworm.

Maybe Sunny McGee is right, I thought grimly. Maybe I really do need an assistant.

"Thank you so much!" Aziza gushed when we'd finished. "I promise I'll do everything you say. You're so good at this!"

I shrugged modestly. To me, taking care of animals is pretty straightforward. Ask the owner some questions, examine the animal, maybe do a few tests. The answers are usually pretty clear.

If only it was that simple dealing with humans—especially the ones whose emotions got so out of hand that they committed murder.

• • •

As I jogged across the parking lot of the Bayside Bistro, where I was meeting Nick and his parents for dinner, I glanced at my watch anxiously. I hadn't paid attention to the time while I was at Aziza's.

It was only ten minutes to seven. I was early.

Yet when I reached the doorway of the restaurant, Dorothy was already standing inside the foyer. Her arms were folded across her chest, and she looked extremely perturbed. Henry, meanwhile, was lounging on a bench that was pushed against one wall.

"You made it," she announced in a shrill voice. "Henry and I were getting worried. In fact, we were wondering if we'd have to eat by ourselves."

I opened my mouth to protest, then snapped it shut. After all, what was the point?

"How was your day?" I asked. "Did you enjoy the wineries?"

"A lot of those places charge for their tastings, you know," Dorothy replied tartly.

They're businesses, I thought, gritting my teeth, not charities for tight-fisted tourists.

I tried changing the subject. "Did you enjoy the scenery?"

She shrugged. "I'm not big on fields."

"How about you, Henry?" I asked, turning my focus to the less offensive half of the Burby duo.

It was only then that I noticed Henry was slumped over in his seat. His eyes were closed and his breathing was raspy.

"Henry?" I cried. "Are you all right?"

"He's fine," Dorothy assured me. "Between all those animals in your house and all that ... that *nature* out east, his allergies have gone berserk. He took a double dose of Benadryl. As usual, it's made him a bit drowsy."

Drowsy! I thought. The man is practically comatose!

"We might as well go inside," Dorothy muttered. "If they haven't already given away our table."

She leaned over Henry's extremely relaxed body so that her face was next to his ear. "Henry?" she hissed. "Naptime is over."

"Wha-a-a?" He opened his eyes and sat up abruptly, looking so disoriented I felt like asking him what year it was and who was president. "Where are we?"

"The overpriced restaurant Jessica picked out," Dorothy informed him. "It's time for dinner, so up and at 'em."

As we walked inside with poor Henry shuffling behind us, she glanced around. I did the same, enjoying the restaurant's sophisticated decor. With its clean lines and subtle use of color, it captured the ambience of an upscale Manhattan eatery.

"Goodness. This place certainly looks ... interesting," Dorothy observed with a look of distaste on her face. "They're obviously in the middle of renovating. That would explain why everything looks so plain."

"I can smell the spices," Henry mumbled.

Grateful for his show of support, I volunteered, "Yes, this place is known for its wonderfully spiced food. In fact—"

"Can't stand spices." If he was trying to imitate a zombie, he was doing a darned good job. "At least, my guts can't. If I eat anything with the least bit of spice in it, it goes right through me."

I was doing my best not to dwell on that particular image when Dorothy asked, "How exactly did you come to choose this particular place, Jessica?"

"Actually, it was Nick's idea," I replied, trying not to sound defensive. "It's one of our—his—favorite places."

"I see." She looked around again before adding, "It seems so...trendy."

She said "trendy" as if Webster's Dictionary defined the word as *bizarre, badly decorated, and filthy enough to be closed by the Board of Health*.

"Speaking of Nick," I said through clenched teeth, "I wonder where he is." For the twentieth time in about thirty seconds, I checked the front door.

"Poor Nicky works so hard," Dorothy said. "Knowing him, he's probably so busy studying he lost track of the time. He doesn't have all that free time that you—"

Fortunately, my fiancé chose that moment to materialize in the doorway of the restaurant.

"Nick!" I cried. "Over here!"

Throw me a life raft! I thought. But having him finally join our chummy little party was the next best thing.

"Hi, everybody," he greeted us breathlessly. "Sorry I'm late."

Me too, I thought.

"Not at all!" Dorothy cooed. "You're right on time. We're the ones who are early. For some reason, Jessica insisted that we get here way before our reservation time."

Before I had a chance to protest, he winked at me. "That's my girl!" he exclaimed. "If it wasn't for Jessie being so organized, I don't know how I'd get through a single day."

"Now, Nicky, you're extremely organized," Dorothy insisted. "I remember when you were in the third grade. Every day, you'd come home from school and—"

"I think our table's ready," I interrupted, anxious to get this family dinner of ours over as quickly as possible. "Isn't the maître d' waving at us?"

Actually, he seemed to be gesturing over something he was telling one of the waiters. But I made a beeline for the only available table in the restaurant, figuring the staff was going to have to use physical force to remove me from my chair if it turned out not to be ours.

Before I'd reached the table, however, the maître d' came rushing over.

"Excuse me, we have another table for you," he said, so politely that, at any other time, I would have reacted as if we were having a normal conversation.

But this wasn't any other time. This was now, when my blood was dangerously close to boiling, thanks to Ma Burby's supernatural ability to get under my skin and somehow turn up the thermostat.

"I want this table," I demanded. "I *need* this table."

"This is the Burby party, isn't it?" he asked.

Is it ever, I thought. "Yes."

"The reservation is for six people. You'll be sitting at that larger table, over in the corner."

"Our reservation is for four," I insisted. "I made it myself."

"But someone called earlier today and added two more."

"That's impossible. There must be some mistake."

I'd barely gotten the words out before a familiar face at the front of the restaurant caught my eye. A lovely warm feeling rushed over me, instantly lowering the temperature of my blood back to normal.

"Betty!" I cried. "What are you doing here?"

I noticed then that Winston was right behind her. "We've come to join you for dinner," he announced as they walked over.

"The more the merrier, right?" Betty added, casting me a conspiratorial look.

I had to resist the urge to hug her right then and there. "Definitely."

In fact, I was already feeling considerably merrier as our group moved toward our table for six. Unfortunately, it was a round table, one that was small enough for everyone to converse at the same time instead of breaking up into little groups.

Still, I waited to see where Dorothy sat before choosing my own seat. Happily, I was able to situate myself between Betty and Nick.

This seemed like a good time to fill Nick in on the latest canine crisis.

"Nick, Mitzi stole Max's pink plastic poodle," I quietly told him as the others were busy taking their seats. I tried to make my tone of voice reflect the severity of the offense. Instead, I sounded like I was whining.

That didn't mean I wasn't annoyed when Nick looked at me as if I'd lost contact with reality. "Jessie, that's ridiculous."

"No, it's not. I noticed before that she was eyeing Max's favorite toy." I took a deep breath before adding, "I think she's evil."

Nick sighed. "Have you been watching the DVD of *The Omen* again?"

"I'm telling you, Nick, Mitzi's taken on your mother's personality."

"Ah. So now we're getting to the crux of the matter. This is really about my mother. It has nothing to do with her dog."

It was true I had issues with Mitzi's mother—uh, owner. Major issues. But this was entirely unrelated.

"Nick, the poodle is gone. Vanished. And poor Max is beside himself."

"Then go out and buy him another poodle!"

"You're missing the point!"

"Jessie, you're imagining this! Dogs don't do nasty things to other dogs for no reason. They're not convicts, for heaven's sake—or junior high school girls!"

I could see this wasn't going anywhere. Nick refused to see Mitzi for what she really was. Come to think of it, ever since his parents had moved in with us, he'd forgotten all his past warnings about how difficult his mother could be. He and I suddenly seemed to be on different teams. Nick, along with Dorothy, Henry, and Mitzi, were the Top Dogs—and my pets and I were the Underdogs.

As for Mitzi's caper, I knew exactly what she was up to. She had planned this whole thing, not only to antagonize a fellow canine but more importantly to create problems between Nick and me.

As if we didn't already have enough of those to deal with.

By that point, everyone had gotten settled. I'd barely had a chance to put my napkin in my lap before Dorothy fixed her eyes on Betty. In a sharp voice, she asked, "Who are you?"

"I'm Betty Vandervoort, a friend of Jessica and Nick's," Betty replied. Her blue eyes twinkling, she added, "I'm also their landlady, so it's important that they stay on my good side. And this is my fiancé, Winston Farnsworth. You must be Nick's parents. I've heard so much about you!"

"No one told me we were having extra people at dinner," Dorothy grumbled. "Did you know about this, Henry?"

Poor Henry was slumped down low in his seat, looking dazed. I had a feeling he'd be snoring long before our waiter brought out the appetizers. I only hoped we'd be able to keep his forehead out of the clam chowder.

All the more reason to make a short night of it.

"Did you say Winston is your fiancé?" Dorothy asked. She snapped her linen napkin and spread it over her lap. "Isn't it a little late for you to be making major life changes?"

"But look at you and Henry!" Betty returned. "You're the perfect example of people our age who have a happy marriage!"

Dorothy's mouth dropped open. Of course she wasn't anywhere near Betty's age, but even she wasn't insensitive enough to correct her.

One point for Betty.

"Tell me, Dorothy," she said, leaning forward and speaking in a chatty, conspiratorial tone. "How do you and Henry manage to keep your marriage so lively?"

All five of us turned our eyes toward Henry. He had leaned his head back against the wall and closed his eyes. His mouth was slightly open, and he'd begun to emit a rasping sound that I suspected was about to escalate into full-scale snoring.

Another point for Betty, I thought gleefully. Maybe this evening won't turn out so badly after all.

"Henry happens to be heavily drugged," Dorothy

returned through clenched teeth. "He's having a very difficult time with all those...those *animals* around."

"Aren't they wonderful?" Betty cooed. "Max and Lou and Cat and little Tinkerbell...And Jessica is so good with them. Of course, she's a professional, so she's used to working with all kinds of animals. When she treats her patients in that marvelous clinic-on-wheels of hers, many of them are feeling stressed or in pain." She looked over at me and beamed. "She sees them at their worst, then makes them feel their best. That's our Jessica!"

"Maybe we should order," I suggested. Even though I was actually having fun now, I felt sorry for Henry. I was also afraid that the maître d' who kept glancing over at us nervously would throw us out—and I was hungry.

When a waiter came by to take our order, Dorothy went first. "These sautéed scallops on the menu—what are they sautéed in?" she asked.

"Butter, of course," the waiter replied, looking confused.

"Ugh. No butter for me. How about the onion soup? Are there a lot of onions in it?"

"A fair amount."

She shook her head disapprovingly. I looked over at Betty and rolled my eyes. She responded with a sympathetic smile.

After Dorothy ordered grilled swordfish, laying out the detailed directions for customizing the entire entrée so that it would meet her standards, the rest of us ordered our meals with amazing speed. I was hoping the arrival of a basket of dinner rolls would keep everyone distracted, at least for a little while.

But as soon as our waiter left, Dorothy zoomed in on Betty. I got the feeling that while the rest of us were ordering, she'd been planning her attack.

"Tell me, Betty," she said, "do you have any children?" Her question might have been completely innocent under different circumstances. But from the way her eyes glittered, it was clear she had an agenda.

"I'm afraid I never had any of my own," Betty replied. "But I've come to think of Jessica and Nick as my children. You don't mind if I borrow your son, do you?"

The look on Dorothy's face said she clearly did mind.

"How tragic that you never experienced the joy of motherhood," she cooed, shaking her head sorrowfully. "How ever did you manage to fill up that long life of yours?"

Betty smiled. "With an exciting and fulfilling career on Broadway, doing the one thing I love most, which is dancing. Traveling all over the world, seeing its wonders and meeting the most fascinating people imaginable. Going to marvelous parties and salons, hobnobbing with the greatest minds of the twentieth century." She reached over and took Winston's hand. "And after an extremely happy and passionate marriage that ended all too quickly, finding the greatest love of my life."

The light in Dorothy's eyes had faded. In fact, she looked as deflated as a balloon the day after the Macy's Thanksgiving Day Parade.

"Nicky, dear," she said, pointedly changing the subject, "would you mind passing the rolls?" She tried to force a smile but didn't quite manage it.

I, however, had to hide my smile behind my napkin.

• • •

"That was fun," Betty said brightly as the six of us walked out of the restaurant. "We'll have to do it again."

Not in my lifetime, I thought—then immediately

realized that, as Nick's wife, having dinner with his parents would be a regular part of my life.

I was wondering how he'd feel about practicing law in Alaska as we all branched off and headed toward our respective cars, calling, "Good night!"

After Betty and Winston had gotten into his cream-colored Rolls-Royce and Dorothy and Henry had climbed into their car, Nick followed me to my VW.

"What was all that about?" he demanded.

"All what?" I asked, frowning in confusion as I unlocked the car door.

"You and Betty ganging up on my mother."

My mouth dropped open. "What are you talking about? Betty and I did no such thing!"

"Oh, no? You mean you didn't pull a fast one by dragging Betty along to help put my mother in her place?"

I could feel anger rising in my chest like a bad cold. "First of all, I didn't 'drag Betty along.' It just so happens she invited herself."

"Why? Because she felt sorry for you, having to put up with your witch of a mother-in-law?"

"*Future* mother-in-law," I corrected him. "And keep in mind that the rest of that sentence consisted of your words, not mine."

"But I bet you gave Betty a real earful before tonight. All about how hard it's been, entertaining my parents for a few days, putting up with your in-laws—even this ridiculous business about Mitzi stealing Max's toy."

"As a matter of fact, I did have a chat with her about it. I needed to vent a little, mainly because your parents are such poor guests!" I hesitated, wondering if I should continue. But the words just kept coming. "And you haven't been much help, catering to your mother's obnoxious habits, not to mention her constant need to insult me."

"They're staying in our house, surrounded by our possessions and your animals and our daily routines—of course they've been finding it stressful!"

"Hey, I'm not the one who insisted they move into our phone booth of a house," I pointed out. "What's wrong with a hotel?"

"Oh, that's really hospitable, isn't it?" Nick retorted. " 'Sure, Mom and Dad, we'd love to have you come visit. But don't think for a minute that you're welcome to stay with us. We'd much rather you check into an impersonal hotel that's miles away from where we live . . .' "

"Would that have been so terrible?" I asked. "Instead of expecting four adults to share one bathroom? Not to mention crawling all over one another every minute of the day—"

" 'Every minute of the day?' " Nick repeated. "You've hardly been home since my parents got here! You've been too busy running around investigating the murder of someone you never even met!"

"I explained the reason for my involvement in investigating Simon Wainwright's murder, and it's a very good one," I returned. "I'm doing it for Betty."

"As if you've ever been able to resist poking your nose in where it doesn't belong. Or maybe it's just an excuse to distance yourself from me."

That last comment threw me. "What are you *talking* about, Nick?"

"Haven't you noticed that every time you and I have a chance to spend some time together, you sabotage it by getting involved in a murder investigation?"

"That's not true!"

"Oh, no? What about Hawaii? What about the time you were in the charge of the Ask-the-Vet booth at that charity dog show in the Bromptons, and we had a chance for a romantic little getaway? But oh, no. You were too busy interviewing suspects to do any of the things normal couples do on vacation, like go sightseeing or snorkeling or—or—"

"Both of those were just a coincidence," I insisted.

"And what about our regular life, when we hardly have any time together at all?" he continued. "With me in law school and you working crazy hours, it's hard enough for us to have much of a life. And then you have to go and complicate things even further by taking on one more thing to do!"

"Nick, that's absolutely not the case!"

"Well, it certainly seems that way to me. And this Simon Whatever-his-name-is is one more example. If you ask me, it's a great way for you to distance yourself from me."

I just stared at him. These accusations were coming from out in left field. I couldn't begin to process them.

Yet as hurt and angry as I was, I couldn't help wondering if maybe there was some truth to them.

I was still trying to run through all the different scenarios that had drawn me into murder investigations in the past when Nick let out a long, deep sigh.

"Look, I've been thinking," he said, slumping against the side of my car. His voice suddenly sounded lower and much more controlled, and he was staring straight ahead so that his eyes were no longer locked on mine. "Maybe you and I should put our engagement on hold for a while."

I stiffened. *"What?"*

He was still gazing off into the distance as he said, "I can see you're not comfortable with it. Maybe you're just not ready."

I was stunned. I couldn't believe what I was hearing.

"I feel like a coerced you into this whole engagement thing," he continued.

"You didn't coerce me." My voice sounded weak and not particularly convincing. All the anger that had gripped me moments before had dissipated.

"Well, it sure seems that way to me. And I think that maybe you need more time. That *we* need more time."

A tidal wave suddenly seemed to be rushing through my head. I felt dizzy and nauseous and, even worse, horribly alone.

Swallowing hard, I said, "Okay, Nick. If that's what you want."

I couldn't be certain, but I thought a look of relief crossed his face. "Yeah," he said. "It is."

By that point, I felt like Dorothy at the beginning of *The Wizard of Oz*. Not only was my house spinning through the air; all the wind had been knocked out of me because of it.

In fact, as I watched Nick stride toward his car, acting as if walking away from me like this was the easiest, most natural thing in the world, I had to remind myself to breathe.

Chapter 11

"What if it was cats who invented technology... would they have TV shows starring rubber squeak toys?"

—Douglas Coupland

Early Thursday morning, I sat at the table— alone—forcing down a third cup of coffee without tasting it. My hope was that an extra large dose of caffeine would diminish the feeling that my head was stuck in a big, thick rain cloud. I also hoped that, somehow, all that coffee would magically infuse me with the energy required to get myself through the day.

"Knock, knock!" Betty called cheerfully, opening the front door a few inches and poking her head inside. "Are you busy? Nick's parents' car isn't here, and I figured he'd already left for school. I thought I might catch you alone."

"Nick's parents are gone," I replied, barely glancing up. "He talked them into staying in New York City for a few nights, then driving home from there. He even found a hotel on the Internet that takes dogs. They left last night."

"You must be happy about that!"

I didn't think I looked happy about that or anything else, but I let her comment pass. "What's up?"

"I'm afraid I have something rather sticky to discuss with you. Is this a good time, Jessica?"

"Come on in," I said dully, even though I wasn't exactly in the mood for company.

"It's so dark in here," Betty commented as she came inside. "Why don't you turn on a light?"

"Is it dark?" I said, without raising my eyes from the rim of my coffee mug. "I hadn't noticed."

As soon as she flipped on a light switch and got a good look at my face, I guess she could tell that this wasn't even close to "a good time."

"Jessica, what's wrong?" she demanded. She sat down at the table and reached for my hand.

As soon as she did, she gasped.

I knew why. I'd taken off my engagement ring. "Nick broke off our engagement last night." I choked out the words. "In fact, he didn't sleep here last night. I guess he stayed in the city with his parents."

Betty's mouth dropped open. "What happened?"

I described the scene that had taken place in the restaurant parking lot the night before, after she and Winston had driven off. When I finished, she shook her head, meanwhile stretching her lips into a thin, straight line.

"I don't believe it," she said staunchly. "It's just a lovers' quarrel. When people get engaged, they have arguments all the time. In fact, I've often wondered if it's simply a way to reinforce their relationship, to demonstrate that even though there are rough patches, they still love each other and will somehow find a way to get through whatever adversity arises.

"Besides," she continued with the same vehemence, "having Nick's parents here put a tremendous strain on you. It put pressure on Nick too, whether he's aware of it or not. Goodness, that Dorothy Burby is enough to make anybody want to move to a deserted island. But this little spat of yours will blow over. I promise. Before you know it, Nick will be standing at the front door with a big bouquet of red roses in his arms."

"Thanks, Betty," I said sincerely. Even though I didn't believe her, it was nice to know that somebody thought our broken engagement was just a glitch, the result of nothing more serious than prewedding jitters.

"So what did you want to talk to me about?" I asked. "You said it was something sticky."

"It hardly seems important right now," she replied.

"Try me. My brain could use something else to think about."

She hesitated for a moment. "It's Chloe, Winston's daughter." Just then, Cat wandered over to say hello by rubbing against Betty's leg. Betty picked her up and put her in her lap. "I'm afraid she's decided that she wants to be my maid of honor. In fact, she was quite insistent when I spoke to her on the phone last night." Stroking Cat distractedly, Betty added, "She practically threw a temper tantrum."

A wave of disappointment swept over me. But it took only about four seconds for me to realize that Chloe's hissy fit meant I wouldn't have to wear the green monster of a dress that was hanging in my closet. The same went for the dyed-to-match high heels that I knew were just waiting to trip me and maliciously break a few bones.

"Betty, the last thing I want to do is make this wedding more stressful for you than it's already turning out to be," I said. "If you want Chloe to be your maid of honor instead of me, I understand completely. After all, she is Winston's daughter."

"But his son James is the best man!" Betty cried. "It only seems fair that if Winston gets to choose his best man, then I should get to choose my maid of honor. And I want you!"

I sighed, contemplating what a stroke of luck it was that both Winston's children happened to live across the sea, far, far away. I only hoped that once the ceremony was over, they'd go back to being completely absorbed in their own lives, the way they usually were, and leave my poor friend alone.

"How does Winston feel about this?" I asked.

"Winston's much too smart to get involved," she told me. "He said he'll leave it up to me to decide."

"Maybe you can have two maids of honor," I suggested. "Or how about having none at all? Maybe we could all just be regular bridesmaids."

Or better yet, I thought, maybe you and Winston can sneak away to Hawaii and get married on a beach—alone.

"No, I feel strongly about this," Betty insisted. "I want you to be my maid of honor and that's that."

"However it turns out, it's fine with me," I assured her. "Planning your wedding should be fun. This is supposed to be a happy time for you. I'll go along with whatever you think is best."

"Thank you, Jessica." Suddenly her facial muscles tensed. "On a much darker note, have you made any headway concerning Simon?" With a sigh, she added, "Winston may be steering clear of my conflict with his daughter, but he certainly hasn't stopped pressuring me to quit the Port Players. As you know, I have my own concerns about there being a killer in our midst, but I'm finding that much less stressful than all the tension Simon's murder has created between Winston and me."

I didn't have the heart to tell her that while my list

of suspects and their possible motivations was growing, I had yet to figure out who had actually killed Simon. It could have been Aziza Zorn, his possessive girlfriend, who might have flown into a rage Friday night because he announced he was ending their relationship. Or Lacey Croft, his jealous ex, who could have finally snapped after weeks of stalking him. Kyle Carlson, his longtime friend, could have been part of a love triangle with Simon—a triangle that was exclusively male and included Ian Norman, who could have been guilty as well. Then there was Gloria Stone, the Broadway producer with a nose for hits and flops, who might have murdered him for reasons that were related to money, rather than passion.

"I've made some progress," I replied. I kept my response intentionally vague, not wanting to add to her worries by naming some of the people she regularly saw at rehearsals. "Simon seems to have been one of those individuals who elicited strong reactions from whoever was around him. From what I can tell, people were just naturally attracted to him. And if they weren't getting enough of him, they felt shortchanged."

"It certainly sounds as if you've gotten a good sense of who he was," Betty commented, "even though you never actually knew him." She shook her head slowly. "I don't mean to pressure you, Jessica. I know you're doing your best. I just thought that maybe you had some idea."

She stood up and carried Cat over to the couch, then deposited the feline on her favorite cushion. "I'm afraid I have to get going. I have an appointment with the caterer this morning." Eyeing me critically, she asked, "Are you sure you'll be okay here all by yourself?"

"I'll be fine," I said. "Besides, I've got some calls to make."

"And we have rehearsal tonight," she reminded me. "I'm sure you'll be feeling better by then. In fact, you'll probably be wearing one of those red roses in your hair."

"Maybe," I said. But I wasn't nearly as optimistic as she was.

As soon as she left, the cottage felt horribly empty. So I was glad when I heard my cell phone calling to me.

My heart thumped wildly as I grabbed it and glanced at the caller ID. But it wasn't Nick. In fact, it was someone I didn't feel much like talking to at all.

I answered anyway.

"Hi, Forrester," I said, trying not to sound glum. "What's up?"

"Nothing much," he replied. "Just a major break in the case."

Despite my gloom, he had definitely caught my attention. "What is it? What happened?"

Instead of answering my question, he asked, "Have you had breakfast yet?"

"Not exactly. Just too much coffee."

"In that case, let's get together and talk. I know a terrific diner that's only about two miles from where you live. I can meet you there in twenty minutes."

"Forrester, this isn't a great time for me. If you could just tell me what—"

"Come on, Popper," he urged. "This is a good excuse for us to spend some quality time together."

Frankly, I wasn't in the mood for spending quality time with anybody, much less Forrester. Still, what difference did it make if I was miserable at home or sitting in a diner? Especially since consuming some so-called "comfort food" might actually turn out to provide me with some comfort?

"Okay," I agreed. "Where should I meet you?"

My reluctance was already fading. Maybe distracting myself with something other than my failed love life would be good for me. Even if that distraction happened to be murder.

• • •

"This is fun," Forrester commented, glancing around the Spartan Diner as he stirred his coffee. "Kind of like a dress rehearsal for our first date."

Startled, I glanced up from the cheese omelet I was doing my best to force down my throat. "What date?" I asked.

"Don't tell me you've forgotten our deal. Which, I'd like to point out, I'm living up to even as we speak."

His words were a powerful wake-up call, doing more to yank me out of my dazed state than all the caffeine I'd consumed. Our deal. Of course. I'd forgotten all about it.

I suddenly understood how foolhardy I'd been.

"Of course, in all my fantasies about the aforementioned first date, you look a lot better than you do right now." Frowning, he looked me up and down, even though doing so required that he stick his head under the table to survey my bottom half.

"What's up, Popper?" he asked, sounding concerned. "You look like something the cat just dragged in—if you don't mind me using a pet-related phrase."

"What's wrong with the way I look?" I shot back.

Grinning, he replied, "Nothing, really, if you happen to be one of those out-of-the-box thinkers who sees no reason for a person's shoes to match."

Horrified, I glanced at my feet. He was right. I was wearing two different shoes. True, they were both black loafer-style shoes. But they weren't from the same pair. When I'd dragged them out of my closet that morning, I hadn't bothered to check.

"Then there are the hygiene issues," Forrester continued.

I stiffened. Bad breath? Body odor? I desperately tried to figure out what he might be referring to.

"I guess you were so busy with your creative approach to footwear this morning that you forgot to brush your hair," he said gently.

"Is *that* all?" I was actually relieved that strangers on the street weren't shrinking away from me in horror as I walked by. Aside from those who happened to be in the hairstyling business. "It's possible," I admitted. "I guess I wasn't all that focused this morning."

"That would certainly explain why you're not about to win the Good Grooming Award." He had that annoying look of amusement on his face, as if he somehow found my personal failings charming.

I realized I had to change the subject as quickly as I could. The last thing I wanted was for Forrester to start speculating about the real reason I was giving new meaning to the phrase *dress-down Friday*. Especially since it was only Thursday.

"Can we please talk about the case?" I asked, sounding as businesslike as I could. "That *is* why I came. What's the big news you wanted to tell me?"

"The police have identified the murder weapon."

I gasped. That *was* big news.

"What is it? A billy club? A metal pipe?"

"Would you believe a ceramic Buddha?"

I blinked. "You're joking."

"I'm not. Apparently it was one of the props the Port Players used in last year's production of *The King and I*. I hadn't realized that Buddhism is the national religion of Thailand, where the musical is set. Anyway, somebody in the cast had noticed it in the props closet and thought it was cute. So she put it in the men's dressing room, just to be funny.

"According to Derek, the cast members were always messing with the props, using them for practical jokes or whatever. It wasn't until the police figured out that the Buddha was the murder weapon that anyone even realized it had vanished from the dressing room."

"Where did the cops find it?" I demanded. "And how do they know it was used to kill Simon?"

"It was way in the back of the props closet."

So Sunny was right, I thought. The murder weapon *was* one of the props—and the killer stashed it in the closet. That girl has a good head on her shoulders.

However, my next thought wasn't nearly as complimentary: What if Theater One's unorthodox cleaning lady knew more than she was letting on?

"As for how they know it was used to kill Simon," Forrester continued, "they found blood, hair, and skin cells that matched Simon's smeared on the surface. The shape of his head wound was also consistent with the contours of the statue."

"But no fingerprints?" I asked.

"Not a one." With a shrug, he said, "Okay, so it's not cut and dried. That doesn't mean you and I can't put our two brilliant heads together and try to figure out who killed Simon. After all, now that we know the murder weapon, we're that much closer to figuring out who the murderer was."

"Are we?" I countered. "Anyone could have smashed poor Simon in the head with that Buddha and then tried to hide it in the props closet. In fact, I have a list of people who could have done exactly that."

He laughed. "I thought you might."

Eagerly, I reached into my purse and pulled out the

list I'd compiled. It occurred to me that it really felt good to have something other than Nick to think about.

"I didn't know you had an actual list," Forrester commented. "I assumed you were talking about a mental list."

"I find it helpful to see the names right in front of me," I explained. Glancing down, I told him, "Lacey Croft is first."

Forrester nodded. "The police have suspected her from the start. But that's mainly because she found his body and called 911."

"She's also the woman scorned."

"So I've heard," he said. "What do you know about her?"

I filled him in on what Aziza had told me about Lacey Croft's brief affair with Simon, as well as the extreme reaction she claimed her rival had had when he came back to her. I also told him about the comments Kyle had made about Lacey and his unwavering insistence that she was the killer.

"When you spoke to Aziza," I asked, "did she tell you about Lacey stalking Simon?"

"She did. She also admitted that she couldn't prove it. I figured I'd ask around and see if anyone else knows anything about that."

"You might try Kyle Carlson," I suggested. "I made a house call to treat his dog Monty a couple of days ago. But I hadn't heard Aziza's claim about the stalking business yet, so I didn't ask him about it.

"Of course, both Kyle and Aziza are on my list of suspects too," I added. "That makes anything they say . . . well, suspect."

"Aziza is high on my list too," Forrester said. Teasingly, he added, "My *mental* list, that is."

"Simply because she is—*was*—Simon's girlfriend?"

"It's always a good idea to look close to home," he replied. "Although I talked to her a couple of days ago and she seemed pretty broken up about Simon's death."

"She's an actress," I pointed out. "Fooling people is something she's particularly good at. She's also a looker, which may have influenced you."

"Aw, my heart's already been stolen," he commented. "I'm not interested in other women."

I chose to ignore him. "Besides, there's something about her I just don't trust. Did you know Aziza isn't her real name? Apparently it's something much more ordinary, like Ann or Anna."

"Nothing wrong with changing your name," Forrester said. "Especially if you're in the *thee*-ah-tah."

"I suppose."

"What about Kyle?" Forrester asked.

"He claims that he and Simon were best friends since their college days. But there's something about him that just doesn't ring true." I thought for a few seconds before adding, "His roommate too. Ian Norman. It's nothing I can put my finger on, but I can't help feeling there's something fishy going on there."

"Maybe Kyle and Simon were more than friends," Forrester said. "Maybe *Ian* and Simon were more than friends. Who knows? Maybe all three of them were more than friends."

"All those possibilities have occurred to me too," I said thoughtfully. "Although that raises the question of why Simon was involved with both Aziza and Lacey over the past few months."

"And don't forget that Kyle has an alibi," Forrester pointed out. "His roommate swears he was with him from late Friday afternoon until the following morning when Simon showed up dead."

"Maybe Ian's just covering for him. Or maybe Kyle's covering for Ian. Why couldn't Ian be the murderer?"

Forrester looked at me skeptically. "A long shot, Popper. What do you know about Ian Norman's history with Simon?"

"Apparently Simon, Ian, and Kyle were all buddies in college," I explained. "Then Kyle and Simon paired off, probably because of their shared love of the theater. As for Ian, he seems to have dropped out of the threesome quite a while ago. But he's back in the picture now that he and Kyle are roomies."

"If not lovers."

"Exactly. At any rate, he's someone I'd definitely like to find out more about. Maybe some old feud from their college days resurfaced. Or maybe something more recent caused bad blood between them."

"Okay, so we'll keep Kyle on the list of suspects, even with his alibi," Forrester said. "Ian too, just in case we're missing something. Who else is on that list? Anybody else from the Port Players?"

"No, but that's only because I've been focusing on people who were especially close to Simon. Do you think there's anyone I've overlooked? The director, Derek Albright? Or Jill D'Angelo, the choreographer? Or anyone else in the cast and crew?"

"Just about everyone in the group who had any sort of relationship with Simon has a solid alibi. According to Falcone, Albright went to the opening of a new Off-Off-Broadway play Friday night. The cast party afterward too. The three people he drove back to Long Island with swear he didn't get home until almost dawn.

"And Jill D'Angelo was with about twenty members of her extended family, celebrating some great-aunt's eightieth birthday. They have videos and everything. Any other ideas?"

"What do you know about Sheldon and Gloria Stone?"

He narrowed his gray-blue eyes. "I've heard of them. Big-time producers on Broadway, right?"

"Exactly. From what I understand, they were getting ready to put Simon's play on Broadway."

"Interesting."

"Very interesting. Especially if you've ever met them. Sheldon comes off as the sweetest, most charming guy you'd ever want to meet. Gloria, meanwhile, is brash, self-centered, and totally obnoxious."

Forrester laughed. "Don't hold back, Popper. Tell me what you really think."

"She's also the one who's generally given credit for having an uncanny instinct for picking hits," I added.

"If they were interested in putting Simon's play on Broadway, is there any reason they would have wanted him dead?"

"I can't answer that," I replied. "But I'm going to try to find out. Simon apparently had a complicated love life. But money is just as likely to be the reason behind a murder. As producers, the Stones weren't only putting their reputation on the line. They would also have been responsible for a lot of money—other people's money. Millions, in fact. I learned that it costs at least ten million dollars to produce a musical on Broadway. Isn't *follow the money* one of the first things you learn as a journalist? Strikes me as a wise thing to do in a murder investigation too."

"Makes sense," Forrester agreed. "Let me know what you find out."

"Will do."

"Got any other suspects? How about someone who wasn't connected to Simon's life in the theater?"

I sighed. "I'm convinced that whoever killed him was involved in that world. It was so much a part of him. In fact, I don't think he had much of a life outside it. Betty told me herself that he was always at Theater One. Apparently he didn't care about anything else, not even his day jobs. They were just a way to finance his passion for acting and writing."

"So that's it?"

"That's all she wrote." I folded up the list and put it back into my purse.

As I did, Forrester reached across the table and grabbed my hand. "Hey, where's the Hope diamond?"

I could feel my cheeks reddening. "I took it off."

"Too heavy to drag around all day?"

I tried to come up with a response. Something clever, or at least something evasive. Instead, I said, "You were right. My engagement didn't last. It's over."

"I see." His voice remained calm, but there was definitely a glint in his eye I hadn't seen before.

Scowling, I added, "I hope you're not going to say, 'I told you so.'"

"Naw. I'm much too classy a guy for that." He hesitated before adding, "I'm not surprised, of course. I've sensed all along how ambivalent you were."

"It wasn't me, okay?" I shot back, loudly enough for the entire clientele of the Spartan Diner to hear me. "It was Nick's idea."

A look of surprise crossed his face. "No kidding." I could practically hear the wheels turning in his head. "His loss. So this means it's time for you to fulfill your part of the deal. You know, the one we made about—"

"I know exactly what you mean, and I can't believe you actually have the bad taste to bring it up," I said crossly. "And here you were just telling me what a classy guy you are."

"Nothing classy about reneging on a deal," he said. "And you and I made an agreement. One that I've been living up to. In fact, just by being here, I'm living up to it. Now it's your turn."

"Forrester, the last thing in the world I want to do is go out with you." Trying to be at least a little diplomatic, I added, "Or anybody else, for that matter."

"That may be true, but a deal's a deal."

I just glowered at him.

"C'mon, Popper. It'll be good for you to get out. It might even be fun."

"I really can't—"

"You can get all dressed up, and I'll take you to one of those fancy restaurants that serves weird food combinations like steak with peanut butter sauce. In fact, I'll even call you Jessica instead of Popper. How does that sound?"

"Like I'd much rather spend the evening with my animals."

He laughed. "We're on for this Saturday night, Popper. I'll pick you up at that little grass shack of yours at seven."

My head was spinning. It sounded like Forrester meant business. And he was right. I *had* made a deal with him. He'd lived up to its terms, and, at least in theory, now it was my turn.

But Nick lived in that little grass shack with me—at least I thought he still did. If Forrester came to pick me up there...

"Can't I at least meet you at the restaurant?" I pleaded.

"Nope. A date, by most people's definitions, involves one party, usually the male, picking up the other party, who's waiting anxiously at the door, all dressed up and ready to party. Seven o'clock, Popper. Sharp."

"Okay, okay," I muttered.

I didn't have any energy left to protest. Not when Forrester had a perfectly valid point. I only hoped Nick would have found something else to do with his Saturday night besides hang around our cottage. I never thought I'd live to see this happen, but I actually found myself wishing his parents would have stayed through the weekend. That way, at least we'd have other people around as a distraction. And when Saturday night rolled around, I was sure they'd want to be out enjoying themselves—with their son.

"And, Popper?" Forrester said, grinning at me as I picked up my fork and attacked my omelet.

"What?"

"Before we go out Saturday night—do me a favor and brush your hair, okay?"

I just cast him the most scathing look I could muster.

• • •

Even though Suzanne was one of my closest friends, I dreaded telling her about Nick and me. After all, the more I talked about it, the more real it became.

But I needed her help with the investigation. Her veterinary practice was on Long Island's South Fork, the bottom fin of what, on a map, looks like a fish tail. Poxabogue, where her office was, was one of the charming towns that made up the chic Bromptons. Because of its fabulous beaches and relative proximity to New York City, the area had been the summer playground of the superrich, the famous, and those who aspired to wealth, fame, or both for over a century. In recent years, more and more celebrities had begun making it their year-round home as well.

Since Suzanne's clientele included many key players in New York's entertainment scene, there was a strong possibility that she was Sheldon and Gloria Stone's veterinarian whenever they were staying at their weekend house on the East End. Even if she wasn't, she was an integral enough part of the community that she was likely either to know where they lived or to know someone else who did.

"Hi, Jess!" she said brightly when she found out who was calling. "It's so great to hear from you!"

"You might not think that once I tell you why I'm calling," I replied. "I'm afraid I've got bad news and worse news."

"In that case, start with the worse news."

"You remember Betty Vandervoort, don't you?" I began.

Suzanne gasped. "Don't tell me something's happened to that lovely landlady of yours!"

"She's fine. She's obsessed with planning her wedding. In fact, she's probably driving the caterer crazy at this very minute, agonizing over which of eighteen different flavors of wedding cake to choose. The really bad news is about a friend of hers, someone who was in her theater group."

" 'Was'?" Suzanne repeated. "You mean he left?"

"I mean he was murdered."

She gasped. "That's awful! Who was it?"

I filled her in on what I'd learned about Simon Wainwright, not only his death but also his life as a talented actor, singer, dancer, playwright, and lyricist.

When I finished, she said, "That's awful, Jess. I read about it in the paper, of course, but it never occurred to me that it was somebody Betty knew. If there's anything I can do—"

"As a matter of fact, there is," I said. "I'm trying to find out whatever I can about a couple of theatrical producers who were apparently planning to back his show on Broadway. Their names are Sheldon and Gloria Stone. I don't suppose they're clients of yours?"

She groaned. "They *were*. At least until Gloria drove me so insane that I told her to find another vet. And believe me, Jess, it's not often that I turn away business. Do you have any idea how high the rents out here are?"

"What was so bad about her?" I asked.

"The woman has an incredible temper. Of course, I didn't know that when she first started bringing her bull terrier here two or three years ago. What was his name? That's right: Bullseye. I seem to recall he was a pretty nice dog.

"Anyway, Bullseye developed severely inflamed skin, probably canine dermatitis. He kept chewing himself, poor guy. I'd treat it with antihistamines and he'd get rid of it for a while. But then it would come back and she'd get mad at me. I tried to explain that it could be an allergy to a certain food or dust or pollen—and that some dogs are even allergic to human dander. I told her that allergies are chronic, and that unless you address the source of the allergies, the problem is going to keep recurring."

She sighed tiredly, as though just thinking about her experience with Gloria Stone sapped her energy. "Look, you and I both know it takes time and effort to do the food allergy elimination trials and the blood tests that are required to find out what the dog is allergic to. But she refused to make the commitment to figure out the underlying cause. I don't even think it was the money, because it's not that expensive. It was more like she couldn't be bothered. She wanted a quick, easy answer—and she was furious at me for not simply making the problem go away.

"The last time she came in—and I remember it like it was yesterday—she started screaming at me about how I was making all this up just to rip her off. I tried showing her some articles from professional journals, but she wouldn't even look at them. She was too busy acting like I was some kind of scam artist or something.

"On her way out, my receptionist innocently asked her if she needed to schedule another appointment. Gloria went absolutely ballistic! She started yelling and throwing magazines around the waiting room. When she knocked over a lamp and I came running out to see what the noise was all about, I saw her chuck the *Ladies' Home Journal* at my receptionist. It was at that point I suggested we part company."

Suzanne's report was chilling. Here I'd thought Gloria Stone was just rude. Instead, she sounded like a psychopath. How her seemingly charming, even-tempered husband managed to put up with her was beyond me.

"That was at least six months ago," Suzanne concluded, "and I haven't seen her since. Good riddance!"

"Do you still have her address on file?" I asked.

"I'm sure I do. And I'd be happy to give it to you— especially if you intend to go over there and start throwing rotten tomatoes at Gloria Stone's house." She hesitated before adding, "Okay, so if that's the really bad news—and a friend of Betty's being murdered certainly fits into that category—what's the news that's bad but not *as* bad?"

I swallowed hard. As I expected, this piece of news was even harder to deliver. "Nick and I broke off our engagement."

"*What?*" she shrieked. "You're kidding, right? Please tell me you're kidding, Jess!"

I took a deep breath, hoping I could manage to talk without sounding as if I was about to choke. "I'm afraid not."

"Jessie, I know you're the type to get cold feet. But you're making the biggest mistake of your life! Go back and tell him that you changed your mind about breaking up, and—"

"It wasn't my decision," I explained. "It was his."

"*Oh.*" All of a sudden, Suzanne was speechless.

"I feel like a complete idiot," I went on, desperate to fill the silence, "but I made this stupid deal, and now I have to go out on a date Saturday night."

"A date?" she repeated, obviously confused. "And what do you mean, a deal?"

"Forrester Sloan agreed to share whatever he learned about Simon Wainwright's murder if I agreed to go out with him if Nick and I ever broke off our engagement. Of course, I never thought it would happen. But . . ." Rather than continuing, I simply sighed.

"Forrester Sloan. He's that *Newsday* reporter, right?" Suzanne asked. "The one who's so crazy about you?"

Before I had a chance to protest, I realized her characterization was pretty accurate.

"It's just one date," I said lamely. "We'll go out, grab a burger, maybe see a movie, and I'll be done with it."

"From what I understand, this guy isn't likely to see it that way," she countered. "But you know what I'm thinking? That going out with a man who's really into you might be the best thing that could happen right now."

"How's that?" I asked, genuinely surprised.

"It'll help your morale, for one thing," she replied. "It also might not hurt if Nick is reminded that he's not the only fish in the sea.

"Besides," she continued, "this could be the start of a beautiful new relationship. If you go into it with the right mind-set, that is."

At the moment, my mind-set was that nothing

sounded better than spending Saturday night with a pint of Cherry Garcia, my beloved pets, and a good book. It was a comforting scene.

And definitely one that had no room for Forrester Sloan.

Chapter 12

"Dogs are not our whole life, but they make our lives whole."

—Roger Caras

Once Suzanne gave me the address of the Stones' weekend house in East Brompton, I could hardly wait to get out there. But first I had my own foray into show biz to deal with.

I thought I'd pretty much mastered the basics by this point. But as soon as I walked into Theater One with Betty for the Thursday evening rehearsal, I gasped.

The entire theater was in chaos. Tremendous canvas drop cloths covered the rows of center seats, and long metal bars were laid across the arms. So were dozens of heavy-looking metal lights. Large cardboard boxes haphazardly packed with scenery, props, and even costumes cluttered the aisles. So did the dozens of fat black cables that snaked around the seats menacingly. A tall ladder I'd noticed stashed backstage stretched up to the ceiling. Plastic trash bags stuffed to capacity were scattered everywhere, along with wadded up bits of paper and strips of cardboard that hadn't made it inside.

"What's going on?" I demanded as soon as I emerged from my state of shock. "Is there a leak in the roof? Has there been a flood?"

I cast a look of desperation at Betty. For some reason, she looked amused. "None of the above, Jessica. It's tech week."

A young man dressed in jeans and a *Rent* T-shirt had just wandered by. "You noticed," he said, laughing.

I guess I still looked confused, because he explained, "The tech people descend upon the theater about a week before opening night to set up the lighting, the sound, and all the other behind-the-scenes stuff that's required to make the show run smoothly."

"Corey is the lighting designer," Betty noted.

"That's right," he said. Pointing toward the ceiling, he added, "See all those lights up there?"

I glanced up and for the first time noticed that metal bars just like the ones lying on the seats had been attached to the ceiling, with lights hanging at different intervals.

"Those are all the lights we need for the show," Corey explained. "They're controlled by the lighting board. It'll take me three or four days in total to set up the lighting cues."

" 'Lighting cues'? " I repeated.

"The lighting configuration keeps changing throughout the performance, depending on who's onstage and what's happening," he went on. "Each light up there—and there'll be about a hundred twenty of them by the time I'm done—is positioned to hit a specific spot onstage. The audience may not notice, but the lighting keeps changing throughout the production. And it's all planned out in excruciating detail during tech week."

"No wonder it takes four days!" I commented.

Grinning, Corey said, "On Broadway, the lighting crew can spend four hours setting up two minutes' worth of cues. The cast, meanwhile, is patiently standing onstage to make sure they're being lit properly.

"Once the combinations of lights have been computerized, it's all controlled by the lighting board." He pointed to the oversize metal board in front of him that was covered with buttons. "The night of the performance, the stage manager sits with the lighting-board operator. Her script is marked with all the lighting changes. Every time one comes up, she says, 'Go,' and the lighting-board operator hits this button—which, appropriately enough, is called the go button. That changes the lighting according to what's been programmed in."

"I think I get it," I remarked.

"There's more. The lighting is coordinated with sound, which operates pretty much the same way. During tech week, we set the levels, meaning how loud or soft each mike should be. But we also program in the sound effects. In this show, for example, we add in the roaring airplane engines. We have a dozen speakers throughout the theater, so we can make it sound as if the plane is moving across the sky."

Every aspect of the theater was turning out to be fascinating. As a member of the audience, I'd never given a thought to all the details that went into putting on a play. But the more I found out, the more amazed I was that an entire production could ever go off without a hitch.

"Jessie, into the dressing room for your final costume fitting, please," Derek called, interrupting my lesson in the technical aspects of theater.

That was fine with me, since costumes were something else I found interesting. The costume designer too. I had found Aziza's claim that Lacey had been stalking Simon hard to believe. It was nearly impossible to imagine the sweet-faced young woman with the big brown eyes in that role. I hoped that talking to her again would give me a chance to uncover her dark side, if she actually had one.

"Hi, Jessie!" Lacey greeted me brightly as I stepped into the women's dressing room. Once again, she was wearing her oversize burgundy sweater, and her hair looked as if she'd pinned it up without bothering to look at a mirror. "Have you decided on a class for your nieces yet?"

It took me a few seconds to figure out what she was talking about and to remember that we'd discussed the Yellow Brick Road's courses at length at the last rehearsal. "Uh, not yet. I still haven't had a chance to discuss it with their mother."

"Whatever you pick, you can't go wrong," she assured me. "All the classes are terrific." She studied the aviator outfit she'd just taken off the rack. "I hope you don't mind trying this on one last time. I'm pretty sure I made all the adjustments it'll need."

I pulled on the beige knickers and matching hooded shirt that comprised my costume. Then, standing in front of the full-length mirror lining the back of the door, I put on the goggles and leather helmet that completed the look.

"It fits great!" Lacey announced happily, her big brown eyes lighting up and her dimples dotting her cheeks. "See, I took it in a little here, and I moved this button a quarter of an inch..."

Standing alone with Lacey behind closed doors gave me the opportunity I'd been hoping for.

"It must be hard, being here in the dressing rooms," I commented, turning away from the mirror to face her. "Since that's where you found Simon last Saturday."

The light in her eyes instantly dimmed. "You have

no idea," she said in a choked voice. "This past week has been one of the worst of my life. I've tried my best to put up a good front, but underneath..."

She hesitated before adding, "Jessie, there's something that's been gnawing at me. I keep wondering if I should tell somebody, but I don't know who I can trust. Since you just joined the company last week, you never knew Simon and or any of the people who were closely involved with him."

My heart was pounding fiercely as I waited for her to go on.

"Simon called me last Thursday night," she said, her voice lowered to a whisper. "The night before he was murdered. He was really upset. He said he needed someone to talk to, and he wanted me to meet him somewhere."

What about Aziza? I thought, surprised.

"I know what you're thinking," Lacey said. "What about Aziza, right? But that's exactly what I was talking about the other day. I always believed that, deep down, he knew she wasn't right for him—and that it was only a question of time before he came back to me."

I wondered if deep down Aziza knew that too.

"What was Simon so upset about?" I asked.

"I never found out," Lacey replied mournfully. "I couldn't meet him. I wasn't at the Port Players' rehearsal that night, because I had a rehearsal for the Yellow Brick Road's spring recital. In fact, when he called me on my cell phone, I was right in the middle of it. I couldn't just leave! I'd be letting my little girls down.

"I knew Simon wasn't going to be at rehearsal that night either, since I'd overheard him telling Derek a few nights before," she continued. "But he didn't mention where he'd gone. The only thing he did tell me was that whatever he was so upset about had something to do with Gloria Stone."

Gloria! I could feel the adrenaline rushing through my veins. Ever since I'd gone to the library the day before and discovered just how powerful the two Broadway producers were, I'd been anxious to find out more about their relationship with Simon. Especially Gloria, whose behavior at the wake had been absolutely chilling.

"I keep wondering 'What if?' " Lacey went on in the same woeful voice. "What if I'd met him that night? What if I'd been able to help him? What if whatever he wanted to talk to me about is the reason he was murdered?"

I took a deep breath. "Lacey," I said, "are you saying you think Gloria killed him?"

She blinked away the tears that were pooling in her eyes. "I'd hate to think that of anyone, Jessie," she replied earnestly. "Especially Gloria. She was about to do so much for him. Putting *She's Flying High* on Broadway, giving him a starring role—she was on the verge of making all his dreams come true."

"In that case," I wondered aloud, "why *would* she have killed him?"

"I don't know. It doesn't make any sense. But somebody wanted him dead, and I can't help thinking that whatever Simon was so desperate to talk to me about that night is the reason."

"Lacey, have you told the police about Simon's phone call?"

She shook her head. "I guess I didn't want anyone to know what a bad friend I'd been to Simon. I was too ashamed to admit that when he reached out to me for help, I wasn't there for him." Choking on her words, she added, "And that maybe I was somehow responsible for what happened."

I was about to suggest that Lacey might be wise to go to the police when I heard Derek call, "Attention, please!" He clapped his hands loudly. "If everyone will please assemble onstage, I'd like to introduce you to a very special visitor."

Curious, I followed Lacey back onto the stage. I was shocked when I saw who was sitting in the front row with her legs crossed and her arms stretched across the tops of the seats on either side.

"Speak of the devil," I muttered in disbelief, exchanging a look of surprise with Lacey.

"Everyone, this is Gloria Stone, a true diamond on the glittering Great White Way," Derek gushed. "I'm sure you know all about her, but in case anyone's been living in a cave for the past couple of decades, Gloria and her husband, Sheldon, have produced some of the biggest hits on Broadway. They include *The Hottest Summer, Elizabeth the Queen,* and *Sad-Faced Clowns,* just to name a few."

He broke into applause. After realizing he was the only one clapping, several of the cast members, including me, felt obligated to join in. I glanced at Gloria, expecting her to be glowing. Instead, she simply looked bored.

"Gloria?" Derek finally prodded. "Perhaps you'd like to say a few words?"

Reluctantly, she rose to her feet. "Not really," she drawled. "I just wanted to stop by and see what this Theater One business was all about, since I've never been here before." She glanced around, curling her lip disapprovingly. "It's certainly small, isn't it? I mean, even for a community theater."

Derek looked crestfallen. "We've enjoyed quite a bit of success," he said, trying to sound proud but instead sounding defensive. "The local paper raved about our last production. Even *Newsday* gave it a positive review."

"I see," Gloria said dryly. "Well, I suppose I don't know much about the standards out here in the *suburbs*." She uttered the word *suburbs* with the same contempt she'd shown at Simon's funeral. Just hearing her made me want to run her over with a lawn mower. "And this, I suppose, is your cast?"

"My energetic, talented, dedicated cast!" Derek exclaimed.

"Ye-e-es" was all she said.

"Do stay and watch us rehearse," Derek insisted. "That is, if you have the time."

"Oh, I have the time," she replied. "Frankly, it's the inclination I lack."

With that, she grabbed her purse, the one emblazoned with PRADA in billboard-size letters, and headed toward the lobby.

"Please come back opening night," Derek called after her. "It's next Friday, a week from tomorrow. I'd love for you to see what a fabulous job we do!"

She didn't answer. She was too hell-bent on hightailing it out of there.

When she was gone, a heavy silence fell over the theater. It seemed to last an embarrassingly long time.

"Wasn't that a thrill!" Derek finally exclaimed.

Up until that point, I'd only seen him in his role as director. But now I realized he also possessed quite a talent for acting.

"Okay, people," he said, clapping his hands once again. But this time he was back to being the no-nonsense head of this production. "The clock is ticking. Opening night is only a week away. Our goal for today is to do as close to a full run as we possibly can. We'll stop only for a train wreck. Onstage, please. Let's go to places for the beginning of Act One. And I want to see lots of energy. Dazzle me!"

The actors scrambled into their places. But somehow, the cast and crew's usual exuberance had faded. Even with her short visit, Gloria Stone had managed to leave behind a bad feeling. In fact, it lingered in the air like the faint scent of her Chanel No. 5.

She's certainly easy to dislike, I thought, crossing the stage. And apparently Simon had come to the same conclusion.

As I got into my beginning position for Act One, I made a mental note to find out more about what had gone on between them in Simon's final days. I believed Lacey's claim that there had been bad blood between them. The question was whether it had been extreme enough to cause real blood to spill.

• • •

It wasn't until Friday morning that I remembered I'd assigned Patti the task of finding me an animal mannequin for my CPR demonstration. As I pulled into the parking lot of the Sunshine Media building, the home of Channel 14 News, I suddenly got that wrenching I-forgot-to-do-my-homework feeling in the pit of my stomach.

I should have called to remind her, I thought. My mind raced as I tried to come up with a way of doing my *Pet People* segment without a suitable patient to perform CPR on. I wasn't having any luck.

After signing in at the front desk, I dashed into Studio A. It was actually a pretty misleading name, considering the fact that the station had only one studio. The large room, its walls painted black, housed three different sets. One featured a big, important-looking desk at which two anchors sat and delivered the news. A second set was much homier, with two up-holstered chairs and a table for more casual interviews.

My set consisted of a counter that was elevated by a platform, with a wall of animals along the back. They happened to be stuffed animals, most of them in garish colors. I took my place on the stool behind the counter, positioning myself between a fuzzy pink elephant and a zebra with rainbow stripes.

"Did you get the mannequin?" I asked anxiously as soon as Patti, the show's producer, and Marlene, the production assistant, strolled in. "The one I need to demonstrate CPR?"

Patti turned to Marlene. "Marlene, where's our demo dummy?"

Marlene grabbed a big black plastic bag, which I took as a good sign. So they *had* remembered. But then she pulled out a large, fluffy, orange stuffed animal with black stripes, huge eyes, and the biggest, cheesiest smile I'd ever seen. "Here you go, Jessie."

I blinked. "You expect me to perform CPR on Garfield?"

"He's big enough, isn't he?" Marlene asked with concern. "And his orange fur will look great on TV."

"But it's—it's *Garfield*!"

Marlene looked indignant. "Garfield is entitled to the same high-quality medical care as any other animal, isn't he? I mean, he *is* a celebrity."

"But that's the problem!" I insisted. "He's—"

"He also happens to be very comfortable appearing on television," Marlene continued. "How many cats actually have their own TV show?"

I can't believe I'm having this discussion, I thought, trying not to panic. I wondered why on earth I had en-trusted this task to people who saw the world only in terms of teasers and sound bites.

But there was no time to agonize over the situation.

As seemed to be the case all too often lately, it was showtime. The cameras were pointed right at me and the bright lights flashed on. I stashed Garfield under the counter as Patti began counting down the seconds before we went on the air live.

"Five, four, three..." She held up two fingers, then one, as she mouthed the rest of the countdown.

"I'm Dr. Jessica Popper," I said brightly, reading the show's scripted introduction from the teleprompter. "Welcome to *Pet People*, the program for people who are passionate about their pets." Patti the perky producer was plainly passionate about the letter *P*.

"Today I'd like to talk about CPR—cardiopulmonary resuscitation," I went on. "I'm sure most of you have heard about using this valuable lifesaving technique on humans, but you may not realize it can also be used on animals. In fact, it's a good idea for cat and dog owners to familiarize themselves with this technique in case they ever run into an emergency situation.

"First, exactly what is CPR? It's a way of helping an animal breathe in the event that his normal respiration fails and to keep blood circulating through his body if his heart stops doing its job. It's important to note that CPR is performed on animals only when they're unconscious and have little chance of survival, since there's a risk of breaking their ribs while performing the procedure."

I did my best to maintain a dignified demeanor as I pulled Garfield out from under the counter.

"I'd like to demonstrate how it's done on this, uh, cat," I continued.

I held Garfield in front of the camera as if I was introducing him. Glancing up at the monitor, I saw that he was grinning at the folks out in TV land, looking as if he was loving all the attention. "As you can see, our, uh, patient looks as if he's in pretty good health. So we're going to have to use our imaginations and pretend he's in respiratory or cardiac arrest. To help determine that this is the case, check for pale gums and dilated pupils."

I glanced at Garfield, noting that his pupils and gums looked just fine. But at least he wasn't breathing, as far as I could tell. I laid him down on his back, so that his four fuzzy orange paws stuck up in the air.

"Okay, the thing to remember is A, B, C," I went on. "The first step, A, stands for *airway*. Start by pulling out the animal's tongue and looking for obstructions. If there are any, remove them with your finger. The next step, B, stands for *breathing*. The technique I'm going to demonstrate is often referred to as 'mouth to snout.' Hold the animal's mouth closed, inhale, and place your mouth over his nose and exhale. Then remove your mouth to give his lungs a chance to deflate."

As I put my mouth over my patient's hard plastic nose, it collided with his large plastic teeth. But that wasn't half as bad as getting a mouthful of fake fur. I wondered exactly where Marlene had gotten this particular Garfield, since he was molting like a canary.

I finished my demonstration, then focused on the camera once again. Out of the corner of my eye, I noticed that Patti was gesturing wildly, brushing her top lip. It took me a few seconds to figure out that she was trying to tell me to do the same. When I did, I discovered my own top lip was covered with orange Garfield fur.

So much for maintaining my dignity, I thought.

Still, I forged ahead. "Uh, next comes circulation, which is what the letter C stands for. Place both hands at the fourth through sixth rib, which is the area about a third of the way up the chest, starting at the sternum. Push downward firmly and steadily, like this. . . ."

At least Garfield's overstuffed chest gave way, enabling me to show how quickly the technique needed to be done. Still, I could imagine the response we'd get from viewers during the show's call-in segment. I could practically hear the disgruntled moms calling to complain about how traumatized their children were over seeing a vet performing emergency procedures on their beloved cartoon cat.

What else could possibly go wrong? I wondered.

I had to remind myself that that question was *always* dangerous to ask.

• • •

With that week's TV spot out of the way, the next major hurdle in my life—my upcoming date with Forrester—hovered over me like a rain cloud. As if I wasn't already upset enough about what had happened between Nick and me, I now had to endure an entire evening with another man.

At this point, I didn't even want to think about it. In fact, I was glad I'd scheduled a bunch of appointments on Long Island's South Fork for that day. Not only was work one of my favorite distractions; spending Friday afternoon on the island's East End put me conveniently close to the Stones' East Brompton home.

I decided to use their dog, Bullseye, as my excuse for popping over. My cover story would be that I was soliciting new clients. I hoped that using the bull terrier's name would be enough to get me in the door.

It was mid-afternoon by the time I turned onto Parrish Avenue. Finding the right street turned out to be the easy part. Locating the actual numbers on the mansions, meanwhile, was a much bigger challenge than I'd anticipated. The people who lived in this neighborhood hadn't exactly put out welcome mats. In fact, the houses were all hidden behind tall hedges or even taller chain-link fences that looked like overstock from Leavenworth.

Even so, when I spotted the house at the end of the street, I had a feeling I'd found the right place. Given the Stones' reputation as two of the brightest lights on Broadway, I pegged the largest, showiest house on the block as theirs. Of course, it didn't hurt that the front gate's design incorporated a swirling wrought-iron *S*.

I couldn't believe my luck when I saw that the gate was open. I drove through, parked in the semicircular driveway, and rang the doorbell. While I waited, I surveyed the tremendous, modernist residence, which was made of up several different levels that jutted out in what struck me as the strangest places. The front lawn was like green velvet, and there was a large fountain smack in the middle. Not my taste, but I could see how it might be Gloria's.

The door was opened by a very tall, very lean African-American man. He was dressed in slacks and a pale blue V-neck sweater with nothing on underneath. If I had to venture a guess, I'd have said the sweater was cashmere and the pants were Armani or some other equally expensive designer.

I did a better job of identifying the spunky bull terrier standing at his side. True to his breed, Bullseye had tiny brown eyes deeply set at the end of his long curved nose, perfectly erect ears, and a sturdy, muscular body. While many bull terriers are white, this one's back, legs, and ears were brindle, a mixture of gray and brown. The breed is known for its ability to fight other dogs, but most bull terriers are extremely playful when they're around people. From the way Bullseye was wagging his tail, I got the feeling this was one dog who knew his way around a Frisbee.

"Is Sheldon Stone here?" I asked politely.

"Sheldon's not here. Neither is Glo, in case she was your second choice." The man sniffed, then muttered, "Although it's hard to imagine why she would be."

My ears pricked up like Max's when he hears the *hrmph, hrmph* of a box of Milk-Bones being shaken. Still, I knew I had to proceed with caution. This gentleman appeared to have useful information about Gloria, and it was information he wasn't shy about sharing. I didn't want to scare him off before I'd even found out who he was.

"I'm Jessie Popper," I said. "I'm a veterinarian, and I'm here about Bullseye."

He stuck out his hand to shake. I noticed his fingernails had been carefully filed and buffed, and they appeared to be coated with clear polish. "I'm Cecil Callow, the Stones' assistant. Is there anything I can help you with?"

I handed him one of my business cards. "I have a mobile veterinary unit—a clinic-on-wheels," I explained. "I have a number of clients in the area, and since the Stones have a dog, I thought they might want to consider using my services."

Cecil glanced at the card. "*Reigning Cats and Dogs,*" he read aloud. Peering over my shoulder at my van, he asked, "Is that your clinic?"

"That's right. It has everything I'd need to treat Bullseye right inside. A mobile office like mine doesn't only save the client time; it's also less stressful for the animal. A lot of dogs and cats find the experience of going to a vet's office frightening, so having me come right to their home makes it a lot easier."

"How absolutely fabulous!" Cecil exclaimed. "And lately I've been getting stuck bringing Bullseye to the vet. I'll be sure to tell them about you. Not that I have any power. Like I said, I'm just the assistant. And believe me, Gloria Stone isn't big on taking advice from underlings."

Cecil was vocal enough about his attitude toward his employer that I decided to take a chance. "It doesn't sound as if you're experiencing a very high level of job satisfaction."

"Which is the main reason I'm only going to be here until I can find something else," he replied sharply. "I've been working for the Stones for less than three months, but frankly, it's been the longest three months of my life."

"I guess that's not surprising," I commented. "I've heard that Gloria—Glo—isn't the easiest person in the world to get along with."

He snorted. "No kidding. Why do you think people call her Glo-Worm? It's not exactly meant as a term of endearment."

From somewhere inside the house, the phone rang.

"I really have to get that," Cecil said, grimacing. "Glo has a hissy fit if I miss a single call. I'm hardly even allowed to go to the bathroom. You'd think no one had ever invented the answering machine. Look, why don't you come in for a minute?"

Before I had a chance to respond, he hurried off. As I stepped inside, I saw that the interior was just as modern as the outside. The tremendous living room was furnished with stark, uncomfortable-looking furniture like angular couches and chairs upholstered in white and small, oddly-shaped tables on spindly legs. The tall glass sculpture looming in one corner looked as if it would break into a million pieces if you dared walk by it, while the oversize coffee table book on Provence was probably too heavy for anyone actually interested in looking at pictures of the south of France to lift. The huge fireplace that covered one wall had clearly never been used. Either that or whoever cleaned it had worked in a hospital before coming to the Stones'.

Through the sliding glass doors that ran along the back of the house, I could see a large turquoise swimming pool. The water on two sides seemed to disappear, cascading over the side of the pool like a waterfall. Thanks to the Home & Garden Channel, I knew they were called vanishing edges—and that "infinity pools," as they were known, were currently all the rage.

While I waited, Bullseye and I became buddies, mainly because I'm such an expert at scratching dogs in all the right spots. After a minute or two, Cecil came striding back into the room, grumbling, "That stupid phone hasn't stopped ringing all week. Everyone's anxious about the Stones' latest production."

"Which production is that?" I asked, putting on my innocent act.

"A new musical they're producing on Broadway." He lowered himself onto one of the snow-white chairs, then gestured for me to do the same. "It was written by an unknown, which makes it riskier than usual. But it also makes it more exciting. The theater world is totally psyched about this show. A lot of people expect it to be the biggest hit since *Cats*. The usual fat cats have been lining up to invest, certain they're going to make a ton of money."

He sighed tiredly. "That's why they keep calling here every five seconds. They're dying to know what's going to happen with it."

"Why is its future suddenly in question?" I kept stroking Bullseye's ears, hoping to give the impression I was more interested in the Stones' dog than in the information I was pumping out of their assistant.

"The person who wrote it, Simon Wainwright, just died," Cecil explained. "There's a lot of concern that his death might bring it to a halt. You see, Simon didn't just write it; he was also supposed to star in it. Now that he's gone, people are wondering if Gloria's lost interest."

"Has she?" I asked.

"*Au contraire,*" he replied with a haughty toss of his head. "The Glo-Worm is absolutely *thrilled* that Simon is suddenly out of the picture."

"Why?" I didn't even try to hide my surprise.

"Between you and me?" Cecil replied, lowering his voice conspiratorially. "Gloria had had second thoughts about Simon. *Big* time."

Once again, my ears pricked up like Max's.

"When negotiations began," he continued, "Simon insisted on playing George Putnam, the male lead. Glo was so convinced she had a surefire hit on her hands that she was willing to agree to anything in order to make a deal. But as soon as the Stones signed on the dotted line, big name Broadway actors started coming out of the woodwork, begging for that role.

"Gloria began to wonder if she'd made a mistake in agreeing to let an unknown like Simon Wainwright star in the show. She decided it was safer to go with a name. Chucky Winthrop, in fact. Not only had she and Shel worked with him before; he also won two Tony Awards, one of them for their production of *The Hottest Summer.*"

"When did she have this change of heart?" I asked.

"A couple of weeks ago. And once she'd decided she didn't want Simon in the show, she and Shel argued about it nonstop. He kept insisting that Simon was perfect for the part. But eventually the usual thing happened: Glo worked on her poor husband until he finally agreed with her.

"The problem was, they had a contract with Simon that specified he'd play George Putnam. They couldn't get out of it unless Simon agreed. So Gloria came up with the bright idea of inviting him to the house, allegedly for a nice sociable dinner. But the real purpose was to drop the bomb about wanting to eliminate him from the cast."

"Were you at that dinner, Cecil?"

"Unfortunately, I was." Rolling his eyes, he said, "Believe me, I took plenty of antacids before I sat down to *that* meal."

"What was Simon's reaction?" I asked.

He looked at me as if I'd just asked the stupidest question in the world. "Are you kidding? Simon had been trying to make it as an actor for years. There was no way he was going to walk away from an opportunity like this!

"He and Glo ended up having a horrible fight. Sheldon didn't get involved, of course. He's one of the least confrontational people I've ever met. But Glo threw a major temper tantrum. By the time the entrées were served, she was screaming and pounding the table and threatening to sic her lawyers on him."

Not unlike her reaction in Suzanne's waiting room, I reflected. "How did the evening end?"

"With Simon stalking out of here in a rage," Cecil replied. "It was a total nightmare. Glo didn't calm down for days. In fact, she did nothing but stomp around the house, fuming. Sheldon tried to calm her down, of course, but she kept insisting she'd find a way to keep Simon out of the show." With a shudder, he added, "She said horrible things like, 'I'll see Simon Wainwright dead before I see him in any production that's got my name on it!' "

"Cecil," I asked, my heart pounding, "when did this dinner take place?"

"Hmm, let me think." Cecil grasped his chin with his hand, doing an impromptu imitation of the great Rodin sculpture "The Thinker." "Not this week. It was the week before. Wednesday, I think. No, Thursday. It must have been Thursday."

Thursday, I thought. The night Simon had called Lacey, desperate to talk about something he was extremely upset about. It was also the night before he was murdered.

"It sounds as if Gloria is really as nasty as people say," I observed, straining to sound matter-of-fact. Cecil clearly knew the Stones a lot better than I did. So I was anxious to find out whether he felt that in addition to having an instinct for theaterical hits, Gloria Stone also possessed a killer instinct.

"Are you kidding? The woman makes Marie Antoinette look like Mother Teresa," he replied, spitting out his words. "I've seen her reduce her maid to tears because she used a cleaning product that had the wrong scent. I swear, her gardener, who was an illegal alien, sneaked across the border *back* into Mexico after working for her for a few weeks."

Pointing at the terrier glued to my side, he added, "She even named her dog Bullseye, for heaven's sake."

"I don't understand the significance," I admitted. I'd just assumed the Stones had chosen it because it was a cute name.

Cecil raised his eyebrows. "Bill Sykes also has a bull terrier named Bullseye."

"Who's Bill Sykes?"

A look of disbelief, no doubt over my appalling ignorance, crossed his face. "Bill Sykes is a truly evil character in the Dickens' novel *Oliver Twist*, as well as in the musical version, *Oliver!* He plots to kill Oliver, then kills his own girlfriend, Nancy."

In that case, I thought, it really was an interesting choice.

"What about Sheldon?" I asked. "What's he like?" Despite his reputation as a real sweetheart, there could be another side to his personality.

"Sheldon's great," Cecil insisted. "If anything, he's

too nice. He'll do anything to keep his Wicked Wife of the West happy."

I wondered if "anything" included finding a way to get Simon out of the picture.

I was about to solicit his opinion about that possibility when Cecil suddenly muttered, "Uh-oh. Here comes trouble."

I followed his gaze to one of the tremendous front windows that overlooked the driveway.

"What kind of trouble?" I asked nervously.

"The Gloria Stone kind."

He was already dashing over to the door. As he flung it open, he was all smiles. "Glo, what a lovely surprise!" he gushed. "I wasn't expecting you."

Me either, I thought. I had to remind myself that having the chance to talk to her was a *good* thing.

"Cecil, get Harvey Gomberg on the phone," she commanded, marching into the house like General Patton. "Wait—before you do, go into the files in my study and get the figures for last week's ticket sales for *The Hottest Summer.* We've got to start promoting the hell out of this new show."

"Of course, Gloria," he said fawningly. He cast me a knowing look, then hurried out of the room.

She suddenly appeared to notice me. "Who are you?" she asked, looking me up and down as if I was something that had crawled in under the door.

"Jessica Popper," I said as evenly as I could. "We met at Simon's wake."

"Really? I don't remember you." She frowned. "What are you doing here?"

"I'm a veterinarian," I replied. "You couldn't have missed my mobile clinic, which is parked in your driveway. I have a lot of clients out here on the East End, and I know that busy people like you can appreciate the convenience of having a vet who makes house calls."

Her eyes narrowed. "Now I remember you from the wake. I saw you at the Theater One rehearsal last night too. You're friends with that aging tap dancer. The one who was close to Simon. Betty Vandervoort. Isn't that her name?"

I was glad Cecil had left the room, given the way I'd feigned total innocence during our little gossip session about Simon Wainwright and *She's Flying High*.

"Yes. That's right. Betty and I are good friends. But I stopped by today to tell you about my practice, since it's something you might consider—"

"I don't get involved with those horrid medical things anymore," she said, waving her hand in the air disgustedly. "Cecil takes care of all that. Talk to him."

I thought I was off the hook until she turned back to me and said, "I understand you're trying to find out who killed Simon Wainwright."

I was so startled I didn't know how to respond. "Who told you that?" I finally gasped.

"That lovely man Lieutenant Falcone," she replied. "I invited him to a little dinner party I threw here at the house a few nights ago. My way of thanking him for all the wonderful work he's doing investigating poor Simon's murder."

Terrific, I thought. Falcone's decided to get me out of the picture by telling the suspects what I'm up to.

Or maybe he didn't consider Gloria Stone a suspect.

But I certainly did. Especially after I'd learned from her own assistant that she had recently decided she was against having Simon star in the Broadway production of *She's Flying High*.

Dead set against it.

• • •

Given what I'd learned about Gloria Stone over the past twenty-four hours, I was convinced she deserved a prominent place on my list of suspects. The timing certainly fit.

According to Cecil, she had fought with Simon on Thursday night about whether or not he'd be in the Broadway cast of *She's Flying High*. He'd been so upset that he called Lacey, wanting to vent. Friday night, Gloria could have come to Theater One—a place she'd made a point of saying she'd never visited before—anticipating that he'd be there. I could picture her pressuring him to cancel their contract—and I could see their conversation erupting into another argument, which Sunny overheard. Later in the evening, Gloria could have come up with the perfect solution to her predicament: grabbing the Buddha and killing poor Simon.

Thinking about such a horrific series of events was exhausting. I looked forward to going home and putting it out of my mind—at least until I let myself into my cottage and realized I now had to deal with spending a Friday evening alone.

In the pre-Nick days, Fridays were for unwinding at home or calling a friend and going out for dinner or a movie. After he moved in, weekend evenings became a chance for us to spend some time together, since we were both so busy the rest of the week.

But I'd seen neither hide nor hair of Nick since our argument in the restaurant parking lot two nights before. And as I wandered around my empty cottage, I suddenly felt very much alone.

So after letting out the dogs, checking all the water bowls, and doling out dinner to all my pets, I strolled over to the Big House to see if Betty and Winston were willing to let me tag along on whatever the two soon-to-be-wed lovebirds had planned. I found Betty sitting on the couch with Frederick curled up in her lap, studying a catalog with such intensity she appeared to be cramming for a quiz. Various pages had been flagged with Post-its.

"You're just in time to give me some advice," she said. "I'm trying to decide on gifts for my bridesmaids. Do you think I should go with these engraved bangle bracelets or is a silver picture frame more practical?"

"I'm sorry, Betty," I replied, "but I'm not really in the mood for anything that's even remotely related to weddings, engagements, love, or even dating."

She frowned. "In that case, would you like to practice your dance steps?"

"I'm *really* not in the mood for that," I replied.

The ringing of the phone interrupted us.

"I'd better get that," Betty said apologetically, dashing off to answer. "It's probably Winston, calling from the tuxedo shop to get advice on what sort of cummerbund to choose."

I fondled Frederick's ears distractedly, half-listening as she padded down the hall toward the phone.

"Hello?" I heard her say.

And then, nothing.

I expected her to report that it was a wrong number. But when she walked back into the room, her face was ashen.

"What's wrong?" I asked. "Who called?"

"It sounded like a threat," Betty replied in a tight voice. "From a woman. I think I recognized her voice, but I can't place it."

"What do you mean, a threat?" I demanded. "From a woman? What did she say?"

"Actually, it sounded like a taped message. And I believe it was a line from a movie."

Before I had a chance to fire more questions at her, she added, "The tape simply said, 'Be afraid. Be very afraid.'"

Chapter 13

"When the mouse laughs at the cat, there is a hole nearby."

—Nigerian Proverb

I know that line," I told Betty. At this point, my voice sounded as strained as hers. "It's from a horror film called *The Fly* that was made in the mid-eighties. It was loosely based on a classic movie with the same title that was made in the 1950s."

"That explains why the woman's voice sounded familiar," Betty commented. "She's probably someone famous."

I concentrated hard for a few seconds, then snapped my fingers. "Geena Davis," I announced.

"The actress who played the President on that television series?"

"That's the one. She starred in *The Fly* with Jeff Goldblum. And she said the famous line. I believe it was also used in the promos for the film."

"What do you think that phone call means?" Betty's voice still sounded pinched. "Do you think it was a joke? Or a wrong number?"

"Probably one or the other," I replied. "Somebody

must have been playing a trick on a friend, except he dialed your number by mistake."

"I'm sure you're right," she agreed.

I knew she didn't believe my explanation for a minute. Neither did I. I was certain that her initial assumption—that she'd just received a threat—was correct. And I suspected that even though she was the one who'd gotten the call, its message was directed at me. The person behind it had decided the best way to scare me away from the investigation was by threatening someone I cared about.

The question was, who *was* that person?

I thought hard about which of the people on my list of suspects knew that Betty and I were friends. The entire cast and crew of the Port Players, of course. The two of us had arrived together at every single rehearsal, since we drove to the theater in the same car. In addition, we usually gravitated toward each other during breaks, sitting together and chatting. That meant Lacey, Kyle, and everyone else involved in the production, from Derek to Jill to the members of the chorus to the stage manager. Aziza too, since I'd told her myself that Betty was the one who'd gotten me involved in the first place.

It was possible that Ian Norman knew Betty and I were close, even though he'd never met her. All it would have taken was a casual comment from his roommate, Kyle—something about the new cast member, meaning me, who'd been brought in by one of the regulars, Betty Vandervoort.

Gloria Stone also knew that Betty and I were friends. She'd mentioned it herself when she'd found me talking to her assistant at her weekend house in the Bromptons. And thanks to my good buddy Anthony Falcone, she knew I was poking my nose around Simon's murder.

Any one of them could have tracked down Betty's telephone number. She was listed in the Norfolk County phone book, for heaven's sake. And it would have been easy enough for anyone to record the famous line from a DVD.

Whoever had made this call, however, had specifically chosen a threat.

A wave of utter despair suddenly swept over me. I wished I could talk to Nick about what was going on. But of course I couldn't. I couldn't talk to Nick about anything.

Forrester? I thought of him next, since he was as interested in who'd killed Simon as I was. However, I certainly didn't want to make any moves that could be interpreted as encouraging his crush.

Falcone? Another dead end.

At the moment, I realized, I was pretty much on my own when it came to this unofficial investigation of Simon Wainwright's murder.

Except for Betty, of course. She was in on it too. As of a few minutes ago, this was one point that had been made perfectly clear.

• • •

I tried to push aside the uneasiness Betty's mysterious telephone call had left behind. Either fortunately or unfortunately, depending on how you looked at it, I had the perfect distraction: my dinner with Forrester Sloan, only twenty-four hours away.

Merely thinking about going on a date with Forrester practically made me break out in hives. My buddy Suzanne, meanwhile, saw the appearance of someone new in my life as an exciting challenge.

In fact, she showed up on my doorstep, unannounced and unexpected, early on Saturday afternoon. The minute I opened the door, I felt as if I'd been ensnared by the posse of gay guys from *Queer Eye*. She was carrying a pile of dresses in her arms, with four different pocketbooks and three pairs of shoes balanced on top.

"What are you doing?" I demanded.

"Preparing you for the harsh world of dating," she replied firmly. "Jessie, you have no idea what it's like out there. Fortunately, help has arrived."

"It's not really a date," I insisted.

She didn't appear to have heard me. Not if the way she came barreling into my living room like a member of a SWAT team was any indication.

"Okay, we've got a busy day ahead of us," she announced. She draped the dresses across the back of my upholstered chair, then gently placed the shoes and the bags on the seat.

Predictably, Max thought the idea of turning the living room into a dressing room was great fun. My Westie thrived on anything new and exciting, and he pranced around gleefully like the party animal he was. Tinkerbell also thought all the commotion signaled playtime. When a satin ribbon floated to the floor after coming loose from Suzanne's fashion treasure trove, she pounced on it and began toying with it as if it was the best invention since catnip. Lou, however, perceived anything out of the ordinary as a potential threat. He treated the mound of accessories and clothing from Suzanne's closet as the enemy. He began growling at the colorful collection of fabric and leather, meanwhile keeping a safe distance away.

"Calm down, Lou," Suzanne instructed matter-of-factly. "This is all for a good cause, I assure you."

I wasn't any more convinced than my Dalmatian. In fact, I was tempted to growl at the mountain of alien clothing myself.

"O-kay," she announced, rubbing her hands together. "The clock is ticking, so let's not waste any time."

"Actually," I told her, doing my best to remain calm, "I thought I'd spend the afternoon catching up on my reading. I've got a stack of veterinary journals that—"

"Not today," she replied firmly. "We have to get your hair cut, find a decent manicurist, buy you some makeup..."

That last word made me cringe. I've never been big on makeup. Whenever I put on lipstick, I get this smudgy line around my mouth that makes me look as if I've been eating tomato sauce. As for eye makeup, I usually rub most of it off before I've even left the house. It's not until I glance in a mirror and see a raccoon staring back at me that I realize what I've done.

Suzanne leaned forward and scrutinized my face in a manner that made me extremely uncomfortable. "When's the last time you had your eyebrows done?"

"It's been a while," I admitted. "Like never."

She shook her head sadly, as if she was too disappointed in me to speak. "Maybe we should start by trying on the dresses. That will give us a solid base to start from."

Why someone needed "a solid base" to go out and eat a cheeseburger with a guy who'd coerced that particular someone into doing so was beyond me. But I could tell by the determined gleam in Suzanne's eye that she wasn't about to take no for an answer.

Still, I couldn't resist gasping in horror when she held up the first dress she'd brought.

"You actually expect me to wear that?" I cried.

"It's Donna Karan," she replied. I got the feeling there was a "Don't you know *anything*?" hiding somewhere in that sentence.

The fact that it had a designer label sewn into it

didn't make it any less weird. And it wasn't even the big, bright flowers splashed all over it that troubled me. What I really had a problem with was the huge fake flower that was glommed onto the shoulder, a floppy pink thing the size of a cabbage.

The dress was also short. So short that I couldn't imagine wearing it while sitting at a table unless the restaurant happened to have extremely large napkins.

"Don't you have anything with a little more fabric?" I hated the pleading tone I heard in my voice.

"There's nothing wrong with showing some flesh," she insisted.

"It's dinner, not an orgy," I pointed out.

I don't know why I even bothered. I could see how fixated Suzanne was on her task for the day: making me presentable—at least, in her eyes. Frankly, I found her doggedness a bit intimidating.

Even so, I nixed the next two without even trying them on. One looked like a large blue rubber band. The other had ruffles. I happen to have a very strict policy about ruffles.

I was about to make the outrageous suggestion that I wear something from my own closet when she held up the last dress. I had to admit, it wasn't bad. It was plain black, for one thing, without any ruffles or flounces or other geegaws that were likely to make me want to spend the entire evening hiding in the ladies' room. It also looked as if it would cover enough of my person to allow me to move like my real self instead of a robot.

"I guess I could try on that one," I said.

I slipped it on, surprised by how good the silky lining felt. It was almost as sensuous as flannel.

"What do you think?" I asked Suzanne, planting myself in front of her with my arms held out.

She smiled. "You look like Audrey Hepburn. Go find yourself a mirror."

Frankly, I'd always identified much more with Katharine Hepburn. And it wasn't only because she happened to have graduated from the same institution of higher learning Suzanne and I had both attended, Bryn Mawr College. Still, when I checked the full-length mirror on the back of the bedroom closet door, I had to admit that I looked like someone who was about to go on a real date, if not an actual *Roman Holiday*.

Not that I fell into either category, of course.

"So?" Suzanne demanded when I returned to the living room.

"You're right," I admitted. "I'm the new Audrey."

"We've got our dress!" she proclaimed triumphantly. "Which means we'll go with these shoes and this purse..." She glanced at her watch and frowned. "Goodness, I didn't realize it was so late! We'd better go. Jaimee hates it if his clients are late. He's always saying his time is much too precious to waste. And, believe me, you want to stay on his good side. When it comes to tress distress, he's the absolute master."

"Who's James?" I asked.

"Not James. Jaimee. J-A-I-M-E-E. And he happens to be the best hairstylist on Long Island, as far as I'm concerned. He owns Hair Explosion of London."

Why a place of business that wasn't actually in London had *London* in its name was beyond me. Frankly, it seemed like a good way to confuse the customers.

But I didn't push it. I didn't even comment on the fact that the exterior of Jaimee's establishment was painted to look like a giant Union Jack. The dazzling red, white, and blue facade was enough of a statement to incite a second revolution.

I just hoped I didn't come out of there looking all punky. Or like a character out of an Austin Powers movie.

I was somewhat reassured by the fact that, inside, Hair Explosions of London looked like an ordinary hair salon. Unfortunately, I couldn't say the same for Jaimee, since he didn't fall into the ordinary category at all. His hair was yellow. Not blond—yellow. And through the magic of gel or flash-freezing or some other mysterious process, it stuck up in a hundred different directions, kind of like crabgrass. Oddly enough, it complemented his bright turquoise silk shirt, which had full sleeves the likes of which I hadn't seen since my last pirate movie.

"So what are we doing today?" Jaimee asked in a lilting, obviously American voice once he'd gotten me into a chair.

I noticed he was talking to Suzanne, not to me. I hate being ignored. Especially when the future of some of my favorite body parts, like my hair and my fingernails and my eyebrows, is on the line.

"A cut, definitely," Suzanne replied thoughtfully. She hovered behind me with her arms folded across her chest, studying my reflection in the mirror. "I think we'll go with some highlights too."

"Honey is very popular right now," Jaimee cooed. "I think honey highlights would look great on her."

"Honey highlights sound perfect," Suzanne agreed. "And we have to do something about her eyebrows."

"Goodness, yes!" Jaimee exclaimed, reacting as if someone had just brought up the topic of global warming or something similarly horrific. "And definitely a facial. I'd suggest an apricot scrub. And what about a lip waxing?"

"That's a given." Suzanne was nodding her head furiously.

"Wait a minute," I interjected. "What's that last thing you mentioned?"

Jaimee leaned forward so his nose was practically touching mine. "Sweetie, we have *got* to do something about that mustache."

"What mustache?" I demanded. "I don't have a mustache!"

"Right," he muttered. "Neither does Fidel Castro."

"Isn't this getting expensive?" I asked meekly. What I actually wanted to have done to me or not done to me clearly held no sway. So I thought maybe the threat of not being able to pay for all the treatments on Jaimee's list would give him pause.

"It's on me," Suzanne replied. "My way of saying thank you for getting me off the hook when I was a murder suspect."

"You were suspected of murdering someone?" Jaimee asked. From the way his entire face lit up, I could see he had new respect for Suzanne. "I love that. It's so *CSI*!"

"You really don't have to do all this, Suzanne," I insisted.

"Oh, yes," Jaimee replied seriously, looking me over and pursing his lips. "She does."

The next couple of hours were a whirl of activity. Unfortunately, I was at the center of every minute of it. After my hair was streaked with a shade of blond that was a tad lighter than my natural color, it was washed, conditioned, combed out, blow-dried, and cut. My fingernails and toenails were buffed, de-cuticled, and polished. My eyebrows were waxed, an experience so painful that I vowed to shave them off entirely before I let anybody ever do that to me again.

Suzanne watched the entire process in silence. Then, for some incomprehensible reason, she suddenly got all chatty once Jaimee began smearing my upper lip with a frightening white cream. It smelled like something a janitor would use to clean the men's room at a gas station.

"So tell me more about Forrester Sloan," she insisted. "I hardly know a thing about him aside from the fact he covers a lot of murder cases."

"What's this?" Jaimee cooed. "A new man on the scene?"

"*Mm*-mm!" I hummed, hoping my utterances did an effective job of communicating the words *No way*. I was afraid that if I parted my lips, some of that vile cream might seep into my mouth and down my throat, causing a quick yet extremely painful death.

"He's a reporter for *Newsday*," Suzanne informed Jaimee with pride. "And he's really cute. Tall, blond, and preppy."

"I adore that look!" Jaimee cried. "That whole Abercrombie thing is so sexy."

"Hmm um *nmm*!" I protested, doing my best to communicate, *He is not!*

Not that what I had to say—or hum—mattered. Suzanne and Jaimee were acting as if I were the Thanksgiving turkey that he was basting while she looked on, admiring his skill.

When my ordeal was finally over and all the chemical substances that had been used to improve me had been washed down the drain, Suzanne looked me up and down.

"Jessie, you look absolutely fabulous," she concluded with satisfaction.

When I finally got up the courage to look at a mirror, I had to agree. My hair was shorter, bouncier, and brighter than ever before. My skin positively glowed. Even my eyebrows looked better, now that they were perfectly symmetrical.

But I didn't feel fabulous. Not when my first

thought was, I can't wait for Nick to see how I look—
and my second thought was, Not gonna happen.

In fact, as Jaimee and Suzanne high-fived each other
over the success of their makeover, I felt strangely
empty, sad, and very, very lonely.

• • •

Once I was out of Jolly Olde England, I hoped the
worst of this nightmarish episode was over. Compared
to being waxed, polished, and highlighted, going out
with Forrester was starting to sound like a breeze. But
as soon as Suzanne and I got back to the cottage, she
dropped another bomb in my lap.

"When Forrester shows up, I'll just hang around in
the background," she announced. "That way, I won't
overshadow you."

I froze. "Wait a minute. You're planning on being
here when he arrives?"

"Definitely."

"Why?"

"Because I want to check this guy out," Suzanne
replied. Casting me a sly smile, she added, "Besides, I
want to make sure you behave yourself. Now put the
dress on so we can see the whole effect."

Great, I thought as I wriggled into my Audrey
Hepburn costume for the second time that day. Not
only do I have to worry about Prometheus saying
something embarrassing, I also have to worry about
Suzanne. I could picture her ushering Forrester and
me out the door, burbling, "Don't do anything I
wouldn't do!"

I was about to exercise some damage control when
there was a knock at the door.

"Knock, knock," Betty called cheerfully as she
poked her head in. "I noticed Suzanne's car outside, so
I thought I'd stop in to say hello."

I instantly felt myself descending into the panic zone. I'd always suspected that Betty was capable of reading minds, especially when I was thinking something I didn't want her to know I was thinking. And the last thing I wanted was for her to find out about my plans for the evening.

I decided the safest thing to do was not mention them.

However, the moment she saw the two of us standing there, me looking like a Barbie doll and Suzanne beaming with pride over her handiwork, she set her bright red mouth into a thin, straight line.

"What are you two up to?" she demanded.

"Nothing!" I insisted at the exact same time Suzanne piped up, "Jessie has a date!"

Unfortunately, Betty zoomed in on Suzanne's response, not mine.

"A date?" she repeated. "With whom?"

"No one," I tried, this time much less forcefully.

"Forrester Sloan," Suzanne chirped in unison.

The corners of Betty's mouth immediately turned downward. Instead of a straight line, her lips now formed a disapproving frown.

"You mean that newspaper reporter." She practically spat out the words.

I was tempted to explain that the only reason I was in this position was that I'd foolishly negotiated what had turned out to be a very bad deal, all in the name of investigating Simon Wainwright's murder. And Betty was the one who'd gotten me involved in *that* in the first place.

But I suspected she wouldn't be particularly sympathetic. Not when she was absolutely crazy about Nick and utterly convinced that he and I belonged together like salt and pepper, Romeo and Juliet, and, well, Betty and Winston. She'd also thought from the very start that Forrester Sloan had designs on me. Designs she didn't approve of.

"I try not to think of myself as old-fashioned," she continued, her words strained and her demeanor icy, "but could someone please tell me when it became the custom for engaged women to date men other than their fiancé?"

"But Jessie's not engaged anymore," Suzanne replied, sounding surprised that I hadn't shared this little tidbit with my landlady and confidante.

"Oh, yes, she is," Betty insisted.

Suzanne glanced over at me, confused. "But Nick broke it off."

"Nothing but a silly little lovers' quarrel," Betty insisted. "Happens all the time. In fact, it would be strange if it didn't.

"Speaking of which," she added, her bright blue eyes darting around the room, "where *is* Nick?"

"He's been making himself scarce," I replied. I couldn't resist adding, "Ever since he decided he didn't want to be engaged to me anymore."

"Jessica, you know he didn't mean that," Betty said indignantly. "I don't know why you insist on being so—"

"This really isn't the best time to discuss the trials and tribulations of my love life," I said pleadingly. "Can we talk about it later?"

Especially since Forrester is due in an alarmingly short time, I thought, and it's bad enough that he's going to find Suzanne here, much less an entire committee of well-meaning friends and associates.

"Oh, yes," she assured me, practically spewing forth icicles. "I can assure you that we will." She stalked toward the door, then stopped when she reached it. "Have a nice time, Jessica," she said over her shoulder. "But not too nice."

How do I get myself into these situations? I wondered.

But I didn't have an opportunity to contemplate that cosmic question, since Suzanne checked her watch again and declared that it was time for makeup. Her timing was excellent. She'd barely finished what turned out to be an amazingly lengthy process when there was another knock at the door.

"It's him!" Suzanne squealed.

By that point, all I wanted was to get the evening over with.

I opened the door and found an unusually spiffed-up, unusually nice-smelling version of Forrester. In one hand he held a single red rose.

But strangely enough, he was the one who looked impressed.

"Wow!" he said breathlessly as he presented me with the rose. "You look great!"

"Thanks," I said halfheartedly.

I felt something sharp dig into my side. I immediately identified it as Suzanne's elbow.

"I mean, thank you, Forrester!" I said, hoping I sounded enthusiastic enough to avoid additional bodily injury. Just to be sure, I added, "You don't look too bad yourself."

By that point, Max and Lou had come charging over. As usual, they couldn't contain their excitement over the arrival of a potential playmate. Max grabbed the pink poodle I'd bought to replace the purloined one and used it to slime the leg of Forrester's pants. Lou, as usual, acted as if it he was completely starved for attention. He planted himself in front of our houseguest and pressed his head against Forrester's hand.

Even the cats wandered over to check out the interloper. And Prometheus predictably burst into wild chatter, although this particular monologue happened to be a string of unrelated phrases that made no sense at all.

"Sorry about all this," I apologized. I reached for Max, planning to scoop him up, but Suzanne stepped between us.

"Let me get the dogs," she suggested. "After all, we wouldn't want any harm to come to that lovely Calvin Klein dress of yours, would we?"

Once she had Max in her arms and Lou by the collar, she looked Forrester up and down.

"I'm Jessie's friend Suzanne," she said brightly. "I'm sure you remember me from that horrible incident on the North Fork."

"Sure, I remember you," Forrester said. A moment of awkwardness followed, probably because what he knew her from was covering a murder case in which she was the cops' number one suspect. "And, listen, I'm really glad everything turned out so well."

"Yes, thanks to Jessie," Suzanne replied. "She's the absolute best, and I'll never be able to pay her back. But I can start by getting out of your hair."

She gave me a big, obvious wink, then settled Max on the floor next to Lou. And then she grabbed her purse and headed for the door.

"Have fun, you two!" she called over her shoulder. "And don't do anything I wouldn't do!"

"I think she liked me," Forrester observed with a grin after she was gone.

"Suzanne isn't exactly known for her great taste in men," I commented.

It wasn't until I'd made the statement that I realized how bad it sounded. I was actually thinking about her latest boyfriend, Marcus Scruggs, who happened to have a primo spot on my list of least favorite people.

Fortunately, Forrester didn't seem to have noticed. He was too busy devouring me with his eyes.

"Shall we got to the restaurant?" I suggested, hoping to focus his appetites on something more appropriate.

"Actually, I thought you might offer me a drink. To give us a chance to talk and, well, get to know each other a little."

"I don't have anything to drink." I hoped he wouldn't check the refrigerator and discover the open bottle of merlot that was right next to a carton of orange juice, a bottle of ginger ale, and half a dozen other liquids that definitely fell into the drink category. "Sorry. Maybe we can get something at the restaurant."

He looked startled. "Sure," he finally said. If he'd figured out that I was plotting to keep us from spending time alone together, he was too polite to mention it.

The restaurant he'd chosen was one of the trendiest in Norfolk County, so popular that even I'd heard of it. It was called Blue Fish, and, true to its name, it specialized in both seafood and the color blue. The walls were powder blue, the tablecloths were navy blue, and the dishes were white but edged in cobalt blue. The music playing in the background was—you guessed it—the blues.

Since it was Saturday night, the place was packed. The women were dressed to the nines, many of them in outfits that made the selections from Suzanne's closet look positively plain. I was actually glad that I'd let her transform me. At least I would blend in.

Between the loud music and the crowd, the noise level made communication difficult. I considered that a plus.

"Want to sit at the bar?" Forrester screamed.

"Sure!" I yelled back.

Actually, it was too crowded to sit. With people

huddled three deep along the edge, we ended up standing a good distance away, trying to hang on to our drinks without spilling them. Within seconds, a man in a dark business suit came over and slapped Forrester on the back.

"Hey, Forrester!" he boomed, shaking his hand energetically. "How's it going over at *Newsday*?"

"Great," he returned. "Ernie Wilson, this is Jessica Popper. I did a piece on Ernie's company a few weeks ago. They recently started providing their employees with shuttle service to the train station. The idea is to cut down on traffic and car pollution."

"Pleased to meet you," I said politely.

"Jessica Popper," Ernie repeated, squinting. "You look familiar. Do I know you?"

"I'm a veterinarian," I replied. "I may have treated one of your pets."

"Naw, I don't have any. No time. No patience either."

"Maybe you've seen her on TV," Forrester interjected. "*Pet People*? On Channel Fourteen?"

"That's right!" Ernie exclaimed. "That vet show, where all those crazy people call in."

As soon as he left, Forrester turned to me and grinned. "See that? You're famous."

"Right," I replied dryly. "People recognize me as soon as you explain to them in explicit detail who I am."

He'd just begun to protest when a petite dark-haired woman tapped him on the shoulder.

"Forrester!" she cried. "What a lovely surprise!"

"Hi, Jean," he greeted her.

"Did I ever thank you for the fabulous piece you did on the Long Island Food Bank?" she asked, beaming.

He just smiled modestly. "Glad it worked out."

"Call me!" And then, much to my amazement, she departed with the words, "We'll do lunch!"

"She certainly seems to like you," I observed. "So does everybody else. In fact, is there anybody here who doesn't know you?"

Forrester grinned apologetically. "Maybe this restaurant wasn't the best choice. Next time we'll go someplace where we can be alone, without being interrupted every thirty seconds."

I opened my mouth to comment on the part about "next time." But the hostess had just called Forrester's name. I was relieved that she led us to a table way in back.

It was actually quiet for a few minutes as Forrester and I scanned our menus.

"I've had the scallops here and they're amazing," he commented. "In fact, their recipe was featured in *Gourmet* magazine."

I realized then that Forrester had put a lot of thought into this date. And it *was* a date. Getting all dressed up, getting picked up at home and driven to a restaurant . . . I could no longer deny it.

As soon as I admitted to myself that I was, indeed, on a date with Forrester Sloan, I was overcome with anxiety. I didn't *belong* on a date with Forrester Sloan—or anybody else, for that matter. I was glad the bottle of wine he'd ordered arrived quickly.

As soon as our waiter poured us each a glass and disappeared to give us time to decide what to order, Forrester held his glass in the air.

"I propose a toast," he said, clinking the rim of his against mine.

"What kind of toast?" I asked nervously.

"C'mon, Popper—I mean, Jessie. Work with me here." Even though he sounded serious, there was a distinct look of merriment in his eyes. He was clearly enjoying every minute of this.

I wished I could say the same. But before I managed to say anything at all, a large-stomached, middle-aged man appeared at our table.

"Hey, Mr. Sloan!" he cried, slapping Forrester on the back.

"Mr. Phillips. What's up?"

"Same old, same old. Hey, when are you gonna write about all the great things the Knights of Columbus are doing?"

"Call me Monday," Forrester replied. "I'll see if I can set something up."

As soon as the Knight of Columbus left, I said, "Goodness, Forrester. Maybe you should think of running for public office."

Even though some of the exasperation I was feeling leaked out, he didn't acknowledge it. Instead, he just shrugged. "What can I say? I'm a popular guy."

"I can see that."

"We could go somewhere quieter, if you'd prefer," he offered. "In fact, I know this great little out-of-the-way place—"

"This is fine," I assured him. "It's just that I never realized you were such a celebrity."

"I'm not. I happen to know a lot of people, that's all. It comes with the job."

Without the least bit of warning, he reached across the table and took both my hands in his. "But let's talk about us."

I did my best not to fall off my chair. But at least I had the presence of mind to insist, "Forrester, there is no 'us.'" Unfortunately, my voice sounded weak. And for some reason, my hands stayed exactly where they were: grasped tightly in his.

"Not yet," he agreed. "But I think we've got great

potential. For one thing, I'm absolutely crazy about you, Jessie."

I squirmed in my seat, which suddenly felt ridiculously hard and uncomfortable. Maybe falling off it wouldn't have been such a bad idea. "Please don't be crazy about me, Forrester." My voice was strangely hoarse. In fact, it was practically a whisper.

"Why not?"

"Because . . . because . . ."

I wanted to explain that I couldn't possibly cope with anyone being crazy about me—anyone other than Nick, at least. How could I, when I still didn't know what was going on with me, much less with Nick and me as a couple? But before I had a chance to say any of that, our waiter reappeared.

"Are you ready or do you need more time?" he asked pleasantly.

More time, I thought, fighting off the panicked feeling that simply would not go away. Definitely much more time.

When Forrester asked, "What would you like, Jessica?" it took me a few seconds to realize he was talking about something as mundane as dinner.

"The scallops," I replied automatically.

After Forrester ordered, he said, "I'm sorry about all these people who keep interrupting us, Jess. The last thing I want to do is make you uncomfortable. Maybe we should talk about the usual first date things."

I gulped. At the moment, I couldn't think of a single topic that people were likely to discuss on a first date.

"So, how about those Mets?" Forrester tried.

I had to laugh. "A much safer topic. Unfortunately, it's one I know absolutely nothing about. How about Simon Wainwright's murder?"

"How about anything *but* Simon Wainwright's murder?" he returned.

"Fair enough," I admitted.

"Okay, then let's go through the list. Favorite books, any good movies or DVDs either of us has seen lately, various acquaintances we might have in common, hopes and dreams for the future, astrological signs—any of those strike your fancy, Jess?"

I had to admit, Forrester Sloan had a certain amount of charm. In fact, I felt kind of sorry for him. I mean, here he was, obviously trying his best to be a good date. He had picked out a nice restaurant, he ordered good wine, he was working hard to make sure the conversation went smoothly—what more could I ask for?

Unfortunately, the answer to that question was all too obvious. Nick.

"I'm sorry," I told Forrester sincerely. I could feel my face growing warm, a sure sign that it was an embarrassing shade of red. With a deep sigh, I added, "This isn't going very well, is it?"

"Let's put it this way: This evening isn't likely to make it into the Dating Hall of Fame." He hesitated before adding, "I think I may have overestimated my capabilities."

"What do you mean?"

"I thought that given half a chance, I could win you over with the old Sloan charm. That somehow I could find a way to make you forget all about that Nick character. But I can see that no matter how much I want that to happen, you're too much in love with him."

I was about to protest, simply because it seemed like the polite thing to do. But I knew he was right. The fact that I'd never wanted to go out on this stupid date with Forrester in the first place wasn't even the point.

The point was that I was crazy about Nick. He was the One.

Betty knew it. Forrester knew it. And deep down inside, I knew it.

I decided it was time to make sure that Nick knew it too.

• • •

One of the nicest things about having so many animals was that I never came home to an empty house. Even so, as I stood in the doorway after Forrester dropped me off, the cottage *felt* empty, even with Max and Lou scampering around at my feet.

I scanned the living room, trying to put my finger on what was different. It took me only a few seconds to figure out what it was.

Nick's things. They were gone.

"Nick?" I cried, hoping that somehow I was mistaken.

I headed into the kitchen. There was a big empty space on the counter where Nick's Mr. Healthybody Super-Juicer had once been, and his *Instant Human! Just Add Coffee* mug was missing from the drain board.

"Nick?" I called again, my voice cracking.

I dashed into the bathroom, still hoping I was misreading what I was seeing. Instead, I noticed that his toothbrush was gone. Mine looked horribly lonely, sitting all alone in the ceramic toothbrush holder.

It wasn't until I came back into the living room that I saw the note.

I hesitated before picking up the white sheet of paper that was sitting in the middle of the coffee table. Biting my lip, I began to read.

Dear Jess,
Since we've decided to give ourselves some time

to figure out where we're going, I thought it might help both of us to have a little breathing space. I'll be staying at Ollie's for a while. I took some of my stuff, but I hope you don't mind that I didn't take all of it. His place is pretty small.

He'd signed it simply *N.*

At least, that was what I thought the note said. To be honest, the tears in my eyes made it a little hard to read.

Chapter 14

"No matter how little money and how few possessions you own, having a dog makes you rich."

—Louis Sabin

Sunday may not have been the most depressing day of my life, but it definitely made the top ten. The house seemed so empty now that Nick was gone. Since he'd left some of his stuff behind, I saw signs of him everywhere I looked. His bathrobe hung on the back of the bathroom door, the shape of his left shoulder still molded into the fabric. His half-full bottle of Red Bull sat in the refrigerator, next to the milk. One of his black socks that had been missing for days finally turned up under his pillow.

Even my animals missed him. They seemed to pick up on my mood, sensing that this wasn't just another day on which Nick had toddled off to law school. Lou spent the entire morning lying by the front door, as if he couldn't even think about enjoying himself until Nick walked in. Max chewed on his new pink rubber poodle halfheartedly, so that it made soft wheezing sounds instead of its usual hysterical squeaks.

Cat also seemed more subdued than usual. She barely left her favorite spot on the couch—her domain once again, now that Mitzi was out of our lives. As for Prometheus, he insisted on singing every song Nick had ever taught him, including "Happy Birthday" and that stupid ditty that goes, "Yo ho, yo ho, the pirate's life for me."

I was glad when Monday morning finally rolled around, since a day jam-packed with house calls was the ideal way of forgetting my cares and woes. I was equally glad I had rehearsal that night, since the prospect of hanging around an empty house all evening struck me as absolutely deadly.

I didn't anticipate that the one topic I was trying to avoid thinking about was the same one Betty couldn't wait to bring up.

Early that evening, as soon as she got into my red VW so I could drive us to rehearsal, she opened with, "Is this a good time to talk about what's going on with you and Nick—and how absurd it is for you to be going out with someone else?"

"Not really," I returned, backing out of the driveway.

"Jessica, I don't like the idea of you going out on dates, especially with that newspaper reporter," she continued, pointedly ignoring what I'd said. "He clearly knows what he wants, and he's been interested in you for a long time. Still, I suppose no real harm has been done—at least, not yet. I noticed you came home fairly early Saturday night. Alone."

I gasped. "You were *spying* on me?"

"I just wanted to make sure you got home safely," she replied, sounding defensive. But she quickly added, "Actually, Jessica, you're right. I *was* spying. But only because I wanted to make sure you didn't do anything you'll regret once this ridiculous argument blows over and you and Nick both come to your senses."

We happened to have stopped at a red light, and I reached over and took her hand. "Betty, I know you're trying to make me feel better," I said, "but I really don't think that's going to happen."

"Of course it's going to happen," she insisted. "You and Nick love each other. You always have, even during your ups and downs. All this foolishness is just a normal part of prewedding jitters—both Nick's and yours. There's no doubt in my mind that before you know it, that bouquet of roses will be arriving, along with an apology for acting so impetuously—"

"Betty," I interrupted, "there's something you should know." My voice sounded strangely thick. I put my hand back on the steering wheel and stared straight ahead. "Nick moved out."

"What do you mean, he moved out?" she demanded. "Where would he go?"

"He's staying with a friend from law school," I said. "He took most of his things with him."

"That's—that's utterly ridiculous," Betty sputtered. "He's simply trying to make a point." She was thoughtful for a few moments, then added, "Would you like me to talk to him?"

I smiled sadly, touched by her concern. "Thank you, Betty. If I thought it would help, I'd say give it a try. But this was more than just an argument. In fact, I don't think Nick's decision to break off our engagement and move out had anything at all to do with his parents coming to visit. I think it's because Nick senses that, deep down, I'm just not ready."

We drove in silence for a long time before she said, "Jessica, a love like the one you and Nick have doesn't come along very often. Some people are never lucky enough to experience it at all. Surely the two of you must recognize that you may never experience it again."

I was glad that I'd just pulled into a parking space outside Theater One. The fact that Betty had verbalized one of the sad truths that had been plaguing me since the breakup made it difficult for me to talk. Without my words coming out as sobs, that is.

"Well, I guess we'd better go in," she said with forced cheerfulness. "Derek hates it if anyone's late. But you already know that, don't you?"

She reached over and took my hand. When she gave it a squeeze, I squeezed right back.

• • •

"Okay, I want Amelia and Anita downstage for the flying lesson scene," Derek announced, clapping his hands to bring the prerehearsal chatter to an end.

I took a few steps closer to the edge of the stage, surprised at how quickly following the director's instructions had become second nature—and once again glad I had something other than my broken engagement to think about. Now that I was on my own, I was more determined than ever to throw myself into both the play and the murder investigation that had gotten me onstage in the first place.

I had to admit that it was rewarding to see how well the production was coming together. By this point, the dance numbers were smooth and the singers' voices were strong and in tune. The actors were delivering their lines almost perfectly.

Even I was feeling much more comfortable onstage. Once I had the confidence that I could remember my lines and do a competent job with the dance steps—thanks to my private coach, Betty—it actually became fun. True, wearing costumes, as we were doing now that opening night was only four nights away, made moving around more difficult. But even that was starting to feel more natural.

"Anita, let's start with your line," Derek commanded. "Amelia, I want you to react. Give me a nod or a change in facial expression when she says, 'Let's show these men...'"

After my few lines of dialogue, Amelia and I got into the plane. Actually, we climbed through a hole in the hand-painted wooden cutout that was supposed to look like a plane, taking care not to knock it over. Then, I gave her a flying lesson amid the clouds created onstage by the fog machine that Sunny had pointed out to me in the props closet.

We finished our few lines of dialogue, delivered with Corey's airplane engine sound effects rumbling in the background. Then the chorus broke into song. From my elevated seat in the airplane, I had a pretty good view of the entire theater, despite the fake clouds. Kyle was onstage, dressed in a pair of knickers with red suspenders and singing his heart out with all the others. I spotted Lacey in the wings, fluttering around a group of women from the chorus who played society ladies in the next scene, pinning flowers onto their dresses and adjusting their sashes.

At the moment, neither Lacey nor Kyle struck me as capable of murdering anyone, least of all Simon.

"Let's take a ten-minute break," Derek called after we'd run through the entire first act, with very few glitches. "If any of you are still having costume issues, this would be a good time to check in with Lacey."

Most of the cast members scattered around the theater, settling into the red velvet seats and chatting with one another. A few dashed out to the delicatessen around the corner, while another group headed toward the lobby to rehearse the "They Call Her Lady Lindy" number by themselves. Some of the crew members, meanwhile, pulled open the three trapdoors onstage to make technical adjustments in the basement. As a safety precaution, they yelled, "Opening trapdoor!" every time they did.

As for me, I had other plans. I needed to consult with Lacey about the fact that my knickers kept riding up over my knees. The last thing I wanted to be doing onstage was tugging at my costume.

Lacey was no longer in the wings, so I assumed she was backstage, probably making adjustments to other people's costumes. I had just stepped inside the women's dressing room, which I was dismayed to find empty, when I heard a muffled voice remark, "But that was so like Simon."

I froze, realizing immediately that the voice was coming from the other side of the wall. It took me only a few seconds to identify the speaker as Jill. She had to be in the dressing room next door. Even though the door that opened onto the hallway was closed, the wall between the two rooms was thin enough for me to hear most of what was being said.

It occurred to me that I was standing in the exact same spot Sunny had been in when she'd overheard Simon arguing with an unidentified woman shortly before he was murdered.

I moved closer, straining to hear the conversation on the other side of the wall.

"Yes, Simon had a heart of gold," a second voice said. That speaker was definitely Derek. "Even when it came to her."

"He never learned, did he?" Jill commented.

Derek sighed loudly. "I hate to say it, since she's done so much for this theater company, but she'd really started acting crazy right before Simon was murdered."

"I know," Jill agreed. "We all saw what was going on."

Lacey, I thought. Derek and Jill are saying the same

thing that Kyle and Aziza said: that Lacey went off the deep end after Simon broke up with her.

"I suppose I wasn't even that surprised when she dropped out," Derek continued, "although I'll never forgive her for leaving me with two weeks until opening night and no one to play Amelia Earhart."

Aziza! If I hadn't been standing close enough to hear every single word, I wouldn't have believed that Derek and Jill were talking about Aziza rather than Lacey.

"You'd think she would have learned her lesson after Simon dropped her and took up with Lacey," Jill said.

"Especially given how pathetic she was, the way she begged him to take her back," Derek added. "Heavens, it was so embarrassing! The more he insisted he was tired of her theatrics and her tantrums and her possessiveness, the more she kept swearing up and down that she'd change."

"And of course she went right back to being the same old Aziza as soon as he agreed to give their relationship another chance," Jill said scornfully.

Derek sniffed. "It was only a question of time before he dumped her again. I know that over these past few weeks he pretended things were going well. But between you and me, he confided in me that he'd had enough of her theatrics. Simon told me he was planning to break up with her again."

"I had no idea!" Jill cried. "Do you think she suspected?"

By that point, I was reeling. I'd been surprised enough to learn that Simon Wainwright had two women after him, Aziza and Lacey. But it seemed he wasn't planning to stick with either one of them. From what Derek was saying, even Aziza, who'd been playing the role of the bereaved girlfriend to the hilt, wasn't going to be in Simon's life much longer.

I froze as what suddenly seemed like an obvious scenario popped into my head. Simon could have broken up with Aziza that Friday night, while the two of them were alone in the theater. She could have been the woman Sunny heard him arguing with. And Aziza could have been so furious, so unwilling to accept what he was telling her, that she grabbed the ceramic Buddha and whacked him in the head with it.

Suddenly, the events of that horrible evening played inside my head with amazing clarity. Aziza Zorn, the woman scorned, had means, motive, and opportunity—the three ingredients homicide professionals looked for when trying to identify a murderer.

On top of that, she had the acting ability to pretend that she was completely heartbroken over Simon's death. If that wasn't a worthwhile use of a person's acting lessons, I didn't know what was.

All I had to do was prove it.

• • •

Tuesday morning brought rain. I was actually pleased that the weather matched my mood. Somehow, the gray skies and relentless drizzle made me feel much more comfortable wallowing in my own misery.

I was more than ready to throw myself into my work, hoping that keeping busy would help me forget all about my mess of a social life. In fact, I was actually doing a decent job of getting myself into that mind-set when I heard a vehicle crunch into my driveway.

Glancing out the window, I saw that the white van that had pulled up in front of my cottage had the name *Flora's Florals* hand-painted in lavender script on the side.

Calm down, I instructed myself, even as my heart went into overdrive. Maybe Betty sent flowers. Or Suzanne. Or even Winston.

At that point, I wasn't willing to entertain the idea that Betty may have been right, that Nick already missed me and wanted to undo what he'd recently done.

I tried to keep my expectations in check as I flung open the front door and found a man who was barely out of his teens, dressed in jeans and a *Flora's Florals* T-shirt, standing there. Yet when I saw the huge white box in his arms, all my resolve instantly vanished.

"Delivery for Jessica Popper," he said. He actually sounded bored, as if even at his young age he'd already brought joy into people's lives too many times.

"Thank you, thank you!" I cried, pressing a ten-dollar bill into his hand.

"Wow, thanks!" It was obviously a bigger tip than he was used to. So big that it actually managed to break through the boredom.

Excitedly I carried the box over to the table. Inside were two dozen long-stemmed red roses. Of course they were absolutely beautiful. But it wasn't their appearance that was the point. It was the point that Nick had sent them.

I thrashed through the cloud of green tissue paper until I found the small white envelope I knew had to be in there somewhere. Sure enough, it was tucked between two of the spindly stems.

I felt like singing as I tore it open.

Then felt my heart turn to lead when I read the note inside.

As hard as I try, I can't stop thinking about you was scrawled across the card. Underneath, it was signed *Forrester.*

I dropped the card, blinking away the stinging in my eyes. Through the tears that insisted on pushing their way through, I stared at the flowers, amazed at how quickly they'd lost their beauty.

When I heard a knock at the door, my first thought was that it was the guy from the florist, coming back to tell me there'd been a mistake. But it was Betty who popped her head in.

"As I was walking over just now, I couldn't help noticing that a florist made a delivery here," she said in a merry, singsong voice. "I was right about your little spat with Nick, wasn't I? It turned out to be nothing more than a lovers' quarrel."

"I'm afraid not," I told her, swiping at my damp eyes with the heels of my hands.

Her smile faded instantly. "What do you mean?"

"It wasn't Nick who sent me flowers."

"Who was it, then?"

I hesitated before 'fessing up. "Forrester Sloan."

"That *Newsday* reporter?" She practically spat out the words.

"Yup."

"Why is he sending you flowers?" she demanded.

"Probably because our date Saturday night went so poorly," I replied. "He was the one who made the observation that I'm still too much in love with Nick to be good company for anyone else. I thought he'd given up on me."

Betty frowned. "I've never heard of a man sending a woman flowers because he'd given up on her."

She peered into the long, white box. "These should be in water," she said. "Where do you keep your vases?"

"Will you do me a favor?" I asked. "Will you take them back to your house? I—I don't particularly want them around."

"Of course." She didn't even look surprised. "But before I go, I have some good news. Sharing it with you was actually my original reason for coming by."

"I could use some good news," I commented.

264 • Cynthia Baxter

"Winston's daughter has decided she doesn't mind you being the maid of honor after all. Of course, Chloe being Chloe, there's one condition: that I let her daughter be the flower girl."

"That's wonderful, Betty. I'm glad it worked out. Now you can stop worrying about Chloe and go back to planning your special day." Surprisingly, it felt good to talk about somebody else's love life. Especially one that was actually working out.

"Yes, and little Fiona is adorable. She's six years old and guaranteed to upstage the bride."

I laughed.

"It's good to hear you laughing," Betty said. Her voice growing serious, she added, "Jessica, are you going to be all right?"

"Of course," I told her. "I'm fine."

And then I forced a smile, proving to myself that I was a much better actress than I thought.

● ● ●

I was about to climb into my van and head off to my first appointment of the day when my cell phone trilled. Glancing at the caller-ID screen, I saw that someone from Channel 14 was calling.

Great, I thought, bracing myself for the strong possibility that a day that had started out badly was about to get even worse. The station has probably been getting calls from the Garfield Anti-Defamation League. Or else the celebrity cat's stable of lawyers.

I was relieved that Marlene Fitzgerald, *Pet People*'s production assistant, sounded like her usual cheerful self.

"Sorry to bother you, Jessie," she chirped, "but somebody left you a message on the station's voicemail system last night. Want me to read it to you?"

"That would be good," I replied.

"It says, *Please tell Jessica Popper to come to Theater One at one o'clock Tuesday afternoon. I have some important things to go over.*"

"Who's it from?" I asked, jotting *Theater One today @ 1:00* on the first scrap of paper I could find.

"The caller didn't leave a name. Or at least the receptionist didn't write it down."

It had to be either Derek or Jill, I thought. "Was it a man or a woman?"

"I don't know that either. Sorry."

"It's not important," I assured her, wondering when corporate message-taking had gotten so lax. Maybe it was an outgrowth of dress-down Friday. "By the way, while I've got you on the phone, I might as well run my idea for this week's show by you. I thought I'd talk about breaking dogs and cats of bad habits…"

Fortunately, my midday appointments were all in the area, making it possible for me to squeeze in a last-minute rehearsal. Still, I was surprised at the short notice. And I wondered why Derek or Jill or whoever had contacted me from the Port Players hadn't called me on my cell phone.

As I pulled out of the gravel driveway, I told myself there could be a dozen different explanations. Besides, I wasn't about to start asking questions. *She's Flying High* was opening in only three more days, and I knew I needed all the help I could get before the curtain went up and I found myself standing on the stage, gazing out at a real, live audience.

Chapter 15

"Curiosity killed the cat, but for a while I was a suspect."

—Steven Wright

O nce again, work proved to be a welcome distraction from my messed-up love life. Apparently Sigmund Freud was right about the importance of love and work. But I wondered if the good doctor ever realized how good one could be at compensating for a lack of the other.

My Tuesday schedule included another follow-up with Kyle Carlson's dog early that afternoon, which I saw as an opportunity to do a little more snooping. True, at that point, three women topped my list of suspects. Aziza currently held the number one spot, thanks to Derek's claim that Simon had intended to break up with her—and that she was likely to react badly. Gloria was a close second, since I now knew she had been more than anxious to get Simon out of the way so that a well-known actor could play the male lead in the Broadway production of *She's Flying High*. And while the more I talked to Lacey, the less convinced I was that she was capable of murder, she *was*

Simon's ex, and it was clearly a role she was having difficulty accepting.

But I hadn't ruled out the possibility that on the night Simon was killed, a man had arrived at the theater sometime after Simon's argument with a woman and committed the heinous act. And even though Kyle and Ian had provided each other with an alibi, I still believed one of them could have been the murderer.

As I neared the front door of their house, I could hear Monty inside, barking. With a doorbell like that, it wasn't surprising that his master had already opened the door by the time I reached the front steps.

"You're right on time," Kyle greeted me, smiling. "Come on in."

Monty seemed equally pleased to see me. Just like both of the other times I'd come by, he gave me a hero's welcome, wagging his entire butt and sliding around on the wooden floor like an ice skater gone out of control. When I crouched down to return his greeting, the muscular Weimaraner lunged forward to lick my face and sent me sprawling onto the floor.

"Not my most dignified moment," I said, laughing. "Guess I should have seen that coming."

Kyle grinned. "Believe me, Monty's decked people a lot bigger and stronger than you," he said proudly. "That's 'cause he's such a friendly guy."

He knelt down on the floor. "You're a really friendly guy, aren't you, Monty?" he said in the same playful voice he'd used to communicate with his favorite canine the first time I'd seen the two of them together. "You're nothing but a big goofus, right? That's right, a big goofus. You're my favorite woofus, foofus, soofus ..."

The heartwarming interaction between a boy and his dog was a real Hallmark moment, even though the boy in question had said good-bye to thirty long before.

"Monty may look big and tough," I observed, "but you're right: He's an absolute teddy bear."

When the two of them had finally finished bonding, Kyle stood up and brushed at his shirt and pants. Looking a little sheepish, he said, "Sorry about that. I know I get a little carried away. It's just that I'm crazy about the guy, y'know?"

"Most animal owners feel the exact same way," I said. "In fact, I don't know where we'd be without our pets."

"Speaking of which," he said, "let's make sure this guy is on the mend. I'm actually on my lunch break right now, so I don't have much time before I have to get back to work."

"Ian's not here?" I asked casually, glancing around the tiny house.

He shook his head. "He had an appointment with a client. By the way, thanks for coming by to check on Monty the other day, even though I wasn't home."

"No problem," I assured him. "It was a stroke of luck that Ian was here to fill in. I was glad it worked out." I looked down at Monty. "And I can see even from here that he's doing well."

Crouching beside Monty, I examined the two gashes on his right thigh. The fact that there was plenty of healthy pink granulation tissue was a sign that both wounds were healing nicely.

"He looks great," I told Kyle. "Just keep up with the same routine, and he'll be one hundred percent again in no time. In fact, there's no need to keep him housebound anymore. I'm sure the big guy would much rather be outside, running around. Just keep away from those squirrels, okay, Monty?"

"What a relief," Kyle said. "How much do I owe you for the follow-up?"

"Nothing," I told him. Realizing I'd just run out of

reasons to linger, I added, "But I could use something cold to drink. Even a glass of water would be fine."

"I've got some bottled water in the fridge."

He led me into the kitchen at the back of house. It turned out to be surprisingly neat for a bachelors' pad. Then again, maybe Kyle and his roommate preferred takeout to home cooking. I leaned against the counter, making a few notes in his dog's chart as he poured me a glass of water.

"Here you go, Dr. Popper," he said, handing it to me.

"Thanks—and please call me Jessie," I corrected him.

"At the theater, it's Jessie. When you're treating Monty, it's Dr. Popper." He frowned. "Speaking of the theater, do you happen to know if the police have made any progress with the investigation? Have they got any new leads or suspects?"

"Not that I've heard," I replied.

Dropping into a chair tiredly, he said, "That's what I thought. I've been following the articles in *Newsday*, and the cops don't exactly seem to be knocking themselves out trying to solve this thing."

He shook his head. "I can't believe how dense they are," he said, his tone bitter. "I mean, could it be any more obvious that Lacey's the one who killed Simon? Why don't they just arrest her? What are they waiting for?"

So Kyle was still convinced that Lacey had murdered Simon. His words from the first time we'd spoken at that Monday night rehearsal echoed through my head. *There was a lot going on between those two,* he'd said about Simon and Lacey. *Believe me, I know. Simon gave me an earful, especially over the last couple of weeks. That woman is not stable.*

It had been the first time I'd heard Lacey characterized that way. The second time had been during my conversation with Aziza. But of course she was also a suspect, which made me question anything she said.

"Kyle," I asked hesitantly, sitting down opposite him at the kitchen table, "you mentioned that Lacey was acting strange the last few weeks before Simon was murdered. What exactly did you mean by that?"

He looked surprised. "I guess you'd have to know her to see that she was going off the deep end. She just couldn't accept the fact that Simon had dumped her."

"I've heard the same thing from other people." I chose my words carefully, not wanting to give out any clues about who I'd been speaking with. "I don't know Lacey very well, but it's hard for me to imagine her stalking Simon."

"But that's exactly what she did!"

"So you knew about that?"

"Of course. Simon told me all about it." Narrowing his eyes slightly, he asked, "How did *you* know?"

I did some fast thinking. "From Betty," I replied. "Aziza told her all about them, and after Simon was killed, Betty mentioned them to me. Kyle, did you actually see any of the letters Lacey wrote to Simon?"

He was silent for what seemed like a very long time. "This is kind of hard to admit," he finally said, picking up the salt shaker sitting in the middle of the table and fiddling with it. "Simon never actually showed them to me, but I managed to see some of them anyway."

I stared at him, not comprehending his meaning.

"Let's just say I did a little spying," he finally explained. "I'm not proud of it, but I couldn't help being curious. I guess I was disturbed by the fact that Simon didn't seem to take any of it very seriously. I was hoping to get a sense of exactly how far gone Lacey really was. I wanted to find out if she was sending him teary letters pleading with him to take her back or something more onerous.

"So once, when he was over here a couple of weeks ago and was busy with Ian, looking at some computer thing, I took advantage of the opportunity to go into his backpack. He'd left it lying on the floor with some of the pockets unzipped, and I could see he'd stashed some papers inside. There were a few envelopes sticking out that could have only been letters." Kyle swallowed hard, his Adam's apple bobbing up and down along his neck. "So I read them."

"And they turned out to be from Lacey?" I asked. I tried to sound matter-of-fact. The last thing I wanted was to sound judgmental about his method of investigation.

He nodded. "They were pretty creepy, for lack of a more descriptive word."

I tried to hide my excitement over having Aziza's story corroborated. "I understand some of them even said things like, *I'd rather see you dead than with her.*"

"That sounds about right," Kyle agreed. "I don't remember exactly how they were worded, but I'm pretty sure it was something like that. You know, I wasn't even that surprised. Like I told you, I already knew she was unstable."

"It certainly sounds like she was having a hard time coming to grips with the breakup," I noted.

Kyle sighed. "What I didn't get was that Simon didn't seem to understand how serious all this was. I could see that Lacey was dangerous, but like I said, Simon refused to believe me."

"Did you suggest that he go to the police?" I asked.

"Of course I did. Ian thought that was what Simon should do too. I remember the three of us sitting around this very table late into the night, with me and Ian working on Simon. We kept trying to convince him to take action. But he was such a nice guy he couldn't imagine anyone having even an ounce of evil in them. Especially someone he used to care about."

His voice broke as he added, "Unfortunately, he had to find out the hard way."

As I said good-bye to Kyle and fondled Monty's smooth silver-gray ears one last time, I was as convinced as Kyle was that Lacey had killed Simon Wainwright. It was hard not to be, when I just heard him verify what Aziza had told me about Lacey stalking Simon in the weeks that preceded his murder.

And if Derek had been telling the truth—if Simon really had broken up with Aziza in his last days—Lacey wouldn't necessarily have known about it. Besides, just because Simon's relationship with Aziza was over, that didn't mean he had a place in his life for Lacey again. Lacey being the killer made perfect sense.

But as I climbed into my van, a thought that had been nagging at me from somewhere in the back of my mind stubbornly pushed its way to the surface.

Had Kyle really verified Aziza's claim that Lacey was stalking Simon? I wondered. Or had I completely misread what just transpired between him and me?

Sitting in the driver's seat, I struggled to reconstruct our conversation. As I replayed it in my head, I tried to figure out whether Kyle had actually volunteered any information about Lacey and the letters she'd purportedly sent Simon—or if he'd simply agreed with what I'd told him, then proceeded to embellish. I was frustrated over my inability to recall every single word that I'd said and every word he'd said.

One thing he'd said stood out in my mind: his story about peeking into Simon's backpack and reading his mail, stumbling upon a letter that happened to fit the description of the letter I was talking about exactly. At the time it had certainly sounded convincing.

Then again, Kyle was trained as an actor.

The problem was that almost everybody I was dealing with who'd had anything to do with Simon

Wainwright had a background in the theater. And given his circle of acquaintances' dedication to mastering the art of deception, how was I supposed to know who I could believe?

All the world's a stage, William Shakespeare said. Yet it wasn't until the past couple of weeks that I'd come to realize just how right he was.

• • •

Even though I did my darnedest to get to Theater One on time, it was ten minutes after one by the time I pulled my van into the parking lot. I hurried inside, knowing that Derek hated his cast members to be late, even though in this particular instance he'd given me ridiculously short notice.

The outer doors of the theater were unlocked, as they usually were during the day. I passed through the lobby, expecting to find Derek or Jill sitting in the front row or onstage, waiting for me—I hoped not too impatiently. Instead, the theater was dark except for the dim light that filtered through the open doors that led to the lobby. I patted the wall just inside the entrance, looking for a switch. No luck. The glowing exit signs helped, but not much.

That's strange, I thought, wondering if somehow I'd gotten the time wrong. Frowning, I checked my watch again. But it was too dark to see.

I slid one hand along the edges of the seats as I gingerly made my way up the aisle in the semidarkness. I exercised the same wariness as I climbed the stairs to the stage.

No signs of life here either.

I poked my head into the wings, figuring that was the next most likely place to find whoever was expecting me. It was dark there too.

I'd just returned to the stage when I heard a creak that sounded like a footstep on an old wooden floor.

"Hello?" I called, my voice echoing through the empty theater. "Is someone here?"

Silence.

I decided that what I was hearing was nothing more than the shifting and creaking of an old building. In fact, I told myself to stop making such a big deal over being alone in an empty theater. In the middle of the day, no less.

When I heard a door slam, I froze.

Okay, I thought. Enough.

I walked across the stage, determined to find out who had come in. There was something unsettling about finding yourself alone in a building except for one other person when you didn't know who that one other person was.

"Derek? Is that you?" I called into the darkness as I crept down the stairs. The pounding of my heart made it difficult for me to hear. "Jill?" I tried, my voice breaking.

Again, silence.

And then, out of the corner of my eye, I noticed a shadow pass by in the doorway that opened onto the lobby.

I was right, I thought. Somebody *is* here in the building. But for some reason, that person is acting as if he or she doesn't want me to know it.

But another voice in my head, a much saner one, interceded. Don't be ridiculous, it said. Someone arranged to meet you here, remember? Why would that person be hiding? Any minute now Derek or Jill or maybe someone else from the cast is going to pop out with a big smile and an apology for being late and suggest that we run some lines or work on my dance moves.

In fact, there was no reason to wait. Deciding it was

time to be more proactive, I strode down the aisle with a confidence that I frankly didn't feel. I really was getting better at this acting thing.

When I reached the doors to the lobby, I burst through them. I immediately glanced from side to side like a member of a SWAT team, blinking in the bright light that was such a sharp contrast to the darkness of the theater.

I was alone.

Unless, of course, someone really was trying to hide.

I looked around a bit more, checking inside the box office and even outside the theater. Not a soul. I finally decided I was blowing this way out of proportion. A creaky old theater with doors that slammed shut by themselves, a passing car that cast a shadow—under normal circumstances I wouldn't even have noticed such common occurrences.

I forced myself to turn around and go back inside.

The theater seemed much darker than before, now that my eyes had readjusted to the light. It suddenly occurred to me that the electrical switches were probably in the wings. I made my way up the aisle slowly, then felt each step with my feet as I went up the stairs cautiously. I even took special care not to trip as I walked across the stage.

It wasn't until I suddenly stepped into nothingness and felt myself in a terrifying state of free fall that I realized one of the trapdoors had been left open.

Even though I could have sworn that, minutes earlier when I'd crossed the stage, they'd all been closed.

But I didn't have time to dwell on how surprised I was.

"Oomph!" I cried, all the air violently pushed out of my lungs as I made contact with something hard. But at least it wasn't as hard as I expected. Although I'd tumbled down a distance of a full story, from the stage to the basement floor, something had cushioned my fall.

I grabbed a chunk of whatever it was, peering at it in the dim light. But I didn't need to see it. The squishy feeling and the distinctive smell told me it was foam rubber. Large misshapen chunks of the stuff, probably the leftovers from the fake bushes and trees the construction crew had sculpted for the outdoor scenes.

As soon as I caught my breath, I did a quick body check to see if anything was broken, twisted, or sprained. As far as I could tell, I'd suffered nothing but a few bruises.

The next step was to get myself the heck out of there.

I staggered to the door that I knew led to the back room of the basement, the section with the stairs up to the backstage area. No harm done, I insisted to myself. I'll just get myself out of this dark creepy space, and—

By that point, I'd grasped the doorknob. And discovered that it wouldn't budge more than a quarter turn.

It was locked.

My head buzzed as I put the pieces together. The creaking floor and the shadow and the slamming door had all been signs that someone was in the building. And I'd been right that that person didn't want to be seen. It had to have been the same person who'd lured me here with that anonymous phone call to the TV station.

The person who'd captured me in a cellar by opening the trapdoor on a very dark stage.

I have to get out of here, I thought. Frantically, I rummaged through my purse, relieved when my fingers finally curled around my cell phone.

I whipped it out and dialed 911. Its unresponsiveness prompted me to check the screen. CALL FAILED, it announced. Snapping it shut, I saw that I wasn't getting a signal.

What did you expect, I thought morosely, trying to make a phone call from a basement?

A feeling of panic swept over me as I realized I was a sitting duck. I tossed my useless cell phone back into my purse and lowered myself onto the cold, hard concrete floor, resting my chin on my bent knees. And then I waited, listening to the blood throb in my temples. Anything could happen, I thought, and there's not much I can do about it.

Yet with each minute that passed, my panic lessened. Whoever had deliberately opened the trapdoor, hoping to ensnare me, had to have realized by now that he or she had been successful. In that case, where was he?

By the time twenty minutes or so had gone by, I realized that it was unlikely anything else was going to happen to me, at least here and now. I figured the person who'd arranged for me to tumble down the rabbit hole had no plans for a face-to-face and was probably long gone. From the looks of things, this was just a warning. A very obvious warning, granted, but a message designed to let me know that someone was becoming very annoyed about my involvement in the investigation of Simon Wainwright's murder.

The murderer, no doubt.

The longer I sat there, the more my butt hurt—and the angrier I became. Okay, you, you...coldhearted killer, I thought. If you think you can scare me away with some cheap trick like sending me plummeting into a locked basement, you clearly don't know me very well. I'm a lot more determined than that. And a lot tougher than you think.

It was then that I heard the scratching.

It wasn't a human sound. It was the haphazard movement of an animal.

Nobody loves animals more than I do. But I had a feeling that any animal that lived in the basement of a hundred-year-old theater wasn't likely to be the cute, cuddly kind.

When something gray, furry and four-legged sprinted by less than three feet in front of where I was sitting, I let out a shriek. I'm not exactly the Betty Boop type, jumping onto a chair and screeching "E-e-ek!" at the drop of a hat. But there's something about a rat that brings out the worst in just about everybody.

I froze at the sound of footsteps above me. Not sneaky-sounding ones, but loud, assertive ones heading across the stage toward the trapdoor.

I jerked my head upward, trying to brace myself for the sight of just about anything. But I wasn't at all prepared for what I actually saw.

"Forrester?" I croaked, blinking.

"Jessie?" Even though it was dark, I could see that the expression on his face was one of total confusion. "What are you *doing* down there?"

"Surprisingly, I'm not here by choice," I replied, my voice dripping with sarcasm. "And if you'd be so kind as to help me find a way out, I'd be extremely grateful."

"Uh, sure." He glanced around, then disappeared for a few seconds. When he returned, he was dragging a ladder with him.

"Thank goodness!" I exclaimed. As soon as he lowered it, I scrambled up the rungs. I was so glad to be out of that dungeon that I ignored the fact that Forrester had positioned himself at the top. He was primarily standing there to hold it in place. But it also put him in a primo spot to catch me in his arms.

"Gotcha!" he cried gleefully, clutching me tightly against him.

Fortunately, so much adrenaline was shooting through my veins that I was stronger than he was. Probably stronger than a bear, in fact. But it turned out that not that much muscle power was required.

"How did you know you'd find me here at the theater?" I asked once I'd squirmed out of his grasp.

"Just a lucky guess. That, and spotting your van parked outside as I drove by. I was hoping I'd get lucky and catch that cleaning lady with the weird name. But finding you here was even better.

"Of course," he added, grinning, "I didn't anticipate that you'd be trying so hard to hide from me that you'd hurl yourself into a dank and dusty old basement."

"I told you, I wasn't down there on pur—oh, forget it. Thanks for getting me out."

"Glad to be of service." He hesitated for a moment before asking, "But, honestly, what *were* you doing down there?"

"I fell in," I snapped, brushing nonexistent cobwebs off my clothes. "Or to be more accurate, somebody arranged for me to fall in by opening the trapdoor in a dark theater."

"'Somebody'?" Forrester frowned. "Like maybe Simon Wainwright's murderer?"

"Seems like the most obvious candidate," I replied. "It's not the first time he tried to scare me away. I wasn't going to mention this, but a few days ago he or she tried to scare me away from investigating Simon's murder with a threatening phone call—"

Before I had a chance to go into detail, he interrupted, "Jess, does Falcone know about all this? I really think you should let him know what's going on."

"Right," I said disdainfully. "As if I have something to gain by listening to another lecture."

"Falling through a trapdoor that's, well, a trap that somebody set for you is pretty serious."

I shot him a wary look. "Falcone may not be the sharpest tack on the bulletin board, but I'm sure even he knows that the person we're dealing with isn't exactly up for *Time* magazine's Person of the Year."

"Suit yourself," Forrester said with a shrug. "By the way," he added, softening his tone, "did you get the roses I sent?"

"Yes, I did." I swallowed hard. "Thank you, Forrester. They're beautiful, but you shouldn't have."

He shrugged. "It was nothing."

"No, really. You shouldn't have. I hate to be blunt, Forrester, but there's no future in this relationship. Even though Nick and I are no longer together, that doesn't mean that you and I—"

"I understand exactly how you feel," he interrupted.

His spirit of cooperation took me completely off guard. "You do?"

"Yes. And I don't blame you one bit."

"You don't?"

"Of course not. After all, we didn't really get a chance to get to know each other Saturday night," he continued. "Too much noise and too many interruptions. I demand a rematch, Jessie. I want another chance."

Forrester sashayed over to a wooden chair that I hadn't even noticed in the dim light. He draped his jacket over the back, as if he was planning on staying awhile. I noticed then how quiet the theater was. But instead of being relieved that the cat in the cat-and-mouse game that had landed me in the basement was probably gone, I felt uneasy over being here all alone with Forrester. And it had nothing to do with my personal safety.

"Let me take you out for dinner again, Jessie," he said, strolling back toward me. "This time, we'll go to a quiet, casual place where we can really talk. In fact," he went on, his voice softening, "we can do some talking right now."

"But we talk all the time!" I protested. "About Simon and Lieutenant Falcone and...and current events that are in the news..."

"That's not what I want to talk about," he replied, his voice as soft and sweet as a melting marshmallow. "At least not at the moment."

"Forrester, this really isn't the best time to—"

He ignored my protests. In fact, he leaned in a little closer. Even though we were surrounded by near-darkness, I could see a distinctive gleam in his gray-blue eyes. A gleam I definitely did not like.

In a soft, seductive voice, he said, "Y'know, Popper, I've been thinking."

"Thinking is good," I said, nodding. "I do some of that myself every now and then."

He laughed. "Don't try to change the subject."

"I didn't know there was a subject. That you and I were discussing, I mean. I thought we were just making conversation."

"We were talking about us. At least I was."

"But there's no such thing as us!" I cried.

"I know there's not, and that's the point. I really want there to be an us, Jessie. As strange as our date last Saturday night was, I had a good time. There's something about you, kiddo. I can't quite put my finger on it, but I like it. Maybe it's your spirit, maybe it's your intelligence, but whatever it is, I can't stop thinking about you."

"I'm not that intelligent," I insisted, my voice high-pitched. "And what you call 'spirit' is really just nervous energy. You see, whenever I—"

"I shouldn't have given up so quickly last weekend," he went on. His eyes had now taken on a new intensity, and his voice had gotten deep. Oddly husky too. "It's obvious that you still have feelings for Nick, but from what you've told me, that's over. Sooner or later you're going to accept that all that's in the past. And I want to make sure that I'm in the picture whenever you come to that realization. It's time for you to start looking ahead to the future." He gently clasped my shoulders. "I really want to be part of that future, Jessie."

He leaned forward to kiss me.

I could feel the panic rising inside me. I knew I had to stop him.

Then suddenly I heard, "Ohmygosh, I'm so *sorry*!"

The sound of something so unexpected caused Forrester to step backward, nearly tripping over his own two feet.

I looked down, even though I knew that the person who had saved me was Sunny McGee.

"Honest, Jessie, I didn't mean to interrupt you!" she cried. She was standing at the foot of the stage, no more than five feet away. Even in the dim light I could see that her face was flushed. "I had no idea you were here with your boyfriend!"

"He's not my boyfriend!" I cried.

"And at this rate," Forrester muttered, "I never will be."

"I—I was driving by and I saw your van parked outside," Sunny went on, still flustered. "I thought I'd pop in to tell you about this cool idea I had. But we can talk some other time. I could call you or—"

"No! Let's talk right now!" I said. "This is a great time. In fact, Forrester was just saying that he wanted to talk to you. Isn't this a stroke of luck?"

Forrester cast me a wary look. "You're not making this easy, Jess."

I could see the disappointment in his face. For the first time, I felt sorry for him. I was struck by the fact that he was doing a lot more than flirting. He really did have strong feelings for me.

And I certainly knew how it felt to want somebody who didn't want you back.

"Do you guys mind if I turn on some lights?" Sunny asked. "It's so dark in here." She made a beeline for the wall and flipped a switch. The entire theater was immediately as bright as day.

Blinking, I turned to Forrester. "I'm sorry," I told him sincerely. "I just can't do this."

"Now—or ever?" he asked.

"Look, how about if I give you a call later, Jessie?" Sunny still sounded breathless. "I can see you two are . . . have stuff to talk about."

"No, don't go, Sunny," I told her. But my eyes were still locked with Forrester's. "I just need a minute."

"I think you need a lot more than a minute," Forrester said somberly.

He ambled back to the chair and picked up his jacket. "Jessie, the ball is now officially in your court. You know where I stand. Call me when—if—you change your mind."

"Okay," I replied in a near-whisper.

Turning to Sunny, he said, "I've been trying to track you down. My name is Forrester Sloan, and I'm covering the Simon Wainwright case for *Newsday*. Can I have a few minutes of your time?"

"Sure," Sunny replied uncertainly. "Just let me talk to Jessie for a second. I'll meet you in the lobby, okay?"

"I'll be waiting." Glancing back at me, he added, "That happens to be something I'm really good at."

As I watched him walk away, I wondered if there was even a chance for Forrester and me. At the moment, I knew I was still too much in love with Nick to consider anyone else. I had no idea whether he would ever want me back. But I knew with more certainty than I'd ever felt before that I wanted him.

I took a couple of deep breaths and turned to Sunny. "So what's up? What's this cool idea of yours?"

"That you let me come work for you on a trial basis," she said excitedly. "We can pick a time period, like two weeks or something. I'll come along with you on your calls and you can teach me stuff. After the two weeks, if you think it's working out, then we can talk about maybe—you know, making it, like, a permanent thing."

"Let me think about it," I told her. Right now I wasn't in a state of mind to focus on my job. I was too overwhelmed by the chaotic state of my love life, not to mention the fact that, from the looks of things, a murderer had just sent me a no-nonsense warning, one that happened to involve rats.

"Great!" she said brightly. "And, listen, I really am sorry that I interrupted you and that guy. Forrester, or whatever his name is."

"That's okay," I reassured her. "In fact, you did me a favor."

It was only then that I realized my hands were shaking. How much of that was due to falling through a trapdoor and finding myself locked in the basement of the theater and how much was due to fending off the unexpected advances of Forrester Sloan, I couldn't say.

Chapter 16

"A boy can learn a lot from a dog: obedience,
loyalty, and the importance of turning around
three times before lying down."

—Robert Benchley

As I turned off Minnesauke Lane late that afternoon, I jerked my van to a halt in front of the
two mailboxes that poked out of the overgrowth
lining the driveway. Before driving on, I leafed through
the usual assortment of junk mail, marveling over how
many banks I'd never even heard of in states I'd never
even been to were eager to offer me credit cards. I was
actually startled when I came across an envelope that
didn't appear to be just one more unwanted solicita-
tion.

It was a standard white business-size envelope, ad-
dressed by hand. There was no return address, and the
handwriting in which my name and address had been
carefully printed wasn't familiar. Each letter had been
meticulously formed, the way kids learn cursive writing in school, without any of the flourishes most people add over time. I wondered if whoever had written
it had purposely disguised his or her writing.

You're blowing this way out of proportion, I scolded myself, putting the van into drive and continuing toward my cottage. It's probably a check from one of your clients or even one of those personal thank-you notes you get from time to time.

Still, as soon as I went through the usual welcome-home routine with my pets, I got a knife and carefully slit the mysterious envelope open. I found a single sheet of white 8½-by-11-inch paper inside, folded into thirds and again in half. Nothing too unusual there, aside from the fact that I still couldn't figure out who'd sent it.

As soon as I started reading, a chill ran through me. *My dearest Simon,* the one-page typed letter began. It ended, *Love forever and ever, Lacey.*

My heard pounded wildly as I read the entire letter.

My dearest Simon,
I know you think I should just accept your decision to go back to that BITCH and crawl away. There's probably nothing you'd like better than having me DISAPPEAR.

But that's not going to happen. It's not only because you BROKE MY HEART. It's because I know that you and I belong TOGETHER. You love me and I love you. SHE is just a distraction. It's like she cast a SPELL on you.

I will make you understand that it's ME you love. I can't STAND knowing you're with HER.

I would rather see you DEAD than with HER. That's how deep my LOVE for you is.

I will make you understand, my dearest Simon. No matter what it takes.

Love forever and ever,
Lacey

The piece of paper in front of me was exactly what Aziza had described: a threat disguised as a love letter. The wording even included the exact same phrase she'd mentioned: *I would rather see you dead than with her*.

Yet it wasn't signed. The name *Lacey* at the bottom was typed, just like the rest of the letter.

That meant that while it could have been written by Lacey, it could also be a fake.

I sank onto the couch, still holding the letter and still unconvinced that it served as proof that Lacey had been stalking Simon. Obviously, that was exactly what the person who had sent it to me wanted me to believe. As for who that person was, there were at least two contenders: Aziza and Kyle, the two people with whom I'd discussed Lacey's alleged stalking of Simon.

But anyone could have sent me this letter.

I decided I had no choice but to hand it over to Lieutenant Falcone. Maybe Norfolk County Homicide would be able to do more with it than I could. After all, the department had the tools required to dust it for fingerprints—other than my own, of course—and even to match it to the computer printers that Lacey had access to, as well as the other suspects' printers.

Which would hopefully help determine if Lacey Croft really had killed Simon—or if this was simply a case of the real murderer trying to set her up.

• • •

While Lacey Croft held a prominent place on my list of suspects, she wasn't alone. Thanks to my ongoing distrust of both Kyle and Ian, I remained anxious to find out everything I could about the threesome that had begun referring to themselves as the Three Musk-Actors after a close encounter with too much tequila.

Heading off to the college at which they'd met seemed like an excellent way to start the next morning.

"Office of the Registrar," a female voice answered crisply after I dialed the number I'd found on Brookside University's Web site.

"Good morning," I began. "I'm trying to verify that two students named Kyle Carlson and Ian Norman attended Brookside as undergraduates. I'm not sure of the exact year, but I believe they would have been there about fifteen years ago."

"I'll check," she replied. "Do you mind if I put you on hold?"

"Not at all."

While I waited, I slipped the letter that Lacey had allegedly written into a large envelope, figuring I'd drop it off at the Norfolk County Homicide office the first chance I got. I'd barely had a chance to scrawl Lieutenant Falcone's name across the front when the woman got back on the phone.

"Thanks for waiting," she said. "I can verify that Kyle Carlson attended school here. He graduated in 1991. But I'm afraid I have no record of anyone named Ian Norman graduating from Brookside. And according to the law, I'm not allowed to give out any information about a student unless he or she actually graduated."

"Really." That was a technicality I hadn't heard about before. My voice reflected my disappointment as I asked, "You mean you can't even tell me what years he was there?"

"I'm afraid I can't tell you anything," she replied, sounding genuinely apologetic. She hesitated, then added, "But you might try talking to someone on the faculty. Somebody is bound to remember something."

After I thanked her and hung up, I immediately headed back to my computer—and the school's Web site. I deposited Tinkerbell into my lap, enjoying the show as she amused herself with the metal button on my jeans. Then I clicked around until I located the theater department's home page.

In addition to information about upcoming productions, audition dates, and requirements for theater majors, the home page had a link to the list of the department's faculty. I read the biographies of all six members. Only one of them had been there for more than a few years. In fact, Professor Garth Hendricks had been there for over twenty.

I jotted down his name and phone number, then dialed, even though I had yet to figure out exactly what I was going to say.

After five rings, a tape came on. *"This is Garth Hendricks, chair of the Brookside University theater department. I'm not in my office, so please leave a message after the tone. Cast and crew members of our current production, just a reminder that there's a dress rehearsal this evening, Wednesday, at eight o'clock in Morgan Hall. Cast call is an hour before."*

Since I couldn't reach Professor Hendricks by phone, I decided to pay him a visit. After all, I was feeling pretty comfortable around theater folk these days. If there was a rehearsal that night, I'd be there.

Once again, the theater beckoned.

• • •

The few times I'd visited the Brookside University campus had been during the day. At night, the maze of roads, parking lots, and imposing buildings had an unfamiliar feeling. I kept checking the map I'd printed off the Internet, peering at the tiny print in the dim overhead light of my VW.

Morgan Hall was located in the center of campus, a five-minute walk from the nearest parking lot. It was only seven-thirty as I trekked across the quad, and students were still streaming along the pathways that crisscrossed the stretches of grass. I kept checking their faces, both hoping and dreading that one of them would turn out to be Nick's. None did.

Reminding myself that I was here for a much nobler reason than staging an unexpected encounter with my former fiancé, I marched purposefully up the concrete steps that led to Morgan Hall. When I pulled open the heavy doors, I found myself in the lobby of the Michelmore Theater.

I grabbed the first person I found, a young woman wearing jeans and a black turtleneck and clutching a clipboard.

"Excuse me," I said. "I'm looking for Professor Hendricks."

"Check the dressing rooms," she answered automatically. "They're down that hallway." Then, peering at me, she added, "We're doing a run-through in about twenty minutes. This isn't the best time."

"I'll be quick," I assured her. I knew firsthand how raw nerves could be when opening night was getting close.

I headed backstage, where people in costumes were dashing around. The atmosphere was frantic. Or at least that was my impression, now that I was able to appreciate everything that went into making the production onstage look seamless.

"Is Professor Hendricks here?" I asked one of the few people who didn't look overly harried. I figured that the young man, probably a student, was part of the technical crew.

"Garth? He's right in there," he replied, pointing at one of the doorways.

"Thanks."

But when I glanced inside, instead of Professor

Hendricks, I spotted a woman. One who happened to be unusually unattractive, I couldn't help thinking. Despite her large frame, she was wearing an unflattering dress splashed with huge flowers in clashing shades of orange, yellow, and green. The thick stockings that encased her beefy calves gave her skin an orange tinge, and her wide feet looked as if they'd been stuffed into her clunky-heeled shoes with a garden spade. Her large head of curly hair was the same brassy shade of orange as her legs. And while I was no expert on theatrical makeup, even I could tell she'd gone overboard with her thick false eyelashes, iridescent blue eye shadow, and bright red lipstick.

"I'm sorry," I said, backing away. "I was looking for Professor Hendricks. I don't suppose—"

"How can I help you?" the woman asked in a husky voice.

"It's actually Professor Hendricks I need to speak with."

"You've got him."

I blinked, not certain how to continue this conversation, which was starting to sound a lot like the famous "Who's On First?" routine. Then, slowly, I figured out what was happening.

"You're Professor Hendricks, aren't you." It was a statement, not a question.

"That's right." A look of amusement crossed his face. "My costume. Of course. That's what confused you."

"Sort of," I admitted.

"Good heavens. Tonight's the dress rehearsal for *La Cage Aux Folles*. I'm playing the role of Albin Mougeotte. My character's in drag during the second act, playing his alter ego Zaza Napoli. That's why I'm dressed like this."

Now that I knew I was actually speaking to the man

I'd come to see, I didn't know whether to be relieved or shocked. I decided to go with the former.

"Professor Hendricks, I can see you're busy, so I'll be quick. I understand you've been on the faculty of Brookside's theater department for a long time."

"Since it was founded," he said proudly. "That was back in the mid-eighties."

"I wanted to ask you about a few theater students who were here at Brookside about fifteen years ago," I continued. "Do you remember a student named Simon Wainwright?"

"Of course I remember Simon," he replied, his expression softening. "How could I ever forget him? Of all the students I've had, he was the one who impressed me most. He was incredibly talented, not only as an actor but also as a playwright. He also had amazing determination and drive."

Professor Hendricks frowned. "But you probably knew all that. At least, if you read the papers. What happened to poor Simon is an unspeakable tragedy."

"Yes, it is," I agreed somberly. "What about a student named Kyle Carlson? He and Simon were friends."

"I remember him too. Kyle still had a lot to learn, but I remember that he had great potential. He didn't exactly have what some people call star quality, and my feeling was that he'd never make it as a leading man. But he was quite good at playing character parts. I remember him doing a fabulous job as Alfred Doolittle, Eliza Doolittle's humorously tipsy father, in *My Fair Lady*. He was quite convincing. In fact, I remember thinking he'd be able to carve out a decent career for himself playing secondary roles."

Professor Hendricks frowned. "He did have a bit of a temper, however."

My ears pricked up like Max's did whenever I uttered the magic words, "Want to go for a ride?"

"What do you mean?" I asked cautiously. I held my breath, hoping Professor Hendricks wouldn't consider it inappropriate to divulge this type of information about a former student.

Instead, his eyes glazed, as if he was drifting back in time. "I remember how he reacted when he tried out for a lead role in *Waiting for Godot*. You know, the Samuel Beckett play? As always, I posted the results of the audition on the bulletin board outside the department office. I happened to be in there when he came by, and when he saw that he hadn't gotten the part of Estragon, he practically threw a temper tantrum."

"I see." This was certainly a side of Kyle Carlson that I hadn't seen. Then again, it was possible that by now he'd outgrown such childish behavior. Fifteen years was a long time.

"What about a student named Ian Norman?" I continued. "I believe he was friends with both Simon and—"

"Damn!"

"What?" I asked anxiously. The fact that I'd obviously hit a raw nerve made my heart flutter.

"There's a run in my stocking!"

"Clear nail polish," I said automatically. "What about Ian Norman?"

"Really? Nail polish?" Professor Hendricks sounded impressed. "That's ingenious."

No, it's something most girls learn while they're growing up, I thought.

"Professor Hendricks," I tried again, "do you remember a student named Ian Norman?"

He thought for a few seconds, then shook his head, sending his wigful of curls dancing. "Can't say I do."

Confused, I said, "But you remember Simon and Kyle. And the three of them were close friends. They took acting classes together here at Brookside. They even called themselves the Three Musk-Actors."

"I'm sorry. The name doesn't mean a thing to me."

"But the three of them were inseparable. Surely you must have—"

Clearly losing patience, he said, "I'm afraid I simply don't remember him. I've taught so many students over the years. Frankly, it's the really good ones and the really bad ones I remember best."

The fact that Professor Hendricks knew Simon and Kyle but didn't remember Ian Norman gave me pause. It also made me suspicious. From the start, I'd sensed that there was something about Ian that didn't quite ring true. The possibility that he'd lied about going to college with Kyle and Simon only increased my doubts about him.

"Have you kept your records from back then?" I asked. "Class lists or grading sheets or any other documents with the names of all your students?"

"I've kept everything. But, frankly, I don't have the time to go through them. Not when *La Cage* opens in only two more days."

"In that case, would you mind if I went through them?"

"I'm afraid I would," he replied. "We'd both be committing a federal offense, since school records are considered privileged information under the Family Educational Rights and Privacy Act."

I sighed, unable to hide my frustration. "Professor Hendricks, is there any other way I could find out whether Ian Norman really took theater classes with Kyle and Simon?"

His heavily-lipsticked mouth turned downward. "Not that I can think of . . ."

I was about to admit to myself that I'd hit a dead end when he suddenly cried, "Wait! There is one way."

"Yes?" I asked, not yet daring to feel optimistic.

"The programs."

"What programs?"

"Any student who enrolls in an acting class at Brookside has to participate in at least one production," he explained. "That includes Introduction to Acting, which is a requirement for every other course in the department. I've taught that class since the beginning. For each production, I make up a program with a list of the cast and crew members, and I've saved every single one. There's no federal law against someone like you looking at old programs."

"That sounds perfect," I told him. "And the sooner, the better. When can I see them?"

"Whenever you want," Professor Hendricks said with a little shrug. "They're stored over in Quattrock—that's the main library—in the university archives. That's a collection of all the materials created over the years by the faculty, the staff, and the students. Most people don't even know it exists, much less where it is. Everything you can think of is saved and stored: campus newspapers, yearbooks, posters from lectures and concerts, technical reports, you name it."

"And the original programs are all there?" I asked anxiously.

"That's right. They're filed chronologically. Unfortunately, I don't remember the exact years Simon and Kyle were here, so you'd have to go through them until you found the right ones."

I could hardly wait. "Do you know how late the library stays open?"

"I'm pretty sure it closes at midnight."

"Thank you so much," I told him sincerely. "You have no idea how helpful you've been. And, uh, break a leg."

"Thank *you*," he returned, looking pleased. "Now,

I wonder where I can get hold of some clear nail polish?"

• • •

According to my map, Quattrock Library was a few buildings away from Morgan Hall. As I trudged over, I noticed that at this time of night, few students were wandering along the dark pathways. The lighting on this part of campus wasn't very good, and once or twice I jumped at the sight of my own shadow.

Reaching the library was a relief. I scanned the roster posted right inside the main entrance, reading through the list of departments: *Architecture and Fine Arts, Engineering, Life Sciences, Special Collections . . .*

University Archives, Lower Level.

In other words, the basement.

I've already spent too much time in a basement this week, I thought with chagrin. But I headed for the staircase next to the information desk.

As I tromped down the stairs, my footsteps echoed through the stairwell. The door at the bottom opened onto a single large room striped with row after row of shelves. The basement of the library didn't appear to be one of the more popular spots on campus. In fact, the only sound was the hum of the fluorescent lights.

I wasn't exactly crazy about being here alone at night.

Still, I had a mission to accomplish. Spotting a row of doors along the wall, I made a beeline for the one with the plaque that read UNIVERSITY ARCHIVES.

Please don't be locked, I begged silently.

The room certainly looked locked, since the windows lining the door—two long, narrow panels made of thick, pebbly glass—were dark. But the doorknob turned easily in my hand.

I flipped on the light switch, expecting to find a dignified homage to the university's past. Thick carpeting, dark paneling, the whole works. Instead, the small room I stepped into was stark and uninviting. Its mustard-yellow cinder block walls were lined with floor-to-ceiling gray metal shelving, and the floor was covered with beige speckled linoleum. The only furniture was a gray metal desk with a swivel chair tucked underneath.

Cardboard boxes and vertical magazine files were crammed onto the shelves. Still, it was clear that there was a system in place, primarily because of the neat, handwritten labels identifying the contents of each one. Thanks to a hand-drawn floor plan posted on the wall, I easily located the section allocated to the theater department.

On a shelf just above eye level, I found a row of blue plastic magazine files labeled *Theater Arts Department—Programs*. Just as Professor Hendricks had promised, they were in chronological order, beginning in 1987 and continuing up to the previous year.

I pulled down the file from fifteen years ago and brought it over to the desk. Perching on the edge of the swivel chair, I plucked out a wad of programs from the front. The one on top was from a production of Shakespeare's *As You Like It,* dated November 20 through 23. I scanned the cast list but didn't see any names I recognized.

I tried the next one, then the one after that. Still no luck. When I'd looked through every program in that folder, I put it back on the shelf and grabbed the next one.

Finally, in the third folder I checked, I found a program for Thornton Wilder's *The Skin of Our Teeth*, one of the plays Ian had mentioned he and Simon and Kyle were in together.

Bingo. I spotted Simon Wainwright's name in the cast list right away. He was playing the male lead, the role of Mr. Antrobus. Kyle Carlson was also listed. Interestingly, he was playing Simon's son, Henry Antrobus.

Ian Norman's name was nowhere to be found.

I checked the list of crew members. I didn't see it there either.

That's just one production, I told myself.

I grabbed the next program. This one was for another play Ian had mentioned, David Mamet's *Glengarry Glen Ross.* I knew it was about the workings of a real estate office, since I'd seen the movie. Checking through the cast list, I saw that Simon had played Ricky Roma, Al Pacino's role in the film version. Kyle had played Kevin Spacey's part, John Williamson.

Once again, there was no mention of Ian Norman anywhere.

I went on to the next one, then another. Simon's and Kyle's names appeared in the five or six programs that followed. And Ian's failed to appear in any of them.

Finally, I got to the point where I didn't recognize any of the names. I returned the last magazine file to the shelf and contemplated what I'd found—and, even more interestingly, what I hadn't found.

Had I misunderstood what Ian told me? I wondered. It seemed impossible that I'd misconstrued what he'd said about Simon, Kyle, and him taking theater courses together and having so much fun that they'd even come up with a nickname for their happy little trio.

Besides, Professor Hendricks had told me himself that every student who took an acting class was required to be in at least one production. That included the most basic course, Introduction to Acting. Even if

Ian had taken only one course in the department and exaggerated about all the plays he'd been in, his name would have appeared in at least one program.

If Ian hadn't gone to school with Simon and Kyle, why on earth would he have lied?

And if Ian wasn't an old friend of theirs, then who was he?

I was still trying to wrap my head around that question when I heard a door slam. My heart instantly began pounding with the speed and ferocity of a jackhammer.

Relax! I told myself. You're in a public place. A library, no less. You're not the only person who has a right to be down here. You're simply reacting to your last visit to a basement. Besides, this time you're on a university campus, not in an empty theater. A place of learning that's filled with earnest students and dedicated teachers.

My heart didn't appear to be listening. My brain either. It clearly wasn't about to relax, at least not until I found out who had joined me in the otherwise deserted basement.

I stuck my head out the door, expecting to see a scowling college student wandering around, looking for some obscure document that was required for an assignment. Or perhaps a librarian type who wore an ID tag and looked very much at home.

I didn't see anyone.

It's a big place, scolded that same voice, the one that struggled to find logical explanations for things. With all these rows of shelves, there's an excellent chance that whoever else is down here would be hidden from view.

All of a sudden, the lights went out.

In the big room, at least. Yet it was hours before closing time. Which made it likely that the person who had just joined me in the basement had decided to make it a *dark* basement.

But the lights in the archives were still on. Which meant whoever was out there now knew exactly where I was.

A sudden burst of adrenaline catapulted me into action. I pushed the door closed and locked it, then flipped off the light.

I immediately heard footsteps. Fast, determined footsteps that were heading my way.

Acting on the same instinct, I crouched behind the metal desk. By that point, my eyes had begun to adjust to the darkness of the small room. As they did, I realized that dim light was coming through the mottled glass alongside the door.

It was probably from exit signs glowing somewhere in the main room, I figured. It didn't provide much illumination, but at least I could see out better than the other person could see in.

I kept my eyes glued to the windows, trying to brace myself for whatever was to come. But I still gasped when a silhouette suddenly appeared in the translucent window in the door. The thickness of the glass, as well as its uneven texture, made the silhouette look ghostly, with no clear edges. I couldn't make out who it was— or even whether it belonged to a male or a female.

And then I heard the doorknob click.

My stalker was trying to open the door.

I rummaged through my purse, trying to find my cell phone. Not an easy task, given how hard my hands were shaking. *Call the police,* I thought. But I knew it would take the police forever to get here.

I was sure my pursuer realized that too.

The doorknob began to rattle. Loudly. Angrily. The person on the other side of the door was clearly growing increasingly frustrated over being locked out.

By that point, so much adrenaline was shooting through my veins that I felt nauseous. The lock on the door hadn't struck me as particularly strong. And the two glass panels were thick, but not exactly impenetrable.

I needed a way out—fast. Preferably one that didn't involve flinging open the door and confronting my stalker face-to-face.

Chapter 17

"When the old dog barks it is time to watch."
—Latin Proverb

Slowly I raised my head above the edge of the desk. I could still see the wavy silhouette of whoever had followed me into the library's archives. He or she was out there, waiting—no doubt thinking that sooner or later I'd have to come out.

You've got to stop spending so much time in deserted basements, I told myself.

But this wasn't exactly the best time for contemplating lifestyle changes. Frantically, I scanned the desktop, hoping I'd find some way of escaping—safely. But all I saw were the usual office items: a neat stack of file folders, a pencil mug, a telephone...

All of sudden, a burst of optimism exploded inside me like a firecracker. The solution was right in front of me.

It came in the form of a small white sticker that was affixed to the phone. It read, *For Campus Security, Dial 4-3232.*

I made a point of speaking loudly as I told the dispatcher that I was in the basement of Quattrock

Library and that I wanted a security guard to walk me to my car. Just as I expected, the silhouette disappeared almost as soon as I got the words out.

The moment I heard footsteps heading away briskly, I dashed over to the door and opened it, just a crack. But from that vantage point, I couldn't see anybody.

Still, the fact that he or she was now running away from me, instead of toward me, gave me confidence. I was suddenly angry that this mysterious person had been causing so much trouble in my life lately.

If I could only get a good look, I thought, even if it's just from the back...

Treading as softly as Cat, I took a few steps into the big room, then immediately cozied up to a tall shelf that I knew would keep me hidden. Even in the dim light, I could see that I was having a close encounter with the complete history of *Rules for Dormitory Living at Brookside University*. Cautiously, I peered around the side.

I caught sight of my stalker, all right—at least, his or her left foot, clad in a white sneaker, right before it disappeared behind the door to the stairwell along with the rest of the body attached to it.

My thoughts raced as the sound of footsteps hurrying up the steps grew fainter and fainter.

To chase or not to chase? I thought.

Before I'd even made a conscious decision, I found myself heading toward the door and racing up the same stairs. When I reached the top, I threw open the door.

And found at least twenty people coming into the library, leaving the library, or holding casual conversations in the entryway.

At least half of them wore white sneakers—and not one of them looked familiar.

I dashed to the front entrance and out into the night. But none of the few souls I saw wandering around campus had on white sneakers.

I decided to wait for the security guard I knew was on his way. Calling the campus security office and requesting an escort had just been a ploy designed to scare away my stalker. But having a little company on this dark, unfamiliar campus suddenly seemed like a good idea.

• • •

"I should never have asked you to get involved, Jessica," Betty said with a sigh as the two of us crossed the Theater One parking lot the following evening. "Too many frightening things have happened. First I got that strange threatening phone call from that actress. Then you were lured to the theater under false pretenses and trapped in the basement. And now you're telling me that last night someone at the Brookside University campus was following you."

"But, Betty, how can we be sure any of those events were related to Simon Wainwright's murder?" I asked. Not that I believed for a moment that they weren't. Still, I was looking for a way to soothe Betty's anxieties. Now that I'd come clean about the mysterious goings-on of the last two days, she blamed herself.

I regretted having told her anything at all. Ordinarily, I would have done my best to protect her. Then again, ordinarily I would have had Nick to confide in. With no one else to talk to, I'd given in to the temptation to tell Betty. I realized immediately that I'd made a big mistake.

"Such terrible occurrences," Betty continued as we strode through the lobby. "I can't help but wonder what's next."

That was a question I'd learned never to ask. And the wisdom of subscribing to that policy was reinforced as soon as we walked into the theater.

"Oh, my goodness!" Betty cried, her hands flying to her cheeks. "Look at this place! What happened?"

The entire theater was in chaos. My first thought was that maybe this was just another case of tech week wreaking havoc. But if Betty's reaction wasn't enough to tell me otherwise, all I had to do was look around to figure out that the theater had been vandalized.

Signs of destruction were everywhere. The scenery at the back of the stage had been smashed, loose cables dangled from the ceiling, and the pieces from broken props littered the floor. The newspaper with the headlines LADY LINDY LOST had been torn into strips, and the carefully crafted bushes had been ripped completely apart, the blobs of foam strewn about like giant pieces of green popcorn. The red velvet upholstery on at least a dozen seats had been slashed.

Even the costumes had been shredded. I immediately recognized the ball gowns Lacey had so lovingly festooned with sashes and flowers. Only now they had been reduced to bits of fabric and crushed ribbons that were mixed in with the debris scattered throughout the theater.

Most of the other cast and crew members had already arrived. Like Betty, they were milling around the theater, looking stunned. No one spoke. It was as if the entire company had gone into shock.

"My costumes!" Lacey shrieked as she appeared in the doorway. "Look at them! All that work for nothing!"

"Where's Derek?" I asked, my voice a hoarse whisper. "He must be crushed."

Before Betty or anyone else had a chance to answer,

Corey, the lighting designer, cried out, "The lighting board! Somebody fried it!"

I turned and saw Corey and Derek at the back of the theater, sitting at what had once been the control board for the entire theater's lighting system.

Derek moaned, "That lighting board cost fifteen thousand dollars!"

"Not to mention all the hours that went into programming the computer, setting up the cues," added Jill, who stood in the aisle, looking stricken.

I turned back to Betty. "What does he mean, 'somebody fried it'?"

Corey heard my question. "It means somebody totally destroyed it," he explained in a choked voice. "It's not even that difficult. All you have to do is shove one end of a bare wire into a wall socket and touch the other end to the metal of the lighting board. The resulting power surge is enough to blow up the motherboard."

"Look!" Jill exclaimed, glancing up at the ceiling. "Somebody took a long stick and pushed all the lights out of place!"

"Wow," Kyle observed. Like everyone else, he sounded dazed. "It'll take hours to reset them all!"

"It's over," Derek said in a dull voice, sinking into one of seats that was still intact. "The entire production. It's done."

"You don't mean that!" Betty protested.

"Betty, there's no way we can open in twenty-four hours," Jill said mournfully. "Not when practically everything in the entire theater has been destroyed."

I had to agree. Looking around, I couldn't imagine how we could even clean the place up, much less put together new sets and costumes and lighting and everything else that was required to stage the production in such a short time. Then there was the fact that all those things required money, something I suspected was in pretty short supply.

And the most horrifying part was that all this destruction was intentional. Someone had worked hard to make sure *She's Flying High* wouldn't open on Friday night—someone who clearly felt the show mustn't go on.

The entire company remained silent for what seemed like a very long time. And then Wendy, the little girl who played Amelia as a child, piped up in her sweet voice, "Derek? I don't know if this would help, but I have a dress at home that's the same style as my costume. I could wear that tomorrow night."

"Thanks, Wendy," Derek replied tiredly. "But I don't think—"

"I have a long dress that looks a lot like my costume in the Presidential reception scene," one of the other female cast members volunteered.

"We could probably throw something together for sets," the stage manager said. "It wouldn't be as nice, of course. But still, we have all day tomorrow to work on it."

"And we can rent a new lighting board," Jill interjected. "A sound board too."

"If I spend the next twenty-four hours doing nothing else, not even sleeping, I can probably redo all the lighting," Corey offered. For the first time, I detected a note of optimism in his voice.

Slowly, Derek rose to his feet. His face flushed, he said, "I can't tell you how much this means to me. There's nothing I want more than to see Simon's production come to life on the Theater One stage. I meant it when I said it's the best way I can think of to honor his talent and his creativity. If there really is some way we could pull this off..." His voice became too choked for him to continue.

It didn't matter, since everyone else in the room filled in for him. The theater was suddenly buzzing with the excited chatter of the cast and crew as they shared their plans, each one coming up with ways to contribute to the reconstruction of what had been so brutally destroyed.

I had to admit, I was touched by their commitment to bringing Simon Wainwright's production to life. Derek was right. Simon deserved this.

He also deserved justice. Reminding myself of that simple fact banished any feelings of defeat I may have been feeling. Instead, I felt energized. The horrifying destruction laid out before me only made me more determined than ever to find out who his killer was.

• • •

Friday morning passed in a blur. On *Pet People,* I did a segment on techniques for breaking dogs and cats of bad habits. The whole time I was on the air, I hoped desperately that no one would call in to blab that it wasn't exactly a skill I'd mastered with my own menagerie. I couldn't forget the day Nick's parents had shown up at my cottage to find that Hurricane Max and Hurricane Lou had struck simultaneously.

I spent the rest of the day zigzagging around Long Island, making back-to-back house calls. So it wasn't until late afternoon that I managed to make the one stop I'd been thinking about all day.

As I pulled up in front of the house Kyle and Ian shared, my heart was pounding and my mouth was dry. Frankly, I wasn't sure what I was going to say or do. I didn't even know if I'd find anyone at home.

But I wasn't about to let any of that stop me. Especially when Ian, the man who currently held the number one spot on my list of suspects, answered the door. I was curious about why it took almost three minutes of knocking, accompanied by Monty's loud barking from out in the backyard, for him to open it. Still, there could have been a million different things he was busy with.

"Jessica," he greeted me, sounding surprised. "I wasn't expecting you. Did you set up an appointment with Kyle that he forgot to tell me about?"

As usual, I found his English accent disarming. But I tried not to let it distract me.

"I just made a house call nearby," I said, hoping my lying skills were up to snuff. "I figured I'd stop by and take another look at Monty. I hope I didn't disturb you."

"Not at all," he assured me.

Still, I noticed that he looked distracted. His wire-rimmed glasses were slightly askew, as was the baseball cap he was wearing once again. His hair was in disarray as well. Something about him seemed off balance somehow. "Do you mind if I come in?" I asked after what seemed like an awfully long silence. "Or I could go around back and check on Monty out there."

"No need," he chirped. "I'll let him in. Please, come inside—and I hope you'll forgive my rudeness. I was just on the phone with a rather irate client, one of those people who's impossible to please. I'm afraid I have a tendency to let that sort of thing get to me."

The inside of the small house looked pretty much the same way I remembered it from my other visits. What did you expect? I asked myself. A copy of *How to Murder Your Best Friend* lying open on the floor? Blood-soaked weapons? A half-written confession letter sitting on the coffee table?

"Difficult clients are definitely the hardest part of being in business for yourself," I said, trying to make conversation. Or, more accurately, trying to lead the conversation around to the topic I realized I had to broach. "But the appreciative clients make it all worthwhile. Fortunately, there are some I've had for nearly a decade, ever since I started practicing medicine."

Before he had a chance to make a comment that would steer the conversation off in a different direction, I continued, "Speaking of people we've known for a long time, a funny thing happened to me the other day. I ran into someone from your past."

"Really?" Ian asked, his English accent making the word sound more like *Rally?* "Who was that?"

I took a deep breath. "A professor from Brookside University. Someone in the theater department. I treated his, uh, his cat."

"What's his name?"

"Professor Hendricks. I think his first name is Garvin." I studied his face, searching for signs of confusion.

Instead, he said, "Garth, not Garvin. Garth Hendricks. And of course I know him. Quite well, in fact. At least I used to, back in my college days."

"Did you take any courses with him?" I probed.

"Yes. Several. I was in a number of his productions as well. That was a requirement in all his acting classes."

I was trying to think of a response when Ian retreated to the kitchen. A few seconds later, Monty came bounding into the house, leaping around and wagging his tail and barking gleefully.

"Here's our boy," Ian exclaimed, sounding as happy as the Weimaraner. As soon as he ruffled his ears, Monty lay down on his back, no doubt looking for a good tummy-scratching.

"Come here, you funny goofus," Ian said in a deep,

throaty voice—without even a trace of an English accent. "Moofus, woofus. Moofus, goofus..."

I froze. I recognized those words. Even more, I recognized the voice.

It belonged to Kyle, not Ian.

And it didn't have even a trace of an English accent.

A chill ran through me as, in a blinding flash, I understood what I was seeing.

Kyle and Ian were the same person.

Even though my head was buzzing, I could hear Professor Hendricks's words in my head, as if someone was playing a tape of something I'd heard before. He had said that Kyle was particularly good at playing character parts.

In other words, Kyle was a first-rate actor.

Something else he'd said suddenly stood out most in my mind.

I remember him doing a fabulous job as Alfred Doolittle, Eliza Doolittle's humorously tipsy father, in My Fair Lady, Kyle's former theater professor had commented. *He was quite convincing.*

My Fair Lady was set in London—and Alfred Doolittle had a strong Cockney accent.

Which meant Kyle was good at imitating accents. Especially English accents.

Like Ian's.

As I studied Ian more closely, watching him cavort with Monty on the floor, I realized why his hair looked strange, not to mention slightly off balance.

It was a wig.

I looked past the beard and past the glasses and realized that the features on that face belonged to Kyle Carlson. And while the last time I'd met Ian, on a scheduled visit, his eyes had been dark, this time they were blue. Like Kyle's. As if he hadn't had time to put in his tinted contact lenses.

My stomach was suddenly lurching as if I was a passenger on the *Titanic*.

Is it really possible? I wondered, questioning the words I was hearing and the image I was seeing. Could Ian Norman really be no more than somebody Kyle created, playing the role of his fictitious roommate in the same way he played a character onstage?

Except this character was designed to do more than entertain. He had been created to provide Kyle Carlson with an alibi for the night of the murder.

As this unbelievable truth came into clearer and clearer focus, something else kept nagging at me. After a few seconds, the fog cleared and I knew what it was.

That *it* began with Lieutenant Falcone—and his New York accent. The way he dropped his Rs at the end of most words. I remembered thinking, *Somewhere out there, there's a tremendous warehouse filled with all the Rs that people living in the New York area have discarded.*

Kyle's "roommate" was named Ian Michael Norman. If someone pronounced his last name without the *R*, it became *no man*.

I thought about his first two names, remembering the way he'd made a point of telling me his middle name. Ian Michael. Which meant his initials were *I. M.*

Put them all together and you ended up with *I Am No Man*.

I felt as if a jolt of electricity had just gone through me. He had me fooled. *All* of us, in fact, including Lieutenant Falcone.

There was no such person as Ian Norman. Kyle's "roommate" was really Kyle, wearing a wig and a fake beard and using the English accent he'd already mastered by the time he went to college.

Which means Kyle must have killed Simon, I concluded, my mind racing. Why else would he have gone to all the trouble of inventing a fake roommate to provide him with an alibi?

I thought fast, trying to remember all the other pieces of the investigation that suddenly made sense.

When the Port Players first learned that Simon was dead, Kyle was one of the few who insisted the production should come to a halt. Then it suddenly seemed as if he'd changed his mind. But in the eleventh hour, someone destroyed the theater, making it seemingly impossible for *She's Flying High* to open after all.

Kyle had also insisted all along that Lacey was the killer. He'd been the only person aside from Aziza who claimed that Lacey had been stalking Simon during the last weeks he was alive. And that had been only with my prompting. He could easily have made up the story about finding one of Lacey's threatening letters in Simon's backpack—and he could have reconstructed the type of letter we had talked about, then sent it to me anonymously.

He could have followed me to the Brookside University campus the night I went there to find Professor Hendricks too. Perhaps he had even guessed that sooner or later my snooping would lead me there. He could have also set me up at Theater One by leaving me an anonymous message to meet him there, then sending me a warning by sneaking around in the dark and leaving the trapdoor open on a dark stage. He certainly knew his way around the theater well enough.

Which meant he would have known about the props closet and the eclectic assortment of items stored inside—including a ceramic Buddha that was heavy enough to kill a man with a single blow. And he possessed the physical strength to drag his victim over to a trunk and push him into it.

It all made perfect sense. For the moment, however, I knew I had to concentrate on getting myself out of there without letting on that I'd finally seen through Kyle's charade—despite his skill as an actor.

"I can see from here that Monty's wounds look great," I said, hoping that whatever I'd learned about acting over the past two weeks was helping me sound the way I usually did. "Here, let me get a better look."

I crouched down and saw that his cuts were, indeed, practically healed.

"Monty's in great shape," I announced with an air of finality as I stood up. "Ian, would you do me a favor and tell Kyle to continue with the antibiotics I gave him until they're all gone?"

Usually I would have explained how important it was to complete the entire course in order to keep the bacteria from building up resistance and over time reducing their efficacy. But I just didn't have the heart.

Not when I knew the next thing I had to do was contact Lieutenant Falcone and tell him that Kyle Carlson had murdered Simon Wainwright—even though a major piece of the puzzle was missing, and that was *why*.

• • •

I wasn't surprised that I couldn't get Lieutenant Falcone on the phone, since after five o'clock on a Friday evening wasn't exactly prime time for communicating with anyone. But that didn't mean I wasn't frustrated.

I left him a message on his voice mail, begging him to call me back as soon as possible. Then, after thinking about it for about eight seconds, I called back and left him a second message. This time I told him the reason it was really important that he call me back right away was that I'd figured out who had killed Simon Wainwright.

I dashed home to let Max and Lou out, feed my entire menagerie, and take a quick shower. By that point, it was close enough to cast call that I figured I might as well go over to the theater. After all, I wasn't about to find anything productive to do with the little time I had left. Especially since I was already feeling pretty jittery.

I was about to knock on Betty's door when I remembered that she'd spent the whole day at Theater One, helping reconstruct scenery and throw together costumes. So I drove to Port Townsend in my red VW by myself, aware that more and more butterflies were gathering in my stomach with each passing mile.

As I walked into the theater, I expected to find it throbbing with activity. Instead, it was deserted.

But I was astonished by how far it had come in the past twenty-four hours. New scenery replaced the fake trees and hand-painted backdrops that had been destroyed. Even though the substitutes were much simpler, they certainly did the job. The torn seats had been repaired with duct tape, and the cables that had been hanging from the ceiling were nowhere in sight. I noticed a new lighting board and a new sound board, both slightly different models than what I remembered seeing before. And a rack of costumes stood on the stage. They weren't nearly as elaborate as the ones Lacey had spent weeks making. But they would do.

When I heard someone clear his throat behind me, I turned and saw Corey wrapping a length of cable around one arm.

"Where is everyone?" I asked.

"Dinner break," he replied. "In fact, I'm off to meet the rest of the group. Want to come along?"

"No, thanks." By that point, my stomach was in such turmoil I couldn't imagine putting even a single morsel of food into it.

Instead, I figured I'd spend my time getting used to the idea that in only a couple of hours, this empty theater would be filled with a living, breathing audience.

I decided that one of the best ways to do that was by getting into costume. As soon as I said good-bye to Corey, I rummaged through the rack of costumes until I found the one that duplicated my aviator suit. Actually, it was nothing more than a white blouse and a pair of khaki-colored Dockers that had been shortened to capri length, with elastic sewn into each hem. But at least my goggles and my leather helmet, both looped onto the hanger, had survived the heartbreaking assault on Theater One.

I'd just brought the outfit into the women's dressing room when I heard a door slam.

"Corey?" I called, surprised that I wasn't alone after all.

But no one answered.

I realized immediately that it couldn't be Corey. The door I'd heard bang shut was close by. In fact, it had to have been the door to the men's dressing room.

"Hello?" I called, wondering who else besides me had stayed behind. "Who's there?"

Once again, there was no response.

"Derek?"

Nothing but silence.

"Doug?" I tried again, this time using the names of other male members of the cast and crew. "Brent? Robert?"

In a choking voice, I added, "Kyle?"

I let out a little scream when somebody suddenly leaped into the doorway of the women's dressing room.

But it wasn't Derek or anyone else from the Port Players. Instead, the man standing just a few feet away from me was Ian Michael Norman, complete with his curly reddish-brown wig, fake beard, wire-rimmed glasses, and tinted contact lenses, just like all the other times I'd been in his company.

This time, however, there was one thing about Ian that was distinctively different. He was clutching a knife the size of a machete.

Chapter 18

"All of the animals excepting man know that the principal business of life is to enjoy it."

—Samuel Butler

Ian!" I cried, my mind racing as I tried to come up with the right thing to say to someone who was brandishing a knife. "How nice to see you. Are you, uh, here for the show?"

Desperate to pretend that absolutely nothing out of the ordinary was happening, I turned toward the mirror and picked up a tube of lipstick. I only hoped he was far enough away that he couldn't see how badly my hands were shaking.

I even dared to wonder, just for a second, if perhaps the knife in his hand was just a prop. But when he grabbed me roughly from behind and held it against my throat, I knew from the sharpness of the blade that this was no fake. This was the real thing.

I could see in the mirror that thanks to his jolting movements, his wig had been pushed askew, revealing a large patch of Kyle Carlson's sandy-colored hair. He might have looked humorous if it wasn't for the fury burning in his eyes.

"The whole cast will be back any minute now!" I cried. "Ian, why don't you just go into the theater and—"

I stopped talking when he pressed the blade more closely against my flesh. In the mirror, I saw that a tiny red line had appeared just above the blade.

"You figured the whole thing out, didn't you?" he hissed in my ear. "I could see it in your eyes today when you were at the house. *My* house. The house I live in alone."

"But Ian!" I tried again.

Once again, he used his knife to make his point. "Stop pretending!" he demanded.

I was hardly in a position to argue. "You're right," I admitted breathlessly. "I know that Ian isn't real. He's someone you invented to prove what a terrific actor you are."

"I think you know the real reason," he shot back.

"No, I—"

He drove home his sense of urgency with the stainless steel blade, cutting a second red line into my flesh.

"All right!" I gasped. "I do know the real reason. You made up Ian to give yourself an alibi."

"Aren't you smart," Kyle snarled. By this point, the wig had slipped off his head completely. I also noticed that his fake beard was coming loose on one side of his face. "The problem is, you're a little too smart. Unfortunately, it's going to cost you."

"But why?" I asked in a shrill voice. "Why did you kill Simon?"

"Because he stole it!" he yelled into my ear.

I instinctively lurched forward. As I did, I felt the terrifyingly sharp blade push even deeper into my skin.

"*She's Flying High* was *my* play, not Simon's!" he cried. "I came up with the idea of writing a musical based on Amelia Earhart's life back when we were just out of college. I'm the one who wrote it, not him! And I finally got tired of listening to everybody talk about how great he was. What a *genius* he was.

"*I'm* the genius!" he exclaimed. "*I'm* the one who stayed up until two or three, night after night, perfecting the script. *I'm* the one who came up with the clever lyrics! *She's Flying High* is *my* creation!"

"Why didn't you just tell everyone the truth?" By that point, my words came out as wheezing sounds. "Derek and the Stones and...and everyone else who was involved with the production?"

"Because I had no way of proving it. Ten years ago, right after I finished it, I showed it to Simon. I was actually trembling as I handed him a copy. His opinion meant so much to me. I hoped he'd read it and tell me it was great. Instead, his reaction devastated me. He told me he thought that parts of it showed promise, but that overall it just wasn't good enough.

"And I *believed* him! In fact, I burned every copy I had. I was devastated, of course, but I trusted him so much I didn't question him. It never even occurred to me that he'd squirrel his copy away and that, when the time was right, he'd put *his* name on it!"

"But that's exactly what he did," I said, doing my best to sound sympathetic. If there had ever been a time I wanted to convince someone I was on his side, this was it. "Simon betrayed you! And you thought he was your friend. I don't blame you for being angry!"

"It was the first time I'd ever seen him do anything that selfish," Kyle continued. I had the feeling he was talking to himself, not to me. "That evil, conniving bastard. I confronted him, of course. As soon as I realized what he'd done, I demanded that he come clean.

"But Simon could be very persuasive once he turned on the charm. He insisted he was simply paving the way. At that point, he already had Derek and everyone else in the company under his spell. He'd also caught the attention of the Stones. See, he was great at crashing parties and making contacts and networking, things I've never been good at. He kept saying that since he was the one who was pitching it to the people who really mattered, he couldn't very well let on that someone else had written it. He assured me that once things were firmly under way, he'd tell everyone the truth.

"I waited and waited, but that moment never came. Finally, when we were only two weeks away from opening night, I confronted Simon again, this time at the theater. I knew he'd show up here that Friday evening, even though there was no rehearsal. He liked to run through his lines on his own, and he preferred to do it on the same stage where he'd be performing. He told me he'd arranged to meet Aziza here so they could rehearse together.

"But by the time I got here, she was long gone. He told me he'd just broken up with her, and naturally they had a huge fight. She stormed out of the theater, but he stayed to rehearse, the way he planned. He acted as if nothing was out of the ordinary. He could be like that—so determined to get what he wanted that nothing else mattered.

"I was glad I'd gotten him alone, since I figured that without Aziza and Lacey and the rest of his entourage crowding him, I'd have a chance to talk some sense into him. Instead, when I demanded that once and for all he give me credit for the musical *I'd* written, he started giving me the same old story about how the timing wasn't right. And standing there in the dressing room with him, I suddenly realized that the timing would *never* be right. I finally saw Simon Wainwright for what he really was."

"No wonder you were devastated!" I exclaimed.

"I saw red," Kyle agreed coldly. "The more he tried to explain why it made sense for him to take credit for my creation, the more enraged I became. Finally, I lost it. Simon turned his back on me, as if our discussion was over and he was going to walk out.

"Before I even knew what I was doing, I grabbed the first heavy thing I saw, a statue of Buddha, and smacked him in the head with it. I didn't even think about the repercussions. It was an instinctive reaction. So I was astonished when I looked down and saw him lying on the floor. I knelt by his side and called his name, over and over. Then I started to cry. Even though I was furious with him, he'd been one of my closest friends for years. We studied together, we auditioned together, we even lived together. Simon and I shared the same dream, and we supported each other as we both went after it. I loved him like a brother.

"I couldn't believe I'd killed him." By now Kyle was practically whispering. It was as if he was reliving the entire scene. "I panicked, then instinctively tried to hide what I'd done. I noticed the dusty old trunk in the corner of the dressing room, and I dragged it out and stuffed Simon inside it. Then I did my best to wipe the fingerprints off everything I could remember touching, especially the trunk and the Buddha. And I was careful to put the Buddha back into the props closet. I figured whoever had taken it out would just assume that the cleaning lady had put it back where it belonged. And then I ran like hell.

"As I drove home, I was shaking. I'm amazed that I didn't have an accident. But as upset as I was, I knew I needed an alibi. That was when I came up with the idea of Ian. I knew I had the acting ability to pull it off. All I had to do was create a roommate and construct a solid story to go with it. I thought it was the cleverest idea I'd ever come up with. I even chose a name that would honor my creation: I. M. Norman. *I am no man.*"

This didn't seem like the best time to mention that I'd already figured that one out—and that he wasn't nearly as clever as he seemed to think he was. The last thing I wanted to do was provoke him.

"When the police called me down to the station as Kyle," he continued, "I was pretty nervous. But when they called me in as Ian, I was frantic. I knew this was going to be the biggest acting challenge of my life. Not only did I have to convince the cops that Ian was a real person, I had to convince them that he was telling the truth.

"Somehow, I did it. I must say, I was flying pretty high myself when I came out of there. I'd actually made them believe I had an airtight alibi for the time Simon was killed. But then I realized I had to keep Ian alive, at least for a little while. Sure, I'd pulled him from out of thin air. But now that I was done with him, I couldn't just have him vanish *back* into thin air.

"That's where you came in. I wanted to let you get to know Ian, and Monty was the perfect excuse. As soon as you told me you were a veterinarian who made house calls, I knew I'd found the ideal way to keep Ian going. See, I hardly ever have anybody over to the house. I'm too much of a loner for that. But I knew you'd come over for only a short time, and I figured you weren't likely to ask too many questions.

"But I was wrong. You kept coming around to check on Monty. I was also wrong about you not asking questions. You asked plenty. I wasn't sure what you were up to, but I thought I'd be safe as long as you believed Ian was real. And if I could convince you and everybody else that Lacey was the killer, I'd get off scot-free. She certainly had the motive. And Aziza's claim that Lacey had been stalking Simon before he was murdered was the perfect way to make her look guilty. So when you told me about it, I jumped right on it.

"I also realized pretty quickly that instead of leaving the production, I'd be better off sticking with the show," he went on. "That way, I'd have a better chance of sabotaging it. The last thing I wanted was for the show Simon stole from me to be produced on a real stage without anyone knowing that I was really the one who deserved all the credit.

"My entire plan went fine until this afternoon. I could see from the look on your face that you'd realized that Ian and Kyle were one and the same. And you're smart enough to figure out why I'd go to the trouble of creating a fake person—one who just happened to provide me with an alibi."

"I guess I'm not a very good actor, after all," I commented weakly.

"Actually, you're not half bad. But the moment I started talking to Monty in that silly voice I use only with him, I realized what I'd done. It was the first mistake I made. Still, I didn't let on. I didn't want you to know I realized the charade was over.

"And now," he concluded, tightening his grip on me, "there's only one thing for me to do. I have to get rid of you. Otherwise, you'll go to the police and tell them everything."

I was about to swear up and down that I had absolutely no intention of doing that when I heard a female voice call, "Hello? Anybody here?"

We both froze.

Thank goodness! I thought. Someone's here!

I opened my mouth to scream. But Kyle covered my mouth with his forearm, still clutching the knife in his hand.

"Great," he muttered. "Now what I am going to—I know."

"Hello!" we heard once again. "Where the heck is everybody?"

Sunny, I thought, recognizing her voice.

But figuring out who had come into the theater didn't do much to help me—or to prevent Kyle from dragging me down the short hallway I knew led to the props closet. I thought of trying to break out of his grasp, but I could feel how strong he was. Besides, there was that tiny problem of a sharp stainless steel blade that happened to be situated dangerously close to my windpipe.

As we neared the props closet, I began to panic. Not only was the closet a small, dark space guaranteed to make anyone who was kept in there long enough claustrophobic. It was also the perfect place for Kyle to use his knife on me, leave me inside, and then slip out of the theater before anyone knew what had happened.

So when we reached the closet door, I couldn't help whimpering. It was the same sound Max made when he was standing at the window, watching a squirrel he knew he couldn't get to.

"Quiet!" Kyle hissed in my ear.

He dragged me into the closet without loosening his grip. It was pretty tight once the two of us were stuffed inside. And it was fairly dark, with the only illumination coming from the thin strip of light underneath the door.

"Don't make a sound," he warned. As if wanting to remind me how serious he was, he pushed the knife harder against my throat.

"Hello?" Sunny called again. "Derek, are you here?"

The sound of her voice enabled me to keep track of

where she was. And from what I could tell, she was coming closer.

In fact, I could hear her walking around in the hall-way, probably no more than fifteen feet away from where Kyle was holding me at knifepoint.

"Don't make a peep," Kyle whispered, his breath hot against my ear.

Come on, Sunny, I thought. Open the door. Please, *please* think of some reason you need to check inside.

"Hello?" I heard Sunny call once again. "Anybody here?"

By this point, she was standing directly in front of the door.

"If you let her know we're in here," Kyle said so quietly I could barely make out the words, "I'll kill you before she has a chance to open the door."

As he spoke, he yanked me more tightly against him. The sudden movement caused me to lose my balance, and my foot struck something hard.

I immediately realized what it was. The fog machine.

I suddenly had an idea. Even though I wasn't sure I could pull it off, I maneuvered my foot around the edge, trying to find the switch Sunny had told me she'd flipped accidentally. That meant it couldn't be that difficult to turn on....

"Stop fidgeting!" Kyle insisted.

"I have a cramp in my leg," I whispered back.

Hoping he'd buy my excuse, I made a few more attempts at flicking on the switch. I finally felt something move, but I still couldn't be sure I'd succeeded. Not without turning on the light and crouching down to get a better look.

And even if I could, that would completely ruin my plan.

Please work, I thought, clamping my eyes shut.

Outside, I could hear footsteps moving away from the props closet. Sunny was still in the backstage area, wandering around. If only she would stay nearby . . .

It seemed as if Kyle and I stood in that closet forever. I could hear his rasping breaths in my ear and could smell his sweat. He must have been getting tired of holding the knife at my throat, because he rested his arm on my shoulder.

While I'd pretty much lost my sense of time, I figured at least five minutes must have passed since the time I fiddled with the fog machine. Suddenly, even in the dim light, I could make out wisps of white smoke wafting along the bottom of the closet. I held my breath, hoping for it to thicken, hoping for the billows of fog to start drifting underneath the door.

"Oh, my God!" Sunny cried. "Fire!"

"Fire!" I repeated in a breathy voice. "Look, the closet's on fire! Kyle, we have to get out of here!"

As I'd hoped, the word *fire* worked like magic. My captor reacted automatically, flinging open the closet door.

In fact, his instinct for survival seemed to make him forget all about me. He pushed me aside and dashed out of the closet. As I followed right behind him, I suddenly heard an earsplitting clanging that reverberated through the entire building.

I spotted Sunny standing at the end of the hall, her hand still poised above the fire alarm.

"Grab him!" I cried, yelling over the loud noise. "He killed Simon!"

Sunny didn't stop to ask questions. Instead, she sprinted after him. As I ran into the wings, I saw that she'd almost caught up with him as they neared the edge of the stage. When he jumped off, my heart sank.

She lost him! I thought miserably.

Instead, she leaped on him from above, falling onto his back and grabbing him around the neck.

"What the—!" he cried, nearly toppling over.

I took advantage of his surprise by following suit. I jumped off the stage, then swooped down and wrapped my arms around his knees. The two of us were too much for him, and he crumpled to the floor.

Sunny couldn't have weighed more than a hundred pounds, but between her weight and mine, we managed to hold him down. As she straddled him, she pulled off the leather belt she wore with her black jeans and did an impressive job of tying his hands behind his back. Then, using my belt, we tied his feet, looping the leather around one of the seats to limit his mobility.

"See, Jessie?" she said proudly as the two of us sat side by side, me on his back and her on his butt. "I really am good at helping out."

"You can certainly think on your feet," I agreed, still trying to catch my breath. "I guess you and I make a pretty good team."

"So what about my idea?" she asked. "You know, about me working for you? Or at least giving it a try?"

I had to smile. "Now that I've seen how good you are in a crisis," I replied, "maybe it's not such a bad idea."

It took under eight minutes for the fire department to arrive. Still sitting side by side on Kyle to hold him down, Sunny and I exchanged relieved glances as we heard the sound of sirens right outside the building. Seconds later, we heard yelling and the stomping of feet.

"Back here!" I yelled to the firefighters who had tromped into the lobby. "There's no fire, but we need your help!"

The two firefighters in black raincoats and boots

who found us looked both relieved and surprised at the same time.

"What's going on here?" one of them demanded. "There's no fire?"

"It's a long story," I told him. "But right now, we're desperate for your assistance. This man is a murderer, and he's about to be arrested. If you can find a way to get Lieutenant Anthony Falcone on the phone, he'll send somebody down here as fast as he can."

The fact that Kyle's giant knife was lying on the ground, just out of reach, must have convinced them that I knew what I was talking about. He also kept demanding a lawyer, which didn't help his case much either.

When one of the firefighters somehow used his clout to get hold of Falcone and tried to explain what was going on, I interrupted, "Let me talk to him."

"What the hell are you doing, Dr. Popper?" Falcone demanded as soon as I'd said hello.

"Catching Simon Wainwright's murderer," I replied. "It's Kyle Carlson. He confessed."

"But what about his roommate? The one who provided his alibi?"

"When I tell you the whole story," I told him, "you're not going to believe it. Unless you keep in mind that Kyle Carlson is an actor.

"In fact," I added, "it turns out that he's actually a surprisingly good actor."

●   ●   ●

Betty and Winston's wedding day was the perfect spring day. Early that morning, I stood in the open doorway of my cottage, clasping a mug of breakfast coffee and basking in the warmth of the May sun. It seemed to be smiling down from the cloudless blue sky.

The flowers in the garden were in full bloom, filling the air with their fragrance.

The ceremony was scheduled to begin in the early afternoon, with the reception immediately afterward. The caterers had already arrived and were setting up tables and chairs under the big white tent that had arrived the day before. As I sipped my coffee and Max and Lou frolicked in the grass, I watched the crew drape pale pink linen tablecloths over a dozen big round tables, then set each place with matching napkins and Betty's fine white china and silverware.

Then the florist drove up. She busily set about placing a crystal vase of pink and white roses at the center of each table. Meanwhile, a group of her employees fastened pink roses onto the white gazebo that had been delivered along with the tent. Another group festooned the walkway with lengths of white netting dotted with more pink roses.

That was my last moment of peace the entire morning. Betty had arranged for two women from a local salon to come to the house to do our hair and makeup. I was afraid I'd end up looking like Marge Simpson. Instead, the two of them performed something close to magic.

Suzanne showed up late that morning to help me dress. She insisted she couldn't wait for the actual ceremony to see how I looked, but I think she wanted to make sure I didn't walk down the aisle with toilet paper stuck to the bottom of my shoe.

"You're going to look fabulous," she gushed as she slipped the mint green monstrosity of a bridesmaid's dress over my head. "The only thing I'm worried about is how you're going to handle yourself in those shoes. Maybe you should have practiced walking in heels all week."

"Nothing wrong with adding a little comic relief to

the occasion," I commented, my voice muffled by the endless folds of fabric that still swarmed around my head.

After tugging at the dress a few times and pushing a stray strand of hair behind my ear, Suzanne stood back and studied me. Her silence was driving me crazy.

"What do you think?" I finally asked, unnerved by her expressionless face.

She considered my question for what seemed like a very long time. "I think . . . I think Nick was nuts to let you get away." She pulled me toward the full-length mirror in the bedroom. "Take a look for yourself."

I held my breath, dreading the sight of Kermit the Frog in drag. Instead, I did a double take. I'm not big on vanity, but I was astonished that the elegant-looking woman in the mirror was actually me. I took a few baby steps, just to see how the skirt swirled when I moved. The effect was dazzling. Gabriella Bertucci was an absolute genius.

"Speaking of Nick," Suzanne continued, clearly trying to sound casual, "what's up with him? Isn't he in the wedding party?"

I nodded, still unable to take my eyes off the astounding image in the mirror. "He's walking Betty down the aisle."

"Did you see him at the rehearsal?"

"Yup. Last night's rehearsal dinner too. We made a point of ignoring each other the whole time."

She sighed. "I don't know which one of you is more stubborn."

Fortunately, we didn't have time for any further discussion of my character flaws. I happened to glance at the clock next to my bed, then let out a shriek.

"It's time!" I cried.

I actually had butterflies in my stomach as I joined the other members of the wedding party who were assembling in Betty's front parlor—minus the bride herself, of course, who was following the tradition of staying hidden until the very last minute. Winston looked wonderfully dignified in his tuxedo. Happy too. And I had to admit that the other bridesmaids looked lovely. One was dressed in pale blue, one in yellow, and one in lavender. Little Fiona, Chloe's daughter, wore pink, and her waist-length blond hair was tied back with a matching ribbon. All those pastels together reminded me of a bouquet of flowers.

Not that the bridesmaids necessarily acted the part. Chloe, who stood nearly six feet tall and in her yellow dress reminded me of a giant banana, was scolding her husband. She acted as if he, like her daughter, was six years old. The blasé expressions of Winston's son, James, and his wife, Grace, said they'd seen all this before.

Watching the interactions was fascinating. Yet I suddenly got the strange feeling that someone was staring at me. I turned and discovered that somebody's eyes were, indeed, boring into me.

They belonged to Nick.

Whatever mushy sentimentality I was feeling over Betty's wedding day disappeared—fast. My heart began racing and I stood frozen to the spot.

Nick, however, had not lost his powers of mobility. In fact, he was heading right in my direction.

He looked pretty darned good too. His tuxedo fit him perfectly, and he'd actually managed to tame the lock of dark hair that was always falling into his eyes. Actually, I kind of missed it.

"Hi," he said simply.

"Hi," I returned.

"You look...amazing." He'd barely gotten the words out before patches of red broke out on his cheeks.

"You look nice too," I replied. I suspected my own face was a matching shade of crimson.

We were both silent for what seemed like a really long time. "Betty told me you've been doing a terrific job in the play," Nick finally said.

I grimaced. "I've been muddling through. Opening night was a little scary, but it gets easier each time."

"Does that mean you'll be going to Broadway when it opens in the fall?"

"I think I'll stick with the veterinarian biz," I said. "But it really has been fun. And it turned out to be worthwhile too. I can't tell you how rewarding it was watching Lieutenant Falcone arrest Simon Wainwright's murderer."

"Yeah, Betty told me all about that too." Nick swallowed, making a loud gulping sound. "Listen, Jessie. I—"

Just then the string quartet sitting next to the gazebo broke into the opening bars of Vivaldi's *Four Seasons,* our cue that the ceremony was about to begin.

"We should probably get into our places," I suggested.

"Right," he replied. "And I'd better go find Betty. I don't want to keep the bride waiting on her big day."

As a result of that short, meaningless conversation, my head was spinning as I began strolling down the aisle in time to the music, clutching a bouquet of white roses tied together with a mint green satin ribbon. I forced myself to concentrate on what was going on around me. I scanned the faces of the hundred or so guests sitting in the chairs lined up in front of the gazebo, craning their necks to watch the procession. Suzanne smiled and nodded approvingly as I walked by. I noted that Derek and Jill and several other people from the Port Players were in attendance, along with some of Winston's friends whom I'd met while treating their polo ponies and house pets.

Speaking of house pets, the three dogs who were invited guests sat in front, kept in line by a young man from the catering company. I had to admit that Betty had also been right about their fashion statement. Max and Lou looked adorable in their bright red bow ties. I'd bathed them both the day before, and Max looked like a fuzzy white teddy bear. Lou's white fur gleamed so brightly that it was hard to believe that less than three weeks before I'd been afraid he'd spend the rest of his life as orange as Garfield. Meanwhile, Frederick's soft light brown fur served as a nice contrast to all that blinding white. And the sunshine-yellow bow tie complemented it perfectly.

As I reached the gazebo, the string quartet broke into "Here Comes the Bride," a sign that Betty was about to start down the aisle. The guests stood and we all turned to watch her grand entrance.

She looked absolutely beautiful, mainly because she was as radiant as every bride should be. Her sapphire-blue eyes were shining, and a serene smile played at her lips. In short, her expression was one of pure joy.

And her white satin dress was like something out of a fairy tale. The long-sleeved bodice was made of Belgian lace, and a row of tiny beads ran down the front. It also had just a touch of theatricality: a skirt that was full enough to swirl around her ankles, making her look as if she was waiting for Fred Astaire to join her in a dance.

Just looking at her made my eyes mist over.

As Betty began to walk slowly down the aisle on Nick's arm, I glanced at Winston. He, too, looked as if he was about to burst.

The ceremony was short but personal. Betty and Winston each recited vows they'd written, pledging their love and their loyalty. I only hoped all the eye makeup I was wearing was waterproof.

"By the power vested in me by the State of New York," the justice of the peace boomed, "I now pronounce you husband and wife. You may kiss the bride."

Winston leaned forward and gave Betty a chaste kiss. She responded by throwing her arms around his neck and planting a big wet one on his mouth.

Everyone laughed, then burst into applause.

Once the ceremony was over, the guests swarmed around the garden. I thought I was done with my part. But before long, Chloe clapped her hands for attention.

"Come, come, ladies," Chloe insisted. She may have been dressed in swirls of yellow satin, but she sounded like the drill sergeant in a World War II movie. "Betty's ready to throw the bouquet. You, stand here. You, over there."

Reluctantly I allowed Chloe to shepherd me to the back of the garden along with all the other single women. They included her six-year-old daughter. Since Fiona had youth on her side, I was betting on her catching the bouquet.

Then Betty pranced over, cradling her bouquet in her arms and beaming. Still, there was a look of determination in her eye that made me nervous. Keeping my head low, I shuffled toward the back, hoping no one would notice me. Especially Betty. I parked myself two or three feet behind the rest of the group, hoping all the towering heads with their elaborate hairdos would keep me hidden.

Big mistake. Standing apart from the crowd only made it that much easier for Betty to hurl her bouquet right at me. You'd have thought she was playing shortstop for the Yankees.

"Oomph!" I cried as I caught it in both hands. I had

to. Otherwise, it would have smacked me in the solar plexus with such force I probably would have been rushed to the nearest emergency room.

I glanced down at the bouquet I was clutching, the symbol for *You're next*. And wondered how I'd managed to let this happen.

"Hey, that was rigged," Nick commented, appearing from out of nowhere.

"Exactly what I was thinking," I replied. Somehow I couldn't bring myself to look him in the eye.

"It looks like Betty refuses to give up on you." He swallowed, then added, "Just like me."

I turned to him, all my defenses suddenly dissolving. "Oh, Nick, I'm so sorry," I said. "I acted like a jerk."

"Or maybe you acted like somebody who's nervous about getting married," he returned lightly. "But you don't have to be afraid, Jess. It's just me. Deep down, you've got to believe as strongly as I do that if there were ever two people who could live happily ever after, it's you and me."

I nodded. "I do."

He laughed. "Can I hold you to that?"

"Yes," I replied. "Absolutely."

And then, just like Betty, I threw my arms around the man of my dreams and planted a big wet kiss on his mouth.

About the Author

Cynthia Baxter is a native of Long Island, New York. She currently resides on the North Shore, where she is at work on her next mystery, *Monkey See, Monkey Die,* which Bantam will publish in summer 2008. Visit her on the Web at www.cynthiabaxter.com.

Dear Reader,

In the next *Reigning Cats & Dogs* mystery, MONKEY SEE, MONKEY DIE, Jessie is drawn into her most dangerous investigation yet when she receives an urgent phone call from an old veterinary school friend—who soon turns up murdered. Nick plays a starring role in the case, of course, along with ever-flirtatious reporter Forrester Sloan and Jessie's close friend Suzanne. Even Marcus Scruggs reappears, this time promoting a questionable new business venture involving diamond dog collars and gourmet cat food!

I'm equally excited about my brand-new series, which I'm thrilled to introduce to you for the very first time! In the *Murder Packs a Suitcase* mystery series, recently widowed spitfire Mallory Marlowe embarks on a new career as a travel writer—and inadvertently ends up with an even more unexpected occupation: amateur sleuth. In each book, Mallory explores a different destination in search of hot travel tips for a magazine article—but her knack for discovering secrets and her sense of adventure soon land her somewhere she never imagined she'd visit: smack in the middle of a murder investigation. Even if you've never been a tourist or armchair traveler, I think you'll find Mal a delightful mystery tour guide. A sample from the first book follows. I hope fans of the *Reigning Cats & Dogs* mysteries enjoy the new *Murder Packs a Suitcase* mystery series just as much!

Until next time,

Cynthia Baxter

DON'T MISS
THESE TWO EXCITING
NEW MYSTERIES
FROM
CYNTHIA BAXTER!

READ ON FOR AN EXCLUSIVE SNEAK PEEK
AT

MONKEY SEE, MONKEY DIE

A New *Reigning Cats & Dogs* Mystery
On sale August 2008

and

The First Book in the Brand-New
***Murder Packs a Suitcase* Mystery Series**
On sale December 2008

MONKEY SEE, MONKEY DIE
On sale August 2008

Chapter 1

"Whenever you observe an animal closely, you feel as if a human being sitting inside were making fun of you."

—Elias Canetti, _The Human Province_

Jessie? I'm sorry for calling so early. I know I probably woke you up. But I don't have your cell phone number, only your home number. And I wanted to make sure I got hold of you before you left for the day."

What a lot of words to be hit with at—what time was it? I forced my eyes open long enough to look at the alarm clock next to my bed.

Five-thirty. In the _morning_.

"I'm sorry, who is this?" I asked groggily.

Whoever had dragged me out of my sleep at this ridiculous hour certainly sounded as if she knew who I was. The problem was, I had no idea who *she* was. And given the fact that only seconds before, I had been lost in a wonderful dream starring Brad Pitt *and* George Clooney, I wasn't exactly in the mood to play guessing games.

"Erin Walsh," the caller replied breathlessly. "Remember me? From vet school?"

It took me a few seconds to connect the name with my years at Cornell University's veterinary college. More than a decade had passed since I'd been a student there. But slowly, even through the thick wad of tissue paper still wrapped around my brain, I managed to attach a face to the name. An entire identity, in fact.

"Sure I remember you, Erin," I said through a mouth that felt as if it were coated with glue. "You and I crammed for the neuroanatomy final together, right? I seem to remember the two of us pulling an all-nighter in the basement of the vet school library. Didn't we keep ourselves awake by eating a different candy bar from one of the vending machines every hour . . . ?"

"That's right. Jessie, the reason I'm calling—"

"You married somebody else who was in our class, didn't you? Bill or Brad . . ."

"Ben Chandler," Erin corrected me, rather abruptly. In fact, I realized that she'd sounded as if she was in a hurry ever since I'd answered the phone. "But I'm afraid I didn't call to reminisce. I need to see you. Right away. Like, this morning."

I turned to glance at the figure lying beside me, fast asleep. Fortunately, I hadn't woken up

Nick. He was so tangled up in the sheets you'd have thought he'd been dreaming about alligator wrestling. Personally, I'd take the Brad Pitt–George Clooney dream any day.

By this point my head was clear enough that I did some calculations. I hadn't spoken to Erin Walsh for more than five years. If I remembered correctly, the last time I'd seen her was at my five-year Cornell reunion. She and Ben were newlyweds back then, both of them glowing like fluorescent lightbulbs as they chattered away about their fabulous wedding and their honeymoon in Barbados and their plans to open a practice together.

"What's the hurry?" I asked.

"Believe me, Jessie, I wouldn't be doing this if it wasn't really important. Please say you'll meet me this morning. It's crucial that I talk to somebody like you!"

Somebody like me? What did *that* mean?

"Where are you?" I asked, still confused.

"On Long Island." She was still talking way too fast. "It's a long story, but Ben and I have been living in Bay Terrace for the past couple of years. We're probably no more than ten miles from where you live. I can meet you anywhere. Just name the time and place. A diner, a street-corner . . . but the sooner, the better."

Mentally I ran through the calls I had scheduled for that morning. My first appointment was a spaying in Metchogue at eight o'clock. Given the fact that it was still practically the middle of the night, that gave me plenty of time to meet Erin for breakfast.

"How about six-thirty at the Spartan Diner?" I suggested. "It's in Niamogue, right on Route forty-seven."

"I know the place. I'll be there. And Jess? Please don't say anything about this to anybody, okay?"

"Erin," I asked, struck by the bizarreness of this entire conversation, "is everything okay?"

"That's the thing, Jessie," she replied with a nervous laugh. "I don't think it is."

"Can you at least give me an idea of what all this is—?"

She never answered my question. In fact, she'd already hung up.

With a loud sigh, I dragged myself out of bed and embarked on my morning pilgrimage to worship at the feet of Mr. Coffee. As usual, my two dogs, Max and Lou, were already in high gear, scampering around my feet with much more energy than any living being should have before the sun has risen. My two cats were just coming to life, stretching and yawning. As for my blue-and-gold macaw, he was already wide awake. Prometheus was always up with the birds, mainly because he is one. My Jackson's chameleon, Leilani, was awake, too, blinking at me from inside her glass tank with the eye that was on the side of her head facing me.

But I was still too busy ruminating about the strange phone call from Erin to pay any of them much attention.

What's with all this cloak-and-dagger non-

sense? I wondered as I shuffled into the kitchen.

My old vet school buddy had sounded as if she was smack in the middle of a drama—and frankly, the last thing I wanted was to be recruited for a supporting role.

Out with the old, in with the new, Mallory thought as she sat in the waiting area at JFK Airport early Sunday morning. She wondered if she was being overly dramatic by imagining that the plane she was about to board would carry her away from her old life and into a brand-new life, one in which she played the role of travel writer.

A very busy travel writer. The last seventy-two hours had been the whirlwind she'd anticipated. She'd freshened up warm-weather clothes that hadn't seen the outside of a cardboard box since September. She'd gotten a haircut along with the leg waxing and, as a last-minute splurge, a pedicure. She'd bought three different guidebooks, then spent both Friday and Saturday nights reading them cover to cover, flagging the important pages.

But instead of having the chance to enjoy any of it, she'd carried out all her preparations under the watchful and disapproving eye of her daughter. A daughter who trailed after her the same way she had when she was four years old, talking nonstop about the pros and cons of business versus law. Mallory had no idea an identity crisis could be so noisy. She only hoped she hadn't been so distracted that she hadn't packed sensibly. She could imagine opening her suitcase in Orlando and finding it contained six pairs of pajamas, two tubes of toothpaste, and a woolen ski sweater.

As for Jordan, he demonstrated his annoyance that his mother was making an attempt at reestablishing a life for herself by acting like one of Orlando's best-known residents: Grumpy. He made a point of letting out a loud sigh every few minutes. He also refused to engage in any of their conversations, including the few that Mallory managed to steer away from the topic of Amanda's career.

As she climbed into the airport van before the sun came up, she felt as if she finally had a chance to catch her breath for the first time since before her job interview. But that didn't mean she was leaving her apprehensions behind with her sleeping children.

True, it was hard to imagine a destination more user-friendly than Orlando. She told herself the folks from the mega-corporations that dominated central Florida's tourism industry undoubtedly put a great deal of time, effort, and money into making sure that nothing bad ever happened to visitors.

But she hadn't been to that part of the country since Amanda was eight and Jordan was six. And on that trip, the Marlowes stuck to the theme parks. There had been little decision-making, much less risk, since their trip had consisted primarily of shuttling from their Disney hotel to the various parks on a monorail, waiting in line for one attraction after another, and consuming every single one of their meals on Disney property. In fact, the most daring thing she could recall doing on that trip was riding the Space Mountain roller coaster.

Now, as she waited to board the plane, her stomach was in knots. The fact that she seemed to be odd man out didn't help. Not surprisingly, she was the only person sitting alone amid a crowd of couples, families, and every other possible combination of travelers. She kept reminding herself that there was something to be said for the feeling of autonomy that came from traveling alone, something she hadn't experienced since before she'd married David. She certainly didn't envy the parents of children who were too young to contain their excitement. Case in point was the frazzled-looking mother of the four-year-old boy wearing a pair of Mickey Mouse ears. "I want Goofy *now*!" he screamed during his category-five temper tantrum.

Mallory tried to focus on the fact that she was here on a mission.

You have work to do, she told herself, whipping out the small notebook she'd brought along in her purse. Tensing the muscles in her forehead, she jotted down the ideas that had occurred to her on the drive to the airport.

"Go to a theme dinner show," she wrote after realizing that the theatrical productions she'd read about in her guidebooks, evenings that centered around medieval jousting or 1920s gangsters or Arabian horses, undoubtedly offered a good opportunity for some over-the-top experiences that she could include in her article. "Check out other hotels re: décor, etc.," she added, remembering a poster advertising Disney's new Animal Kingdom resort that she'd spotted next to the ladies' room.

And then she had a brainstorm: rating the attractions she visited. She would turn herself into the Roger Ebert of travel. And rather than ranking them with stars or thumbs that went up or down the way restaurant or movie critics did, she would use her own version: one to five flamingos. After all, what screamed "old Florida" more than flamingos?

She was relieved when it was time to board. After all, as long as she was earthbound, she could still back out. She shuffled through the plane behind the other passengers, checking the seat numbers.

As she neared 12C, she saw that the aisle seat was already occupied. Quite comfortably, too. Sprawled across it was a tall man in his late fifties or early sixties, his face gaunt with leathery skin and his longish gray hair slicked back over his head. He looked like a caricature of a tourist, thanks to his gaudy Hawaiian shirt, splashed with orange, yellow, and green parrots, and his khaki Bermuda shorts that had so many pockets he probably hadn't needed luggage.

"Excuse me," she said politely. "I believe you're sitting in my seat."

He didn't even glance up.

"Excuse me," she repeated, this time in a louder voice. "I believe you're—"

"I heard you the first time," he shot back.

"Then, why are you still sitting there?" she countered. She hadn't meant to sound so cranky. She realized the tension that had been accumulating over the past few days was catching up with her.

"You can take my seat," the man told her. "Twenty-three B."

"I don't want a middle seat. I want an aisle seat—like this one."

"Hey, I've got long legs. I need an aisle seat." To prove his point, he stuck out both legs. They were long, all right. They also had exceptionally knobby knees and pasty white skin that looked as if it hadn't been exposed to sunlight in months.

"In that case," Mallory said, letting her impatience show, "you should have requested an aisle seat when you made your reservation."

"Is there a problem?" the flight attendant asked.

"There doesn't have to be," the man said. "Not if this lady will go sit in twenty-three B."

"This is my seat," Mallory said. "See? Here's my boarding pass."

The flight attendant glanced at it. "Sir, I'm afraid you'll have to move. This isn't your seat."

"What difference does it make?" he growled. "I have long legs and I need to sit on the aisle."

"I'm sorry, sir, but this seat belongs to this woman." By this point, most of the other passengers in the vicinity had stopped chattering. The altercation that had brought the boarding process to a standstill was evidently much more interesting than anything they had to say to their traveling companions.

"Why can't she just sit in twenty-three B?" the man demanded.

"She's made it quite clear that she prefers the seat she was assigned." The flight attendant looked ready to strangle him with one of those oxygen masks that drops from the ceiling in the event of an emergency. "Now if you'll please get up and go back to your own—"

"I'm writing down your name," the man barked. "I'm going to notify the airline of your unprofessional behavior as soon as we land. You obviously don't know who I am, do you?"

"Sir, our policy is the same for everyone," the flight attendant insisted.

"Whatever." He stalked off to his assigned seat, muttering under his breath the entire time.

Mallory had a feeling she wasn't the only one who was relieved. She was also glad his seat wasn't anywhere near hers.

As she sat down in the seat she'd fought so hard for, she tried to push the uncomfortable interlude out of her mind. In fact, she forced herself to picture a relaxing setting, the way Amanda had taught her, even though she hadn't had much luck with it the last time around. She was determined to do everything she could to make this trip a success, not only to prove to Trevor Pierce that she could do it, but also to prove it to herself.

She settled back and fastened her seat belt. It was time to take off.